Destined to
Fail *but*
Ordained to
Glory

MarSha Andrus

Destined to Fail but Ordained to Glory

Copyright © 2014 by MarSha Andrus

Cover Photo: Samuel Leger

Scripture quotations are taken from the HOLY BIBLE, NEW INTERNATIONAL VERSION®. NIV®. Copyright© 1973, 1978, 1984 by International Bible Society.

ISBN#: 978-0692235362
0692235361

Printed in the United States of America

Dedicated to my firstborn. Had it not been for you I would not be the person I am today. I love you Quinsha.

Acknowledgement

I would like to first and foremost acknowledge my Creator for allowing me to live such an interesting life and yet still remain pure and intact; my husband, in whom I find great delight for always challenging me to admit my feelings and be ok with them; my daughter, for never giving up on me and not letting me give up on her even when I did not know what to do or how to do it; my two handsome sons for being simply mine. Although distance is between us the two of you prove every day that what I have instilled in you both will carry over for a lifetime; my friends, who stood dear and true through rough times and good times and always held me accountable even when I tried to wiggle my way out of things; my Mom and my sisters for loving me in spite of me.

Last but not least, Wisdom. The process of you coming into this world opened my eyes in a way that I could never imagine. Thank you for allowing me to be a part of your ordained miracle.

Preface

When I was younger, I was told that love was not enough. Something inside of me refused to believe that. I knew if I were capable of giving genuine love then I was capable of receiving genuine love. In my journey to give and receive genuine love I learned that pain produces life and life produces understanding. Many people die from both. In this world there is a lot of trouble, but Christ tells us to take heed for He has overcome the world. I had to learn that I must first receive love before giving it. How could I freely give something that I had not wholeheartedly received or begun to grasp?

In my quest I have learned that God is love and it is only His love that can teach you to give and receive. My hope is that you will learn something from my story and live your life without regrets for there is purpose in each path that we choose.

After I moved to Houston from Louisiana, my life changed drastically. I was no longer near my Dad, and my Mom worked like crazy. As far as God was concerned, the only thing I knew was that He was up there somewhere and I had to thank Him every night and every morning. I also knew if I did not feel good, He would make me feel better if I asked.

Once I had what is called the whooping cough, which is basically a contagious bacterial disease that causes out of control coughing. This cough caused my ribs to hurt every time I breathed. While watching an episode of the cartoon "Beetle Juice" I saw how when something hurt him, he would take that body part off and massage it or do all manner of things to it until it no longer hurt. I decided to ask God to take out my ribs and heal them. In the morning when I awakened, I felt a hand leaving my chest. I stretched and took a deep breath and there was not any pain. I looked up to the ceiling and said, "Thank You, Lord." I was healed just like that. I told my mother and sisters what happened but as always they just nodded and said "Okay, that's good." This was not the first encounter I had with God. At an early age I began having dreams and seeing different visions that actually happened. Some of the things I saw scared me, so my Mom told me to pray and ask God to take the dreams and visions away. I prayed, but I soon realized that God does not answer every prayer with a yes. As I got older I learned to be thankful for the no's as well as the yes's. Keep living and you will soon learn that God knows best and loves you enough not to give you what can only cause you eternal harm.

After those cute tender years from age 5 to 10, life seemed to begin moving extremely fast. At that time my mother worked so much and was back in school to get her degree in business, and I was left at home with my two older twin sisters. They loved me but had a real funny way of showing it. I was more of the always-outside-type while they stayed in. One thing we did share in common though was our love for music. We would dance and sing like there was no tomorrow, so much that my mother decided to put us in front of people at church. Now this was odd to us because we talked about parents like this—you know, the ones that lie to their children and tell them they can sing and then the children embarrass themselves on national TV all because their mother said, "Gone Baby, sang that song."

Not only was singing not a talent of mine but cleaning was not either. I was somewhat of a well-kept child. Most people would use the word spoiled, but being that I am neither rotten nor distasteful I choose to describe it as being well-kept. My older sisters would fix the beds, wash the dishes, clean the bathroom, etc. I, on the other hand got away with a lot while doing nothing, which caused unspoken strife between my sisters and me. This seemingly small and innocent act led me to believe later in life that it was okay to get by with others doing things for you. When I left home at age 14, I realized that was nowhere near being true. Out there away from home no one was willing to baby me, and I realized if someone did do something for me their reason for doing so was indeed questionable.

The lessons I learned were not voluntary at all. They were choices I made and things that I did because I felt like my back was against the wall. I felt alone and like there was nobody who loved me but me and if I did not take care of me, I would die a lonely cold person.

Isn't it amazing how it seemed to be okay when we were children to listen to any kind of music and hang out at Mom's card games, listening to the grownups talk and allowing people to speak things over our lives such as, "Oh, you are going be just like your Daddy or just like so and so." We were raised to complete high school, go to college, get married, and have children. No one ever told us to have fun, save your money, travel, see the world, open your own business; but most of all have fun (except for that crazy Aunt or Uncle who either drank too much or smoked too much weed).

The problems that most of us face today are because of some ignorant, unintentional, demonically-influenced words that have been spoken over our lives that we have yet to declare victory over. Some of us as youth fall deeply in love with music. Our lives begin to be carried on the wave of a beat and on the thump of the drum with the lyrics being our guiding light, not even realizing where the initial rhythm was rooted from. We tend to take this music and these words and shape our lives around them unintentionally.

On this day and however many more days it takes you to finish this book, find the beat with me, catch the rhythm and flow to the everlasting thump of Judah. In composing music there are a lot of strings and chords and just as you must have an ear to hear what goes where to make the beat successful, I hope that you will have an ear to hear what is being said and make the rhythm in your life the flow that it has been created to be. It is up to us to choose the Composer that we will follow. Although some chords seem right in certain places there may be a string that would fit perfectly if we would only surrender our lyrics.

My story begins with a beat and the thump of a drum, so as you flow through on the waves of these writings catch the beat and feel the rhythm then ask yourself, whom will I surrender my lyric to?

To God be the glory!

Introduction

Sitting on the curb in front of the Price Buster Food Store, my best friend Joy turned to me while patting my back and said, "Everything is going to be alright. Don't let this get you down. You will get her back soon, okay?" Shaking my head while holding back tears I stood up just as Derrick pulled into the parking lot.

"Man, how did all this happen?" I asked, while getting into the car.

Joy climbed into the back seat with me and said, "Girl I don't even know. Life can be a trip. You never know what your destiny holds."

"What are you doing?" Derrick asked Joy.

"What? I am sitting back here with Reyne," Joy said while holding me in her arms.

Letting her hand go, I said, "Go ahead and get in the front Boo, I am going to try and go to sleep anyway."

Joy climbed in the front seat with Derrick and asked him to stop at Jack in the Box for she knew a burger would cheer me up just a little.

As "Creeping on a Come Up" bumped out of those Pioneer speakers I thought back to the beginning of the weekend.

I was lying in bed on the phone with my legs up against the wall.

"I have not seen my baby girl in about five months now, since Christmas. I hope she remembers who I am. I really miss her. Her birthday is tomorrow and…"

Joy cut me off. "I know when my god-daughter's birthday is. Are we going to take her to the mall to get her ears pierced? Forever 21 is having a sale." I rolled my eyes. "Yes, that is the plan. I requested the weekend off so we can hang out and spend time with my baby. I have to go. Big Sis is honking the horn again like she crazy and we got to get to the bus station."

As I got into the car Lacey snapped, "What took you so long?"

"I was on the phone." I rolled my eyes at her.

She smacked her lips and drove off. The ride was silent the rest of the way and the tension was thick. As we entered the crowded, smelly, bus station all I could think of was how much I missed my baby girl and what she looked like now. Looking around trying to spot them, I noticed Lacey seemed quite irritated. Finally, I spotted them and walked over.

"Hi Momma," I said giving her a hug.

"Hey Boo," she replied and hugged me back.

I looked at my baby and said, "Wow, she looks so different." I frowned and wondered why my mother had not combed her hair.

"What is wrong?" my mother asked with a hint of attitude while she picked up her luggage.

"Nothing," I said, while shaking my head and reaching for the bags.

Mom gave me a shove. "Well, pick her up and come on. Don't just stand there. I have been waiting in this place long enough. Let's go."

Looking around Lacey asks, "Where is Tanya?"

"She is coming. She went to the bathroom," Mom said.

As she finished her sentence, Tanya ran up and gave me a big hug almost knocking Elizabeth out of my arms. "Hey Boo, be careful. I almost dropped my baby."

"I missed you so much," Tanya said while picking up her suitcase.

"I missed you too, Sweetie," I say hugging her as we all walk to the car.

"Reyne, can Momma and me come live with you please?" Tanya asked me as I was locking Elizabeth in her car seat.

I patted her on the back and told her, "Not right now Sweetie, I have some things to take care of first."

I helped her get in the car. The ride home was quiet. Mom broke the silence while asking, "What do you plan on doing for Elizabeth's first birthday Reyne?"

"Joy and I are taking her to the mall to get her ears pierced," I replied while playing with Elizabeth's hand.

"So, you are not going to giving her a party?"

"No, I am taking her to see Joy. We can do cake and ice-cream when I get back," I said irritably rolling my eyes in the back of my head. Once we arrived back at the house I told everyone goodnight and took Elizabeth to her room. Holding her in my arms I looked at her and said, "Hi there, Sweetie. We have a big day tomorrow," I said while laying her down in the bed. Peeking my head out the door I yell, "Mom did you bring all of her stuff with you?"

"Yeah, I have to see if Roger is going to bring her bed."

"Um, how is Mr. Roger anyway?" I asked sarcastically. I really didn't care about the answer.

"He is fine," she snapped and gave me an ugly look.

"Well, anyway goodnight," I said. "Goodnight Lacey."

"Um huh goodnight," she said back with an attitude rolling her eyes.

"What is wrong with you?" I asked as I stepped out of the room.

"Nothing, I said goodnight," she snapped back.

"You need to lose the attitude because no one did anything to you," I said while stepping closer to her.

"Get out of my face and shut up," she said angrily while stepping aside.

"No, you shut up," I said standing in front of her again.

"I am not sure what your problem is," she said while getting closer to my face. My Mom stood up and yelled, "Both of yawl shut the hell up. It is late and I am ready to go to bed." I look Lacey up and down and said "goodnight." She grumbled "goodnight" back to me and walked in her room.

What the hell is her problem? I thought to myself as I lay down next to my baby girl who was already fast asleep. Oh well, she will be alright. She is probably just mad because I would not talk to her about trying to kill myself. It is not like she cared anyway, I thought as I closed my eyes and drifted off to sleep.

I rose up with tears and frustration in my eyes and said to myself, "There has to be a better way than this."

Joy reached back and offered support by rubbing my leg. I lay back down and said, "God, help me please. I got to get my baby back as soon as possible." One Day you're here the Next Day Your Gone by UGK was playing from the tape player. I closed my eyes and meditated on the words of the song and began to think about how as early as six-years-old I began experiencing loss. It seems like I have been separated from the ones I love all of my life. It all started when we moved to Houston from Louisiana. That was one of the most horrible experiences of my life.

Table of Contents

CHAPTER 1 1

The Beginning or Shall I say the End 1

CHAPTER 2 19

Growing Up...19

CHAPTER 3 79

Rebellious Teen..79

CHAPTER 4 103

Stolen Values and Life Lessons 103

CHAPTER 5 143

Mi Casa Es Su Casa Until you Piss me Off.............................143

CHAPTER 6 165

From the Pole to the Cross...165

CHAPTER 7 215

Out of Ignorance into Bondage...215

CHAPTER 8 265

Counterfeits: Confused but not Condemned 265

CHAPTER 9 279

Total Submission 279

CHAPTER 10..303

The End or Shall I say the Beginning 303

Epilogue 327

CHAPTER 1

The Beginning or Shall I say the End

"Bad enough she beat me and lock me in the closet, then you come over here the total next day and tell her all she has to do is open the capsule and put it in my food," I said to my Daddy. I was livid and hurt both physically and emotionally. "How could you forget about me?" I was now crying. "I thought you had bought me some new candy. I did not know that was medicine. I thought they were pink M&M's. And why didn't you come to the hospital?" I asked while hitting him and still crying.

"Ahh Baby girl, Daddy's sorry that I could not get here until this morning, well, this afternoon," he said as he looked at his watch while hugging my head to his chest. "Besides Mice, you know I always bring you orange slices not chocolate. I tell you what, let's go for a ride. We can go to Checkers and get some lunch then Dairy Queen for a snicker blizzard. Now you go and clean your face and put some shoes on," he said as he kissed me on the forehead and gave me a little push towards the bathroom. He turned towards the kitchen and told my mother we were going out for a little while and would be back shortly.

She yelled back, "Do not even talk to me. Your child was in the hospital getting her stomach pumped and you were somewhere pumping. It is bad enough I have to be second but all these others. Please just go."

"But Eva," Dad started.

"Get the hell out of here Edward, now!"

Walking out of the bedroom, Stacey and Lacey came running up to my Dad and asked him if they could come along. My Dad looked at me and I quickly shook my head no. I did not want to share my time with the two sisters who watched me get whipped and stuck in the closet and did not even bother to help.

"Daddy can you come on, I am ready to go," I innocently stated as I stood by the door. He bent down, gave them both a hug and a dollar. He told them that they could not go this time but he would bring them something back.

"I need to talk to Mice in private. She is still mad at me," he whispered.

I was now frustrated. "Daddy let's go!" and I headed out the door. As we were walking out I heard Stacey said, "That boney cow makes me sick."

"Yeah," said Lacey. "She always gets what she wants but one day she won't."

In the car I asked, "Daddy when can I go to your house? Stacey'nem is mean to me and they always call me names and never want to go outside and play with me."

"Well, Baby, right now coming to my house is out of the question. I'm always in and out. That is why I come to see you."

I looked out the window and smelled the odor from the sugar factory. "Daddy who is that woman that stands at the door when Uncle Sean or my Poraine (God-Father) brings me to see you?" He began to shrug uncomfortably while searching for an answer. Relieved he pulled into the Checker's parking lot saying, "Uh Mice look who's here, and it's your friend Melissa."

I jumped out of the car and ran and gave her a hug. "Hi, Melissa," I said excitedly.

"Hi, Reyne. Hi, Mr. Edward," her Mom and Dad spoke to us.

"What are you doing today?" Melissa asked.

"I am going to get some ice cream after I leave here and maybe go to the park," I said excitedly.

"Oh, Mama, please can I go?" Melissa begged. She turned to her Dad and cried, "Father please? Mr. Edward can bring me home."

"We would hate to impose," Melissa's mother said as she pulled her back. My Daddy reached out his hand and said, "Oh, no, it will not be a problem. I will have them back in a few hours."

Melissa's Dad knelt down and told her, "Okay Melissa, you mind Mr. Edward now."

She grabbed my hand and squealed, "Yes, Daddy."

I said, "Oh trust me she will." We ran to the counter to order our favorites.

"Thank you. I will make sure they do not eat too much," said my Daddy as he shook her father's hand and bid them a good day. Unknowingly, we were actually helping them out big time by keeping Melissa for a few hours which worked in both Melissa and my favor. Her parents were surprising her with a puppy for her sixth birthday and it turned out to be quite a surprise. Melissa had this thing where she liked to put French fries in her pocket to eat as a snack later. While she was doing that, we laughed and talked about the park and what we wanted to do. After we ate until our bellies were content we went to the park. My Daddy pushed us on the swings and merry go rounds until we couldn't yell any more. On our way to Melissa's house, we stopped and got our blizzards. Melissa asked for an extra cone for her Mom, because Dairy Queen was her Mom's favorite place. We pulled up to the house and my Daddy opened the door for us. We ran to the porch and her Dad came from the backyard with a puppy in his arms. The puppy obviously smelled those fries in Melissa's pocket because just as she was handing her Mom her ice cream cone, the puppy jumped down and attacked her pocket. Ice cream went everywhere. One landed on Melissa's Mom's head and the other--well let's just say chocolate ice cream all over a steamy red white man is not a pretty sight. Melissa's Dad was livid, and all the while Melissa and I rolled around in laughter on the porch as the puppy devoured the fries and the cone. Melissa and I played with the puppy while our dads discussed grown up stuff. Time flew by and it was time to say good bye.

"What did you guys decide to name him?" asked her Dad.

Proudly we both yelled out, "Small Fry, because we all love French fries."

"Yeah" said Melissa, "and we are all best friends for life," she said giving me a hug. "I love you,"

"I love you, too," I said closing the hug and smashing the puppy in the middle. He began to bark and we said, "Yeah, yeah we love you, too."

My Daddy said, "Alright Small Fry numbers 1, 2, and 3 it is time to go." He patted each one of us on the head. "I promise I'll bring her back soon so you all can play again."

"Bye everybody," I said waving while walking to the car holding my Daddy's hand. "I had so much fun. Thank you, Daddy," I gave him a big hug as we got out the car back at the house. I looked forward to our next outing with them but unfortunately I never saw Melissa or the puppy again.

That night my parents had an argument and my Mom made him leave. As he was walking out the door, I heard my mother crying like a child and I became very angry. I took one of my Dad's shoes from behind the door and threw it at him. It hit him in the head.

"Baby girl why did you do that?" he asks while he rubbed his head.

"You made my Mama cry," I said angrily. I cried, slammed the door and locked it as he headed to me with opens arms while saying he was sorry. I waited until I heard him drive off and went to check on my Mom, but she was nowhere to be found. I went in to talk to my sisters but they were already asleep. I lay down for a bit but a loud rumbling noise startled me. My stomach was growling. Going into the kitchen I saw a shadow holding up a big knife. "Momma, Momma," I called out half asleep and half awake, unsure of what I was seeing. "I'm hungry," I said rubbing my eyes.

Startled, she dropped the knife in the sink looked at me again and asked, "What do you want to eat?"

Climbing up on the chair I said, "I don't know. What'cha got?" I asked with a huge smile. I did not know until years later after my own suicide attempt, that I had saved my mother's life. Somewhere in that moment of looking into my eyes, and hearing my tiny, hungry voice, she was jerked back into reality. Within the next few weeks, we were packed up and on our way to Houston. I didn't even get to tell my Daddy, Melissa, or Small Fry good-bye. My Dad told me that after that weekend we went to the park, Melissa came down with poison ivy and was restricted to her bed for two weeks. Small Fry slept by her door until she got better.

We moved to Houston in the middle of the school semester. First through the third grade was a blur. I cried every day and was teased because I talked funny and wore lots of pigtails. My Mom finally decided to put me in cheerleading my fourth grade year. That way I could stay after school while she went to class and my sisters worked at the post office. By this time I had stopped crying and was extremely good at cheering. My desire for dancing returned. One day after practice while waiting for my sisters to pick me up, I was practicing my routine when suddenly a bag fell on my head   "Ow!" I said, rubbing my head.

"I am so sorry. Are you okay?" asked this lanky boy.

"Yes, I am fine," I said, bending down to pick up the bag that pummeled me just seconds ago. "Is this yours?" I asked.

"Oh yeah, thank you," he said. He looked at my head while he took his bag.

"Are you sure you're okay?"

"Yes."

"Uh, I think I see a knot forming, but then again your head is a little big," he said with a grin.

"What? You have some nerve calling my head big!" I put my hand on my hip and rolled my neck. "You…"

"Hey," he said cutting me off, "I am just playing. I just wanted to make you laugh. My mother said laughing brings healing to the soul."

"Funny, but my head is still not big," I said as I sat under the tree.

"What is your name anyway," he asked? "My name is Reyne, I replied.

"Reyne! What, he giggled. I spelled it out r-e-y-n-e.

I quickly said, "Unless you want your head to swell, you better stop teasing me."

"Ooh so feisty like a cat, not a tiger. Roarrrrrr! So how did you get your name? I know everybody probably calls you Renee," he asked.

"Yeah, you're right, they do but I correct them every time, even my mother. See, when I was born…" He interrupted.

"I'm sorry. Do you want one of my Twinkies and some root beer?"

"Sure," I said taking the Twinkie. "Now listen, when I was born, my mother was knocked out asleep from the medication they had given her. So when the nurse came in to do my birth certificate, her best friend filled it out and pronounced it Renee although it is spelled Reyne you know the N makes the E long. So when my Daddy and the rest of the family came to see me she told everybody my name was Renee. By the time my mother woke up in her right mind and was no longer out of it, the whole family was calling and still does call me Renee."

"Ahh man, I bet that sucks."

"Yeah it does, so when I got older, well really about a year or so ago, when I saw my birth certificate she explained it to me. I took it upon myself to declare my name to rightfully be as she had chosen it to be in the first place."

He raised his hand and yelled it out with me. "Reyne!"

Laughing uncontrollably, I said, "Yes, Reyne. So what's your name?"

"My family calls me Tree, because I am so tall."

"And skinny! What, dude you are skinny and your head is so small it looks like a small bush, especially the hair."

"Not funny Baby Renee."

"Ahh, come on. What happened to laughing bringing healing to the soul?" I poked him in the side. He began tickling me and we laughed until our stomachs ached. We met underneath that tree for a month every day after school. Strangely, I would never see him in school. Then one day close to the end of my 4th grade year, coming from the nurse's office, I saw Tree and this really huge lady coming out of the principal's office. I ran to catch up, and I yelled out his name but I was stopped by a hall monitor. Tree looked back and with tears in those big brown eyes, he waved good-bye. I finally got loose from the hall monitor but by the time I got outside, the car pulled off. Once again I was alone. After school I walked home by myself because my sisters thought my Mom was picking me up, I went straight to my room and cried.

"What is she crying for now," yelled one twin to the other as Lacey was coming down the hall.

"I don't know," she probably didn't get her way." said Stacey.

I got up and slammed the door and began talking to God. "God, if you can hear me, I'm alone, please bring Tree back." I did this for several weeks. I didn't know that my mother heard me pleading. One Saturday, a few months later, my mom told us to pack our things because we were moving. This new apartment did not have as much space as the other one. The units were really close together. It was summertime and I was looking forward to seeing Melissa when my Daddy came to get me. We were all settled in, school was out and the summer had just begun.

"Mom, when is my Daddy coming?" I asked.

"Soon Baby, go outside and play." she said.

While I was outside playing, a girl walked up to me and said "Hi." As I stood to shake her hand, she disappeared right before my eyes. Immediately, I went inside and told my Mom that I was sleepy and wanted to take a nap.

"Sure Baby, go ahead," she said.

The house was quiet. My sisters were away at pre-college camp at Prairie View A&M University. Cuddled comfortably under my teddy bear, I instantly fell into a deep sleep. Suddenly, the little girl reappeared but this time she looked different, in a weird way. Almost transparent, like a distant memory, almost as if I knew her. She chased after a red ball right into the street. As she bent over to pick it up, a car smashed right into her. I immediately began screaming and the next thing I knew was my mother was shaking me and waking me up. She asked, "What's wrong?" The phone started to ring as I stared into my mother's eyes. I was trembling. She grabbed the phone with one hand while still holding me with the other. "Hello, hello?" she said frantically into the phone.

"Hey Eva, this is David." Uncle David is my Mom's youngest brother. "What is going on?" I asked looking at her as he spoke. "Okay,

I will tell her," she said nodding her head. They talked for a few more minutes, and then she hung up the phone and propped me up.

"Baby, I have something to tell you, but first tell me why you were screaming."

As I began to recite the dream to my mother, she began to cry lightly. Small tears ran down her face as she told me that my best friend, Melissa, had just been hit by a car while trying to catch Small Fry as he chased his favorite red ball. At that moment, my world ended. My mother just held me and swore that she would never let me have a dog. I sat speechless and the feeling of being alone came rushing back once again. To make matters worse my Daddy was not able to visit like he said he would.

Fifth grade was a blur. Right before school let out for the next summer we went to Louisiana for another funeral. We were not able to make Melissa's funeral but in all honesty I really did not want to. This time my cousin had been shot. At the store, I saw the man that shot him and screamed furiously that he killed my cousin. My Dad quieted me, because this man was the cop I had seen in another dream. My sisters took me to the car. They later told my Mom that one night while she was working late before we got the call about the funeral that I had another dream. By this time, my mother thought I was weird but she told me that if I was afraid, pray and ask God to take the dreams away. I did that but in my 6th grade year, at a second school, and in a new house, I had another one. This one was different. In my new classes, as well as in my neighborhood, I was the only chocolate sister in the bunch--other than my biology teacher who might as well have been white because she was high yellow. People looked at me differently. I never knew there was a difference between whites and blacks. Besides, my best friend was white. One evening I spent the night at the neighbor's house. It was New Year's Eve night and these were not your average 10, 11, and 12-year-old little girls. Bedtime came and we climbed in bed and the next thing I know, one of them began moving up and down on the other. The 11-year old asked me if I wanted to try it. She said it's called "hunching." I told her no, it just did not look right. She then told me try it on the pillow and to watch her first. She gave me a pillow and I began to mock what she did to her pillow. Suddenly a certain feeling came over me and it felt like I was peeing on myself, and although there was no water, my panties were wet. Yet, I could not stop hunching the pillow. Finally after about three times, I stopped. The three of them were all excited and touching each other. I got up, grabbed my stuff and went home. Although it was weird, it kind of felt good and I slept like a baby. I was so tired. The next morning, I got up, ate and went back to sleep. My mother knocked on my door.

"Reyne, what are you doing here? I thought you were staying at Jessica's"

"I don't like it over there, they are bad."

"Did anything happen? Did someone touch you?" I was really nervous about my answer because somehow I knew what had happened was wrong but I just did not know how wrong.

"No ma'am, I just do not want to play with them."

"Well okay, I am going to sleep" said Mom.

"I think I am going to take a nap, too."

I tried and tried to go back to sleep. I kept tossing and turning, and seeing them hunching each other. Finally, I pulled out my pillow and tried it again until I felt the rush of wetness and fell straight to sleep. No faster than I fell asleep, I jumped up about to scream when I saw what I thought to be a girl hanging, then realizing that I was only in my panties with a pillow between my legs. I thought I better not. Sweating frantically with tears in my eyes, I looked out my window only to see that it was dark. I had slept the whole day. I washed up, changed my panties, got dressed, and opened my door to find my sister Stacey about to knock on it.

"Hey, I was coming to wake you up. Mama said come eat."

"Okay, I'm coming," I said as I put my head down so she could not see my tears. I grasped my soiled panties into a fist behind my back. "I need to use the restroom." Turning away, she said "Okay, hurry up. We are going to watch 'Coming to America' after we eat."

I closed the bathroom door. I rinsed out my panties and washed my face. Coming out of my room from hanging them to dry, my sister Lacey yelled, "Girl come on here, the food is getting cold."

"I'm coming." I yelled back.

After dinner, we sat down to watch the movie.

"Hey T-Bone," called Stacey "did you have fun last night with your new friends?" "No, I did not and stop calling me T-Bone."

"Oh, I'm sorry Woo-Ann, did I offend you?"

"Huh? Naah!" I said distractedly trying not to think about the girl I saw hanging.

"She's probably mad because she has to get them naps combed later," said the other twin. "Whatever," I said and got up and stomped out. In my room, I cried myself to sleep with memories of the dream I had earlier about the girl hanging. The next day my Mom watched me strangely with curiosity written all over her face as she drove me to school.

"Are you okay?" she asked. "Yeah Mom, I'm fine, just sleepy."

"Well, you slept all day yesterday." she said.

"It probably was the rain. You know how I get when it rains," I said looking out of the window.

"Yeah, I do. I know you are really happy to have your own room."

"Yes Momma. I am glad that we have a house; I just wish my Daddy was here. That would make it great--one big family."

"Well Hon, sometimes things just do not happen that way, but you do not have to worry about that because you will finish school, get married and have children of your own one day," she said as we pulled up to the school.

I just looked at her and smiled "Bye, Mom, love you," I finally said after pondering the look in her eyes.

"Love you, too, Baby. See you when I get off work." She grabbed my arm and asked one last time, "Are you sure you're okay?"

I pulled my arm back, "I'm fine Momma. Now, have a good day at work." I leaned in to her to kiss her cheek. I got out the car and entered what should have been a loud, busy school only to find it quiet and gloomy. The students as well as the teachers had tears in their eyes. I wondered what was going on. I reached homeroom and just as the bell rang, the principal came over the loud speaker and said one of the eighth graders was found dead in her room last night from an apparent suicide. According to the school nurse, where I found myself shortly after seeing a picture of the 8th grader and realizing that was the girl from my dream the night before, this was one of the saddest incidents to happen in Palmer Village since the school fire a few years back according to some of the teachers. I could not keep anything on my stomach. I begged the nurse not to call my mother, but she had to because I had a fever. Not even a good two hours had passed since she dropped me off and now she had to leave work and come get me. She was not happy, but understanding when the nurse told her about the suicide. At home, I just went to sleep. I did not want to talk, and was too weak to eat. The next day I stayed home alone. She locked the doors from the outside so no one could get in or out unless they had a key. My sisters made it home at about noon that day. My Mom had instructed my sister Stacey to wash my hair. While washing it, she noticed little red bumps on my back and she saw that I was scratching uncontrollably.

"What is wrong with you?" she asked.

"I don't know, but I don't feel good." I collapsed in her arms. Lacey called Momma. The oldest twin picked up the phone as the other carried me to the couch. I vaguely heard her say, "Okay, okay thank you," as she hung up the phone. "They said she left for the day."

"Uh uh, hell no, I am not taking a whipping for this." Grabbing me out of my sister's arm, the oldest twin, Stacey, begin smacking me, shaking me, and screaming "wake up, wake up, I am not taking any more whippings for you."

My eyes opened slowly and I squealed, "I can't breathe." Just as Lacey was giving me some water, my mother walked in. Lacey jumped up, dropped the water along with my head saying, "I did not touch her."

Stacey then jumped in, "Momma, I promise we did not do anything."

I tried to stand on my feet and speak. "Momma, they did not do any…." That's as far as I got. I fell to the floor. Immediately, she grabbed me, commanded them to put some shoes on me and off to the emergency room we went. Finally after two hours of waiting, the doctor told my Mom that I had the shingles. "The what?" she asked. "Shingles, it is a nervous reaction of the chicken pox. Did something scare her or frighten her recently?" asked the doctor.

No, not that I am aware of, her behavior has not changed other than her sleeping more but I thought she was just tired." said my Mom.

"Well, look here. Reyne can you raise your shirt please?" the doctor asked. I raised it up and she gasped while covering her mouth. The doctor began to speak very softly. Okay, now this is a very serious disease. If these bumps connect she will die. Right now they are at the middle of her chest and her back and some are coming around the side. "Whatever happened, it must have been bad, because she had to be really frightened for the bumps to spread so rapidly. Please give her the medicine, but if you don't find out what happened, the condition could worsen. The medicine will make her sleepy, but it is for nausea and light headedness. She cannot go to school, and no, it is not contagious. My mother quickly remembered my first episode with pills and she asked,

"Could the pills come in a capsule form?" The doctor said yes and needless to say we both were relieved. On the way home my Stacey laid me on her lap. I could feel her tears fall on my arm. At that moment, I knew she loved me although sometimes she had a real funny way of showing it.

The next morning, Stacey woke me up by climbing next to me in bed. She raised my shirt up and saw that the bumps were spreading rapidly to my side. She then motioned for my other sister, Lacey, the second twin to come in. Lacey kneeled on the opposite side of the bed and began sucking her thumb like she always does when she is between sleepiness and contemplating something of importance. Stacey said, "Look," and she showed her my side. Instantly, Lacey eyes welled up with tears, "Reyne, not calling me Renee, what happened to you?"

"The doctor said something scared you," said Stacey.

"What is it?" they asked. I just shook my head and tried to lie back down. The more they questioned me, the more I began to cry and then Stacey said, "You know we found those panties in your closet. Were you bleeding?"

"Bleeding?" I asked, my eyes now open wide. "Why would I be bleeding? I do not have any scabs on my butt."

"No, not from your butt, from your private," said Lacey.

"Now that is just nasty. No, I was not bleeding. I used the restroom a little on myself and I did not want Momma or y'all to know." I lied, hoping that would stop the badgering. Finally they gave up and at the same time as they did quite often said, "Well something scared you and you better tell us quick."

"Yeah, said Stacey. We are seniors and cannot miss any more school to stay home with you, and Momma cannot keep missing work. Get up and come take your medicine." Because the medicine was so strong, I slept all day. The second day, my sisters stayed home with me again. On the third day, I woke up drenched in sweat and crying. Before I could even sit up good, my mother was in the room. She was known for having super ears. Her room was all the way across the other side of the house in the front, whereas mine was in the back. She grabbed me as I tried to lift my shirt off but could not get it off due to the stickiness from the sweat.

She said, "Here let me." Gasping for air, she uttered a small prayer. God must have heard her because by the time I got to the mirror I had begun to cry. My mother stood behind me and in the kindest voice I had ever heard, she said, "Renee (giving me a look), I mean Reyne. You have to tell me what happened. If these bumps connect, you are going to die." She turned me around to face her, kneeled down and looked into my eyes. She said, "I am Mommy and I love you. Please tell me what happened." I shook my head and put my shirt down. She lifted it back up and said, "Tell me this: if you die, who will be the first woman president of the United States of America? Hmmm? And something else--who will make me peanut butter cookies after a hard day at work?" That caused me to smile softly.

"Do you promise not to be mad at me and not to whip me?" I asked.

"Well that all depends on what it is now," said Mom. I put my head down again but she picked it back up and said, "I tell you what. I promise not to kill you myself, how is that?"

She had a gentle look in her eyes and a firm grip on my cheeks. I knew she was growing impatient. "Okay Momma." I walked over to the bed and tapped the mattress for her to sit next to me. With my head slightly held down I told her everything. Starting from New Year's Eve with Jessica and her little freaky cousins to the dream of the girl lying dead in bed to the girl found dead in her room the next morning at school that caused all of this to happen. She listened without saying a word. She cleared her throat and said it was time for us to have a talk, and she began to explain about the birds and the bees and the flow, which I later decided to call Aunt Flo.

Apparently she caught on to something my sisters said. "So that is what Stacey'nem was talking about."

"What?" I asked.

"Never mind tell me more." As my mother and I sat there and talked, the fever went away and the bumps began to vanish, patch by patch. The more we talked the better I began to feel. My mother noticed it as well and rubbed her hand over my back ushering me to the mirror. Rubbing my chest I said, so let me get this straight. One day because I am a girl that will one day grow up to be a beautiful woman I will bleed once a month for three to seven days from my private."

"Yes dear," she replied.

"Oh, but why, I don't want to bleed." I began to pout and sulk. "I want to be a boy. Yeah that's it, boys don't bleed, right? And they don't grow titties? Can I be a boy? I will ask God to turn me into a boy that way you will have a son and two girls. Please Momma may I?"

"No, you cannot," she said. She held me in the center of my chest and my back where the last of the bumps were. "You are a girl and a very beautiful one. Your beauty is your joy because it comes from within, but there is one thing you can pray for."

"What?" I asked.

"Do those dreams scare you?"

"Yes ma'am, they do."

"Why don't you pray and ask God to remove them from you so that you will not be scared anymore?" She turned me around to face the mirror and removed her hands. Just as she did that, I felt a burning in my chest and my back. The bumps turned bright red orange looking and as fast as the burning sensation came it went away. She rubbed the last six bumps on my chest and grabbed my hand. I knew then that she felt the heat from the burning sensation because her hand was red hot.

She gave me a hug and told me to go take a bath while she fixed us some dinner. As she walked out of the room, I said, "Please do not tell anybody about the, you know, the hunching."

"Oh okay, I won't Baby. Your secrets are always safe with Momma. Just do not do it again."

I then smiled broadly. "Okay, Momma, I love you."

"Love you, too." she said.

Needless to say, I was healed from that one-on-one mother-daughter conversation. After my bath, I was really thankful to have gotten that stuff off my chest. It was literally killing me. I learned from that point on, do not hold stuff in, tell somebody.

After a few days, things were back to normal. I was back at school, my Mom went to work, and Stacey'nem had their activities. Running home one Friday, I came to a dead stop when I saw the U-Haul parked in the driveway and my sisters loading boxes. I ran to the door and demanded to know what was going on. My mother came out of the kitchen and said "Put your stuff in the boxes that are in your room. We are moving."

I followed her into her room. "But why I like my room I don't want to move. Why do we have to keep moving?"

She swiftly turned around. "Look child, we have to be out of here in less than two hours and the truck has to be back in an hour and a half. Get your room packed and let's go. We are going to stay with Mom for a while."

"Momma!" I yelled loudly.

She came towards me with her hand raised. "Girl, if you don't go do what I said …"

I scurried out and down the hall to my room and saw that my bed and dressers were already gone. I packed my clothes, my bears and books and loaded them up. At the foot of the yard were my sit-down table and various other items that I would have preferred to take with me.

"Mom, why is my table over there where the trash goes?" I asked.

"There is not enough room for it or that other stuff at Momma's house."

"But I want…"

"Look, it's just a vanity table. Someday you will get another one. Come on let's go." As I climbed in the back of that old yellow station wagon I hugged my bear tightly and thought to myself now we have lost the house too. First my Daddy, second Melissa and Small Fry, then Tree, now my room and my vanity table where I played pretty. Looking at my bear I began to cry and fell asleep for the long journey ahead.

CHAPTER 2

Growing Up

"Um, are we there yet?" I asked.

"Naah, sleepy head go back to sleep," said Joy. She looked back and reached for my hand. "Are you okay?"

I gripped her hand and nodded. "I'm good."

"Ahh, enough with the mushy stuff already," said Derrick. "Here, look who called, Javier!" He threw his pager into the backseat. Smiling, I glanced at Joy in the mirror and she gave me that look and I nodded in agreement.

We both said together, "Murder time." I laughed wickedly, and gave Derrick his pager back and begin to think back to my first kiss. I drifted off again.

Staying with my grandma was not pretty. One day when I came home from school, she was out on the porch. I walked up there right as she was going into the house. She said something negative about us staying there and I started to smack my lips, while rolling my eyes and turning away. Before I could complete the smack and roll just one eye, her hands were around my throat. I began losing air and growing weak. I silently whispered for help and I began to feel fire burning in my chest and my back. Obviously, she felt it too, because she immediately backed away from me very slowly and went into the house never losing the astonished, yet evil gaze she had on me. I gasped for air and went to the apartment house in the back. My sisters heard me crying and came to the stairs. "What is wrong?" she screamed reaching for me.

"Granny, yawl's grandma, Momma's mommy, just tried to kill me."

"What? Why? She crazy!" stated Lacey. She helped me inside, and when she placed her hand on my back, it was hot to the touch. "Ouch," she yelled and quickly moved it away. "Why are you so hot?"

"Oh," I said fiddling at my backpack, "I ran back here and I guess I just got hot."

"Um, well I'm calling Momma," said Lacey, with her thumb in her mouth as she picked up the phone.

"No," said Stacey, as she snatched the phone away. "This is why she lost her last job, always having to take off to see about us." Lacey covered her mouth and gestured towards me.

"Shhh! Don't say that. Momma said it's not her fault." I looked up at that point and realized that they were talking about me. The rest of that evening, I did my homework in silence, wondering if I was the reason my mother lost her job as administrative assistant at the college and our house. Finally, Momma came home, exhausted. My sisters tried to tell her that Granny tried to kill me but she silenced them and told me to come over to her. Out of fear, I came forth. She looked at my neck and asked me if I was okay.

"Yes ma'am," I answered.

"Good, because you all are going to need your energy. We are moving tomorrow." At the same time we all yelled, "Yes!"

"I cannot take any more of Momma's crap, I got to get out of here," she said shaking her head and taking off her shoes.

We were all rejoicing. Then just as we started together we stopped together. We looked at her. "What?" she yelled. There was a guilty look on her face as she looked up at the three of us. As if she was our spokesperson, Stacey stepped up and said, "We don't have to change schools again? I mean I understand if we do, it is just that this is our senior year and well we kind of want to finish there and Renee, I mean Reyne (she glanced at me) is back at Kingsley with her friends from elementary as well."

"No, you all do not have to change schools," she glanced in my direction.

"I was actually okay with it. I mean seeing everyone from elementary is cool but Tree is not there, so it's not the same. Plus, they tease me because we live here and not to mention these 50 plats in my head. Come on Mom, I'm in sixth grade," I said pulling at my pigtails. "Yeah Mom it's time to come on up to the 90's, says Stacey.

"I got your 90's. Who is going to get up and comb her hair?"

"I'll comb it," I said. They all looked at me and said, "Uh No!" and roared with laughter.

The next few months were great. I got my own room back; my sisters got a limo for their prom that I got to ride around the block in. My mother promised me that for my prom, I could get one, too. I even went to Louisiana for the summer. I saw my Daddy, but I could not stay with him. I had to stay with my Mom's best friend Ms. Shirley who would be moving to Houston at the end of the month. She had three daughters and two sons that stayed with her and Mr. Harry. He was a real nice man, and he and my Daddy talked a lot. One afternoon her son Wayne, which I told everyone, was my cousin, wanted to race. He was 12 years old, a year older than I. We had been told we could only play for a little while because it was going to rain. We went all the way to the end of the street as the sky grew gray and the thunder roared slightly. With no shoes on, in the middle of Opelousas, Louisiana on Blanchard Street, we took off. Wayne took the lead but I quickly caught up. Suddenly there was a sound like a lion roaring. We looked back and saw that we were being chased by the rain. We screamed and ran as fast as we could to the house. We were four houses away when the rain overtook us. On the porch, soaking wet, we both got spankings and were made to bathe, eat dinner, and go to bed. That night I slept in the room with Debra. Suddenly I heard a noise. I quickly opened my eyes but did not take the cover off my head.

"Shhh! Quiet, or you will wake up the child," Debra said. She shook me to make sure I was asleep. "Good, she's knocked out. These children sleep like logs," she said.

I then heard a bunch of smacking and what sounded like something being slapped together. I peeked from under the cover and there to my amazement was the guy from the store earlier that day on top of Debra hunching her and kissing her and saying she was beautiful, and he was going to marry her. Debra then flipped him over and said "sex me." Things got a little hectic after that, so I quietly slid out of bed and through the door, down the hall to Roderick's room. Roderick was Ms. Shirley's 16-year-old son. He was so cute and I really liked hanging out with him because he always called me beautiful and kissed me on the cheek. He called me his best girl and would always bring me back candy from the store. Quietly opening the door, I walked in. "Hey Beautiful, what's wrong? Couldn't sleep?"

"Well no it's just…"

"Oh, let me guess, Debra has company?"

"Yes."

"You want to sleep in here?"

"Yes." I lit up like a light bright doll.

He pulled back the covers and said "Come on." I got in the bed with my bear and snuggled right under Roderick. I turned and switched sides then went back to the other side. Finally I got comfortable and went right to sleep.

In the morning, I had one leg out of the bed and the other on him only something did not feel right. I rose up and there was something hard in his shorts and my leg was all wet. He awakened, looked at his shorts, and the wet stuff on my leg. He jumped up, grabbed himself and said "Oh no!"

He said, "I'm sorry" and he quickly grabbed his shirt and wiped off my leg. He examined the rest of me, handed me a big towel and told me to go in the bathroom and clean up with some soap and water. "Do not let anybody see you. If they do, tell them you peed on yourself--look you're all wet."

"No, I didn't, I...." I stopped in mid-sentence, when I noticed the embarrassed look in his eyes. I later discovered that my leg was the victim of a wet dream. I still laugh when I think about it. At breakfast, Debra looked very refreshed. "Hey Reyne, walk with me to the store." I know she was up to something because she called me Reyne and not Renee. I went to the store anyway because I wanted some candy. As I walked to the door, Roderick slid me a dollar bill and told me to buy as much penny candy as I wanted. He kissed me on the cheek and winked his eye. Once out the door, I ran back in and told him "Don't worry, your secret is safe with me. I won't tell anybody you peed on yourself last night for another dollar and then one every day until I go back home." He handed me another dollar.

Once we made it around the corner from the house, Debra stopped and grabbed me by my shirt.

"Did you tell anyone what you saw last night," she asked while jack-ing me up some more.

"No, I promise I didn't," I said as I pushed her away. She pushing me back says, "Good and you better not or I'll get you."

"Okay, I won't," I said as I fixed my shirt. Walking slowly behind her, I realized that bribery only worked for some, but to put fear in one's heart always gets results. Inside the store, the guy who is also the bagger from last night was all over Debra like white on rice. I walked around her and he stopped kissing her instantly and loosened his embrace. She almost fell into the nearby empty baskets as he kneeled down and kissed my hand.

"Who is this? She is beautiful." She grabbed him by the chin and raised him up.

"This is my little cousin, Reyne," she half-introduced us.

"Anybody ever tell you how beautiful you are?" Tommy asked. I blushed.

"Come on here," said Debra. "I am the only one you call beautiful."

"Oh Baby come on, she is just a child. Nobody can take your place," he said while kissing her on the lips. He looked over at me and said, "She is beautiful though. If I were about 8 years younger boy I'd ..." Debra gave him a look as they walked on ahead of me.

"Is it okay if I buy her something?" He pulled out a twenty and told me to get whatever I wanted. I got lots of candy and I kept the change.

I left there that summer with a total of $85.00, an arch enemy--Debra, and a secret on Roderick that would always generate a dollar or two, whenever I come back around again. Back home my mother was happy that her best friend and her family were moving to Houston. I was happy that my Daddy would be here too, when they came in three weeks. In time, the dreams came back.

My Mom was busy getting my sisters' graduation party together when my grandmother came running in frantically. She had been looking for my uncle. "Have yawl seen Tim?" she asked distractedly gazing around.

"No Mama," said my Mom not even looking up.

"Well he has been gone since 10 a.m. this morning." said my grandmother with her hands on her hips.

Suddenly all the lights went out. Stacey'nem came running downstairs.

"What is going on? Stacey asked. She opened the front door to let some light in and saw that some of the neighbors were doing the same thing.

"Did you check Aunt Pat house, he goes over there sometime to watch football with Junior?" ask Stacey

"Yeah, he was not there." says Grandma.

"Okay, well come on, we'll go down to the police station and report him missing. Stacey, yawl watch your sister, get some candles and the flashlights, it will be dark in an hour, says my Mom." "Can I go outside?" I asked.

"No," Lacey said.

My mother said, "Yeah, but don't go too far and be in the house before dark."

I stuck my tongue out at my sister and headed out the back door. I waved at my mother and grandmother as they sped off to the police station. It seemed like everybody's lights were off in the neighborhood because everybody was outside.

"Hey, Wayne," I say while walking up to my cousin on the sidewalk. Hey, Reyne, what's up?" he replied without looking up. "What are yawl doing?" I asked. "Playing marbles," said Wayne.

"You want to play?" asked this tall skinny guy.

"Yeah but I can't stay long because it is almost dark."

"Hey, I saw your uncle this morning. He was walking to the store, says Wayne."

I paused and felt the heat begin to rise in my chest. I shook my head in an attempt to make the heat go away. I said "Really? My Mom and grandmother are going to look for him right now."

"Is something wrong?" asked the skinny guy kneeling next to me.

"No. Why?" I ask squirming uncomfortably.

"I don't know. You seem hot as if fire is coming off of you." he said touching my shoulder.

I jumped up and said, "Look, I have to go." He grabbed my hand.

"Wait, you're really pretty. Can I have your phone number?"

Snatching his hand away, Wayne said, "Naah man, get back! You can't talk to my little cousin." As I was walking off, I heard, "Hey Reyne, is something wrong with your uncle? You know is he slow or something," asked the skinny guy?"

"Yeah, I think he has some kind of mental problem. Why?" I asked while walking back towards them. "I tried talking to him and it was like he could not even hear what I was saying." he said hunching his shoulders kneeling back down to play with the marbles.

I could feel the burning increase. I said, "I don't know, I have to go. I'll see yawl tomorrow."

"Bye," said the skinny guy. He looked at Wayne while touching his hand. "Man she's hot."

Wayne hit him in the head and said, "Whatever man, let's finish this game, so I can whip you again."

Back in the house I leaned on the door and took deep breaths with my eyes closed. Lacey peeped around the corner. "What's wrong with you?" she asked. Startled, I explained to her that I was just tired. "I'm going take a bath. Is Mom back yet?" "No, and Stacey is in the tub, so you will have to wait." "Okay, well I'll just wait right here on the couch. Can we close the front door?" I asked motioning towards the door. "No, there are no more candles and I am using the flashlight to fix the food," said Lacey.

I lay down on the couch and as soon as my head hit the pillow I began to dream. In my dream, I saw a freeway and a lot of cars. Suddenly a man appeared walking on the freeway. He was crying. As he cried, I begin to cry in my sleep while dodging the lights from the cars. I squealed, "Oh God, help me please. Help him please," I began to speak out as I slept. Soon, Lacey was shaking me. I could vaguely hear the phone ringing as my mother came through the door screaming "Answer the phone, answer the phone." Stacey came and sat me up in her arms. I opened my eyes only to look into my mother's eyes filled with tears. Lacey quickly ran to her side to find out what was wrong. The heat in my chest began to fade as my mother hung up the phone. "That was Aunt Trish. They found Tim," my mother said. "Where?" asked my grandmother. "He was walking on the freeway," I blurted out.

I turned to my grandmother and she gasped and looked at me with that same cold evil stare and backed out of the house saying "I will go home and wait for Trish to bring him." As soon as she turned to walk away the lights came back on. Lacey closed and locked the door. I buried my head in Stacey's chest and started crying. My mother was astonished.

"Reyne, baby, did you have another dream?" she asked while coming to sit next to me.

I rose up. "Yes, Momma, but he is okay. Li'l-T is going to bring him home, he's not hurt, just scared." She gave me a hug, told me everything was going to be okay and ordered my sisters to fix me some food and prepare for bed.

After dinner, we all ate ice-cream and said our prayers. Although I really did not have an appetite I always seem to find room for milk chocolate ice-cream and bananas. Needless to say, I did not sleep in my room that night. I slept in the bed between my sisters.

The graduation party went well and Ms. Shirley decided to host a fish fry in my sisters' honor. While cleaning up after the party, Wayne and his skinny friend came over to where I was standing. "Are you coming to the fish fry tonight?" I asked. "Yeah, I'll be there," Wayne said. I'll be there, too, and I sure wouldn't mind dancing with you," the skinny boy said. The DJ cleared his throat and said. "Excuse me pretty lady. Are these two young men bothering you?" I blushing and batting my eyes, swaying from side to side was about to speak but was interrupted by Skinny.

"Excuse me Mr. DJ or whatever your name is. She and I were just about to dance." I yanked my arm back and said. "Actually no we weren't." Wayne stepped in and said, "Let's let the lady decide." I smoothly stood up straight, looked at the skinny guy, turned and said, "Mr. DJ, I will gladly take this dance. I gave him my arm and we turned to the dance floor."

Skinny man's mouth dropped opened and he said, "By the way my name is Jacob." I shooed him off and began my dance. Wayne put his arm around Jacob and I heard him say, "Don't worry man, the DJ will not be at the fish fry tonight."

Little did he know he would be there? Twirling around to Atlantic Stars, "Play another Slow Jam," Mr. DJ told me that I was the most beautiful girl he's ever seen and called it a privilege to dance with me. When the song was over, he kissed me on my forehead and told me to stay sweet. My Mom took a picture of us and I must say I was looking pretty good in my blue jean ruffled mini-skirt with matching jacket that my Mom got me for my 10th birthday from Mexico.

I was too happy to get to Ms. Shirley's house and see him there. Before I could even get over to him good, Debra was all in his face handing him a coke. Realizing that his gaze was fixed on me, she turned and gave me this evil look, took his hand and I did not see him anymore that night or ever again actually, except once. Standing there looking dumb, Wayne tapped me on the shoulder. "Come on in the room, he was too old for you anyway and besides you don't do the things that Debra does.

You are a good girl," he said while patting me on my back. Once inside the room Jacob patted the seat next to him on the love seat for me to sit next to him. Wayne climbed in the bed behind us with one of the neighbor's daughters while all the other kids played the Nintendo and other board games.

"Hey Marco cut that light off," said Wayne. "You better not turn that light off. My Momma said I cannot be in the room with boys with the light off," I said to Wayne. As I turned to Marco, Wayne motioned to him to turn the light off. Seeing the eye contact, I quickly turned around to Wayne and just as I turned, the light went off and bam! Jacob's lips met mine. "Uh, yuck! I am going to beat your butt!" I yelled. I began beating Jacob like he stole something, which he did and I was not happy about it. As Jacob began screaming like a little girl, my Mom, Wayne's mom and whoever else could fit through the door came running into the room. My Mom switched on the light and pulled me off of Jacob. "What the hell is going on in here?" she yelled. "He tried to kiss me!" I yelled pointing at Jacob. "What?" My Mom grabbed Jacob by the neck and said, "If you ever come near my daughter again, I am going to tear you a new ass hole."

Everyone gasped except Wayne. He fell off the bed laughing even harder than before. My Mom grabbed him and said, "Shut up!" He shut up dry. Then she calmed down. "Come on out of this room," she said, "and somebody get this child some ice for his lips before he bleed to death." I sat in the living room with the other kids and the DJ and Debra came by with their coats on. "Good girl" he said pinching me on my cheek and winking his eye. Then he turned to Jacob and shook his fist at him as they walked out the door. Shortly afterwards, my mother said, "Come on let's go. Baby I'll take you home so I can tell your Mom what happened to your face," she told Jacob all nice and calm, like she did not just threaten his life. He never made eye contact with her but mumbled, "Yes ma'am" while holding his lip. The ride home was silent with the exception of my sisters snickering under their breath the whole way. We arrived in the Village and Jacob got out of the car.

"Umm ma'am, it was really an accident. I would never disrespect you daughter like that. She is really beautiful and well I think I'm in love," protested Jacob.

"Boy if you don't get your narrow ass up to that door I'm going to throw you through it," she said. He ran to the door and knocked on it. His Mom answered. "What happened to your face," she gasped. "Oh nothing, just some love licks from my future wife," he smiled. "Hey Beverly," said my Mom waving to his Mom.

"Hi Eva. What happened?" she asked while walking to the car. "Jacob decided to try and steal a kiss and well that little fireball back there whipped him real good," said my Mom pointing at me in the backseat. Beverly laughed hysterically.

"Well that is what his soon-to-be 12 year old butt deserved. How old is your baby," she asked. "She will be 11 in six months," answered my Mom. "And he's talking about his future wife… these kids," said his Mom shaking her head.

My Mom, dead serious said, "If he likes living, he better stay away from my daughter." Then almost in the same breath she switched tones and said "Goodnight girl. Tell Sarah I said hi." Sarah was Jacob's older sister, and my cousin Roderick's pregnant girlfriend.

I was coming out of the tub getting ready to go to bed when my sisters came running to my door singing "Jacob and Reyne sitting in a tree K-I-S-S-I-N-G first come love then come …" I screamed "Leave me alone" and I slammed the door shut. I could still hear them as they laughed and walked away. My mom yelled, "Leave that girl alone and yawl go to bed."

The last few weeks of summer went by quickly. I do not know who was worst Jacob or JT, the neighbor who also had a crush on me. Seemed like every weekend my Mom had me returning gifts to the both of them. I could have started my own jewelry and teddy bear store. One week before school started, my Mom called my sisters and me into the living room. "We are moving" she said. "Ahh again? Why, did you lose your job?" I asked.

"No they transferred me to another campus and it is too much driving back and forth to get you to and from school. Momma is already living over there and Trish and Aunt Pat are moving this week, too." "Ahh no," we all said. "Are we moving with Grandma again?" I asked.

"No child. We will have our own place." she answered. A sigh of relief came from all of us. "Okay Mom, we'll start packing." I was actually excited about this move and kind of happy to get away from Jacob and JT, but sad to leave my cousin Nancy. It was easy to dodge Jacob but JT lived right across the street and would come to my door singing Baby Face and New Edition songs faithfully every Saturday morning while my Mom was pressing my hair.

We settled in our new place and my cousin Keith was back home and kind of became my running partner except when he would began to tease me in front of his friends. He'd call me skinny and I would call him ears because they were very big. When Nancy would come to visit the three of us together spelled TROUBLE.

At my new school I met a girl name Shonda Brown. We became inseparable. We would write each other notes, dress alike, and share lunch. Cheerleading had boosted me to new heights. Shonda and I were literally at the top of the pyramid. On the weekends, my time was spent teaching cheers and dance moves to the girls in the neighborhood that cheered for the football team. My cousin Keith was head quarterback as well as the fastest runner on the team. One weekend when we did not have a game, I was moping around and sitting on the steps because I could not go to Shonda's house. My Mom never let me stay at other people's houses anymore ever since the shingles incident.

Two girls, whom I had never seen before, came running up to me. One said, "Hey, you're Reyne, Keith's cousin." "Yeah! Why? Who wants to know?" I asked as I jumped up off the stairs. "I'm Keisha and this is my cousin Shaquita."

"Hi" Shaquita said waving one hand with her head down. I said "Hi" back and noticed that her shyness was unlike her cousins' eagerness. "Anyway," said Keisha, "We were wondering if we could meet him?" "I am not sure. You know they don't allow girls at practice." "We will be very quiet, as long as you introduce us afterwards." I looked them both over and I said, "Okay but come back in about an hour from now closer to the end of their practice."

Excitedly Keisha said she would be back. She pushed Shaquita on the shoulder and told her to stay. She then ran off to do only God knows what, while Shaquita and I sat on the stairs and began talking. We realized we had a lot in common and we both missed our dads very much. "You know my cousin is fast," said Shaquita. "Fast" I asked humping my shoulders. "What is that?" "You know, she lets the boys play with her and put their mouth on her chest," said Shaquita.

"Uh yuck, that is disgusting. Why would she do such a thing?" I say shaking my head. "I don't know," she said. "Her Mom does a lot of that stuff and she smokes too."

"Smokes? That is just nasty," I say making a stinky face.

"So what do you do?" Shaquita asked. "Who me?" I shook my head while I was still pondering what she had said previously. "I don't do none of that. Usually I am teaching cheers, reading, or dancing, anxiously waiting for Monday so I can see my best friend, Shonda." "Hey that is my middle name." she said smiling brightly. "Oh cool," I replied. I was really beginning to like her. We seem to laugh a lot together. "So what church do you go to?" she asked. "None right now. My Mom is never home and if she is home on a Sunday, she sleeps. We pray and stuff and oh yeah, I got baptized when I was seven." "Really, how old are you now?" asked Shaquita. "I'm 11 now, but I will be 12 in November," I responded proudly. "November what?" she asked excitedly. "The twenty-fifth." I said. "Oh my gosh, that's my birthday too." she squealed. "For real?" I said excitedly eyes wide. "We should have our parties together, I will be 13," she suggested.

"Sounds good. I will ask my Mom and maybe we can even come to church with you," I responded. "Yeah, that would be great and you could sing with me in the choir," she said stretching out her hand. "You got yourself a partner," I said and shook her hand.

"What is this?" asked Keisha. She walked up looking like a circus clown with too much make-up on. We covered our noses and asked, "What is that smell? Toush it stinks." Swaying from side to side, Keisha said, "Oh that's Chanel #5."

"Well it smells like Lionel under the bridge #5," I said laughing. "Come on" Keisha said as she grabbed Shaquita. "Let's go." "She looks crazy," I said. "Girl, I told you she was fast. The only reason my Mom lets me come over is because she's a nurse and for the most part, she's almost always on call. It just so happens she got called into work this weekend and I got stuck with Keisha." "Ahh that sucks," I say as we head towards the football practice field.

Around the corner up the hill there were the guys chilling on the field.

Looking good and very hot, I must say I missed a lot. Never had I noticed one of them was really cute. Keisha had long ago left us and ran down right into my cousin's face in the middle of the guys. By the time I looked up from fantasizing my cousin had given Keisha the boot. She came over there stomping saying, "Let's go," But Shaquita and I were already making our way down as she was coming back up.

Keith and Aaron were smiling in our faces as we all laughed at how ridiculous Keisha smelled and looked. Keisha stomped away back up the hill. Where are you going after this, asked Aaron to Keith? Touching his stomach he said, I'm kind of hungry." Nudging me Shaquita asked, "Are you hungry?"

"Uh huh," I replied, lost in Aaron's eyes. "Yeah, I could go for some food." Keith said, "Well, that settles it. We'll go home and shower up, get ready and meet y'all by Coach's car in about an hour." "Okay," Shaquita answered and pulled my arm. "Come on, let's go." "Oh, alright, I said and waved bye. Aaron reached out and touched my hand, locking his fingers into mine. "I'll see you later," he said looking me straight in the eye. I almost fainted. I mumbled "okay" and I ran off with Shaquita to get prepared. As we reached the bottom of the hill we could hear them talking as they walked behind us. Keith said, "Are you just going to stand there until Christmas? Come on man, you know Coach will leave us and I am not trying to miss a meal." Aaron was staring over the hill. "Yeah, let's go," he replied.

They began to walk down the hill. He continued, "Man your cousin is beautiful. Where has she been? I've never seen her around here before."

"Boy you crazy. She skinny and has big hair," Keith said and hit him upside the head. "You see her every game. She is the head cheer-leader."

"What?" Aaron shockingly said. "I promise I never noticed her."

"Yeah, that's because you too busy running the ball into the end zone." He grabbed Keith's head and put him in the headlock.

"Yeah but we win every game, don't we? You throw those passes so smooth," said Aaron pretending to catch a pass. "We are like Joe Montana and Jerry Rice. You throw, I catch and bam, Touchdown!" he said bragging. He then asked, "I wonder how I can score a touchdown with your cousin?

Keith replied, "Alright man, don't get your legs broke. My Aunt Eva doesn't play that. She'll cut your man off." "What? Nah, nah, I don't mean like that." Aaron stopped and then starting walking again. "You know I could like bring her home to my mother, bring her to the family reunion, yeah she could meet the family," he said as he walked to his apartment. "Alright now man," Keith said while knocking my door. "Don't trip on those arrows cupid is shooting at you."

"Wait," said Shaquita. "Let me sit down." After she gave me the nod, I went and opened the door for my cousin. Keith comes in and goes straight to the kitchen. Suddenly there is a knock on the door and he yells "I got it." It was Aaron.

He says bad news, "My Mom is waiting for me because we have to go shopping and coach has to find his little brother so we will have to eat another time. Sorry yawl." Keith asked, "Where did Coach Brother go?" "I don't know man some of the other guys say they saw him with some funny smelling girl that looks like a clown," says Aaron. Looking at each other Shaquita said, "It wouldn't happen to be the girl that was talking to Keith earlier would it?" Putting his hand to his face he said, "You know what? Now that I think about it, I did see them walking towards the back of the apartments." "Yep, that's her" said Shaquita. "Oh well." She threw her hands up and sat back on the couch. "You will not see him for a few hours."

"Who is she anyway?" asked Keith with a frown while closing the door behind Aaron. "Oh that's my cousin," Shaquita said and put her head down. "We are not really that close." "Good," he answered and sat next to her on the couch.

"Ahh, let's go," I said pulling them both up. "You know if your Aunt Eva, my momma, walk in here and see you sitting next to her she is going tear both of you a new you-know-what." They jumped up and said, "Let's go play outside."

"Wait, I am still hungry," I said as I rumbled through the fridge. Keith said, "Come on, girl. Grandma is cooking and Uncle John is barbequing hopefully it is finished by now. Aunt Barbara should be over there in a little bit and Uncle Ervin came down from Louisiana."

Excitedly I jumped up. "Oooh yes, my Porain is here! I can get us some candy money. Let's go," I said and locked the door. We headed to my grandmother's apartment. When we got there I ran straight to my Porain and gave him a hug. "Hey Porain!" Keith went inside while I stood patiently smiling knowing my Porain would give me money for goodies. "Hey Baby Girl," he said and kissed me on the forehead. "What you got for me," he asked while moving my hair out of my eyes.

I quickly give him a rundown of my grades and introduced him to Shaquita and stuck my hand out. He gave me $2.50 and gave Shaquita the same and told us to go get some chips or something because all the meat will not be ready until later. I gave him another hug and told him thanks. Inside Grandmother's apartment, we found Keith and asked him to walk us to the store. "Who is that with all that racket?" yelled my Grandmother coming out of the kitchen.

"Hi, Grandma," I said. This is my friend, Shaquita." "I don't care who it is. Get out of my house with all that noise. People are trying to watch T.V." I looked into those cold eyes of hers and told Shaquita, "Come on, let's go." She slammed the door behind us and locked it.

"Wow, is that your grandmother?" Shaquita asked. "Yeah unfortunately," I said and shook my head. "She seems so mean, almost evil." Shaquita shivered her shoulders. "Evil does not even come close to describing that woman," I said as we walked to the stairs. "Oh look, there is my Mom." I walked towards her. "Hey Momma." "Hey, Baby. Where is Stacey'nem?" I ask. "They are coming. They went to take the groceries to the house. Momma this is my friend, Shaquita. Can we please go to church with her and her mom tomorrow?" "Baby, we will see."

"Momma, please?" I beg. "I will let you know. Go on now. Go play. We got all day to be concerned about going to church tomorrow." She kissed me on the cheek and walked towards the door. Smacking her lips with her hand on the knob, she asked, "Why is the door locked?"

"Hey, y'all ready?" yelled Keith coming from around the corner. "Where were you? We were looking for you in the house." "Oh, I had to do something for Uncle John," he said as he handed him a brown paper bag. "Come on, let's go," he said and started walking towards the street. As we were headed out of the apartments Uncle Ben and Aunt Barbara pulled up. "Hey, where are yawl going?" asked Aunt Barbara. "To the store," says Keith "Hey Nancy," I said. Nancy was my favorite cousin who was in the back seat waving madly. "Oooh Momma, can I go too, please?" "Yes, child, go ahead and don't spend all your change on junk. Your Grandmother cooked." "Yes mam," Nancy yelled. She was already out of the car and next to us. "Hey, Keith" she asked. "What's up Sneaky neak?" Keith asked.

"Hi, I'm Nancy. Who are you?" she asked Shaquita while looking her up and down. "I'm Shaquita," she replied and stretched out her hand for a handshake.

"Come on, enough with the introductions already. I just saw the snack truck leave the store so let's get the fresh stuff," Keith said as he grabbed Shaquita's hand. "So are you going to get on the swings today?" asked Nancy.

"Don't start, Nancy. You know I am not fond of that thing." "I'm telling you it's fun. It feels as if you are flying high in the sky, free like a bird," Nancy said while waving her arms in the air. I relented. "Okay, fine. I will try it as long as you do not try and push me. Let me do it by myself." I pointed my finger sternly in her face.

When we reached the house Aunt Barbara was outside going through the cooler. "What took you all so long?" she asked. "You know us. Just walking and talking," Nancy stated hiding her pickle behind her back.

"Come here, girl and give me the butt off that pickle," Aunt Barbara said.

"Ahh Momma," Nancy sulked handing her the pickle saying, "You always take the good part." "Is the food ready yet?" asked Keith. "No," said Grandmother coming out of the house with another pan of meat. Yawl go play at the park and do not get in any fights." She looked mainly at my cousin, Nancy.

As we headed it to the park, Nancy noticed Keith holding Shaquita's hand.

"I've never seen Keith hold a girl's hand before," she said. "Well, there is a first time for everything," I said. I hunched my shoulders and ran ahead. "We are headed to the monkey bars," Keith yelled. "Okay, we are going to the swings," Nancy said. She grabbed my hand and pulled me towards the swings. "Okay, look this is how you start," she said. She climbed on the swing and showed me how it is done. I got onto the swing next to her. "First, you push back and run a little so you can build some height." she said while moving her long legs.

I was trying to understand when suddenly everyone started screaming and running. "Oh no, it's Mad Dog," yelled one of the kids on the other swing.

"Swing higher," Nancy yelled. "I don't know how," I yelled back. "I'm getting off."

"No, girl he will catch you if you run." She put her leg in front of me. "What do I do then? I ask hurriedly. "He is coming." "Look. Put your legs out and when you go back, put your legs in. Hurry," she yelled. In and out, in and out I kept repeating to myself. "Yeah, just like that. You got it, Nancy said. "Oh, no! Here he comes!" I yelled and started pushing harder. "Go higher! Push your back in! Go! Go!" Nancy yelled.

The dog jumped up and down barking and growling. I began to sing, "Ha, ha, you can't get me." I stuck my tongue out at the dog. I had not even realized how high off the ground I was until the dog's master called out to him and the dog tucked his head and went towards him. Finally, I stopped the swing by tapping the ground a few times and Nancy gave me a high five. She said, "Wow you were swinging really high." "Yeah, I guess when it comes down to life and death, fear goes straight out of the window," I replied. "Hey, are you all okay?" I yelled to Shaquita and Keith on top of the monkey bars. "Yeah, we good," they both replied while shaking their heads laughing at how fast everyone scattered when the dog came.

Keith said, "I saw you swinging. You did good." "Thank you," I say smiling happily. My sister Lacey called out, "Hey y'all, come on. It is time to eat." "Hey, Lacey," I said running over to her. "Where were you guys? Yawl missed it. I was swinging." "We went with Momma to the store. Come on, I will race y'all to the house." Keith said, "I am going to win because I smell those ribs from here," and he took off running. As always Keith beat me but I still managed to get my plate first because he headed straight for the sodas once we arrived at the apartment.

Sitting outside on the steps eating, Keisha walked up to let Shaquita know her Mom was there. "Where have you been?" Shaquita asked. "I was kind of busy," Keisha said looking over her shoulder and waving bye to the Coach's brother. Rolling her eyes, Shaquita said, "Come on Reyne, get your Mom so she can meet my Mom. "Momma, come here please, Shaquita's Mom is outside and I want you to meet her," I yell into the house. "Okay I'm coming," my Mom said as she put her plate away.

"So are you coming to church tomorrow, Keith?" asked Shaquita. Keith looking shy says, "Yes, if Aunt Eva goes I will ride with her." "Alright, it was nice meeting you," Shaquita said and gave Keith a hug. "Hi, Mom. I had a wonderful day," said Shaquita while giving her a hug. "This is my friend, Reyne." I shook her hand and said, "Hello. This is my Mom, Eva."

"Hello, Eva. I'm Samantha," says her Mom politely. "Your daughter invited us to church tomorrow," my mother said. "Great, let me give you the directions," she said. As we turned to walk away, I heard her Mom say, "Keisha told me you did not play with her much today."

"Mom, I need to talk to you about something important. Reyne told me that I should not be afraid to come to you." "So, I see you made a new friend," her Mom said as they got into the car. I smiled and held my Mom's hand on the way back to my grandmother's apartment. "Thanks Mom, I love you," I said. She smiled and said, "I love you, too." For some odd reason or another I think my Mom was happy that I asked her about church. It seemed as if she needed a break from working so much.

At church on Sunday, the preacher preached about people coming in and out of your life for a reason and a season at a time and that sometimes we lose people but we never lose their memory. So we should be thankful for the time we have shared with them. As he spoke I sat back and a few tears began to fall as I thought about Melissa, Tree and my Daddy. At the end of church, we ate with the congregation and played outside. Shaquita was happy to see both Keith and me. I was anxious to get to school on Monday and tell Shonda all about my weekend and to hear about hers.

However, Shonda did not come to school until Wednesday and due to the game we did not get a chance to talk until Friday at lunch. I told her all about my weekend and Aaron. "Never kiss, never hug, and if he starts to act like a bug, squish him like the one he is," Shonda said. "Girl, you crazy but I got you." I said laughing and high fiving her. The next two months were great. Shonda and I made honor roll, I joined the choir at church, and I finally got to spend a night at Shonda's house. My Mom called us to the living room one Sunday and told us we would be moving. I immediately began to protest and stated that I was not leaving West Jr. High School. To my surprise she said, "You don't have to change schools. I have switched jobs and I am going to manage some apartments. So rent will be free and maybe by spring break we can make it to Disney World...finally."

To my surprise, within a month we moved from that apartment to a house. Come to find out the management company promised free rent and lights without pay. Let's just say Mom got her month's pay out of the place. For what they would have paid her in wages, they had to pay in damages to their property, after she took out her anger on the place. I must say it was a blast trashing the apartment. I hated living there anyway. Everything was so dirty.

This next place was not fun at all; it was a house in the center of what seemed to be woods. The landlord left me with a very dark and eerie feeling anytime he came around. The rent was cheap and I was still able to go to West Jr. High so we made the best of it. Another month passed and the holidays were soon to come.

One Sunday afternoon I was taking a nap after church and suddenly I began screaming and crying frantically. My sisters shook me to wake me up. At the same time, the phone was ringing. Stacey answered and tears began to well up in the corners of her eyes. I watched in total shock as Lacey turned back and forth asking us both what happened? Stacey whom I was laying on when she answered the phone looked down at me and placed her hand on my chest because she felt the heat rising from me. She thought I would know because in the past when I would cry waking up and the phone would be ringing it would be someone dying exactly or dead just how I was dreaming it when they were waking me up from crying. Before she could speak, Momma walked in the door, dropped the groceries and took the phone from Stacey "Okay, I'll be there," she said and hung up the phone. "Momma, what happened?" I asked. "Aunt Trish lost the baby. It was born still-born and the funeral will be tomorrow. It will be closed-casket. What's wrong with you? Come here," said my Mom. "Be careful Mom, she's burning up," says Stacey. Touching my head my Mom asked me what was wrong. Crying and shaking my head, I asked, "Will I be able see the baby tomorrow?" "Well, honey, no you're not. It is going to be a closed casket funeral."

I screamed I want to see the baby and, ran up to the room and cried myself to sleep. I woke up at about at 9 p.m. to find Lacey by my side. "Where is Momma," I asked. "She and Stacey went to the hospital to help Aunt Trish. Do you want to tell me about the dream?" "No, I don't want to talk about it. I want my Daddy. Can we call him?" "No, we cannot," said Momma coming through the door. "Lacey come here a minute." Closing the door, Momma asked Lacey to tell her exactly what happened.

"I was watching T.V. and I heard Reyne saying, 'No I want to see the baby, I want to see the baby, please let me see her and then she started crying, screaming and wrestling. Shortly after that, the phone rang. It was Aunt Trish."

"Reyne, do you want to talk about it?" My mom asks, peeking her head through the door. "No Momma, I just want to go to sleep."

The next morning, I begged to go to school and not the funeral but of course my mother made me go. I cried the entire time because I couldn't see the baby. It was not until a week later that I found out Aunt Trish had reacted the exact way I had in my dream. After hearing this, I told Mom the entire dream. I explained to her that our family and her best friend's family had gone on a camping trip in the woods. And my god-sister got lost and nobody would let me go outside to find her. I kept screaming I want to see her and they kept telling me no. My god-sister was only a year old but I considered her my little baby, because I would always have her with me when I would visit my Mom's best friend. She told me to ask God to take it away if I were scared. I was not scared, just upset because I couldn't see the baby.

Back at school I finally told Shonda what was going on with the dreams and she told me that she had similar dreams and her grandmother said it was because she was chosen by God, to see things. I asked

Shaquita about it at church and she asked the pastor. The pastor said he would talk to my Mom. Needless to say I never heard anything about it because we stopped going to church due to another move.

One evening after coming from my Grandmother's, we came home to find the house ambushed. The T.V. and the VCR were missing. The radio and the cassette tapes were gone too. On the kitchen table sat the jug of empty Kool-Aid, an empty bread pack, and empty packets of meat and cheese that looked like someone had eaten. My Mom was furious. After she called the cops, she went to the landlord who claimed he didn't see anything. When he came over to the house I looked right into his eyes and saw exactly what had happened.

There he was watching us leave. He came into the house, took our stuff, ate our food and then lied like he didn't do anything. After everyone left, including the cops, I told my mother what I saw. She asked me was I sure and then said that she would handle it. The next few days went by quick. By Wednesday the landlord was in jail and she was preparing us to move; only this time I had to change schools. Oh, I was livid. I cried the whole entire day on Thursday. When I told Shonda at breakfast that morning, we clanged together like two Siamese twins. I cried, she cried, she cried, I cried. It was so bad that when my Mom came to pick me up at 1 o'clock that day, the school had to call Shonda's Mom to pry us apart.

Finally we said our goodbyes, and I never heard from or saw Shonda again. Oh how I miss her. In the car, my Mom said, "Fix your face now. I have to get you registered at your new school."

I protested, "I don't want to go to a new school." "You, my child, don't have any wants," she said grabbing me by my shirt. "I want my Daddy," I said. "Well, that is not going to happen. Your Daddy is not here right now," she said and let my shirt go. We pulled up to the school and I refused to get out of the car. Forgetting what kind of mother I have, I found myself flying out of the car door and into the doorway of the school, not quite remembering how I got there.

After we registered, the lady asked my Mom, "Will she be starting today?" My mother looked at me with compassion in her eyes as if she could feel my hurt. She whispers, "No. She has already missed half a day. She can start tomorrow." My Mom hugged me and said, "Let's go. Baby, I promise our next move will be to a big house with a huge yard and your own room. I promise." Pushing me ahead of her, we headed to the new place.

The next morning was the worst, yet the most defining day of my life. Here I was separated from another person I loved, living in another new place, starting another new school, and I woke up to find a small puddle of blood in my bed. I just sat there screaming. My Mom and my sisters rushed into the room. They asked, "What's wrong with you? Why are you screaming?" "I am bleeding, I am bleeding! Look!" I said throwing back the covers. My sisters took a closer look and said at the same time as they often do as twins, "Oh girl, your cycle started." "My cycle?" I asked looking puzzled. "Mom, you are on your own with this one," they said.

"Get up child. Come on now. Get up and come take a bath quickly, so you won't be late for school. I have to pick up Tina," she said, fiddling through my dresser drawers looking for sheets. "Mom, what is a cycle?" I asked, while preparing my bath. "Well honey I guess you do not remember us talking about this sometime ago," she said as she sat down on the toilet. "A cycle is a cleansing of the body at a certain time of the month. Your body goes through different changes and causes you to bleed for a few days once a month." "Does everybody get it?" I asked.

"Yes Baby," she answered and helped me get out my clothes. "Even boys?"

"No, silly not boys. Only women. Remember I told you about this a while ago and you declared you wanted to be a boy so that you would not have to go through this once a month." "But I'm not a woman, I am only 11." "You will be 12 in two weeks and that's a pre-teen, so it is about that time."

"Why don't boys get it? That's not fair." I stepped into the bathtub and yelled, "I want to be a boy...I want to be a boy!" "Girl if you don't sit down and shut up, I will make you a permanent figure on that wall. "Yes, Ma'am," I softly whispered. "I still want to be a boy." She walked out of the bathroom. Lacey showed me all about the pads and stuff and helped me pack my bag for school. She told me I may get a little cranky and feel some pain in my lower stomach. To my surprise, I did not feel any pain or crankiness. I just noticed I was extremely tired and just could not seem to eat enough chocolate that day or the next three days. Everything was okay except that following Monday when my Mom took me to school.

That previous Friday when it started, I made her pinky promise not to tell anyone. Ha, like everything else that secret went out the window. I had just awoken in the backseat of the car and my Mom and Tina were talking in the front. Through the small hole in my sweater that I slept with over my head, I saw my Mom look back to see if I was still asleep. Then I hear her say, "My baby is not a baby anymore, her cycle started." "For real?" Tina asked. "Yeah, but don't say anything about it. You know she's sensitive and embarrassed." She went on to tell her how I screamed and yelled, "I want to be a boy." I was flabbergasted.

Here it is my own mother telling the very thing she pinkie promised she wouldn't and laughing about it. Upon arrival at the school she shook me. I got up, got out the car, and gave both of them a nice long stare, while they smiled and chuckled and said goodbye. Without a word, I rolled my eyes at the both of them and walked away. As I walked off, I heard Tina say, "Child she got PMS already."

My Mom said, "Yep, I guess so," not even having a clue that I heard her tell the secret. A few months went by and I tried each month not to tell my Mom when my cycle started because I knew she would blab to her friends but I had to because I needed pads.

As if that was not bad enough, in my history class we were learning about American History. In this particular segment we learned about slavery. My stomach ached with sickness as I saw the pictures of black people being hung by white people. I remember thinking to myself how could they be so cruel? Here it is December 1991, my 7th grade year of school. Eight out of 12 of my closest friends are white. Two out of that 12 are Hispanic and the other two are black. This caused a tremendous uproar. As if seeing the shock on my face my friend Jessica, who is white, rubbed me on my back and said, "Its okay. My parents told me those were bad black people. You're not like that." Immediately I jumped up and went to my teacher. "Sir, I don't understand this. How is it that all of us can drink from the same fountain today and things were so bad less than 30 years ago?"

My teacher said some things change and some people don't. I then said, "Almost all of my friends are white, and I love them." Looking up from his work and right into my eyes Mr. Andserson said, "Reyne, I think it's time you got some new friends...some black friends." I gasped and backed away slowly burning with anger. I went back to my desk gathered my things and politely walked out of class. Two of my white friends followed me, "Are you ok?" they asked. Looking up with tears in my eyes, I said, "I just want to be alone right now." I moved their arms of comfort off of me, and walked away. The bell rang, and it was time for lunch, just as I reached the corner, a girl named Latasha pulled me to the side. "Hey are you okay?" she asked. I heard from Laquita what happened. Laquita was a black girl that I was not very fond of. She was fast and loud and always made jokes about me wanting to be white. Latasha on the other hand also known as Twinkie was black and white. I had two other classes with her and enjoyed her friendship. She liked my white friends and was only concerned about her boyfriend, Jed, who did not go to our school and, yep you guessed it, Twinkies. I told her that I did not know what I was angry about, the fact that the teacher said that to me or the fact that most of the white kids already knew about this stuff and my Momma never told me a peep about any of it. I felt like a real idiot. She nodded her head and asked me to sit with them at lunch. I told her okay.

Although I still had a lot of questions, I felt a small sense of comfort surrounded by all black faces at the lunch table. As Becky and Elizabeth passed by, they sort of looked on with shock and amazement. Jessica shoved them on. She rolled her eyes and said, "Leave her to her kind, we are different."

It was sad to say, but Jessica had a point. Until that moment, looking around at the cafeteria, I had not realized how different we all were. I slumped down in sadness again anxiously anticipating the end of the day. My last three classes went by extremely quickly. Running like a cheetah to the car, I told my Mom all about what happened and the mean and horrible comment the teacher made to me. Before I could even get on her case about not telling me about this stuff she was on the phone.

By coincidence, the teacher was out the next two weeks. Our sub, Mr. Estevez was nice and explained the racism issue that was at hand and allowed us to do an in class project where we would interact with one another on the Civil Rights movement. This brought unity back amongst the whites and blacks in my class.

The teacher suggested we watch the television show "Roots" over the Christmas break to get a visual of the beginning of slavery to the end. Needless to say, I was floored. I could only make the first three parts. I then told my mother that was enough. She talked to me briefly about the hatred people have for one another because of the color of

47

their skin but I could tell it was not something she really wanted to discuss. I spent the rest of my break on the phone with Twinkie, her boyfriend, and his cousin, who they were trying to fix me up with. Now I knew how my Mom felt about boys, so I kept this a strict secret.

Back at school, the New Year was full of surprises. Being that Mr. Anderson was back; just about every parent of students in my 7th grade history class was at the school petitioning to have him fired, both white and black. Fired he was and Ms. Estevez, our sub while he was out before the break became our permanent teacher. Everyone was happy about that. One morning while in the courtyard, Shun, Twinkie, and myself were rapping Tonight by DJ Quick when the school bus pulled up. As if by some unexplainable force, all our heads turned towards the bus.

Wow! There he was, skin like sunshine, beautiful eyes, tall and slim. I quickly grabbed (the rolled up notebook) and sang, "And the one with the brown eyes is coming with me." The rest of the girls said, "He's the one." I said, "You bet your bottom dollar." Completing the song, we ran to class not to be late for the first bell. I glanced over at the new guy. We made eye contact and smiled at one another. For some strange reason, I felt like I knew him.

I totally ignored the lesson because I could not get my mind off of those pretty brown eyes. The end of 1st period was rounding up and in walked Pretty Eyes. Due to a cheerleader meeting, I was called out just as he entered.

"Excuse me," he said. "No, excuse me," I said brushing past him and running to my meeting. "Hey slow down," yelled Mrs. Anderson the cheer-leading coach.

Checking my pulse, I said, "I'm fine, just a little weak in the knees," as I remembered how he smelled when I walk by. I held my chest and leaned on the auditorium door. I was eager to see if he would be in any of my other classes.

Unfortunately, at lunch time I had to work on my cheers and was not able to spy on him. At gym class, I was able to catch a glimpse of those strong legs.

As me and the girls checked him out, I wondered how would Jed's cousin take to me looking at another guy. I had not seen him yet anyway, so technically I was not cheating. Besides it was not like I could have a boyfriend anyway. "Girl, can you quit daydreaming and come on?" said Shun, and I gathered my things. It was the end of the school day, and time for our cheerleader try-outs. I was fully confident that I would make the team. I had been at this since 2nd grade. I could jump the highest, split the lowest and had the straightest legs on my cartwheels.

Finally, it was my turn, I did all my stunts properly and shouted accurately and on time but I had one thing against me. The coach, Ms. Anderson, who made the final decisions for who made the team, was the Mr. Anderson's aunt, the history teacher who was fired. Needless to say, I did not make the team. As everyone's parents began to arrive, Jessica came up to me and rubbed my shoulders and said, "Maybe next year." I shrugged and said, "Naah, this is it for me young one. My cheerleading career is up, time to pursue more intellectual matters. I'll see you tomorrow." Not long afterwards, I was the only kid left. The coach rolled down her window and asked, "You need a ride?" "No, thank you my mother will be here soon." She drove off and rolled her window up.

Getting comfortable under the tree, I suddenly heard a voice. "You would have made captain of the team, if it were up to Me."

"What? Who said that?" I jump up and looked around. Pretty Eyes landed from out of the tree. "Oh my gosh, you scared me," I said holding my chest.

"I apologize my lady," he said bowing to me. "I didn't mean to frighten you. Allow me to introduce myself." He grabbed my hand, "My name is, 'beep-beep.'" I couldn't hear the rest of the sentence because of a horn blowing in the distance. "Reyne come on here, let's go!" We released hands. "I'm sorry, I have to go." I gathered my things and ran to the car. "Who was that?" asked Lacey.

"Nobody," I said closing the car door. "Yeah right," said Stacey. "I'm going tell Momma you were out here talking to some boy." "Please don't. I'll do each of yawls dishes for a week." "Deal," said the twins at the same time laughing. When we got home, I ran to Momma and gave her a hug.

"Hey there, you seem to be in good spirits. I take it you made the cheer-leading team," she said. "Actually, I didn't," I said while fixing my crust-less peanut butter and jelly sandwich. It just so happens that Coach Anderson is Mr. Anderson's aunt. "What?" she said moving her neck around? "I'll be up there tomorrow." I almost dropped my sandwich. "No, Momma, please no, do not come. It is okay. I do not want to cheer anymore; I want to pursue my writing plus I will always have dancing. That is like my skin color, it will never change or fade away," I said while swirling around. "Ahh, hush, girl," Lacey said. "I'm happy to see you in good spirits, I thought for sure if you did not make it, we would have to listen to you whine all night. You know how you get when you don't get your way," my Mom said. Lacey and Stacey nodded at the same time.

"Oh mother, I am growing up now. Doesn't the Bible say when I was a child, I thought like a child? I am becoming a young woman now, almost a teenager. I must not hold on to matters that are so trivial." Mother said, "Now I know something is wrong." "Nothing is wrong mother, just growing up," I said as I walked by tapping her on the shoulder. Stacey interrupted, "Reyne, tell Mom about your new friend."

As if fire hit, I immediately burned a glaze towards Stacey and then turned to my mother softly saying, "Oh yeah, we got a new student. Seems like a nice kid, anyhow call me when dinner is ready. I'll be in my room." I turned back to eyeball Stacey again. I couldn't wait to get on my phone. "Hey girl," Twinkie said when she heard my voice. "What's up chic, what are you doing?" I asked. "Waiting for Jed to call me back. Freddy called him all excited about something like an hour ago. I wonder how he looks. Jed said you will probably meet him soon," she said. "Well, I hope so the suspense is killing me," I say impatiently. "Hey did you get a look at the new guy?" asked Twinkie. "I saw him after school," I said. "Really, what is his name?" she asked. "I am not sure, my sisters drove up and I had to go." "Reyne come on down to dinner," said my Mom on the other end of the phone.

"Okay girl, I got to go. See you at school tomorrow," I said hanging up the phone. As I walked to the kitchen I thought to myself I really hope she was not listening to my call.

The next day I had to go to school early because my Mom had an exam to take for school. As I walked in the bathroom, I heard someone crying.

"Hello, are you okay?" I asked peeking under the stalls. The last door opened. It was Gracie. "Gracie, oh Gracie, what's wrong?" I reached out to her. She fell into my arms and wailed loudly. "Oh honey, what's wrong?" I asked again. "Please just don't tell anyone." She looked up at me and showed me scratches all over her neck. "Oh my gosh, Gracie, what happened to you?" I asked franticly. "I don't want anyone to see the bruises," she says while fumbling for her makeup kit.

"Who did this to you?" I asked. She reached for her compact that had fallen to the floor. "I can't tell you." Monica came in and saw us on the floor. She stopped in her tracks. "Oh no, not again," she said and ran to Gracie.

"You know about this?" I asked in amazement. "Yeah, her brother," says Monica.

"No please," Gracie shouted and reached out for Monica trying to get her to be quiet. She started crying all over again. "Oh Gracie, come here." I reached out for her, grabbed her and she placed her head on my shoulder. Monica came and laid her head on Gracie's lap and we all sat there together, weeping for what seems like hours.

Gracie finally said, "Come on. Let's get up before someone comes in here." I said, "Let's fix you up." I swiped her face. Monica picked up her makeup and put it back into her purse. Gracie grabbed my hand and Monica's hand and looked at the both of us and begged, "Please you guys do not tell anyone. This is between us. I will be okay. Please promise?" Monica rolled her eyes and nodded her head "yes." Gracie asked me, "Reyne, do you promise?" "I only promise if I never see you hurt like this again," I say nodding my head. "Deal," Gracie said. We shook on it and the bell sounded. "Oh no, there's the bell," Gracie said as she looked in the mirror. Hey you did a great job with the makeup, Monica, thanks." She hugged us both. "You know y'all are my sisters, right? No matter if I'm Mexican and Monica too, and you're black? We all share the same blood and I love you both."

"We love you, too, Gracie, now let's get to class," Monica said. "You guys go ahead. I'll be out in a minute." I said.

I looked at the floor, picked up Gracie's powder case and made a vow, looking into the mirror that if I ever have to use make-up to cover hurt and pain, I promise to run far away and never look back to what caused such pain. Throwing the case away, I walked out and ran right into Twinkie. "Girl, where have you been? I've been looking for you all over. Come on, I have a surprise for you," she said.

"What surprise?" I asked. "Just come on," she said pulling me to our 1st period class.

"Oh my gosh," I said. I stood in the door entrance with my hand over my mouth.

"Why hello, Ms. Williams, said the new guy as I entered the class room.

"Hello to you," I said as I picked up the paper made roses and the candy off my desk. "What is this all about?"

"Just a token of gratitude to my girl or anyone else girl for that matter." (He was trying to be funny because we were already dating but I did not know it was him yet) "I only talk to one guy and his name is...." He quickly grabbed my hand and said "Freddy. Freddy Jennings it is I, bowing, your knight in brand new Fila's" and he kissed my hand. I jerked my hand back and said, "Many boys have gotten busted lips for that." He grabbed my hand and kissed it again. He said, "Well, that's a fat lip I'm willing to take and a black eye, too, if you will be my girl." I began to blush and giggle and then I quickly jerked my hand back and said, "We'll see."

Off in the distance, I heard hands clapping. "Okay Prince Charming and Princess Di, can we have class now? Ms. Burns asked as she walked in wearing the same dull-colored suit as usual. "I see you've all met our new student, Freddy Jennings." "Hi, Freddy," the class said in unison. He bowed as he took his seat directly across from me. Angel passed me a note that read "I know what has been happening to Gracie Chiles." I looked at her with mixed emotions and I wrote back: "What about it?" She wrote back: "I will tell you later, too many eyes right now."

I looked up to see Freddy looking at me in a weird manner and a few others seemed to have caught my facial expressions.

Ms. Burns cleared her throat. "May I have your attention please?" Freddy raised his hand. "Excuse me Ms. Burns." He got up and pulled something from his desk. Gasping, Ms. Burns sat back. "I wanted to give you this on behalf of the rest of the class to say 'thank you' for taking out the time to teach us and even be concerned about our futures," Freddy said as he handed her a small pot of fresh flowers. I leaned to the side and gave Twinkie one of no he didn't looks. He then took his seat and winked at me. I half smiled and shook my head. Ms. Burns dropped a few tears and quickly went on with the lesson in a low, shy voice. The bell rang and Freddy grabbed my books and my hand and asked me where my next class was. I told him American History and he walked me straight there.

He walked me to and from all of my classes every day after that. A month had passed and this went on non-stop. Gym class was our favorite because we got to run together side-by-side, until his boys started calling him hen-pecked and whipped, so then the competitiveness kicked in. Everything between us became competition. Being a girl, I was determined to win at everything. Everything the guys did, I did better. One day, Freddy missed school and Angel and I hung out the entire day. At lunch, because Twinkie was out that day too, Angel and I sat together. Abruptly, Gracie came up and rudely shoved her way between the two of us. Monica and some other girls sat on the other side.

"So," said Gracie, "What's so important that you all had to sit all the way over here and talk about?" "Nothing," said Angel, as she put her head down.

"Nothing, huh? Get up and come here," Gracie said, grabbing Angelita's arm. She pulled her to the far side of the cafeteria with the other girls following. "Hey wait a minute," I said as I pushed my tray back and got up. "What's going on? Let her go," I protested. Monica grabbed my arm and said "Reyne, there are a lot of things you don't know." "Know or don't know, they are not going to jump my friend," I say jerking my arm away.

"No one is going to fight," said Monica as she tightened her grip on my arm. "Gracie just needed to talk to her." "What do all the other girls want?" I asked and jerked my arm away again and walked towards the girls. I pushed them out of the way. "Move, get back," I said as I got between Gracie and Angel. "What in the hell is going on here?" Quickly the girls dispersed as the principal walked up. Gracie grabbed Angel's arms. "Remember you're in this, too." Then she ran off. I turned to

Angel, only to be grabbed by the assistant principal. "Are you causing trouble?"

"What? No! Let me go!" I said and squirmed away from her. "You better not be and I don't want to see you in my office today," said the assistant principal as she walked off. "Angel, are you alright? I cannot believe Gracie treated you that way. What happened between you two?" Angel looked up and said "nothing" and walked off.

I had two more classes to go to and I could go home and call Freddy. In class I could not focus. I had so much on my mind. The rude principal who was still mad at my Mom for getting Mr. Anderson fired, and Angel and Gracie......

"Ms. Williams, Ms. Williams, which were on the earth first, the dinosaurs or the cows and horses, or humans," asked Mr. Brown interrupting my thoughts.

"Mr. Brown, we go over this every day, and my answer is the same, God created all the animals and Adam named them." "Wrong Ms. Williams, wrong." God did not create man and all the animals."

"Yes, He did."

"No, He didn't."

"Yes, He did."

"No, He didn't."

"Yes, He did and it's true and a fact because that is what the Bible says, and that settles it." I slammed my book on my desk.

"You know what? That's it. I want you out of my classroom," said Mr. Brown as he wrote a disciplinary note to send me to the office. I gathered my books and snatched the note out of his hand and stomped out of the door. Angel raised her hand. "May I go to the restroom," I heard Angel ask. "Yes, Ms. Gonzalez, you may go. Now back to our lesson. Anyone else has a problem?" asked Mr. Brown.

"Reyne, Reyne, pssst Reyne." I heard from behind me. I stopped walking and turned around. "Angel, what's up? What's going on?" "Here read these, the key map is inside. I have to go back to class," she said pushing letters into my hand.

"Okay," I say.

Once inside the office, the assistant principal immediately told Mr. Parks about the incident in the lunch room and showed him the note from Mr. Brown. Yep, you guessed it. I got three swats with the paddle, detention and a note home that had me in my room on punishment the entire weekend. My room was okay because that is where I spent all my free time anyway, but no phone? Boy, I was sick. I cried myself to sleep that night and did not even eat dinner. The next morning I was rummaging through my backpack to find my markers. I checked the pocket on the side and found the letters Angel had given me. I opened the first letter and it had a bunch of stars, hearts and other shapes. I tossed that one to the side and opened the other letter that said "key." On this letter was the alphabet that each shape stood for. At the bottom of the page was written, "PLEASE KEEP MAP SEPERATE FROM LETTER IN CASE ANYONE FINDS THE LETTER." Since I had nothing else to do, I spent the rest of the day decoding the two-page letter.

I fell asleep and awakened only when I heard, "Knock, knock. Are you hungry?" asked Stacey. I jumped up startled and said, "No, I am okay." I listened for her foot steps to leave the door. I rose up and sat on the floor, with the complete decoded letter on my lap.

Dear Reyne, first let me say thank you for having my back at lunch today, I do not know how to tell you this but I hope it gives you a clear view of what is going on. Gracie and I have grown up together since first grade. One night when we were in the 5th grade I spent the night at her house. I woke up in the middle of the night and saw her and her brother arguing. The other brother saw me coming down the hall and dragged me to Gracie's room. Gracie was carried in by her older brother. They began to hold us down and kiss on us. Then he entered me and I began screaming. He covered my mouth and then they switched. Gracie made me promise not to tell anyone and they threatened that if I did, they would hurt me even worse. After that they left. I asked through my tears if this was the first time this happened and she said no, that it had been going on for three years now and she was trying to protect me and was really sorry. That next year in the 6th grade my parents had to go out of town for a week. My mom asked Gracie's mom if I could stay there until they came back. I cried, begged, and pleaded not to go, but my mother insisted and since I could not tell them what happened, I really did not have reason not to go. That entire week night after night her two brothers and her dad repeatedly raped us over and over. As soon as my mom got back I told her. My parents immediately went to her parents and told them what was going on. Gracie denied everything, her dad called me a whore, reminding my parents about the time me and her younger brother kissed in the second grade. My mother suggested that she and Gracie's mother take us to the doctor. We all went and two days later Gracie's mom killed herself and her dad and the family moved out of the neighborhood. The doctor told my mom that I had been opened and … she nearly went insane. Ever since then I've been locked in the house not able to do anything or go anywhere not to mention no boy contact whatsoever. I really do not care if you tell her but I wanted to let you know before you get hurt or the same thing happens to you. I thought it was only fair to warn you. I am okay. My mom put me in counseling and I am okay now. My dad refuses to talk about it and burns with anger anytime we pass by the old house. He does not take week-long trips anymore and if they are going to be gone more than four hours, they take me with them. I love you, Reyne and please be careful, her family is crazy.

There was a knock on the door. I quickly wiped my face and slid the letters under my pillow and sat on it, just as my Mom walked through the door.

"Reyne, what are you doing? You did not come down for lunch." "I am not hungry," I said and looked down at my hands. "Mind if I sit next to you," she asked.

"Come on," I said and patted my other pillow. "Remember when you came to me and told me you wanted to be baptized?" "Yes," I answered.

"I was very happy for you and I let you do it. After that you started having all those visions and hearing things. I did not expect for you to get so smart and begin telling your teachers off." I protested, "But I didn't." Mother raised her hand. "Girl, don't you interrupt me like that again."

"Just because you know something is wrong does not mean you have the right to tell them what is right. Sometimes you need to keep things to yourself rather than blab them out. It will be time for you to say what is right. Right now, you need to keep your mouth shut. You do not have to prove anything to anyone. Do you understand me?" I kept my head down and said, "Yes, ma'am." "And pick up your head when I'm talking to you. Always look a person right in the eyes when you speak to them. You hear me?" "Yes ma'am," I answered. She gave me a hug and walked out of the room.

Needless to say, I cried myself to sleep that night again. I wanted to jump in my mother's arms so badly give her a big hug, but I knew she would not understand. Sunday was a better day. We actually went to Shaquita's church. I told her all about Freddy and she told me that her and my cousin Keith had broken up due to a passion mark. I said, "Hmmm, somebody must be a vampire to get a mark on that black neck," and we both fell out laughing. It was good seeing her and it made me smile which I needed badly.

Back at school I gave Angel a letter in code that I had written to her over my punishment weekend. We hugged and made a silent vow to keep quiet, unless it happened again.

Freddy was so happy to see me that he could not even concentrate in class and in gym he tripped over the track bar trying to watch me do my flips. The rest of the school year was a breeze. Freddy and I grew closer every day. It seemed as if we were more like brother and sister instead of boyfriend and girlfriend though. He was always correcting me and I was always protecting him. It was weird. Finally, summer came and I went to Twinkies 13th birthday party. Freddy was there as well and let's just say we danced the night away, and he sang his favorite songs to me. It was so much fun. The last two months of summer we spent going back and forth to my sisters' programs at Prairie View. Freddy went to Louisiana and Twinkie traveled with her mom.

Back at school, that 8th grade year, it seemed like everyone grew tremendously, especially the boys. Freddy seemed to have grown much taller and a little wider, although he was still skinny. Again the entire crew had 1st period together; Freddy, Twinkie, Angel, Shun, and I, as well as gym class and Pre-Algebra. The year started off great. All was well at home. My sisters were back from Prairie View and it did not seem like we would be moving anytime soon. Although I missed Shonda dearly and quite often wondered how she was doing, things were good. I tried calling her but her number was disconnected shortly after I left the school.

One day, in class, I had a problem understanding a question in Pre-Algebra. The answer was so simple but I just could not get it. After I gave up and went back to my seat, the teacher called Freddy up to solve the problem. He did so in less than one minute and was like, "Duh, Reyne," when he walked back to his seat. I was livid. I refused to talk to him the rest of the day, or the next morning. At lunch, I looked around but did not see him, so I sat by myself not wanting to be bothered. Suddenly a group of guys came towards me, led by Roger Blackmon. With snapping fingers and a drummer on the table across from me, Roger picked me up and sat me on the table and began to sing, "Tell Me

When Will I See You Smile Again." As I looked around at everyone gathering around, Roger moved to the side and Freddy came out, got down on one knee on the bench in front of me and said, "Baby, can I talk to you for a minute? I didn't mean to make you cry, tell me when I will see you smile again?" Roger then climbed on the end of the table and sang the climax of the song, which caused all the girls to fall around him. While everyone was paying attention to Roger, Freddy grabbed me and gave me a big hug and apologized for being so chauvinistic. "You're forgiven," I said.

The rest of the day was smooth sailing. In gym class we sat and talked about our lives and what we wanted to be when we grow up. I, of course, wanted to be the first black woman president. Freddy said while I was out bossing the world he would be making sure the entire universe of women was healthy by being a gynecologist. "A what?" I asked. "I do not think so, baby boom, no man of mine is going to be a gynecologist." "No matter what happens you'll be my best girl," he countered. "Forget best, how about only?" "Okay," he said and put my head in a head-lock. "The one-n-only." I gave him an upper cut in the ribs, and he jumped up and took off running. I quickly caught him and jumped high up on his back.

"Wow, Freddy you got yourself a real tomboy there," Roger said. I quickly jump down, and said shyly, "Oh hi Roger."

Freddy stepped in front of me. "Yeah, hi man, thanks for the song." He grabbed my hand and walked away. "What's he got on me anyway?" asked Freddy, stopping in center of the field and turning towards me.

"What do you mean?" "Why do all the girls flock to him likes as if he is Denzel or something?" I laughed. "Denzel? I would not go that far and not all the girls. I don't flock to him." "Maybe not, but you sit all shy and stuff, when he talks to you," said Freddy, holding his head down. I said, "Hey you," and grabbed his arm. "Stop for a moment and look at me." I placed my hand on his chin and lifted it up. "Who cares if all the girls don't flock to you? You're smart, handsome, a great listener and very mature for your age. You're shaped better than he and furthermore, you have me, something he could never have. Okay?" "Okay! But why do you act shy and all giddy when he comes around?"

"Every seemingly defensive animal acts helpless when confronted by their challenger no matter how charming the challenger may be. Yet, when the challenger thinks they have control, that's when you attack and suck'em dry." (Yep lol) "Wow, Baby Reyne you are a handful. I better watch myself and never get on your bad side," he laughed and put his arm around my shoulders. He looked at me. "What?" I asked. "Honestly, you never had a crush on him?" "Okay," I said nodding my head. "Once I did, but when he could not beat me in track, my crush quickly went away and I was only left with a few fuzzes when I hear him sing. I can't have a boyfriend who cannot even beat me in track. I don't want to have to spend the rest of my life making sure I don't step on his ego by holding myself back. Not cool, I am a lady." I said stroking my hair, "who can fix a sandwich and kick some butt." I punched him in the side and ran back to the gym.

When he finally caught up with me, he said "We are going to work on that lady part. For a lady, you have hands of steel." I caressed and looked at my hands, "These old things, no way," I said and pinched him on the cheek, "see you later."

The holidays came and went and my Dad visited for Thanksgiving. For my birthday, Freddy went all out with flowers, balloons and a poem. For Christmas, we went to Louisiana and stayed with my nanny and her son, named "Donnie," who was never home and always on the phone when he was home.

By the time February rolled around 1st period English and lunch had become a local concert. This girl named Ruby caught Freddy kissing me on the forehead and began to sing "Tender Kisses." She named this our theme song. At the time, I thought the song was beautiful and sang along with it, not knowing that all those tender kisses would soon be gone away just like the song says. Now the school was in frenzy, planning for our 8th grade prom that would be held at the end of March. Great thing, right? Wrong! March 6th was the day we had to do our annual school projects in Science. I hated Science.

I arrived at school early with my project and went to the bathroom to fill my volcano cup with soap and water. I walked in to find Gracie with a busted lip, black eye and her arm was in a sling, trying to cover up the bruises with makeup. "Oh no, not again, this is it!" I exclaimed. I'm telling the school nurse," and I turned to walk out. Gracie grabbed me and yelled in intense pain as I grabbed her hand and told her, "No." I stopped and looked at her purple and blue fingers. "What happened to your hand?" "I was trying to run and they grabbed me and slammed my fingers in the door." I could feel the bones in her fingers were out of place. "Gracie, I think they are broken." "Please, just help me cover this up and don't tell the nurse."

I began helping her apply the makeup. I thought I will never wear this stuff in my life because it only covers the truth. I begin to cry at the thought. Gracie patted me and said, "Reyne, please don't cry, I will be okay. I met a nice guy who is a senior in high school and has his own place. He is going to pick me up from school tomorrow and we will run away together after he graduates. He says he loves me."

My tears dried immediately and I looked up at her and said, "You are out of your mind and you need help. Just because you have bigger boobs than everyone here and look grown, does not mean you need to be running off with some boy you don't know, who claims he loves you."

Gracie straightened up, removed her hand from my shoulder and snatched her makeup kit and said, "Never mind, I'll do it myself. You just think you have it made because you have Freddy who makes your paper roses and has other people sing to you because he cannot sing himself." My mouth dropped and my heart fell in my stomach. Then she said, "I don't like flowers anyway. People can give them to me when I die," then she walked out of the bathroom. I was dumbfounded and did not know what to say or how to feel. I had so many emotions going on all I could do was look up and say, "God, help me please." I finished filling my bottle and went to class right in time for the bell to ring. Freddy was late again that morning and had to go to detention during lunch.

Ruby came and asked us, what colors were we both going to wear for the dance? Byron and I are on the committee list, and we would like to do a tribute to you for keeping us together." Freddy and I looked at each other and back at her at the same time and said, "Ahh, how sweet." Looking back at his paper he said, "Reyne, what color do you want to wear?" I said, "I don't care, you pick," looking at my paper or class work. "Wait a minute," Ruby said. "Are you two arguing?"

We looked up at one another. "Everything is great," said Freddy. "Yeah things are chill," I said giving Freddy another glance.

I just for whatever reason could not get Gracie out of my head. I was no longer excited about the dance or anything else for that matter. I looked up at Freddy again but he did not notice my stare. He, too, seemed pre-occupied, but I could not worry about him. I had to figure out what to do about Gracie. I left out of the classroom and ran into Twinkie. "Hey Reyne, what are you wearing?" asked Twinkie. "Um, I believe Freddy and I agreed on baby blue. Is Jed coming?" I asked. "I am not sure I have not asked him, yet," she said. "Well you better try and hurry up, it is only a few weeks away. I got to go, see you later," I said walking off.

Freddy rushed to catch up with me. "Wait a minute. Oh, Reyne, I am sorry, I was just trying to hurry and get to class. I did not finish my homework last night and I have three problems left." He kissed me on the forehead. "I'll see you later." "Okay, bye." I said. At that moment, I had a flashback of elementary school sitting under the tree talking to my dear friend Tree, whom I missed dearly. Then I saw his face clearly when he was being led out of the school by some grown up. His eyes were so tender and brown. Then it hit me: Freddy and Tree have the same color eyes. Could it possibly be? No it couldn't. Then almost as quickly as I had the thought, it was gone by the sound of Gracie's laughter over by Monica's and my locker.

I walked up only to hear her telling this wild story about the high school boy she mentioned earlier, beating some other boys who were trying to rape her. Just as I got closer, Jessica walked by and said, "Are you sure they tried to rape you? From the length of that skirt it looks like you were willing." She turned to her other friends with a laugh. I walked up to her and slapped her and told her, "You better watch your mouth Missy, because you never know what might happen to you one day."

Jessica held her face and yelled, "I'm telling!" and went straight to the principal's office. Gracie looked at me and grabbed Monica and the other on-lookers and said, "Come on, let's go." I opened my locker, but I did not notice Angel standing there. She looked at me, nodded her head and went into the classroom. I got out everything I needed for class, and made it in the door just as the bell was ringing. "Late again, Ms. Williams." I protested, "I, I…."

"I don't want to hear it," said Mr. Bernstein. "Just take a seat and prepare to do your presentation after I call the roll." I walked to my seat with a mumbled, "Yes sir." I looked up to see Angel, and we both mouthed at the same time, "I need to talk to you!" Nodding, we both said, "Okay."

After Mr. Bernstein called roll, he called me up to show my project. In the middle of my presentation, right when the bubbles were getting ready to come out at the pushing of a button, in walked Mr. Park.

"Excuse me, Mr. Bernstein," he was waving a pink disciplinary notice in his hand and he whispered something in his ear. Mr. Bernstein turned back to the class and said, "Excuse me. Reyne, you need to gather your things and follow Mr. Parks." "Ahhh, come on, can I at least finish? I was almost done." Mr. Parks shouted "No," and motioned for me to head out the door. I stomped to my desk, gathered my things, and threw my project in the trash, smacking my lips out the door. I heard Mr. Bernstein say, "With that attitude, she will not get anywhere."

In the office, I began to plead my case. Mr. Parks looked up at me and said, "Please wait out in the waiting area. I will call you when I'm ready."

"When you're ready? I could have finished my project. What do you mean when you're ready? You walked all the way down there to come and get me in the middle of my presentation, because some dingy broad, who by the way deserved that pop in the mouth, came down here and made it seem like she was the victim." I reached for his paddle. "Ahh nah, baby boom, it is not going down like this. Here," I said and handed him the paddle. "We need to get this over with now." I leaned on the desk, ready for my swats. "Come on now, I have work to do. I do not have time to sit here for this type of nonsense." Mr. Parks stood up, walked around the desk, handed me the paddle, and pointed to the nail it usually hung on. I put it back and he said, "Please wait outside until I call you," and he walked back to his desk. I picked up my books and went out and sat in the lobby. He got up and closed his door and I heard a roar of frustration and what sounded like papers being thrown on the floor. Then there was silence. I looked to my left and saw Angel sitting in the corner shaking her head from side to side.

"What are you doing in here?" I asked. "I told Mr. Bernstein 'up his' for that smart little comment that he made when you left out of the class, and he sent me down here. He said "If I liked you so much, I could rot in detention with you."

"He is such a jerk," I said. "So, you saw Gracie's face huh?"

"Yeah, when I got to school this morning I saw her getting dropped off and all bruised up. She was crying. I tried to help her but she pushed me away telling me to stay away from her. She blames me for her mother's death, you know. She said if I would have never said anything her mom would still be alive." I moved next to Angel and held her hand. "Surely it is not your fault. Her mom killed herself, right?"

Angel looked up at me, "I am not so sure. Remember I told you our mothers took us to the doctor? Well that next night, we heard scream-ing. I ran to the window to see Gracie's mom running to our yard. My dad went to open the door and just as he was opening it Gracie's dad grabbed her mom by the hair and told my dad, if he said anything to anyone he would kill me and my mom. I jumped down out the window just after I looked into Gracie's mom's eyes and my dad slowly closed the door. The next day it was said that she committed suicide." I gasped, "Oh my, why didn't your dad tell the police?" "He was afraid for our safety," said Angel. "What about after they moved?" "I believe he was just happy they were gone." I nodded my head. "We must do something about this. How can we get proof of what's going on?" Just as I finished my statement Mr. Parks came out. "Here, both of you have detention the rest of the day. Go straight there," and then he went back in his office and slammed the door. We both looked at each and shook our head "I wonder what is bugging him?" I said. Angel said, "I don't know." We both hunched our shoulders and headed to detention. Third period was just about over.

When we walked in, Ms. Mahacheik, who told us to pronounce her name My-Hot-Check, my algebra teacher was on duty. "Hey, my two favorite students," she said. I didn't know Freddy was behind me. Angel was puzzled. "I am not in your class," she said. "No Honey, not you, Freddy and Reyne." I looked back and saw Freddy. "Oh, can you two please go and get the SAC lunches for me before the bell rings?" "Sure

Ms. Hot Check Mahachiek," Freddy said. We walked down the hall and I asked, "Honey what's wrong? You don't look too good, today. Your shirt is wrinkled, you do not have on a belt and your hair is not brushed." I grabbed his arm and pulled him back. "Talk to me, what's wrong?" He stepped back, looked at me, took a deep breath, put his head down and said, "Nothing." "Okay fine, well I have a problem." I say. "What is it?" he asked. "I have a friend...." The bell rang.

We ran to the cafeteria and back to the SAC room only to see Ms. My Hot Check with her hands on her waist tapping her foot. "Oh, Ms. My Hot Check, I am so sorry," Freddy said. "I don't want to hear it. Get in here and pass those lunches out," she said. Freddy grabbed the box and started slinging lunches on the table. "Mr. Jennings, are you okay," asked Ms. Mahachiek. "Yes ma'am," he said and took his seat next to me in the back with Angel. She looked over at me and I mouthed "I don't know." I continued with my story. "So as I was saying, I have this friend and she is going through some problems at home and." Freddy cut me off. He was aggravated.

"Look, I have my own problems and I really don't want to hear about anyone else's. If it is that serious, ask your Mom what you should do," he said and he put his head down and went to sleep. I frowned and thought how rude then I looked at Angel and said "That's it. Why didn't I think of this sooner?" I got up and hugged his back. "What would I do without you?" "Um huh, love you too, now let me sleep," he said.

I took my seat and said to Angel, "This is what we will do." We went on to conduct our plan. I woke Freddy up when it was time to go home. My mother was already there early to pick me up, but I did not notice her. Once outside of the school, Freddy stepped down off the steps and stood in front of me, and grabbed my hand. "Baby Reyne please forgive me for my behavior earlier today. I am having a tough time at home right now." Before I had a chance to respond, this big black ugly looking man from a distance, said, "Freddy let's go."

Freddy said, "Remember this, you will always be my best friend and my favorite girl no matter what." The ugly man said, "Boy, I said come on!" Freddy yelled back, "I'm coming!" He reached for my cheeks, looked into my eyes, kissed me on my forehead, and headed towards Big Ugly.

I watched him walk off. I suddenly heard someone clear their throat. I turned around to see my mother standing there with her arms crossed with that "um huh" look in her eyes. I adjusted my position and asked, "Hi Mom, how are you?"

"How am I? How are you and who was your little tall friend?" "That's Freddy," I said as I walked past her towards the car. I turned around, looked at her, and said, "Hello Mom, can we go now?" I motioned her to come on. "Let's go."

Once in the car, I said, "Before you get upset, yes, Freddy is the new kid that Stacey mentioned to you last year. He is so adorably sweet and kind. He is like my best friend, my best, best, best friend."

She shook her head, "This is also the same boy that called you 15 times begging to talk to you when you were on punishment." "What? He called the house?" I said in shock. "Fifteen times," said Mom. "Wow! So you knew all this time?"

"Yep, I just did not say anything. Your grades were not affected and you did not bring home any jewelry and you were always off the phone by the time your curfew was up, so I will let you make it." "Oh Mom, you're the best. He really is nice. I would like to meet his mom, he talks about her a lot and how he helps her cook. He makes flowers for her."

"Makes flowers? So is that where all those paper roses come from all over your room?" I sunk down in the seat and said, "Yes ma'am."

She laughed and said, "Well at least they'll never die." As soon as she said that my smile went away as we pulled into Piccadilly's parking lot. She cut off the car, looked at me, and said, "Come on, let's go eat." Then she asked, "Reyne what's wrong?" I looked up at her from my sunken position and then put my head down and twiddled my fingers. "I need to talk to you." "Okay, Baby what is it?" We began to embrace.

"Can we go inside first, I'm starving. I had SAC today and those stale hard peanut butter and jelly sandwiches were not touching my tummy," I said getting out of the car. "SAC!" my mother yelled as she closed her door. "Yes mother, SAC, I'll explain inside." After we got our food, we sat side by side in a booth, and said grace. "God, thank you for this food and please watch over Gracie tonight and please bless my mother to do the right thing after I tell her this, oh yeah, and God prepare her mind. Amen and thank you, Lord."

"Okay Reyne, what's going on?" she asked while stirring her food. "I have this friend named Gracie and she is in trouble. The first time I found out about it last year, she made me promise not to tell anyone. I told her I would only promise if I never see her hurt again. Well, this morning when you dropped me off, I saw her and she did not look good. I said I was going to tell the nurse and she begged me not to, so I am telling you." I pulled out the letter that I had decoded and showed it to my mother. While she read, I ate and by the time she got through, we were both in tears. When she saw that I noticed her tears, her eyes quickly dried up. She folded the letter back up and put it in her purse along with the decoder. "I will take care of it, come on, wrap up your cookies and let's go." In the car I asked, "Mom, what are you going to do?" "I am going to make sure your friend is not hurt anymore."

Once at home, I called Freddy and we talked for a little bit about the dance. Then I heard a woman yelling for him to get off the phone in the background and he had to go. That next day at school seem to be much more peaceful, until around 3rd period, which was the History class I had with Gracie. I was called down to the office along with about five other students. My Mom, Angel's mom and some people in black suits as well as police officers were all crowded in the office. A search was done in Gracie's locker and two other crumpled letters were found. Once they were decoded, they revealed that Angel had threatened to tell another student's parents whose daughter was supposed to spend the night at Gracie's house, but luckily, she went out of town with her parents.

That girl had gone to Gracie's house after school one day and was almost attacked. Come to find out, Monica had pleaded with Mr. Parks, not to suspend me for slapping Jessica, and that I was only trying to defend our friend Gracie. Well after everyone told what they knew, the police informed Gracie that her father and two brothers were going to be locked away for a long time, and that her and her younger brother were going to be taken into custody by the people in the suits from Child Protective Services. Gracie began yelling in my face, "I hate you, I hate you, and you promised me you would not tell." I began crying and I yelled back, "I did not promise not to tell, I said, only if I never saw you hurt again and I promised not to tell the nurse." Angel put her arms around me and Gracie told her, "This is all your fault. If you would have never written those stupid letters and kept your mouth closed, none of this would have happened." She turned towards Monica, "And you, I cannot believe." She got one of her arms free, and snatched the best friend necklace off of Monica's neck and threw it to the floor smashing it with her foot. "I hate all of you," were her last words, as they carried her out of the school along with her younger brother, who was a 6th grader.

"Are you okay?" I asked my Mom. "Yes ma'am, do you want to go home or stay here?" "I'll stay. I have a test in Algebra." "Well lunch is over, Ms. Haggler, so if you want to go and get her something?" said Mr. Parks. "No, it's okay, I am not hungry," I said as I grabbed Angel's hand. I gave my Mom a hug and Angel hugged her Mom. Angel and I walked out hand in hand. Once we got down the hall, Angel burst out crying and began banging her head on a locker saying repeatedly, "Stupid, stupid, stupid!"

I put my arm behind her head, held her and said, "No, you are not stupid, you did the right thing. We did not know she would have to go to a foster home. God will protect her and her little brother, watch and see, I promise." Through her tears she asked, "Do you, you promise?" "Yes, Angel, I promise, He will." The bell rang and it was time for gym. As we stood up Freddy came around the corner.

"Hey, I've been looking for you all day. Where were you?" He saw the look on my face. "Reyne, are you okay?" he asked hugging me. "Yeah, I'm good."

Angel tapped him on the shoulder and told him thanks for the advice on yesterday. "Advice, what advice?" Freddy asked, looking dumb.

"Never mind, come on before we are late," she said. We all headed to gym.

"Oh no," I said once we got in the locker room. "What's wrong?" Angel asked.

"My Aunt-T is here." "Your what?" "My Aunt, you know, Aunt Flo." "Aunt who?" Angel asked. "My cycle, child. I call it Aunt Flo." "Oh okay. Here, I have some wipes and some pads," said Angel. "Thanks girl, you're a life saver."

"That's what friends are for."

"Speaking of friends," said Monica, coming around the corner, "I cannot believe you told your Mom and the cops what happened to Gracie." She pushed my shoulder. Angel stepped between the two of us and said "So what, you told Mr. Parks." She pushed her back. "Some kind of friend you are," Monica said and walked off. I stepped from behind Angel. "You knew about this before I did and was too scared to say anything. You were closer to her than any of us; you should have spoken up first." Monica said, "Whatever," and continued walking.

Angel said, "Don't worry about it." I went and fixed myself up and we headed for the track.

That weekend my Mom talked to Freddy's mom, and he and I talked about our outfits for the dance. Since we were nominated King and Queen of the Spring Fling, we had to be fly. Once again, all was well. My mother made me pick out a baby blue halter dress with a jacket and some baby blue and white heels. I would have much rather have worn the baby blue shorts set and my new tennis shoes, but she and my sisters said no.

For the next week after school, I practiced walking up and down stairs and dancing in the heels. There was one more week before the week of the dance. I was ready. I had my Michael Jackson, Troop, whop, cabbage patch, and the Kid-n-Play ready in those heels. With the help of my sisters, I even had my turns and spins down. Freddy had talked a really good game and I was ready to tear him up on the dance floor. That Tuesday in 1st period, Ruby asked me if I was ready. I was like, "Yeah, of course." The day before, Freddy had tried to make me look bad by dancing in gym class. Twinkie showed me the material from her dress. It was really pretty and black.

"The material looks really good, Twinkie. I bet the dress is going to be beautiful. Are you making it or your Mom?" I asked. Twinkie was known for making her own clothes. She was one of the most unique people I've ever known. She was the only 8th grader I knew who made her own clothes, and the only person I knew with a strawberry birth mark in the center of her head. It actually looked and felt like a strawberry. It was red and green. "She is going to help me," said Twinkie. "Good," I said, and looked around for Freddy. "Hmm, maybe he is late again." "What?" asked Twinkie. "Oh, nothing girl. Just talking to myself," I say shrugging my shoulders.

By lunch time, Freddy still had not arrived. I was concerned by this time, but I could not worry about it. I had a ton of work to catch up on from missing class last week due to the issue with Gracie. As soon as I got home, I ran straight to the phone. I called but there wasn't an answer. I completed my homework and called again but still no answer. After dinner, you guessed it--no answer. "Mom can I please call Freddy? I know it is past eight, but I have to talk to him." "Yes child, but you only have ten minutes to talk." she said. NO ANSWER again.

I went to school the following day and still no Freddy. I told myself maybe he was sick or something. Thursday rolled around and he still had not arrived. "Twinkie, please tell me you talked to Freddy, Jed or somebody." "Actually I was just about to tell you that last night, Jed called me and said Freddy called him about 6 p.m. yesterday evening, crying." "Crying?" "He said that Freddy said he had to go out of town and was not sure when he was coming back."

"Did he ask about me? Did he say why?" "Jed said he said he could not say why, because his Mom was yelling for him to get off the phone in the background. He asked him if he called you and he said he couldn't, he had to go and then the phone hung up. Jed tried calling back but he says he kept getting a busy signal."

My world was crushed; I sat there in unbelievable amazement. I looked at my fingers and the paper roses on my desk. How could this happen, there has to be some type of explanation. I cleared my throat and sat up straight. I looked Twinkie square in the eye and said, "You know what? He is going to surprise me. That's it, he is going to pop up and surprise me." "Okay, I guess, said Twinkie, turning to do her work." "He will, just wait and see," I said. I thought to myself, He better. The rest of the day was quiet and sad. Finally, the day of the dance, my Mom asked, "Reyne, what's wrong?" She stared at me as I sat at bottom of the stairs. "Oh nothing just…." "Get up, get up, I have a surprise for you," she said as she raised me up.

I plopped back down. "If it is not Freddy in a baby blue suit, I do not care to see it." "What's wrong?" she asked. "I have not seen or talked to Freddy in two weeks. His cousin Jed said that he called him crying saying that he and his mother had to leave immediately to go out of town. Jed has no idea where they went. He's called all the family here in Houston and nobody knows where they are. It is as if he disappeared." "Perk up child and go get dressed and come back down." I did as I was told and when I returned, Lacey said, "Ahh girl cheer up," as she tied a blindfold around my eyes. She walked me outside and I heard Mom ask, "Are you ready?" "Ready for what?" I asked in a low melancholy voice and off came my blindfold. I opened my eyes and adjusted them only to see a black stretch limo in front of the apartment. "Oh my God! Is that for me?" I squealed with excitement.

"Yes honey, Mom said. She was pleased with making me smile. The driver opened my door and I stepped in, but before I got settled, I asked Mom if we could get Twinkie. "As long as she is on the way to the school," she said with a stern look. "Yes, Mom she is, remember we drove her home one day after school when it was raining really bad. I will call her," I said as I got back out. My Mom looked at the driver as if to ask was it ok about the extra stop and proceeded with the directions when he smiled.

"Here, the limo driver said to me as he looked at my Mom, "You can use the car phone so we can get moving." He gave Mom a reassuring look. "I gave her a big hug and stuck my tongue out at my sisters and told the driver "Let's go." I called Twinkie. "Hello, Hello, Hello, Twinkie!" I said excitedly when she answered. "Hold on," she yelled. There was a lot of noise in the background. "Hello? Hey Reyne." "Hey girl, how do I get to your house?" I asked. "I am on my way to pick you up." "Pick me up? I already have a ride." "Trust me when I say you will want to ride with me." I slid my hand over the leather seats. "Okay let me tell my Mom, hold on. Mom, Reyne's Mom is taking us. You do not have to take me." "Twinkie, my Mom is at home, someone else is taking us!"

"Who," she asked. "Come outside and bring your Mom with you." I hung up the phone. Just as Twinkie opened the door, I stepped out of the limo. We both screamed and ran to each other.

"Oh my gosh, oh my gosh, you have a limo!" Twinkie yelled and jumped up and down. "This is way cool; come on let's go. I do not want to be late." She waved bye to her Mom. Once inside the limo, we lay all over the seats and opened every container, being nosy. The driver rolled down the middle window and we both jumped and bumped our heads. "Ouch!" We yelled at the same time holding our heads. "You all are welcome to anything back there," he said. "I will put some music on for y'all."

"Tonight" by DJ Quick began bumping out of the speakers. We popped open a bottle of sparkling soda and a bag of Snickers and began munching down. Once we were settled we sipped out of our wine glasses. I said, "I was at your place for a while. It was just hard parking because we had to go around that big U-Haul. Are your neighbors moving?" I asked.

"Someone is moving, but it is not my neighbors." I stop chewing and my eyes began to well up with tears. Twinkie sat down her glass and said, "I have known for about two weeks now. Friday was my last day of school." I took a hard swallow and stared at her in disbelief. "I am sorry, Baby Reyne. She took my glass and sat it down. "I just did not know how to tell you, you were so worried about Freddy and the stuff that happened with Gracie. I just did not want to add anything else to your plate."

I sank back in the seat and Twinkie laid her head on my shoulder, and began singing "Pretty Brown Eyes." Then it came on the radio and we both started laughing. "You know I am going to miss you," she continued. "We are going all the way to California." "California, that is far. I know you will be happy though. Maybe you can even start making clothes for stars." "Yeah, maybe," she said. "Have you talked to him?"

she asked. "No, not yet," I said. "Well, maybe he will show up tonight." "Maybe." "How Will I Know," came on and we began dancing and singing, trying to forget the sadness ahead and focus on the night at hand.

We arrived at the school and the driver opened our door. Twinkie stepped out first. "Wow," said our first period teacher. "YOU ALL LOOK BEAUTIFUL."

"Hey," said Ruby greeting us as we made it inside. "Where is Freddy?" she asked. Byron headed towards her. "He's probably just late," I said. "Oh okay, well let me know when he gets here. We have to have our couples dance off," she said as she ran towards Byron.

The dance was slamming and they were playing all our jams. The time finally came for the crowning of the king and queen. I looked around intensely for Freddy. I didn't see him. Ruby had the microphone and she began speaking. This song is dedicated to our king and queen. These two came here to Aldine and stole the hearts of many as well as each other. I would like to announce this year's Spring Fling King and Queen, Freddy Jennings and Reyne Williams. Everyone began to applaud as Ruby and Byron began singing "Tender Kisses," by Traci Spencer.

As the crowd stepped aside for me to walk through, I crossed my fingers desperately hoping Freddy would walk up any moment. As I made it to the stage Mrs. Smith our English teacher came up and says, "I am so sorry for the misunderstanding, but Mr. Jennings, Freddy is no longer with us." She moved the microphone and whispered to me that his Mom came and withdrew him last Thursday. I took a deep breath and reached for the microphone while choking back tears. "Thank all of you for this, but on behalf of both Freddy and myself in his absence I would like to present this honor to Byron and Ruby," I said.

I handed them the pillow holding the crowns. I hugged them both and walked off the stage straight to the door. Before I could get out of the door, Angel and Twinkie come to my side, and drug me back to the dance floor, saying this party is not over yet. We danced my troubles away and for a moment the embarrassing moment was non-existent. "Just Want to Hold You," by Jasmine Guy came on and just as I was about to rest, Roger Flemings came up to me and asked to dance with me.

I look into those big brown eyes remembering the day Freddy had him sing to me and I turned my back to walk away saying, "No thank you." He grabbed my arm gently and said, "Look, Freddy is a great guy and very lucky I might add to have you as a friend. I know he cares about you dearly and would not want you dancing alone." I gave in and accepted the dance. We sang along to the song and he dipped me at the end. I laughed and thanked him. He hugged me and told me to keep my head up. The night came to a close and I said my goodbyes.

After dropping off Twinkie and saying goodbye to yet another friend, I asked the driver to take the long way to my house. I was not quite ready to go home yet. I curled up on the seat, just as "Goodbye Love" by Guy began to play. I began to think about all of the friends I had to leave and the ones that left me. "For the Good Times" came on next and I could no longer hold back my tears. I began to think of my Daddy and how he would put me to sleep with Al Green playing in the background. Once at home, Mom was waiting outside. She paid the driver and said thank you. Putting her arm around me she asked if I had a good time. I told her yes other than Freddy not being there and finding out Twinkie was moving half way across the world. She hugged me tightly, kissed me on the cheek and said, "People come and go honey, now get some sleep. Goodnight and don't forget to say your prayers and thank the Lord."

CHAPTER 3

Rebellious Teen

Time went on and although I had other friends I missed Twinkie and Freddy like crazy. Every time Tender Kisses played on the radio I cried. For the rest of the year I stayed in my room most of the time reading books and listening to music. At the time those were the only two things that soothed me.

We moved again at the end of the school year but this time I was in for a huge shocker. As time progressed I just seemed to grow sadder and sadder. I would sit in my room or outside crying, missing my friends, and my Daddy. Sitting there outside not noticing my Mom standing there she just shook her head and said, "Look Reyne you have to get over it. If it is meant to be he will come back and find you. In the meantime you just have to keep busy. You cannot be in boy's faces. Men, boys all of them will always do what they want to do no matter who they hurt," she says shaking her head looking down. Lifting her head and touching my shoulder she continues to say, "If Freddy was your friend then remember the good times. He was your friend, nothing more, nothing less." "Kind of like you and Mr. Roger, just friends?" I ask. Looking down again she says, "Yeah kind of like Roger and me," and got up and walked away. I sat there for a moment watching her walk off and I thought to myself, Freddy and I were more than just friends.

The next morning I woke up screaming and crying. My sister Lacey ran into the room. As she shook me to wake me up the phone began to ring. I jumped up and began screaming "No." I ran past my sister down the stairs only to see my Mom hanging up the phone with tears in her eyes. She told us that Berry our cousin had been shot and killed last night. The funeral would be that Friday and we were going to Louisiana. I fell to the floor and wept like a baby. "Reyne, look at me," she says lifting my head. "I want you to pray and ask God to take those dreams away from you, ok?" I said ok and prayed the prayer. Early Friday morning while it was still dark we headed to Louisiana. I was sort of happy that I would be seeing my Dad but not happy about going to a funeral. After the wake we went to my Nanny's house. Her second son Donnie whom at the time seemed mad cool was talking about moving to Houston now that his brother was dead. He said he, his wife Keisha and their kids would move in about six months. My Mom told him that if he did to be sure to keep in touch and gave him our phone number and address.

At the funeral I sat next to my Daddy. I looked up at him and saw tears coming down his face. I burst into tears and he grabbed me by my hand and led me out of the church. "Daddy please," I pleaded once we got by the big tree. "Please do not make me go to any more funerals." He gave me a big hug and wiped his tears and mine and promised me I would never have to go to another funeral not even his own if I did not want to. Sitting under that tree he told me that the last memory of someone you love should not be them lying lifeless in a casket but should be of them smiling, laughing and having fun because that is what life is all about at the end of the day. "Life is about the bad times that turned into good ones and this is why you should always keep smiling no matter what because everything will work out for the best," he said hugging me.

On the way back to Houston I told my Mom how much it hurt me to see my Daddy crying and that he promised me I would not have to go to another funeral again. She just nodded and kept driving never saying a word. Back at home July rolled around and Mr. Roger had been coming around more and more.

One morning I got up early and went downstairs. I came to a sudden halt when I saw right in front of me my Mom and Mr. Roger wrapped in each other's arms sleeping. I felt heat rise from my chest and something inside of me shattered. I tiptoed back up the stairs and woke up my sisters. They came and peeked and they too were upset and angry. The younger twin Lacey began to cry and sat in the corner sucking her thumb. Stacey began to fuss saying, "All that talk about just being friends and look where she at. Hm! well I am not giving her my money anymore. He can pay the bills now." Lacey broke her tears and yelled out, "Give yeah right you know she go take it." My Mom for as long as I could remember would take their checks from their job and give them only twenty or thirty dollars out of it. I rarely saw my check that I would get from my Daddy unless I got it out of the mailbox.

As they continued to go on and on about that, I went downstairs into the kitchen. I ruffled some things around to make just enough noise to wake them up. I went back into the living room and stood over them until someone opened their eyes. When they did I said, "Good morning Momma, Roger," and rolled my eyes and walked back upstairs.

This was the beginning of my rebellion. It was as if day by day my respect and adoration for my mother went out the window and she did not make it any better. She told us off, for coming downstairs or as she puts it sneaking downstairs seeing her and Roger lying there. She began neglecting and ignoring us all the more. We could not even have seconds anymore when she would cook just so he would have something to eat. Nevertheless she was still using my sister's checks and my check from my Dad to pay stuff. The only helpful thing we ever saw him do was fix the car and even that seemed to break down every other month.

When my sisters and I decided to talk to her about this her only response was that what she does is none of our business and that she is grown and can do what she pleases and we are children and should stay in our place. As we were walking off she says, "Oh yeah by the way I am pregnant. The baby is due next month and it is a girl." Immediately my sisters became emotional and began yelling out different names. I just stood there in shock and astonishment. I knew my Mom had been getting bigger but I just thought the medication she was taking was causing her to swell up because she did mention going to the doctor several times. As she went on about the baby being her decision and as a grown woman she could do what she pleased I turned and went to my room. Needless to say no one even noticed that I left. From that day on I decided I wanted to be grown too then maybe I could move to a place and never have to leave my friends or my Daddy.

At the end of July when things had cooled down my Mom asked me to ride with Roger to pick up his daughter Gina. Now I was 13 and she was 14. My birthday was November 25 and hers was the 17th. This was good information because finally I would have someone my age around. On the way there Roger carried on small talk. He seemed ok but I was not even trying to give him a chance to get close to me. We made it to Dallas and picked her up from the house of her Aunt who had picked her up from the airport. Gina lived in Boston and had flown into Dallas to make the cost easier for her Dad. "How was your flight?" he asked her. "It was straight," she said. He then introduced us. We nodded heads at each other and the rest of the ride was silent.

As I watched her sleep holding her bag tightly I wondered if she even liked her Dad. I had never heard him ever talk about even having children. She did not seem very happy to see him anyway. I know when I see my Dad I light up like the Fourth of July. She just looked like the inside of a tomb. I then remembered overhearing my Mom gossiping on the phone as she so often did about how he had not seen his daughter since she was six and that if she could get her to come and stay with us Roger would not have to pay anymore child support and that would be more money for her.

Once we made it to the house he woke both of us up and I took her to my room to show her where to put her stuff. "I have twin beds so pick the one you want," I said while pointing at the beds. "I'll take the one by the window. It reminds me of home," she said while looking at the window. Getting to know her was not easy; she seemed very territorial and stuck up. Oddly I seemed the same way to her. We would find out later that we both shared similar hurts. One day we got into an argument about a pack of bologna. She would eat and leave the red string on the counter along with the empty pack and I would get blamed for it. The worst part was instead of her saying she did it while my Mom would yell and pop me up-side my head she just sat there, and yet if Roger left something out or put a pot in the refrigerator with food in it she would not say anything. Uggh this really irritated me and left me with no respect for Roger and not much liking for Gina.

On this particular day I told her to throw away her trash. She gets in my face and says make me and pushes me. Why did she do that, there was bologna everywhere. Later that day after my sisters broke up that fight, we had another. This time it was over a guy named Anthony that went to school at the Community College where my Mom worked. Anthony is a very handsome young man that my Mom asked to take my sister to her prom. You see, Lacey had a major crush on Anthony but would not act on it. I told her she was a scary cat. When he saw some mail in our name he said he just decided to hand deliver it since he was our carrier for that week. I was eight years old when I met him and he was eighteen.

Now at 23 he looked even better. I was drawn to him the moment I met him and would cling to him every chance I got. Well obviously Gina felt the same way because right when I was about to get my hug she politely scoots in and introduces herself. Burning with anger I grab her by the arm and say "Excuse me," pull her to the washroom and politely try to stuff her butt in the dryer. Again she is saved by Stacey but by this time Anthony is gone with a promise to return later for dinner. Upon hearing that Gina rushes upstairs and locks herself in the bathroom.

After about forty-five minutes she comes out smelling like a perfume factory and her hair neatly combed. "What are you doing?" I ask as she comes downstairs and stands by the window as if she is waiting for someone or something. I shake my head and I say, "He is not coming back you know." "You don't know that," she spurts out, "and besides Stacey said he was." As the rest of us decided to head to the den after about thirty minutes or so I walked up to her and told her something that I had to learn at an early age. "Gina, you know men always make promises but they rarely keep them." She then put her head down and took her hair out of the clip, ruffled it and said, "Don't I know." "Come on let me show you my pictures from my eighth grade prom. "

Upstairs in my room as we look through my pictures she began to tell me about this dream about this tall light skinned man who would come and rescue her from the rough streets of Boston and move her to a nice settled place and start a family. She shared the pain of seeing her mother abused and having to be responsible for her five other siblings. She also shared how it seems like anytime she got close to someone they were either shot or hauled off to jail, or had to leave town. Then she told me about a guy named Popeye who was her boyfriend/best friend. As she spoke of him I began to think of my would-have-been boyfriend/best friend Freddy. I told her all about him and how he meant the world to me because he understood me. I also told her how one day he was here and the next he was just gone as if he was never here at all. I described how that left a gaping hole in my heart sort of like the one she had in hers. We continued talking all night both saying that maybe one day we would see them again. I looked up at the ceiling before closing my eyes to settle for a good night rest and said, "Yeah maybe one day."

The next day rolled around and I had to get up early for freshman orientation and Gina had a flight to catch. We hugged and cried as we said our goodbyes. Stacey shaking her head said, "Look at these two. You all fought the whole time you were here and now yawl crying like yawl are best friends." We both laugh and hug again and say we are more than best friends, we are sisters. On the way back from orientation I ask Stacey was she really happy about the baby coming? "Yeah I guess so. I just want Momma to be happy because sometimes she seems so sad. Maybe this will cheer her up," says Stacey. "Yeah maybe," I say. "At least Mr. Roger is around." "Yeah not like my Daddy was," says Stacey. "The nerve of him to call Momma from the hospital and tell her to get a ride home. Only to arrive home to an empty house with a nightstand in the middle of the room containing a gun and a note," says Stacey. "I don't ever want to meet him," she says frowning and rolling her eyes. "I wonder why she did not stay with my Daddy." I ask. "Well," says Stacey as we pull up to the house, "your Daddy was still." "Come on lets go," says Lacey running up to the car. "Momma is having the baby. We have to get to the hospital quick," she says climbing in the car. We speed off and arrive just in time to see her at the baby window in the nursery. Immediately my heart melted and I knew from that moment that my Mom would never be lonely again and that I had a best friend for life.

The next week I started high school and everyone seemed much bigger than me. I was so skinny and short. I wore my hair in a leisure curl style and kept in a ponytail. I was already going through a crisis because the beautician who did my hair cutting my split ends and ended up cutting all my pretty long hair off. My Mom thought that if I kept the curl it would at least be curly and I could pin it up. I had her pin it up. I wore my hair in one ponytail my first two months of school. I was happy to be at East High School because a lot of my friends from elementary school were there. As I finally got adjusted to my hair and being the smallest out of the bunch another surprise comes.

One day while sitting in English class while discussing Edgar Allen Poe's The Raven in walks Mr. Freddy Jennings. As the teacher introduces him and the class welcomes him I just stare in utter disbelief. My friend Andrea from elementary school leans over and says," I don't think Chris would like the way you are looking at the new guy." I grab her arm and give it a slight pinch and say, "Well Chris does not have to know and besides he got a girlfriend anyway." "Um, I see someone still has a temper," says Freddy as he takes the seat next to me. Before I can even catch myself I turn and let him have it. "You have some nerve Mister to waltz your lanky booty on your back self-up in here and sit next to me like as if everything is ok." Pointing my finger I say, "You have not call me, wrote me, looked for me or nothing. How dare you."

By this time my teacher comes out of shock and walks over to tell us we are excused to step out in the hallway and have a quieter discussion. Just as I turn around to answer her the bell rings. I grab my things and run straight out of the classroom. My emotions are all over the place and the last conversation that Charity and I had begins rushing back to me. I stop by my lockers only to be bombarded by Freddy saying, "Baby Reyne wait up." I yell "What do you want?" Everything gets quiet and I notice everyone staring. As I look around I take a few deep breaths and look at him and whisper, "What?" He looks around and begins singing Tell Me When Will I See You Smile Again. I groan deeply and turn around and stomp away.

During second period I could not even think straight, I was so upset. Luckily we had a sub and did not cover much material. My 3rd period class was history, one of my favorite subjects. While getting settled and ready to discuss the Revolution, in walks Freddy. I smack my lips and roll my eyes. He walks up to me and says, "For you, Reyne," and hands me a paper rose. I look at it, grab it and say, "Ahh how stupid," and ball it up then proceed to tear it into little bitty pieces and tell him never to call me Baby Reyne again because he lost that privilege. With that said he looked astonished and put his head down and walked to the other side of the room and took his seat. When the bell rang at the end of class he jetted out the door without even a glance back at me. I walked out expecting to see him waiting for me but he was not there. I hump my shoulders and said, "Oh well." Taking a step forward I bump right into Ervin. "Reyne, I thought that was you," he says backing me into the locker. "I knew, I recognize that voice this morning and that walk," he says while staring at me as if I am lunch. "How are you doing?" he asks. "I am doing fine Ervin. How are you?" I say trying to hold my breath from the disgusting smell of alcohol reeking from him. "Ahh Baby, I am much better now, that you're back in my life. You looking real good," he says looking me up and down.

"Now that you're older maybe I could get that kiss," and then pooches out his lips. I kick him right in the balls and run to my next class, bumping right into Freddy as I enter the classroom. He catches me right before I hit the floor. "Are you ok?" he asks helping me stand up straight. "Yeah, I am fine," I say shaking myself together. "Look I am sorry," we both say at the same time and laugh. "You first," we both say again. "Okay 123 go Rock paper scissors." "Scissors beats paper," he says. As we take our seats I tell him about what just happened in the hallway with Ervin. Of course he laughs at me and says if I was not so cute I would not have to worry about deranged guys stalking me.

At lunch it was as if we had never been apart. I told him all about the eighth grade prom that we won KING and QUEEN at and my limo ride as well as us moving and Gina and my new baby sister. He told me they had moved back to Louisiana and had just come back two days ago. After lunch was over we saw Ervin and Freddy moved me to the side and told me to stand still. As Ervin got closer to me Freddy cut him off and kissed me on the forehead and then turned to Ervin with his arm around me and said, "Can I help you man?" Ervin was livid. He looked at me then back at Freddy and was like, "You can have cause she aint given up nothing no way," and walked off. Freddy and I both look at each other after watching him walk away and crack up laughing. "Thank you," I say punching him in the shoulder.

"Ahh what are best friends for?" squeezing me on my cheek. Freddy walked me to the rest of my classes arm in arm. We both had gym class 6th period and walked in arm in arm. I looked up from our conversation we had to see Chris coming across the gym. I quickly moved my arm and stepped away from Freddy. As he gets closer I say, "Hi Chris." He says, "Hi" looking at me and then looking Freddy up and down. After he disappears into the locker room Freddy says,"Uhh huh somebody has a crush on someone." In my defense I quickly say, "No I don't," and walk towards the bleachers. "Yeah you do," says Freddy. "I know that look anywhere."

Scooting closer to me he says, "Need I remind you about Roger, who by the way is a proud Papa now." "What," I say. "No way. You're lying!" "Yes way," says Freddy. When I came back in town I was at the basketball court and he was there playing and then Joann walks up with a baby." "Wow for real," I say. "Yep and they are getting married," says Freddy. "Married, what they are only in the tenth grade," I yell. "I know," Freddy says. "Aren't you happy I came along, that could have been you carrying that baby." "Oh no you didn't," I say jumping on his back and hitting him in the head. Coach Spencer clears his throat with the other guys standing behind him including Chris and says, "Um Mr. Jennings you need to join us guys over here, correct?"

Putting me down gently and trying to get the last lick Freddy says, "Yes Sir," and heads to the other side of the gym. "Ms. Williams." "Yes Coach Spencer," I say. "Don't you need to dress out and join the ladies?" "Yes Sir," I say trying not to look at Chris who is staring at me intensely from behind Coach's back. That night on the phone I told Freddy that I really missed him a lot. He asked me what was up with Chris and I told him we liked each other but Chris could not seem to get rid of his girlfriend and I was not about to play seconds although we did kiss a time or two. Freddy told me that I should leave Chris alone because if he really was a good guy he would not be kissing me knowing that he already has a girlfriend and that if I respected myself I would not have let him. Needless to say that was the end of Chris and me.

Freddy always seemed to have a way at helping me out of what could be a harmful situation. He then asked me where he and I stood. Honestly I could not answer that right then. I cared for Freddy deeply and really loved his company but neither one of us could seem to say we were officially boyfriend and girlfriend, yet we felt bonded together so tightly almost like brother and sister but with a hint of attraction. Over the next few months Freddy seemed to grow pretty popular. To say he had just come to the school three months ago he was pretty well known.

We stuck together like white on rice. It was not easy trying to explain to Chris that Freddy was sort of my ex-boyfriend/ best friend from middle school who suddenly reappeared. Then I remembered what Freddy said and I told him, "Besides you still have not made up your mind if you want to be with me or Shantay." He had nothing to say at that point and left to go to the class. The holidays were coming up and my Mom was happy that Freddy was back in my life. His family and my family got together for Thanksgiving. That year on my birthday Freddy gave me a Bell Biv DeVoe tape with our song on it (Tell Me When Will I See You Smile Again). Music really is a prophecy because in the next month or so I was not smiling at all.

December rolled around and my Mom called a family meeting. She told my sisters that she needed the money they had been saving to use as a down payment on a house due to the recent shootings that went on in our neighborhood. Because of this unexpected move I was not able to join the majorette team. I was so hurt. Ever since the first time I went to the Battle of the Bands with my sisters I said I was going to be a majorette. Well that did not happen. My Mom then said she did have some good news. She told us Gina would be coming back to live with us and that she would be arriving next week. They get out early because of the snow.

Gina came as planned and met her new little sister. I was really happy that Gina was back and staying this time. That Christmas was great. We moved into our new house right before Christmas and had a huge celebration. While out on break Gina and I went to the park across the street and talked and swung until dark sometimes. She told me that Popeye had another girlfriend and was lying to her the whole time. I told her all about Freddy coming back and not to worry about Popeye cause I am sure she would meet someone else in due time. I could not wait for her to meet my Freddy but his family went out of town for Christmas and New Year's.

Gina and I spent almost our whole break talking about Freddy. Little did I know the more I told her of his caring heart and all the wonderful things he would do and say from the moment we met up until now, that cold thick black wall that she had built around her heart came crashing down with each statement . On Gina's first day of school I introduced her to Freddy. He like her knew a lot about her as well. Because I talk to him about everything, from the way she brushes her teeth to her leaving the red string on the bologna on the counter. "Hello Gina," he said. "You are very beautiful," he says shaking her hand. Gina blushes slightly and says, "You are very handsome yourself." Watching these two stare at each other as if they are the only two humans on the earth I grab

Freddy's arm and say, "Ok can we go to class now please?" He lets go her hand and we all say our see you later. Gina was a sophomore and of course she was the total opposite of me. Where I was brown, with a ponytail, straight up and down, Gina was yellow with long black hair and boobs. Freddy decided we should at least walk her to her first class. I felt like I was walking with two strangers. As they said goodbye to one another, Freddy began to look around almost as if he had just remembered something and I waved from across the hall and said,

"Hello I am over here." Walking over to me he begins to talk about how nice she is. "You've only known her five minutes Freddy," I say rolling my eyes. "I know, I know but from all the things you have told me about her and finally putting a face with the name. Man, she is gorgeous," says Freddy. "Yuck," I say sticking my finger in my mouth as if to gag myself. "Come on here before we end up being late." By the end of January, Freddy had been to our house every weekend and once out of each school week.

The last Sunday in January, Anthony and Freddy came over for dinner. While I was pulling Anthony away for one of our private talks as I quite often did when he visited, I saw Gina and Freddy kissing by the car. I told Anthony let's go back inside because it was too cold out. He did not see them. Later that night after everyone left I called Freddy. "Hey Beautiful," he said answering the phone. I said, "Hello to you too." He said, "Reyne, oh I thought you were Gina calling me what's up?" "Oh so you calling her beautiful now," I yell into the phone. "Oh come on Reyne, don't start that. What's wrong?" says Freddy. "I saw you and her kissing. What is up with that?" I ask. "Well, Reyne, I don't know how to tell you this but Gina and I are, well she is my Lady and I am her Man, and I am proud of it," declares Freddy. My heart sank. "You're what and when did this happen?" I ask. Gina walks up and takes the phone and put it on speaker and says, "Well actually before we ever met." "Yeah Reyne," says Freddy. "All the nights that you would spend telling us about one another we would lie on our beds wondering how each other looked." Gina began smiling and says, "Yeah when you introduced us to one another and our hands touched we knew we were meant for one another." I groaned, kicked the phone and left the room.

The next few months were pure hell. I went from sweet and caring to conniving and insensitive. Every time Gina and Freddy would be on the phone, I would pick up the other phone and protest saying, "Freddy you are still my best friend and I need to talk to you. Who is more important me or her?" He would get off the phone with Gina and barely talk to me. At school I no longer got walked to my classes and in the classes we had together all day long he talked about her and wrote her letters. My Mom had given Gina an hour longer on the phone than me because she was older. So where I had to get off at eight, she and Freddy had a whole other hour to fall deeper in love with one another and I could do nothing about it. She completely took over his brother and sister and I was left looking like a fool pouting and whining because the attention was no longer on me and my best friend was no longer mine.

By May my Mom had opened a clothing shop in the local flea market by the house. Freddy transferred to another school so while Gina would be picked up by his Mom on weekends I would work in the shop. On the weekends that I did not work I would hang out with my cousin Donnie. Donnie was a different type of person. He saw life as the more money you have the more power and respect you have. Every weekend that we hung out he would tell me about making money, his way. Being an entrepreneur as he called himself I decided to take notes. I added up the chump change I made sitting up at my Mom's shop to what he said he made in only a few hours and realized that I was definitely in the wrong business.

Although I had met someone who seemed to be a nice guy up there named Walter, I was ready for something different. Walter was way older than I and had two jobs. We talked on the phone a lot and where I was fourteen and not even thinking about sex, he was almost eighteen and that's all he wanted. His best friend Derrick tried to talk to Gina several times but she was of course in love with Freddy plus Derrick reminded her of Popeye so on that alone it was a no go.

After about three weeks Walter and I broke up but remained friends. His Uncle took a liking to my sister and they have been together from 1993 to present day, married with four children. After Walter I met another guy named Gregory. Nice kid and definitely more age appropriate but that did not last long due to the fact that he sold drugs on the corner. Donnie told me never talk to a man that is out on the corner nickel and diming, because that was an easy way to go to jail and you really did not make much money that way. I figured he knew what he was talking about since he had been to jail before and used to nickel and dime himself when he was younger. Donnie would always say you should eliminate the middle man and do it yourself.

By August my baby sister was walking and not long after that the drama began. I thought Freddy would come back to East High School that year but he did not. He and Gina kept in touch though. He would ask about me every now and then and Gina would tell him I was gone with my cousin Donnie. During those next few weeks in the house everyone seemed distant from one another. Although we were never really close it just seemed weird. My sisters would come in and go straight to sleep from work, and by the time they got up it was time to go right back to work. The only time conversation really took place was when my Mom was arguing with them about money. Gina was preoccupied with Freddy's brother and sister. My Mom was so wrapped up into Roger that it seemed as if we really did not exist. The only time she seemed to notice me was when a boy called or came to the house to see me. I spent a little time with my cousins when we had our first annual family reunion right before school started back. My cousin Keith was still a ladies' man and even had Gina showing all thirty-two teeth. Nancy on the other hand was all legs and ready to fight at the drop of a dime. It was a nice day and everyone seemed happy except my Grandmother of course who always seemed to find something negative to say about something. This time she was complaining about a pot of beans.

I waved her off as usual and went inside the house. Walking into the kitchen I see my little sister trying to walk across to the table. "Come here T", I say. She sees me and begins to runs towards me but falls over. I pick her up and go into my room closing the door. "Here sit there and I'll sing you a song." Flipping through my tapes I put on R. Kelly Dedicated. I hold her in my arms and sing and dance with her. She giggles and lays her head on my shoulder. I promise her that I will always be with her and never let anything happen to her.

As time went on, over the next two months the arguing increased between my Mom and my sisters. One evening my mother chewed my head off because I had not cleaned the kitchen. In actuality I had but Roger came in late and warmed up food dirtying up the dishes and left them on the stove. I was livid, I immediately snapped back at her and told her that I did clean the kitchen and it was her so-called man that left those dishes out. She called me a liar, slapped my face, and said "Stop talking back." "I want to go and live with my Daddy," I said. "Huh, your Daddy."

"Well you can't, your Daddy is married and he's been married." "So what," I say, "his wife should know about me right?" "No she does not," says my Mom. "Well tell her." "I am not going to tell her, that is your Dad's job," says Mom. "Well tell him to tell her," I say. "He won't." "Well why not?" I ask. "He just won't and that is the end of it." Turning my back I mumble, "Hm you were bold enough to sleep with him but you're not woman enough to make him tell his wife about me. That is just crazy." Before I even finished my words I was on the floor holding my jaw. My Mom had hit me so hard I felt like my whole face had been turned around to face my back.

My sister reached out for me and my Mom told her she better not touch me or she would knock the hell out of both of us. Gina sat on the couch in tears. Luckily Tanya was asleep. I got up and went to my room and cried out. "God I need a friend, somebody who I can talk to. Someone that likes me for who I am and will not make fun of me or…" Hearing Gina open the door I roll over and say, "…or still my man" (rolling my eyes putting the cover over my head). "Reyne are you ok," asked Gina. "Leave me alone please," I respond. "Your Mom loves you it just hurt her when you said what you said." Gina pleads with me. "Well she told me to speak my mind" (rising up moving the covers back).

"How is it that she can teach me all this stuff about keeping your legs closed and not being in boys faces and not talking to married men when here it is she slept with a married man and has a baby for an engaged man and now does not even spend time with us but yells at us if we don't do something right. That is not fair." Gina comes and sits beside me. "Reyne, my Mom had a lot of issues too. She had different men, neglected us, and I had to take care of my other sisters and brothers because she was running behind a different man all the time."

"It seems like as soon as a man comes into their lives no one else exist not even their own children," says Gina. "What is about a man that makes a woman lose her mind?" I ask. "Girl I do not know but what I do know is that I love being in my man's arms." Turning, looking at the ceiling, and closing her eyes, "It's like no one else is there just you and him me and Freddy and oh it just." I smack my lips, roll my eyes and left her right there in the room by herself dreaming of Freddy. Sitting in the living room alone, the house is quiet. God, I really could use that friend now.

Knock Knock Knock. Jumping up off the couch, "Who is it?" "It's me, Donnie." "What, what time is it?" (Opening the door) "Hey, pretty girl," says Donnie. "What's up cuz?" I say stepping aside so he can enter.

"Who is that at the door?" ask my Mom coming around the corner with Tanya. "It's me, Nan Eva.", says Donnie waving his hand and sitting down. "Oh, hey," says my Mom. Tanya reaches for me. I get her from my Mom and sit down next to Donnie. "What brings you here so early in the morning?" asks my Mom. "I have some tickets to the car show and I wanted to see if Reyne could go with me." "Please Momma, can I go, my room is clean and my homework is done, please." "Yeah she can go but don't be gone all night. Where is Keisha? Oh she at work she gets off at 9 tonight so I will bring her back home before I go to pick her up. Ok well yawl have a good time." Kissing Tanya, handing her to my mother I run and get ready.

Fifteen minutes later, "You sure get ready quick," says Donnie as we rolling in the van. "I was glad you came, I wanted to get away from there. Donnie let me ask you something, what is it that is so good about a man that it makes a woman ignore her children?" He began to laugh and say "Do you really want to know?" "Uh yes I would not be asking if I didn't." "Well it is a little story called the birds and the bees." "Man Donnie don't play with me for real what is it?" "Ok on the real it's like this sometimes a woman who is single and has not gotten any attention from a man in a long time becomes lonely."

"It is not that she does not love her children it is just that she is lonely and feels neglected." "But how can she be lonely when we are right there?" "It is not the same, Reyne. Yawl can't hold your Momma the way a man can. You can't tell her she is beautiful the way a man can. You see there is a difference between being held by a man and being held by your children or friends. Your Mom was lonely and now that she has a man she is just getting what she needs you know." (Looking at me) "Know what? I do not understand. We tell momma she is beautiful all the time, Tanya holds her we hug her when we are not arguing what is the difference?" "The difference is the dick." Covering my mouth, "WHAT? The dick? What is that I mean what do you mean?" "You know sex a man and a woman kissing hugging f---king you know the way your little sister got here." "You mean to tell me that it is so good that it makes you act like that?"

"Sometimes worse than that it all depends on the woman and how lonely or desperate she is," says Donnie. "Well I am never going to be like that ain't no dick that good to make me turn my back on my kids." "Ahh Shi- ," yells Donnie. "What's wrong, I left the tickets on top of the TV." (Turning the truck around) As we pull up to the crib I hop out of the van and head to the bathroom. Donnie stops to talk to some guy working on a car. "Hey Lawrence what's up man?" "Nothing, just trying to fix this old raggedy car," the guy responds. "Who is that?" ask Lawrence. "Oh that is my little cousin, she's cute huh?" says Donnie. "Yeah man she looks good, a little young huh?" "Yeah she is going on 15. Really she looks twelve but has a fine body."

Walking out of the house handing Donnie the keys, "I got the tickets lets ride." "Hey come here," says Donnie grabbing my arm. "This is my boy Lawrence. Lawrence this is…" I stretch out my hand and say "Reyne." He kisses my hand and says hello never taking his eyes off of mine. "Hello to you as well," taking back my hand, "Man get out here with that Romeo shit. You ain't no Mac Daddy." "You're right I am not, I just know how to respect a young lady."

Turning I go and get in the van. As we drive off I say, "Nice to meet you." Riding silently looking at my hand I think to myself, wow now he was fine. Nice muscles no shirt out there working on that car. Man he is sexy. Huh! Jumping from Donnie's thump on my arm, "What are you thinking about?" he asks. "Oh nothing," placing my hand under my leg. "Um somebody has a crush on my boy." "Whatever man it seems to me the other way around. Anyway he is cute." "Cute girl please that boy ugly." "No he's not." "Look at ya hooked already."

"I have to teach you the game you too cute to be out here getting caught up with these lil piss ant niggas that can't even buy a pair of tennis shoes. Unlock that back door," says Donnie. "What are we doing? Whose house is this?" I ask looking around "This is Keisha's sister place her niece Joy is coming with us yawl are about the same age." Looking forward this light skinned girl comes out whose breasts are as big as my two older sisters put together.

"Hey Donnie!" "Hi," she says to me. "Hello," I say. Donnie says, "This is Reyne and Reyne this is Joy." We shake hands and head to the show. Once we arrive Donnie hands us our tickets and says, "Meet me back here at the van in about 3 hours. If I am not back I will be here no later than 3:30." As I was getting out I dropped my change pouch. Reaching under the seat I feel something cold and hard. I look and there are two guns and a long case. I jumped, startled. "What are you doing?" asks Donnie. "Oh, I had dropped my pouch. What is that?" "Nothing." moving me aside he closes the door and steps in front of it. "I have to go take care of something I will be back."

"Here is some cash yawl have fun and I will see yawl in a few." "What grade are you in?" I ask Joy. "Ninth grade what about you?" "I am in the 10th grade I go to East," I say handing the woman the tickets. "I wonder where Donnie had to go." "Girl ain't no telling he always running off going somewhere," says Joy. "Well let's get something to eat. I am hungry." Sitting down eating our Nachos we began talking about our lives. "Do you have a boyfriend?" "Yeah I talk this boy name Sam he is really cute. Do you?" ask Joy. "No I don't but I want one." "Are you an only child?" asks Joy. "No I have two older sisters and a baby sister, oh yeah and a stepsister." I have an older sister," says Joy, "but she lives at home in Louisiana." "Oh! really? I am from Opelousas," I say. "So am I." "My Daddy is still there, Mr. Edward Sam." "Mr. Sam, I know him he is married", says Joy. "Yeah I know I just found that out." I then told her all about the argument my Mom and I had just had the night before. My Mom is dead; she died when I was twelve. She was hit by a car," says Joy. "Ahh man I am sorry to hear that." I am, "Excuse me ladies, can you all take a few pictures with us?"

We both look up and there are four fine brothers standing in front of us. We look at each other and say sure. As we are taking the pictures we realize that the guys are the members of the group All-4-One. Needless to say we are super excited. After we all take pictures the guys head to perform. While performing All-4-One point to us as they sing. After their performance they gave us hugs goodbye and head to their next show. "Wow I cannot believe that," says Joy. "You? I can't they are so cute," I say looking at our pictures. "Man, wait until we tell Donnie." "Tell me what?" says Donnie from behind us. We both turn around and there he is carrying two snow cones and a bag of cotton candy. "When did you get back?" ask Joy. "In time enough to see yawl all over those boys," he says taking the pictures handing us the snow cones. "Come on let's go," he says handing me the pictures as we head back to the van.

"Where are we going now?" asks Joy. "I told Janet I would pick up some crackling and help Sherman Bar-B-Que so to the store and then back over there." While Donnie barbequed Joy and I played outside and talked more and more.

Over the next few weeks Joy and I became like sisters. Each time Donnie would come and get me, Joy would be right there. At home the plot thickened. Lately my Mom seems to have more of an attitude than usual. One month she would be fine than the next week she was a mad woman. She and Stacey, the oldest twin, stayed on each other's nerves. One night after getting off the phone with Walter, I heard my Mom and my sister arguing. Suddenly it sounded like something fell. I ran into the hall way to see my sister and my Mom fighting. My Mom was hitting Stacey in the face and Gina was screaming, "Stop!" I jumped on my Mom and began hitting her telling her to get off my sister. Lacey the younger twin than grabbed me and pushed me off my Mom. I could not believe she had done that as badly as my Mom treated her. "How can you take up for her?" I yelled. Getting up, my Mom tells Stacey to get out. "I am going with you," I say heading to my room to grab my things. Stacey says, "Come on lets go," while grabbing her things.

As I prepare to walk out the door my Mom comes down the hall with a shot gun and puts it to my chest and says, "If you walk out that door I will kill you." Stacey stops in the doorway and says, "Mom let her go. Have you lost your mind?" She then turns and tells Stacey to get out or she will kill us both and proceeds to cock the gun. Stacey walks slowly towards the door and says, "I will come back and get you." I tell her, "I will meet her so wait for me." My mom slams the door in my sisters' face with her foot and pushes the gun closer in my chest.

"The only way you go leave out of her is crawling," and begins beating me with the gun. I try to run into my room but I trip over my bags in the door way. I try to kick her away but she beats my legs with the shot gun yelling and cursing at me. Finally she stops and looks at me. I look up at her and totally forget that she is my mother. As I watch her back out of the room she became a total stranger to me and me to her. Lying there not able to move my leg from the pain I can hear Lacey crying in the bathroom and I can see Gina lying on the floor in the doorway of the other room holding herself like a baby.

I ease up onto the bed and prop myself up. Suddenly I hear steps. My little sister comes in the room with a trail of toilet tissue behind her. She climbs up on me and begins wiping my tears. "Tanya get your ass in this room," yells my mother. She hugs me tight and gives me a kiss on the cheek and rubs my legs kissing them. "I wove you Reyne," says Tanya. "I love you too T," I say as she leaves out running to the bedroom. Whop! I hear a slap and then I hear my mother saying don't ever slap her like that again and popping my little sister and making her go to bed. As the lights went out in the house I vowed to never return to that place. I decided that it was time to go.

The next morning my legs ached so badly I walked with a limp in both of them. As we rode to school Gina ask me was I ok. I told her no but I would be. When I got out of the car Lacey said, "Reyne I love you and please don't run away." I rolled my eyes at her and said, "If you love me you would have helped us and limped away." That day I had my end of the six weeks finals and was thankful that I studied because thinking even hurt. After my last final I asked for a pass to the nurse office to get some ice for my legs. I had to tell the teachers that I fell off a bike.

On my way to the office, I called Donnie from the payphone. "Hello," says Donnie. "Hey it's me can you come get me?" I ask. "Yeah I have been waiting on you to call. Your sister told me what happen. I am on my way." "Ok I will meet you by the gym in 20 minutes," I say hanging up the phone. Next I head to Gina's class and ask the teacher to speak with her for a moment. "Hey I am leaving," I say. "Where are you going?" ask Gina with a concerned look on her face. "I am going to stay with Donnie," I say. "I really do not think that is a good idea Reyne. Isn't he a drug dealer?" she says leaning forward and whispering in my ear. "Yeah, but so what? He will take care of me and besides Momma tried to kill me last night! So who is safer to you, a drug dealer or a crazy lonely woman with a gun I ask?" I say angrily. Shrugging her shoulders Gina says, "Well you be careful. What do you want me to say?" "Just tell her that you could not find me after school." "What about your clothes?" asks Gina? "I will get them later. I have a few in my bag for now," I say. "I love you," says Gina hugging me. "I love you too Gina," I say while hugging her back. "Take care of yourself and Freddy too. Remember keep smiling and stay strong," I say walking off trying not to cry.

Standing there leaning on the pole I began to cry as I watched an eagle flying with its wings stretched out wide. I think to myself, one day I am going to fly like that, high above all of this bull shit I say looking at my legs. Beep beep Donnie honks the horn as he pulls up to the gate. I began limping towards the van and he jumps out to help me. "Dang girl she fucked you up huh?" he says opening the door for me. "Yeah man," I say lifting myself into the van. Donnie closes the door and gets in on the other side. Looking at me, he touches my shoulder and says, "You know there is no going back right?" "Um? Yeah, I know," I say putting my head back and closing my eyes. As Black Monks plays heavily in the background I think to myself looking out of the window seeing that eagle, "this is the end of life as I knew it as a child and the beginning of survival on my own.

CHAPTER 4
Stolen Values and Life Lessons

"Man can you change the music. Do or Die is not who I need to be listening to right now," I ask Derrick stretching while waking up. "Oh yeah I forgot how crazy you are" says Derrick. "Are you strapped now?" "Nah nigga, you know I don't roll like that no mo." "Shid," says Derrick, "let the wrong fool roll up. I know you got something, somewhere." "Nah man for real, I promise I am straight. I'm turning over a new leaf," I say turning over. "Speaking of new leaves I really have to do right by my baby girl," I say drifting off to sleep again. While fading out I could hear Thanks for my Child playing in the background. I mumble as my eyes close, "I remember being pregnant." Uhh I was so sick.

"Reyne wake up, wake up," Donnie says shaking me awake. "Hm! Yeah I'm up," I say rising up to step out of the van. "Come on your leg is bleeding, let's get you cleaned up," says Donnie. Once in the apartment he handed me some cotton balls and peroxide. "Knock Knock," says Lawrence walking through the door. "Man what I done told you about walking in my house like that," says Keisha. "Oh I'm sorry Keisha. I did not know you were home I saw Donnie come in and I was coming to…" he says pausing in mid-sentence. "Oh," he says looking over at me. "I did not see you," he says reaching for my hand. "How are you?" asked Lawrence. "As you can see, I am in a little pain, I say leaning to clean my leg ouching the entire way. "Here," says Lawrence. "Let me." He sits next to me and begins cleaning my leg. "Please be careful it is very sore." I say happy to have someone else do it cause it hurt for me to lean forward being that the barrel of the shotgun landed on my back a few times. "Ah look how sweet," says Donnie. "Say Lawrence I have to go and take Keisha to work and pick up the kids from school. You mind keeping my little cousin company until I get back?" "Nah man I got her," he says looking at me gently. "Alright Lawrence don't make me have to cut you." "That's my girl," says Keisha on her way out the door. "It will be fine," says Lawrence giving Donnie dap as he walks out the door.

Turning back to me he says, "So are you going to tell me what happen to your leg or do I have to guess?" "I really don't want to talk about it," I say flipping through the channels with the remote, rolling my eyes. For what seemed like forever we just sat there in silence. "Why do you keep staring at me and you can stop rubbing my leg now I am fine," I say with an attitude. "I am sorry. It is just that you are so beautiful and well," he says. "Well what? Let me guess you like me and you want to have sex with me so I can start acting crazy and forget the people that mean the most to me. Well, no it aint going to happen now please get out! I will be fine by myself," I say pushing his hand off my leg. "I was just," he says looking confused. "Get out please now. I want to be alone," I say turning away so he will not see my tears.

As he walked out the door I began to cry. I cried myself right to sleep. As I slept I dreamed of being in a dark tunnel. As I walked through that tunnel arms were grabbing at me and voices were screaming my name saying we want you we want you. I tried to run but I fell over a mirror lying on the ground. When I looked into it I saw a bright figure and heard "For my name sake you will come out of this," and then as quickly as it came it was gone. I got up and walked through the dark tunnel and although the hands were still reaching for me and my name was still being called I was no longer afraid. Just as I got to the end of the tunnel I woke up.

"Reyne get up," says Katy, Donnie's oldest daughter. As I get up Kerry and Kyle join Katy in tickling me. "Ohh, be careful my leg," I screech. They all step back and say sorry and kiss my leg. "Thank yawl," I say. "Alright children that is enough. Go and do your homework" say Donnie.

"Are you feeling better? And what happen to Lawrence," asked Donnie. "Oh I asked him to leave I wanted to be alone." Sitting next to me Donnie asked "Are you sure you are ok"? "Yeah I am good. Just everything is so different now. I mean finding out about my Dad was a shocker and then the way my Mom is acting like it is not even a big deal to treat us like this really hurts me," I say shaking my head and rubbing my leg. "Reyne you cannot let anything or anyone hurt you. One thing about survival is to not let anyone or anything get close to you. Every time you do you will get hurt. No one has your back like you do. People can say whatever they want but out here on these streets its KILL OR BE KILLED. You have to have no love out here for real," says Donnie getting up.

"I am going to fix the kids some food. Are you hungry?" asked Donnie turning towards the knock on the door. "Who is it?" he yells. "Oh hey Stacey," says Donnie opening the door. "Hey yawl. What happen to you?" asked Stacey looking at my legs? "Momma beat me with that shotgun after you left." "Ah Reyne, I am so sorry I should have never left you. I will never let anything happen to you again," she says kneeling giving me a hug. "Come on I need to talk to you. Donnie we will be back," says Stacey helping me up. As we walk out the door Lawrence walks up and grabs my hand right when I was about to fall, "Here let me help you," he says. "How are you? My name is Lawrence," he says stretching out a hand to my sister. She shakes it, and says," I am Stacey Reyne's sister." "Nice to meet you. I have to go now but will be back later and maybe we can talk," says Lawrence. I just nod my head as he walks away briskly.

Once in the car I look at my hand and realize that there is a note there. I open it and it says, "Look I know you are going through a lot right now but do not let that turn you away from people that are trying to help you. I want to be your friend and maybe one day your man but right now I can tell you need a friend. Call me and by the way, u is beautiful." I fold the paper back up and smile. "What was that all about?" asks Stacey. "Nothing," I say tucking the paper in my pocket. "Just a note." "A note huh?" says Stacey. We pull into Golden Corral and before we get out my sister looks at me and says, "Do you want to live with Donnie?" Getting out of the car, I hump my shoulders and tell her I am not sure. "Are you staying with me?" I ask. She hesitates as we walk inside.

When we get our food and sit down after grace Stacey says, "Well that is what I wanted to talk to you about. Mitchell asks me to come and live with him at his Mom's house in Pflugerville." "That is good we can stay there, right?" I say excitedly. "Well, actually we can't because it is not enough room," says Stacey eating her food. I sit back and sulk in my seat. "It will only be for a little while and then I will get an apartment and come back and get you. I already talk to Donnie and Keisha last night, and they said they do not mind you staying with them. I have to meet Lacey later to get our clothes," Stacey says happily. I smack my lips and say, "Why are you even talking to her, she did not even help us?" "She is still our sister Reyne just like Momma is still our Momma and we have to love them both," she says. "I do not think that you should have to love a person just because you are born into their family."

"Anyway I am not hungry any more can you take me back to Donnie's house please," I say pushing my plate away. "Why do you have such an attitude?" she asked frowning. "What?" I yell. "You are leaving me for a man just like Momma," I protest. "No I am not. I told you I am going to come back and get you. It is not enough room at Mitchell's mom house or at Donnie's house for the both of us. I love Mitchell and he loves me and I want to be with him. You are always with Donnie'nem every weekend anyway so you might as well stay there." "I guess," I say. "Come on let's go I do not have an appetite any more either," says Stacey shoving her plate aside. "Reyne I am going to come and get you besides you can spend more time with Joy and you are not that far from school," she says pleading her case. "I am not going back to school. You know Momma go come looking for me," I say. "Well I kind of already told her where you were going to be," says Stacey. "Oh great job just hand me over to the crazy woman," I say pointing at my legs as I get in the car. Back at Donnie's Stacey gathers her things and says goodbye. I hug her and look into her eyes. I love you Stacey please don't start acting like Momma because of Mitchell." "I promise you I won't and I will bring your clothes on Saturday," she says hugging me back. We both sigh and go our separate ways.

Finally Friday arrived and Joy came over. She and I babysat while Donnie and Keisha went out and did whatever it is they do. "So what's up with that Lawrence guy?" "He is fine," says Joy. "Yes he is, but I am not sure if I want to talk to him or anyone else for that matter. I mean, I am still trying to figure out what is so good about a man that they make you lose the little piece of mind that you have you know?" "I think you should go for it. You see he comes by here almost every day to try and talk to you. Obviously he likes you." "I know, I'll think about it." The next day, Stacey brings my clothes and leaves just as fast as she came, rushing off saying something about her and Mitchell.

The next week my legs began to feel a lot better. I was able to walk without the limp but running was still not attainable yet. Watching the guys play dominos, I asked Donnie what was that he was rolling up.

"Oh this (raising up a joint), this is called weed. You want some?" "Um, this is not like cigarettes huh, because I cannot stand cigarettes. They make your clothes and your breath stink, and don't they cause cancer?" Lawrence took out his pack of cigarettes and said, "I will quit smoking them if you give me the opportunity to talk to you for an hour." The other guys around the table say, "Man you are stupid, I ain't given up smoking for no woman. There is not a woman in the world worth me giving up my cigarettes." At that comment, Lawrence stood up, opened his pack and broke each cigarette, looked at me with the broken pieces lying in his hand and said, "You are worth me quitting and much, much, much more." I smile shyly and walk in the house. Donnie says, "Man you really like my cousin, huh?" "Yeah, she is beautiful." "There is something really special about her." Licking his lips, Donnie said, "Yeah I know."

Throughout that week, I became Donnie's pet project. He told me if I was going to hang out with the "big dogs" that I must be able to handle myself because he may not always be around to defend me and if I chose Lawrence as a boyfriend he was not the best fighter in the world. First, he started off by rolling three joints. I puffed the first one and coughed a little. The second was smoother and by the time I got to the third one I had the giggles like crazy. Everything was funny except Donnie's face. He immediately grabbed me and took me in the house away from everybody.

"Look at you (standing in the mirror), if you are going to hang out with me, you must toughen up and learn how to handle your weed. Straighten up and walk with one foot in front of the other until I tell you to stop." I stumbled a little at first, but, by that afternoon I had it. By the third day I was able to smoke five joints and drink two 40's and no one would ever know I was buzzing other than the fact that my eyes were low, but then again, when I am sleepy or not feeling well my eyes are low as well.

When Friday rolled around, Joy came back and that is when the alcohol training took place. "Dang Donnie, you bought the whole liquor store" said Joy. "Donnie, are you going to make her drink all of that?" asked Lawrence. "Yep," says Donnie, opening a bottle of Crown Royal. "The key to drinking," says Joy "is to eat something first," popping open a bag of Doritos. "Let's go," says Donnie. On my first swig, "Uh, this stuff is horrible. Can't I just stick to beer," I ask. "No, you have to be able to handle it all." "Ease up man," says Lawrence, reaching for the bottle of gin. "She is just a kid." "A kid, I am not a kid," taking the bottle from Donnie and turning it up, drinking half of it. "UHHHHH, my throat burns."

"Can I please have some water"? "Here you go." "You need to slow down," says Lawrence. "Lawrence, think about it like this," says Donnie. "Look at her, what do you see when you look at her? A sweet, sexy girl that can hang with the fellows, drink, smoke weed, get high and watch this." He puts his machete in my hand and says, "Can rob all of them blind and they will not even expect it," says Donnie. "Man, I see where you're going, but she is so beautiful, she would not hurt anybody," says Lawrence, looking at me with such compassion. "I cannot watch this, I have to go to my Dad's. I'll be back on Tuesday. Here is the number call me ok?" says Lawrence handing me the number. "Ok," I say burping from all the alcohol. By the end of the next week I was able to drink a wino under the table and still do five cartwheels and the split without staggering.

One day Keisha and Donnie were arguing. Donnie stomps out the front door. Keisha says "Reyne I think it is time you start making your own money." Now, I will be at work a lot, but I want you to start running dope with Donnie. We have to make a run out of town. I will show you what to do." She pulls out these maxi-pads and needle and thread. "Hand me that razor behind you," says Keisha. I give her the razor and she cuts a small slit in the center of the lining of the pad. She then places what looks like a T-cake inside of the pad, and sews it back together. "Close your eyes and hold out your hands." I close my eyes and stretch out my hands. "Open them." In my hands are two pads. "Which one has the dope in it?" I looked. "I do not know," I say. "Good. There is $2000 worth of dope in each pad.

She pulls out a box of Swisher Sweets. "In this box is $240 worth of weed. It is supposed to be $250, but I just sold one. This is what we will be traveling with. You will wear two pads and I will wear two. Donnie will take care of the weed. Once we get where we going I will tell you what to do. Is your cycle on?" asked Keisha. "No." "Good I do not want blood all over my dope. Pack your stuff we are leaving tonight." "Is Joy coming?" "No she is not and do not ever ask her to. She is not to have any parts in this."

Outside in the van, I asked Donnie why Joy can't come. He said, "Because she cannot handle the pressure. You passed the entire test and know how to handle the equipment," pointing to the guns in the back. "Why are you angry?" I asked Donnie. "No reason just comes on when it is time to deal. Get in the back." We head out of town and make the drop off. The transition obviously went well. After about two more rounds of this I got pretty used to it and wanted to know why we could not just sell the whole cookie instead of breaking it up. Donnie told me to slow my roll that that lesson would come later, but first he wanted to talk to me about something. "Think about it, if we sell the whole cookie and raise the price to $5000 a pop, we could cut our trips down to one a month."

"That's $10,000 on me and 10 on Keisha." "You are becoming a monster," says Donnie, climbing into the back of the van. "Look, I am just trying to cut down on some of these trips; I miss hanging with Joy every weekend. She has to go to school and we only get to chill for a little bit on Sunday when we come back." "Is that the only person you miss?" says Donnie, looking at me with an evil stare. "Uh well, yeah I miss Lawrence too. I miss him singing to me, holding me, and rubbing my legs." "It has been about two months now since you've been here so that puts you and Lawrence together for about a month and two weeks, because those first two weeks, you made the boy struggle." "Yeah, I did huh," smiling and feeling all funny inside. "Have you fucked him yet?" asked Donnie. "What no, I am a virgin. I can't do that. I don't even know how to kiss." "I can show you," said Donnie, with a hungry look in his eyes.

"Get outta here man! You can't show me that, you are my cousin." "I know that, that is exactly why I can show you. I can teach you everything else," said Donnie. "Yeah, but I do not want to kiss you, your breath stinks." "Have you ever seen a dick before?" "No I haven't." "Do you want to see one?" "I guess, maybe, I don't know. I am not fucking, so I don't need to see it." "Have you kissed Lawrence yet?" "Yes a little." "And how did it make you feel?" "Did you get wet down in your private?" "Yeah, sometimes when he rubs my back or kisses my neck or something." "Do you want to have sex with him?" "Maybe, but I don't know how." "Do you want me to show you?" asked Donnie. "I guess." "Okay, I will be right back." Donnie gets out of the van and come back a minute later with a bag.

"Ok, pull your pants down," he says as he pulls out his thing and puts something on it. "What are you doing?" "I am getting ready," says Donnie. "I know that, but what is that?" "This?" he says, pointing at himself. "This is a penis." "No silly, what are you putting on it?" I ask. "Oh, this is a condom. I put this on so you don't get pregnant." "Pregnant!" "Yeah, you know, the sperm comes out and goes to your egg and makes a baby." "I do not want to have a baby." "You won't, that is why you use these. Remember, if you use one of these, you will not get pregnant." "Ok, come on, get on top of me." "Are you sure we should be doing this?" "How would Keisha feel about you teaching me this?"

"What, come on! She told me to teach you what you needed to know and you don't know right?"

"Ok I guess, but something feels strange about this to me," I said, climbing up. "Here, hold it," says Donnie. "Ok, now sit down on it." "It hurts and that thing feels like rubber." "Well, it is rubber," says Donnie adjusting himself, trying to make it go in. "Ok, I am going to take it off." "But you said you have to wear it so I won't get pregnant." "I will pull out before I nut." "What, pull out, uh uh this is not right." He then grabs me and turns me over and throws me down saying, "Come on girl, you know you want to learn. You can't be with Lawrence and not know what you are doing. Open your legs." He shoves my legs open. "But no, Donnie, I don't want to do it. Please stop! Get off me." He penetrates me and I scream stop. As he takes two strokes he pulls out. "Uh yuck!"

"Why did you do that when I told you I did not want to," I said, reaching for the door with tears in my eyes. "No wait," he grabs me. "Don't tell anyone, people will not understand that I was just trying to teach you and I know you do not want to end up in a foster home somewhere if someone finds out." I look at him and roll my eyes and get out of the van. Sitting in the tub, I began to cry and almost as fast as the tears started, they stopped. I could hear Donnie's voice saying, "Don't cry. Do not show your feelings, crying will get you killed." I look down and see specks of blood flowing from my private in the running water. I clean up and climb on the sofa bed and rock myself to sleep.

I awoke in the middle of the night holding my private area. A part of me was angry with him but another part of me knew he was all I had at the moment. As I thought back on the words he had spoken to me, I remembered him telling me that actions always spoke louder than words. Although I felt it was wrong what he did, I told myself he was only trying to teach me how to survive, just like he was teaching me everything else. I was so young and naive, simply stupid. Here I was being molested by my trusted cousin and I did not try and stop it until his teaching turned into lust and anger. The next day Donnie asks me was I ok. I shrugged my shoulders and told him yes. I began to stay to myself and not around Donnie as much that next week. "Are you mad at me?" he asks. "No, I just wish you would have stopped when I asked you to." "I am sorry," and he gives me a hug and a kiss on the cheek. "You know, I was only trying to teach you how to do it right. I do not want anyone to ever take advantage of you and I know..." Lawrence walks up at that moment and clears his throat, enabling Donnie to finish his statement. "Man, I am going to have to watch you around my girl. Only my lips belong on that beautiful angelic face." Donnie looks at him with one of those evil smirks on his face, and releases me from his embrace. "Reyne, come sit with me for a little bit. My cousin is gone and we can have some alone time."

I ask Donnie and he says it's cool and watches Lawrence and me walk off hand in hand. Keisha reaches around him and says, "Why don't me and you have some alone time." Donnie pushes her hand off of him and says, "Not right now. I got some errands to run," and grabs his keys and leaves. "Your cousin sure has been acting mighty possessive the past few weeks. Is he ok?" asked Lawrence." "Yeah, I guess, you know Donnie crazy." Scooting closer, Lawrence puts his arm around me and begins singing in my ear. I giggle and squirm. "Stop that" I say. "Why do you want me to stop?" he asks kissing my lips. "Because it makes me feel funny inside," I reply. He begins to tickle me and he falls on top of me on the floor. As "Freak Me Baby" by Silk plays in the background, he begins grinding his private against mine and kissing my neck. It feels so good, but suddenly I sit up. "What's wrong?" he asked, sitting on the side of me.

"Nothing, I just want, I don't know...I want it to be special. I am not ready. I'm sorry." I get up to leave and Lawrence takes my hand and kisses it and says "No worry, I am yours forever. We have our whole life to make love." He pulls me to him and caresses my hair and plants one ' on me that leaves me staggering. I stumble towards the door and tell him I will see him later.

When I get back to the house I walk in to find Keisha sitting on the couch looking sad. "What's wrong Keisha?" "Girl, nothing you wouldn't understand." I sit next to her and say," Try me, talk to me." She begins going on and on about how Donnie is not romantic with her anymore and that when they do have sex it is so unromantic. "He just climbs on me and does his business and then it's over. We don't even kiss the same." I began smiling. "What are you smiling about and what that is on your neck?" "What?" I asked, covering my neck. "Oh, Lawrence and I, well, we were, you know kissing and stuff. "Oh, you gave him some of your stuff?" says Keisha. "No, I didn't. We were just bumping and grinding," I said, holding my private.

She jumps up and starts winding her hips singing R. Kelly's Bump and Grind. "Sit down crazy," I said, pulling her back down. "What is romance? I want to do it with Lawrence. He say that he will wait and that we have our whole lives to make love. What is making love? I thought it was called fucking or sex." "No honey child, let me show you," said Keisha. She pulls out these tapes from her closet and says "Hmm where do we begin." She pops in this video of this man walking with a dog. "Ok, what is romantic about a man reading a letter walking with a dog?" I asked her. "Girl, just watch," passing me a bottle of Boones Farm. As the show continues a woman begins telling a story of an affair she is having with this man that does construction work next to her office building. Her husband, at home, is not satisfying her. Keisha says "Hmm, I know what you mean, but Donnie would kill me if he caught me cheating." "Wow look at that. He is big," I say staring at the man's private part. I've never seen one that big." "Yeah, unfortunately I haven't either," says Keisha squeezing her legs together.

As the two began to make love, my body becomes hotter and hotter. "I think I am going to go and see Lawrence now," I say rising up to go out the door. "Girl, no, if you go down there like that for yawls first time he is going to really be hooked. You think he be after you now, child you gonna have him looking for you with a flashlight in the daytime if you go down there like that. Sit down and calm yourself. Let me show you another tape." We watched another tape but this one was not as sensual as the other. They were rougher and there was no story-line just fucking. I do not like this one. We heard a key in the door and Keisha quickly turns it off right when the door opens and her 7 year old son Kyle walks in. "Hey Momma." "Hey minifies." They all run to her and give her a hug, asking, "Are we going to pick up Auntie Joy please, please?" "Yeah, we will all go get her, go change clothes," says Keisha. She walks up to Donnie and grabs his private and says, "I have an appointment with you later at 9:00 PM Baby," and licks him in the ear. He smiles and grabs her butt and says "I'll be there." I laugh and go in the room and help the kids get ready.

Once we pick up Joy we head back to the house. "So, what are you doing for your birthday?" asked Joy. "I do not know yet. I want to go to the R. Kelly concert. That would be nice." "Speaking of Mr. Bump and Grind, have you and Lawrence done it yet?" "Girl, no we just bump and grind." "There yawl go, I have been waiting for you," says Stacey. "What's up?" "Come on and get dressed. I have tickets to the R. Kelly concert." "What, oh my gosh! I just said I wanted to go." "Ok, I am going to get ready." "Wait a minute, do you have a ticket for Joy?" I asked. "Of course, I do here it is," says Stacey. "I don't have anything to wear," says Joy. "Look, the concert starts in an hour so yawl better come on so we can beat traffic. I have to pick up Gina," says Stacey.

In fifteen minutes flat, we were showered and ready to go. In the car, I asked Stacey, "How did you get so many tickets?" "Reyne, now you know we got that call in thing down on the radio to get them tickets." "Oh yeah," turning to Joy, "I forgot." "Hey, remember that time Mr. Roger took us to the MC Hammer concert and then that time we went to see Jodeci and Shai and the guy from Color Me Badd threw me his drumstick?" "Yeah girl, I remember all that." "No, the question is, do you remember" says Stacey, "the time when East had that concert when R. Kelly first came out and you and Gina tried to pull Marques Houston from Immature off the stage?" Laughing loudly, I said "Aww man, I remember that. I did not want to give that ring back either. He was gone have to come to my house and get it."

Beep Beep, "Gina come on," says Stacey honking the horn. "Why isn't Lacey going?" I ask. "She is not feeling well. Those headaches are bothering her again," says Stacey. "Oh, hey Gina, you can get in the front," I said, climbing in the back seat with Joy. "So Reyne, Stacey tells me you have this new boyfriend who sings to you all the time and writes you letters," says Gina. Blushing, I said, "Yeah he is nice, his name is Lawrence but that's all I'm telling you. The last time I told you about my man you stole him."

We all look at each other and fall out laughing. "How is my best friend Freddy doing anyway?" I ask. "He is upset because you have not called him and he is worried about you, I told him about Lawrence." "What you go and do that for?" "Well you know how he is Mr. Protector," says Gina. "Well tell him I am fine and happy." "Guess what yawl?" says Stacey. We all look at her. She yells, "I am not a virgin anymore." "What? Uh uh Stacey you and Mitchell did it?" says Gina. "Did it hurt?" ask Joy. "A little," says Stacey. "So, Gina what about you?" ask Stacey. "Um I really don't want to hear about that right now," I say. "No Reyne I have not, yet but I have been thinking about it," says Gina. "You girls are bad," says Joy. "Joy come on now I know you ain't talking," I say. "What I have not done anything yet," she says looking around innocently. "Ok, nasty girls yawl better keep yawl legs closed and don't be getting all hot listening to Mr. Kelly tonight," says Stacey. We all laugh and say at the same time, "Too late" and start singing I don't see anything wrong with a little bump and grind.

By the time the concert was over Gina had called Freddy three times. Joy was ready to go home and Stacey was like look we will go eat tomorrow. I have to get home to my man. I on the other hand was in another world. The rhythm of the music had overtaken me so I was speechless. My body felt numb I was as high as could be. No weed I had ever smoked gave me the high that I got when I listened and danced to music. We dropped Gina off first, then Joy and then me. I hugged my sister bye and told her thank you for taking us to the concert.

As I walked into the apartment I could hear the sound of Keisha and Donnie doing their thang. I peeked in on the kids to find them knocked out with the TV blasting as usual. Because of Keisha's screams I left it turned up. While in the kitchen drinking a glass of water I thought back to earlier that day when Lawrence was on top of me grinding and singing in my ear. I quickly took a shower and went down to his apartment. Just my luck his cousin was leaving with his girlfriend just as I got to the door. "Hello," he said, "Lawrence is in the bathroom but you can go in we are leaving for the night," says his cousin. "Ok thanks," I say. I walk in and turn to lock the door.

When I turn around Lawrence is standing there with no shirt on with a towel wrapped around his waist. "How are you?" he says. "Fine," I say slipping away from the door making my way to the couch. "I heard the door open back and was coming to see who it was," he says. "Yeah your cousin was leaving and he told me to come on in." "How was the concert?" he asks walking towards me. "It was um, good I had a great time," I say swallowing hard as I see the shape of his manliness while he walks. I think to myself wow look at the size of that thing as he sits next to me smelling so good. "I missed you. I came down there to find you, but Donnie said you went to the concert with your sister," he says stroking my hair. "Yeah I would have come and told you but we were press for time," I say trying not to shudder from his touch. "I had something planned to do for your birthday. I know it is not until tomorrow, well in a few minutes, but I will not be here all day so I wanted to celebrate with you today because I have to go and meet my Dad," he says placing my hand on his chest. "Oh it's ok. I am happy to be here now," I say rubbing his chest. He takes my hand and begins kissing it slowly. He stands me up and dances with me pressing his hardness up against my body. I melt in his arms. Not to mention the remix to Your Body's Calling starts playing. I am really high now.

Before I even realized it my clothes were off. He picked me up and we continued to dance. He then made his way to the couch and laid me down. As we lay on the couch on the side of each other he stroked my hair and sang Happy Birthday to me. I told him thank you, kissed him and went to sleep, only to wake up two hours later and start again. I stretched and turned over only to hear someone banging on the door. It was Donnie. Lawrence gets up and opens the door as I run to the bathroom to get dressed I did not notice it was almost noon. "Is my little cousin here?" asked Donnie. "Hey Cousin," I say coming around the corner. "Girl come on here we got to go to Janet house we been looking all over for you. You were here all night huh?" Donnie says looking around. "I came over after the concert last night," I say looking at Lawrence sheepishly. "Well let's go," says Donnie. "Alright! Bye Lawrence," I say reaching to give him a hug.

He grabs me and puts his tongue down my throat causing me to erupt down there again. I back out of the door still holding his hand. "I will see you later on when I get back," says Lawrence. "Ok Bye." "Bye Baby," he says letting go of my hand. Donnie grabs me and says as we get further down the hall, "You gave him my...I mean your stuff didn't you." "What? Why are you grabbing on me let me go!" I say jerking myself away from Donnie. "Come here Reyne. You know I am just playing with you. I just want to make sure you are ok," he says rubbing my cheek and caressing my back. I jerk away and say "I am fine" and walk off.

The rest of my 15th birthday was spent with Joy telling her about my night and us laughing and talking about our futures. For Christmas that year we went to Louisiana, and by January I was ready to run my own dope as well as weed. I had taken over the swisher sweet sells around the neighborhood and had become the main supplier. Lawrence and I grew closer and he started telling me he loved me. I told him not to tell me that because every time someone did they always ended up leaving me. He promised me that he would never go anywhere and that he loved me for life. Of course I had already warned him about those words and just like everybody else they proved to be fatal.

One day while Joy and I were sitting out in front of the apartment cleaning the machete Lawrence comes running out of his apartment. His cousin has a gun and comes out behind him threatening to shoot him and cursing about some money. The cousin's girlfriend then comes out with a butcher knife and is trying to cut Lawrence. I run in the house and grab the gun and load it. As I cock it back while walking towards them it goes off. I instantly go flying into the wall behind me and the bullet ricochets off of the staircase and goes into the wall. The girlfriend comes towards me with the butcher knife and Joy throws me the Machete. Luckily it was in the case because in landed point down on my leg. I take it out just in time and swing towards her. Lawrence yells no and his cousin drops the gun and they both come running my way. I raise it up to cut her and from behind Donnie grabbed me and took it out of my hand. The girlfriend drops her knife and walks back toward the cousin cursing and yelling all sorts of obscenities. Lawrence's cousin demands for him to come and get his stuff as he checks his crazy girlfriend to be sure I did not cut her. Lawrence looks our way and mouths he is so sorry for everything. Donnie still has a pretty tight grip on me because I am still heated and wanting to fight.

Lawrence comes out of the apartment with his bags and his cousin tells him he never want to see your face again. I yell don't worry you won't still trying to wiggle away from Donnie's grip. "Calm your lil ass down girl," says Donnie and he let me go. "What in the hell is going on? I leave to go bring Keisha to work and I come back and all this craziness is going on." Lawrence walks up and says, "Look man I am sorry my cousin and I got into it and she ran out here with the gun." "The gun…nah man look I do not know what you got going on but if something happens to my cousin that is going to be your ass my nigga for real," says Donnie. "Man, I promise you dog, I would never let anything happen to her," says Lawrence reaching for my hand. "Say, Donnie can I stay here for a few days," ask Lawrence. "Hell nah man you know my wife ain't having that. I got kids. You better come in here and call your Dad," said Donnie. While Lawrence calls his Dad Donnie leaves to take Joy back home and to pick up the kids. "Keep that negro out of my shit. He can wait here for his dad to pick him up but that is it," whispers Donnie in my ear before he leaves. I nod ok and hug Joy goodbye.

"Reyne I have to tell you something," says Lawrence as I walk into the living room. "Don't bother. Let me guess. You're leaving right?" I say rolling my eyes. "Baby it is only temporary. I love you and I promise I will be back. I have to go to Corpus Christi for a little while to work," he says walking towards me. "I told you not to tell me you love me," I say turning away. Coming closer he says, "I promise I am coming back and when I do you and I can get a place and be together, just the two of us. I sat on the couch in his arms in silence until his Dad arrived. Donnie returned right when his Dad pulled up. "I love you Reyne," he pleaded. "Please stop saying that shit. I do not want to hear it just go. If you love me you would not be leaving," I yell. "But I do love you" he says grabbing me trying to kiss me. "Just go man" I say pushing him away. "Just go." "I promise I will be back for you," he says as he walks out the door. I sit in the corner of the couch with no emotion at all. Donnie sits next to me. "Are you ok?" he asked. "Yeah I'm straight. No emotion right," I say getting up going in the bathroom. "No emotion."

That night I sat on the sofa bed alone looking at the calendar. Here it is February 5, 1995 and I am deserted once again. I looked up at the ceiling and made a vow to never be hurt like this again. The next few weeks things got thick. Donnie kept trying to have sex with me and I pushed him away sometimes. The more I resisted him the meaner he became towards me. Whereas before I did not have to do many chores, now I had to clean up. By the end of March my sister kept her word and came to get me. We moved to Rain View to some apartments called Waypoint. Joy would come to visit the first few weekends but then Donnie and Keisha moved back to Louisiana at the end of April. Because I knew all his customers of course I kept the game going. My sister lost her job in April and well Mitchell was not working so between paying the bills and the mall money became funny.

One day in May I was going across the street to Burger King and I heard someone call my name. I ignored it the first time and then I heard it again. This time I turned around and lo and behold guess who it was? Freddy! "What's up man?" I say grabbing his hand and shaking it. He looks at me strangely and says, "What happen to my hug?" "Hug! Nigga I don't do all that hugging shit. That is for them li'l bitches you are use to messing with," I say frowning. "Whoa okay what happen to my sweet innocent friend who does not use that type of language?" he said throwing his hands up. "Hm! I guess she died, so I'm here now," I say. He puts his arm around me and says, "Look we need to talk. Come on let's go sit down and eat. I heard what happen with you and your Mom," says Freddy. "Yeah, but I'm good. I am on my own now and nobody can tell me what to do," I say stuffing French fries in my mouth. "Why didn't you call me?" ask Freddy. "Call you for what? You were so wrapped up into Gina you did not care what was going on with me," I say angrily rolling my eyes. "That is not true Reyne," he says looking at the time. "Come on my Mom has to go to work and I have to watch my little sister and brother," he says reaching for me.

Entering the house his mother sees me and says, "Hey Baby I have not seen you in a while." "Hi, Ms. Monica. How have you been?" I say politely in my sweetest voice possible. Freddy does a double take as if he has just seen a ghost. Hugging me she says, "Look baby I have to get to work. You are welcome to anything in the refrigerator. Freddy, Peter cannot go outside and Samantha is still punished." "Ahh, Momma that is not fair why Freddy always get to have company and do whatever he wants," whines Samantha. "Girl don't talk back to me I'll knock your teeth down your throat now come give me some sugar bye and I will see you later," says Ms. Monica as she kisses her daughter goodbye.

As her Mom walks out the door Samantha turns to Freddy and says, "Does Gina know she's here?" "No and it is none of your business so go in your room," says Freddy. "Hi," says Peter waving shyly. "Hi Peter." I go and give him a hug. "How are you?" I ask. He just stares at me smiling. "I see Peter still does not talk much huh?" I say turning to Freddy. "No," says Freddy. "We have him in speech therapy he is trying though." Freddy's brother has a speech impediment and is a little bit slow. Sweet kid though and he really loves his brother. "So what have you been up to girl," Freddy ask as he begins to clean up. "Hustling just trying to survive, you know trying to make a dollar out of fifteen cents," I say helping him clean. "You sound like a street hustler. What's wrong with you," ask Freddy looking irritated. "What is wrong with me what's wrong with you nigga?" I say dropping the broom. "Girl don't you use that word in this house you now I don't like that word," he says handing me the broom back. "Man look I am out I will catch up with you later," I say pushing past him and the broom. "Why don't you go and call Gina or something," I say shoving the picture of the two of them on the floor and walking out of the door.

Back at the apartment I hear voices and it is Walter talking with his uncle and Stacey. "There you go. I was wondering where you were," says Stacey. "Oh I went to get something to eat." I say hopping on the couch. "Girl let me tell you. I went to the office to tell them I would be late on the rent and they told me it was paid already," says Stacey excitedly. Not looking her in her face I say, "That's cool," turning towards Walter. "What's up Walter?" Laughing he says, "Nothing what's up with you?" "You know just trying to survive." "Come on Stacey let's go," says Mitchell. I look up and roll my eyes and ask them where they are going. "We going hang out for a bit" says Stacey pulling Mitchell out the door.

Pulling out my stash I began rolling up a blunt. "You want some?" I ask Walter. "No I am good. When did you start smoking?" he ask looking confused. I looked up at him and say, "Why you didn't expect a good girl like me to smoke? You would be surprised at the things I do now." "Really," says Walter pulling up a chair sitting down. Throughout the rest of the month, Walter and his two friends Derrick and Javier started coming over more and more. Derrick was tall and dark while Javier was brown and nicely built. Since Stacey was not working she was rarely home because all of her time was spent with Mitchell. When she was home it was to get some clothes and leave again. She and Mitchell were like glue.

Summer time hit and Donnie and my other cousin Byron came to visit for a weekend. Seeing how well I had done while he was gone he decided that he wanted me to come to Louisiana with them. I turn down the offer and said I was waiting for Lawrence to come home. I had talked to him at the beginning of May and he said he would be home by June. "Well you might want to call him because we saw him last night and he said he is not coming back. As a matter of fact he is leaving on Tuesday," says Donnie. "Where did you see him at?" I ask. "At the old spot in Mark Twain, we stopped by last night when we got in town to holler at Cookie'nem and he was at his cousin's house," says Byron. "Really I'll be back," I say walking out of the apartment. I went to the payphone and called. Sure enough Lawrence answered the phone. "How dare you be here in Houston and you have not come to see me yet." I yell. "Reyne?" he questions. "Uh yeah who in the hell else is it going to be?" I say with major attitude. "Hey Baby I…I was going to come see you. It's just that my Dad has the car right now and well I…um have to go back to Corpus until like September."

"I did not know how to tell you so when I saw Donnie last night I asked him to tell you," says Lawrence. I held the phone silently as anger rose up. "Hello, Reyne," says Lawrence. "What?" I say. "I miss you," says Lawrence. "When are you leaving to go back?" I ask. "Tonight but I will try my best to come and see you before I leave." he says. "It is already four in the afternoon. How are you even going to get here?" I ask. "Look I don't know but if I don't see you, you can always call me. I promise I am coming back and I have a good job there making legit money. I'll be back I promise." he proclaims. "So what are you saying you expect me to wait for you?" I ask. "Um. Yeah. I guess! I do not know. I mean it is really not fair for me to ask you to do that," he says. "Would you wait for me?" I ask. "Honestly no and I do not mean that in a bad way but look at you. You're beautiful you cannot tell me that guys have not been trying to pick you up. I know they have" says Lawrence. "What about you? Are you talking to other females?" I ask curiously. "Well I have met people but I love you I am not trying to be with anyone else. I am here to work so I can come home and be with you." he pleads.

"I tell you what Lawrence, I am not going to sit here and wait for you, neither am I going to be available for other men but my door is not closed. I am not saying that I do not care about you but I do not know what you are doing out there. For all I know there could be a broad sitting right next to you right now. Call me when you come back if I am not taken than we will see where it goes but in the meantime I got to take care of me." "I love you Reyne and I do not want anybody else but you" says Lawrence. "I wish I could believe that and if that were true why are you leaving me again?" I say and hang up the phone. Before I even made it back to the house good Donnie's pager had done went off like four times. "Girl will you please call this nigga back. He is blowing up my pager," says Donnie. "Nah, I am good. He will be ok," I said walking back out of the apartment.

"Hi, what's your name?" I turn around to see a young girl standing by the tree. "What's your name? My name is Cat," she says. "Hey I'm Reyne." She sits on the bench next to me and says, "You look sad. Is your Mom giving you a hard time too?" she asks. "What? My Mom? I do not live with my Momma. This is me and my sister's place. Well it might as well be mine because she is never here and I pay all the bills," I say shaking my head. "I want to run away but I do not have anywhere to go. My Mom hits on me and is always cursing me out and stuff" says Cat. "For real? I remember my Mom beat me once. My legs are still kind of tender if I run too much. Hey look I tell you what why don't you try to work it out with your Mom and talk to her. Meet me back here tomorrow at about three and let me know how it went." I say. "I don't get out of summer school until four," she says. "Alright well make it five then. Make sure you tell her how you really feel. If she loves you she will listen," I say and get up and head back to the apartment.

Back in the house Donnie began packing up to head back to Louisiana. "Are you sure you do not want to go? You can make triple the money than what you are doing now." "Nah, I am going to stay here. Lawrence and I broke up so I am just going to chill for a minute." Donnie says, "Alright then but don't miss your paper over no nigga. He gives me a hug and says be good and keep it tight. You know you are the one that holds the power," pointing between my legs. "I am like yeah I know ain't nobody getting it unless I want them to have it," I mock him. As Stacey and I walked them out Donnie goes back in the house to get something he forgot. I went in after him but he came right back out not seeing Stacey standing there. Donnie ask me if I could front him two cookies for the trip. In my mind I am thinking I knew there was a reason he wanted me to go back with him. I ask, "This is why you wanted me to come with you, because you do not have anyone to carry the dope huh?"

As I went in my stash to give him what he ask for Stacey comes in and says, "I knew it." "Knew what I ask?" I ask looking all innocent. "I knew you were selling drugs and in my house get that stuff out of here. Donnie take it all with you," says Stacey." But what are we going to do about the rent and stuff," I say as Donnie grabs my entire stash crack. Donnie says, "Alright I am gone. That is between you and your sister. You could have come with me but you said no." "Hey bring back the weed though," says Stacey grabbing the swisher sweet box from under his arm. Stacey goes and locks the door behind them. "Reyne come here." I come in the living room and sit down pissed because that was the last of my stash that I planned to cover the bills with for the next six months until the lease was up. "Man Stacey do you realize there was over $5,000 worth of goods in there not counting the weed," I say sulking. "I do not care how much was in there. Do you know what that stuff does to people?" ask Stacey. "Yeah man I know, but I am not smoking it," I say humping my shoulders.

"You remember that time you came running home from school when they showed yawl that tape of the people doing drugs. You know the one with the man overdosing in the bathroom," she says. Squirming I say, "Uggh, yeah I remember." "That is what he was doing injecting himself with drugs," she says turning towards me. "Promise me you will not sell these drugs anymore. Promise me" says Stacey. "Ok, ok I won't. It has been kind of getting to me lately anyway. I couldn't even watch New Jack City. Whenever I watch a movie that has drugs in it I get all squeamish inside. But what are we going to do about the bills?" I ask. "You do not worry about that. I want you to go back to school in

August when school starts back," says Stacey. "I know you do. I will maybe," I say looking down.

"I have to go and pick up Mitchell so I will see you later. Are you ok?" asked Stacey looking down at me. "What do you mean?" I ask looking up. "Lawrence," she says. "No emotion right," I say. "Do you want to ride with me?" ask Stacey. "No I am going to visit Freddy. You know he lives right across the street," I tell her. "For real," says Stacey. "Yeah I ran into him last week." "Have fun I will see you later," says Stacey walking out the house. She turns around and tells me, "Remember no more selling drugs. Let me worry about the bills. You just finish school." I nod my head yes.

Walking across the street to Freddy's I see him outside playing ball with his friends. As the quarterback throws the ball I catch it and began to run for the touchdown. Freddy and about three other guys jump out at me and I dodge their efforts to tackle me and I score. I start singing, "You know I'm bad I'm bad you know it." The guys all stop and ask who am I? Freddy puts his sweaty stink arm around me and says, "Fellows this pretty young thing is my best friend all the way from middle school." One of the guys walks up and says, "I can teach you a thing or two," rubbing his hand in my face. I grab his hand and punch him in the chest and say, "No I think I could teach you a thing or two." "Alright alright lady calm down," Freddy grabs me. "Lady, man she hits like a man. She is pretty but she packs a hell of a punch," says the guy holding his chest.

"Freddy, Freddy come on now I got to go to store," yells Mom. The guys make the dud dud dun sound. "Whatever man" says Freddy telling the guys bye. "Are you coming up?" he asked me. "Yeah I can hang out for a minute," I say, walking up the steps. "Freddy your sister and brother and I will be back here in about two to three hours please have the food ready," said Mom. "Ok Mom I got it," Freddy says walking into the kitchen. "No you don't have it. You stink. Go bathe."

"I will do it," I say. Mom hugs us both and leaves out the door. "Hey," Freddy says taking off his shirt as his bath water runs, "You know Gina left." "Yeah I heard Stacey told me she moved back to Boston. How you holding up?" I ask. "Oh, I am good," he says taking off his socks. "How are you and that Lawrence guy doing?" "Well he is not coming back from Corpus until September," I say as I begin cooking. "Are you going to wait for him?" asked Freddy. "That is funny he ask me the same thing. Are you going to wait for Gina," I ask throwing a piece of spaghetti at him. We both look at each other and burst into laughter.

"Hurry up. You are stinking up the house," I say shooing him away with the spatula. "That food sure does smell good," Freddy yells from the bathtub. I walk into the bathroom after finishing the food. Luckily his Mom had already started so it was half way done. "You are not done yet. I thought you were cleaning the tub out. I know I heard the shower go off," I say standing next to the tub. "Yeah I washed off all the dirt in the shower and ran some bath water to relax in. Do you want to join me?" he says patting the water. "No way! I will just climb right here and watch," I say climbing up on the sink as Freddy rinses off. We talk about the good times back in middle school and how abandoned I felt during the homecoming dance. He says, "Yeah I know and again I am so sorry about that. I guess what goes around comes around because now Gina is gone," he says. "Yeah but it is not the same at least you got a chance to say bye," I say hopping off the sink. "Hand me that towel off the bed please" says Freddy standing up in the tub. As I hand him the towel I say, "Wow did Gina see all of this?" "Did Lawrence see all of that?" pointing at my body, asked Freddy. "For me to know and you never to find out," I say as I walk out of the bathroom into his room.

"Hey what is this?" I ask bending over picking up a yearbook on the floor. "Oh that is my year book from elementary school," says Freddy. "Oh what school was it," I ask climbing up on the bed. "West Houston," he says. "West Houston, I went to West Houston," I say. Freddy climbs on the side of me, grabs the book and turns to the picture of the cheerleading team and points me out. "Oh my gosh," I say as he turns to the picture of himself. I gasped and say, "Tree." He says, "Yep that's me." "I knew it! Your eyes were always so kind and kind of sad," I say looking into them remembering the paper roses and how sweet he was to me in middle school.

Freddy sets the yearbook aside and pulls me over on his chest. I lay on him with one leg straddling his body and we talk about what happen to him after he left West Houston. As time went on we fell asleep. About an hour or so later I feel something hard against my leg. I look down and I see his manliness bulging out of his boxers. As I try to move to adjust myself he pulls me back on top of him and begins kissing my neck. As he kisses my neck his hand begins to undo my shorts and I began to think is this for real. Right when he gets my shorts undone we look into each other's eyes and burst out laughing. "Wait a minute," I say rolling off of him placing my hand on his chest and my head on his shoulder, "What are we doing?" Freddy laughs, "Yeah what are we doing? Get off me girl," He says moving his arm. I get up and look at him and laugh uncontrollably. "I cannot believe we were about to do the nasty," I say buttoning my shorts back. "Oo I can't either." he says adjusting himself.

Suddenly there are keys at the door. Freddy jumps up and gets completely dressed, I jump over the couch and grab the remote just as the door opens and Mom and his brother and sister walk in. "Hi Mom," I say. Freddy comes from out of the kitchen and grabs the bags. "Freddy you didn't clean up nothing," she yells as she looks around. "I told him Momma. I cooked. He was just running his mouth." Freddy shakes his fist at me Mom starts fussing at him and I stick out my tongue at him. As she proceeds to pick up books I say, "Well Mom I have to go now. I will see yawl later." I hug Samantha and Peter bye and punch Freddy in the arm.

The next morning I awake to someone banging on my door. I slightly pull the 357 from under the couch and creep to the door. Looking through the peep hole I say, "Who is it?" "It's me Cat." I put the gun up but keep it close. Being that I was out of the game now I expected visitors but luckily for them, I never got any. I open the door and Cat is standing there with a black eye and a fat lip. "What happen to you?" I ask letting her in. She comes in and says, "I told my mother how I really felt." "Wow looks like she showed you how she felt." I say looking at her face. "Can I stay here please?" ask Cat. "I don't care but I do not want any visitors and you cannot be telling people you live here," I say. "Ok. I am hungry," says Cat. "Let's go get something to eat," I say.

That Thursday Walter, Derrick and Javier came over to play Dominos. Cat took a liking to Walter as soon as she saw him. "Reyne come here," says Cat motioning me into the kitchen. "Is that your boyfriend?" she asked. "Who?" I ask. "The light skinned guy. You know the bow-legged one." says Cat. "No, why do you like him?" I ask. "Yeah! I think he is fine," she says. "You can talk to him but you are going to have to fuck," I tell her. "What?" says Cat. "Fuck! He is going to want to do the nasty are you down?" I ask getting irritated. "I guess. I don't know," she says looking lost. "What is it that you don't know? Either you will or you won't it is your body." I tell her even more irritated. "Have you ever fucked him?" ask Cat. "Of course I have but it was just one time for show. So to me it really did not count because I had no feelings for him what so ever and was not even horny," I explain to her. "Well ok. Are you sure you are ok with it?" ask Cat. "Yes, girl and cool I will let him know." I say. "Oh, do I need to get somebody for the other two guys?" ask Cat. "Not Javier, but you can find somebody for Derrick. Javier has a girlfriend." I tell her. "Ok I will be right back," she says heading out of the apartment.

She goes and gets this girl name Shena whom at the time I could not stand. She was so messy and always talking about people but good for the job. Before she even got in the door I told her look if she was not sucking or fucking she could not come in. Derrick immediately was like hell nah he was not touching that girl. I told him he could at least get some head and then send her home. I told Walter that Cat was interested and he asked me what about me. "What about me? I am chilling my man will be back in September," I say sitting on the couch next to Javier rolling a swisher. Derrick says with a sneaky look on his face, "September? What are you going to do from July until then? "Exactly what I am doing now, chilling." Javier turns to me and says, "What you think you something like a pimp or something." "What nigga, I aint no pimp people just do what I say," I say lighting up the weed. "Really, well I aint go do nothing you say. You need to mess with a real man that is going to make you sit your ass down somewhere," he says. "Excuse me," I say rolling my eyes. "There is not a man born that can make me sit down." "Oh yeah! I bet I could tame your but I am going to chill because I do not want to break you li'l skinny tail," he says smiling. "I would break you," I say looking him up and down.

For about a week all Javier and I did was argue about who had the biggest cahoonies. Walter and Cat got closer and Derrick only dealt with Shena on a head basis. One night I was sitting out on the steps when I smelled reefa. Oh it smells so good I thought to myself. Almost as if the guy heard what I said he asked me if I wanted to come up and smoke one with him. I had notice these guys before and I knew their supplier so I knew the weed was good and that it was not laced with anything. So as Bone Thugs n Harmony flowed in the background I smoked one and had a little small talk with the guy. His name was Damon and he had a twin brother name David. Just as we lit up the second blunt a girl walks up.

"What's up Hope," says Damon. "What s up," she says looking at me and giving me the nod I back to her. I pass her the blunt and she nods again. Once the blunt is complete I tell them I am going to call it a

131

night. I shake Damon's hand and give Hope the nod and head downstairs in the house.

After one final argument, I could not take it anymore, Javier and I had become the best of lovers. He had developed a habit of singing Prince Songs when we would do it because he loved the reaction he got from my body when Prince would hit the high notes. Of course Walter and Derrick talked about him for this. All he would say is, "Man yawl don't know like I know what she does when she does what she does." Money had become tight and the bills were barely getting paid. My weed habit had superseded what I was selling and it seemed like my supplier was always running out faster than I could replenish my stock. Walter and Javier wanted to take Cat and me out. Of course I did not have money for a new outfit so Cat says let's just go and steal one from Palais Royal. I was not really comfortable with committing any crimes with Cat especially stealing. She was so goofy and the only thing she seems to be good at was sex. I really only kept her around because it was too hard to try to rob guys without being touched. So with Cat around since she liked it so much she played the guinea pig while I got the goods.

Inside of the dressing room I tell her, "You know something does not feel right." "Come on quit being scared I know you like the outfit. Just put your clothes on top of it and let's go," she says getting dressed. "I do not feel right," I say walking out. I looked up and made eye contact with the security guard. He nodded his head no and I walk back towards the dressing room. I waved for Cat to follow me but her silly butt went out the front door. The security guard immediately went after her. As I was taking off the clothes the manager comes in and grabs me and drags me to the back room. Inside Cat is sitting there begging them not to call her mother. "What is your mother's number," asked the manager? "I do not know," I say. "I don't live with my Momma. I live by myself."

Yeah right she says and decides to just have the police take us to jail. Cat begins to plead, "No please you can call her sister she don't stay with her Momma." I kick her and tell her to shut up. The cop walks in and hand cuffs us both. They put us in separate cars and take us to a girl's juvenile detention center. Inside we were separated and questioned about some break-ins that had been happening around the neighborhood. The security guard told the officers that I took the clothes off and Cat was the one that actually stole. They made me do a week and half worth of time because I was at the scene and attempted. Cat did four weeks and was bailed out by her Mom. Of course my mother had to come get me. When she arrived I saw in her eyes that she was going to beat the hell out of me, so I just prepared myself for the beating. No sooner had we walked in the house she grabs a belt and begins to whip me yelling that I am a thief and a whore and will never be anything. I did not even cry I was so angry all I could see was red.

When she finished I went in my old room and reevaluated the situation. I knew for sure that I did not like jail so I had to get a job and beat Cat's ass as soon as I got back because I told her to take off the damn clothes. I heard my door open and looked up it was Lacey and Tanya. I reached out for Tanya and she came to me. I had not seen here in so long. "She misses you," said Lacey. I roll my eyes at her and play with Tanya's hair. "Look, I am sorry for not jumping in ok I did not know what to do I love all of yawl and Momma. I did not want to fight." says Lacey sincerely. I look at my sister, give her a hug and tell her it is ok I understand. "Are you going to move out?" I ask her as she sits on the bed. "No actually Momma is moving to Louisiana. I am going to keep the house, she says. "What about Roger?" I ask. "He is staying here for a little while and then he is going to go and meet Momma," says Lacey.

"Are you going to stay?" she asked. I looked around and shook my head no. "I am trying to get out of here as fast as possible. I do not ever want to come back to the house while she is here," I say looking towards the hallway. "Look, I love you and be safe out there ok? I am going to bed," says Lacey getting up and walking towards the door. "I guess I'll see you another time." I just looked at her and nodded my head. As she walked out and closed the door Tanya sat up and pointed to the radio. I dug around under the bed and came across my old tape box. And pulled out R. Kelly. I put on Dedicated and we danced around the room as I sang the song to her. We went through that entire tape box singing and dancing to the songs. Momma knocks on the door and opens it just as I turn the music off to tell me dinner is ready. I tell Tanya to go eat and tell my Mom I am not hungry. As she walks out I close the door back and put my music back on.

Listening to Paula Abdul sing Rush Rush I think of Lawrence and if he really plans on coming back to get me like he said. As I began to feel sad I quickly shake it off and began to smile as Adore comes on by Prince. Immediately my thoughts shift from Lawrence to Javier and all I can do is lay back and smile as I think of how good it will be to ride him again and release all this penned up frustration. It was weird but I just felt so free with Javier almost like I was safe and no problems existed.

A week goes by and I realize that I cannot take any more of this. My Mom had taken away my phone privileges so I could not call anyone. I thought out loud man if I could just get to a phone. Before I could even finish the thought, my Mom knocks on the door and brings me the phone. "Your Daddy is on the phone he wants to talk to you." I really did not want to talk to him but I needed the opportunity so I got the phone. "Hello" I said. "Hey my Baby how are you?" he asked. "I am ok," I say closing my room door. "Daddy, why can't I come and live with you?" "Baby now your Momma done told you Ms. Sam don't know nothing about you. That woman will have me hanged if she finds out about you." "Why don't you just tell her," I say smacking my lips.

"Baby I can't. Now why were you trying to steal clothes? Your Momma have not been given you your check?" "What check? You know she ain't go give me no money," I say curious about what he is talking about. "I will tell her to give you fifty dollars each month but you have to behave and listen to her and follow her rules." "Ok Daddy. Thank you I love you." "You too Baby." "Daddy?" "Yes Baby." "Why don't you ever tell me you love me?" "Love is not something you say Baby girl. It is something that you show. Anybody can say they love you. I gotta go tell your Mom I will call her back in ten minutes." "Ok Daddy I love you." "You too Baby," he says hanging up. I quickly call Walter and tell him to come and pick me up at about 1 AM. By that time my Mom is done reading and will be knocked out. I waited until my Dad called back and took my Mom the phone.

After she got off the phone with him she had Tanya come and bring me fifty dollars. I put on my music and danced around my room. Tanya fell asleep on my bed watching me dance. I carried her in my Mom's room and put her in her bed. "Good night Reyne," my Mom says. I look at her and say goodnight. I went back to my room and began packing as much of my stuff as I could. As the music played I twirled around and danced around the room. When it got closer to 1 I turned off my music and began putting my bags out the window. On time Walter pulled up and I was out of the house once again. "What's up jailbird?" said Walter. "Man, just get me out of here please," I say putting on my seatbelt.

Back at the house Derrick and Javier were already there with Stacey and Mitchell. Stacey calls me in the room as soon as I walk through the door. "Reyne we are about to get evicted. I am going to stay with Mitchell at his Mom's house. All this traffic you have running in and out of here has got the apartment people in frenzy," says Stacey. "Where are you going to go?" she asked. "I will just stay with Freddy and his Mom for a little while I guess," I say leaning on the door. "Are you sure, because I am leaving tomorrow," she asks. "Yes," I say moving off the door as Mitchell knocks and walks in. "Reyne you have company at the door," he says with a silly smile on his face.

I walk out and Cat is standing there with a big smile on her face. I walk up to her and push her down. "I told you I did not feel right about the whole thing," I yell kneeling to punch her. Everyone pulls me back and tells her to get up. "Let me go," I protest squirming away. "I am sorry I was just trying to help," she says propping herself up. "Man look I am not cut out to be a petty thief I need to make real money," I say kicking the couch. "No, what you need to do is go back to school," says Stacey. "Man shut up you are only concerned about Mitchell," I say rolling my eyes at her. "You know what I don't care what happens to your little skinny black ass. Momma should have left you at that jail house," says Stacey and walks out the door. Of course Mitchell followed behind her with that same silly grin on his face.

That night I took my frustrations out on Javier. Needless to say, he enjoyed every moment of it. As I laid there on his arm when we finished I began talking to him about the kind of life I really wanted. It was hard to believe that somewhere inside of me after all that had taken place I still had dreams and desires. He listened as he rubbed my eye and told me not to worry I would get everything I desired one day. The next day Cat and I went out to South Park to make some money. She had been telling me about this friend of hers that could help us out.

We get out there and this guy wants us to stand on the corner nickel and diming. I curse out him and Cat. "Look I am in need of real good lick really quick and I heard you know of a load coming tonight," I say to the guy after cursing him. He began laughing and walked away. Cat said she knew where he was going so we waited until night fall then went to where he was. The money we got from his stash was enough to cover the rent owed from August as well as September and the light bill. I figured if I sold the weed and did not smoke it I could by some food and tissue and stuff. Cat's cousin drove us to this hotel and said he would take us home in the morning.

I demanded to go home that night and he said if we were that much in a hurry we could call a cab because he was too messed up to drive. I did not feel right about spending the night there, I had an eerie feeling and no matter how drunk he was I did not care for his roaming eyes looking over my body the way he did. We called a cab and headed home. Once at the house I went upstairs and told Damon I had some weed. He purchased a pound from me and told me he would get another one for his brother tomorrow. September rolled around and my sister came and moved more of her stuff to Mitchell's Mom's house. She asked me again what I was going to do, I told her I would be fine and to go ahead and go. She said she was not moving completely until they actually evicted us. Until then she would try to pay the rent and she would come and talk to Freddy's Mom sometime that week.

Everything was chill. Javier and I were getting along fine. I really enjoyed the arrangement we had. I was in full control and was not tied down in any kind of way. We both could come and go as we pleased plus I could talk to him about anything and he actually listened. Donnie was still in Louisiana and the game had picked back up so I had some change saved up for emergencies. One day when Stacey and I had come back from seeing Joy, Cat came running through the door. "Girl what the hell is wrong with you. You could get stabbed like that," I say holding the machete in my hand. "Hide me Hide me," she says. "What?" "Just...oh no," she says as someone knocks on the door. "Please do not open the door," she pleads crouching behind the couch.

I open the door and there stood Hope the girl I had smoked with upstairs about two months ago and about 12 other girls. "Where she at?" says Hope, looking around me. "Hold on. You not go walk up in here like that," I say stepping in front of her. One girl from the back yells there she is and before I know it they charge Cat and Hope starts beating her up in the middle of the hallway. Stacey comes out of her room and breaks them apart. "What in the hell is going on? Get off of her," yells Stacey. I am holding back the other three girls that ran in the house with Hope as Hope continues to hit Cat. Once Stacey gets Hope off of Cat, I let them go and ask what the problem is. Cat begins saying as she tries to stand up, it was not her it was Shena that started the mess. "I did not do anything," she protested catching her balance. "I knew it. Come on here," I say walking out the door with all the girls following me.

I knock on Shena's door and as she opens it I punch her right in the mouth. "You always got something to say. I promise you after tonight you will not talk for a month." I say as I rear back to punch her again. Hope grabbed my arm and said, "Please let me get her." I told her have at it and stepped back. Cat comes busting through the crowd and kicks Shena as Hope is punching her, and yells, "It is your fault that I got beat up. You are going around here putting my name in all this mess." Hope eases up off of Shena and tells Cat to get her one. One of the girls yells, "Hope your Mom is coming." All of the girls run around the corner and Hope gives me dap and tells me she will be back later. She looks at Cat and balls up her fist and tells her she is one lucky little bitch.

Later that night after Stacey's lecture I had to fire up a blunt. That was too much action not to get blown away. I was really trying to avoid smoking my stash but man all that drama caused my head to hurt. Just as I was about to pull out my stash, Damon knocks on the door and says let me get another pound and come smoke with me. Hope comes around the corner and joins us. She introduces herself properly and apologizes for bo-guarding my crib like that. I told her it was cool and I enjoyed whipping Shena's ass. I had been waiting for an opportunity to get in that ass anyway. Damon gave me a blunt and told me to release some of that tension. I had a lot of tension ever since Javier's girlfriend had come back and school started back. I did not see him as much.

The last time I had gotten laid was 2 weeks ago and Javier had surgery on his knee so we couldn't get really freaky like usual. Money started getting low, so Cat called her cousin again. We went out to South Park that following week. Hope could not go because she had school. Before we left she pulled me to the side and told me to watch Cat. "I've known her for a while and she is not as innocent as she proclaims to be. She will get you if you are slipping." she whispered. I told her good looking out and headed to the bus stop. "What was that all about," ask Cat? "Nothing, just clearing up some shit. What does your cousin have planned?" I ask her. "I am not sure. He just said something about these Puerto Ricans coming in with a lot of dope." she said.

As we get closer there I began getting an eerie feeling. "What's wrong?" asked Cat. "Nothing. I am cool let's just hurry up I am ready to go home," I say getting off the bus. "You are always ready to go home," she says laughing. I look at her and roll my eyes.

Her cousin picks us up at the bus top and takes us to this hotel. "Why are we going here?" I ask. "This is where it is going down at," said the cousin. "Where what is going down?" I ask. "Just come on," he says opening the door to the car. "Look you and Cat are going to distract them and I am going to rob them while you know yawl do what yawl do," says the cousin. "What are you talking about what yawl do? I do the robbing," I say stopping in the middle of the walk way. "Not tonight sweetie. We will split everything when yawl are done. I will meet yawl at the corner in 45 minutes." As we walk into the room that feeling grows stronger and stronger.

The cousin starts talking to one of the guys and says, "Yeah man that one right there she need somebody to break her back. She thinks she macho woman or some shit." Cat had made herself comfortable on the lap of one of the guys in the corner. The cousin sat on the bed while the other guy kept trying to lead me over to the bed but I refuse and kept my back towards the door watching everyone around me. "Man fuck this. I thought you said these bitches was go fuck?" says the guy trying to have me come closer to him. Cat says, "I am down but you have to let my girl warm up." "Man, they will but you at least got to be gentle their ladies," says the cousin running his hand over my cheek. The guy grabs my arm and says, "Lady this," and puts my hand on his dick. I grab it and began to twist his balls. As he tries to get a loose I punch him in the head.

The cousin cuts off the light and the next thing I heard was Cat laughing. I remembered that the lamp was next to me I grab it and hit the cousin who had tried to grab me from behind. I head butted him and kicked the other guy in front of me again. I got the door open and ran until I could not run anymore. I do not know how I felt. I was so angry and scared. I did not know if I wanted to cry or scream. I did not have any money on me nor was I strapped. I was slipping for real. I walked until I could not walk anymore. I was lost and had no money. I saw a cab at a gas station and I asked him to take home. He saw that my clothes were ruffled up a little bit so I made up some lame lie about my Mom and Dad fighting and I was trying to get to my sisters but her phone was off so I could not call her. He took me home for free. He insisted on walking me to my door but I told him I could manage from there and thanked him.

Once inside I broke down. I cried so much and was so angry I screamed and punched a hole in the wall. In my moment of rage there was a knock on the door. I pulled myself together and went to the door. "Who is it?" I say. "It's me Hope." I open the door and she asked me if I was alright. "Hell no I aint all right. I am going to kill that little bitch if I ever see her again," I say pulling my machete from under the couch. Hope sits down and pulls out a blunt. "I told you she was no good." "Yeah thanks for the warning," I say taking a hit off the blunt.

As we sat and smoke I told her what happened. Knock Knock. Damon knocks at the door. Hope opens the door. "Hey I bought you some of those cookies I know you like from Wendy's. I just got off work," he says handing me the bag. Damon had been being like extremely nice to me. As time went on him and I began talking. Cat never showed back up and just when I thought Damon maybe a pretty nice guy he disappears. I find out two weeks later that his baby's Mom is back and they were getting married. I was crushed. All I could think was I guess my cousin Donnie was right, men are full of shit and love really was not enough.

I listen to Aliyah Street Thang over and over wondering if I would ever really find somebody to sing these songs about. Javier came to mind and as I told Hope who I was thinking about she pulled harder on the blunt and said, "Hey you never know what the future may hold for you two but for right now fuck all of them. Let's get blowed away." Hope and I became like sisters. I would go and get her out of school with fake phone calls. We would chill the whole day eating and getting high, talking about life and what we wanted.

I went to see Freddy one day but when I got there they were packing the U-Haul. "Where are yawl going?" Freddy looking sad said, "We are moving again. I will keep in touch though I have your address." He gave me a hug and they drove off. At least I got to say bye this time. Once again I watched those tender sad eyes as they drove away. If matters could not get any worse when I got back to the apartment Stacey was packing for real this time. She handed me the letter. The letter said we had to be gone by Monday. It was Thursday. "Can you still go and stay with Freddy?" she asked. "Um no. Not really. They moved," I said. "What are you going to do?" she says looking frantic. Hope walks up and says, "Do about what?" I hand her the letter. Shaking her head she says, "Man this is fucked up. You can come and stay with me." "Are you sure?" asked Stacey. "Yes my Momma don't care. She will not even notice," says Hope. "Well I need to talk to her," says Stacey. "Well, um she is out of town right now for work but I can have her call you," says Hope. Stacey says ok and hugs me goodbye. She tells me to be safe and stay out of trouble and that she expects me to be back in school soon. I hug her back and say ok while mouthing yeah right to Hope.

CHAPTER 5
Mi Casa Es Su Casa–
Until you Piss me Off

Hope and I gathered my things and took them to her house. We tucked them away neatly because of course she has not confirmed this with her Mom yet. Hope makes room in the dresser drawer for my clothes. "Ok this is the deal my Mom cannot know you are here right off. I am going to have to like prepare her for it and talk to her about it, kind of like a 'what if' situation," says Hope. I just nod okay and lay down for a quick nap.

For two weeks straight I hid in Hope's closet when she would leave for school. Her Mom asked her one day what is wrong with her because she sure was eating a lot lately. "Are you pregnant?" asked her Mom. In the room I crack up laughing in the pillow so her Mom cannot hear me. "Nah Momma! I aint pregnant just hungry," Hope says walking in the room closing the door. I burst out laughing. As nightfall came for some reason I could not sleep. The next morning I felt even stranger than I felt that night. Hope felt it too but she told me to chill out and don't worry because no matter what everything would be alright. As I climbed into my spot in the closet I said, "You better be right." Sitting there I felt so weird. I wanted to get out but I could not because her Mom had not left for work yet.

Suddenly Hope's room door opens and I hear her Mom talking. "Now Lord I know I am not crazy. Somebody is in here and in the name of Jesus I am going to find them." She began looking behind the door, under the bed and in the closet. My heart began to race like a train. The pounding was so loud in my ears I just knew she could hear it. She stopped and turned her head to the side as if she was listening to something. She began speaking some language I did not understand and then moved the covers back and yelled, "I knew it. Get up. Get up right now," she yelled pulling all of the covers off of me. I was totally exposed and she kept switching from English to that weird sounding language. I climbed out of the closet and she asked me who I was and just how long had I been there. Before I could open my mouth Hope came rushing in and told her Mom to let her explain.

I was so happy to see her I did not know what to do. We all went and sat down in the living room. As Hope began to explain how I got there her Mom's face began to soften. "Mom please? Can she stay? Can I keep her?" pleads Hope. "Hope she is not a dog and no I have to call her mother," her Mom says reaching for the phone. "She is not going to care anyway. She beat me and I ran away," I say with my head down. "I still have to call her. If your mother finds out you are here she could take me to court and all kind of craziness. Hope, you know I am really tired of you always doing stuff without thinking. I do not know what is wrong with you. I let you do whatever you want. I buy you everything you ask me for. You go to the movies, skating, etc. Why do you have to constantly get me into trouble?" she asked with tears in her eyes.

As she reached for the phone I sat back and thought man if my Momma did all of that I would never get in trouble. "What is your number?" she turns and asks me. I reach for the phone and dial my Mom's number. "Hello," says my Mom. "Hey Mama," I say. There is an awkward silence after she hears that it is me on the line. "Hello," I say again. "Yeah, I am here. What is it?" says my Mom. "Someone wants to talk to you," I say handing Hope's Mom the phone. "Hi." "Her name is Eva," I whisper. "Hi Ms. Eva my name is Betty Burns. I have your daughter here." "Let me guess. She is in trouble," says my mother. "Uh no, not exactly. You see my daughter has been hiding her in the closet for quite some time now and I need you to come and get her," says Hope's Mom. "I am not coming to get her she can stay gone for all I care. She ran away. She has a home but does not want to be here," says my Mom with much attitude. "Well Ma'am no disrespect but she says you beat her with a shotgun," says Hope's Mom hesitantly. "You got damn right I did and I will do it again if her ass comes back here," says my Mom in her matter of fact tone. Appalled Hope's Mom's mouth drops and she says, "Do you mind if she stays with me?" "I do not care where she lives as long as she does not bother me," says my Mom. "Ok, well I will need to get her shot records and stuff to get her in school," says Ms. Betty. "She is still registered for school all she has to do is go," says my mother impatiently. "Ok well thank you Ma'am. This is my number you can call her and check on her anytime," says Ms. Betty cautiously. "Thank you and goodbye" says my Mom and she hangs up the phone.

Hope's Mom looks at the phone in shock. "Look I have to get to work. Do you have somewhere to go while Hope goes to school?" she asks shaking putting the phone down and standing up. "Yes Ma'am I will manage," I say trying to hold in my excitement and gratefulness. "So can she stay?" asked Hope getting all excited. "I guess so we have no other option. We will discuss the rules when I get home from work," she says walking out the door motioning for us to come on. I go to the old apartment and try the key while Hope's Mom drops her off at school and heads to work. Luckily the key still worked. I went in and fixed me a sandwich with the last of the bread. After about an hour or so I left to go and get Hope out of class.

We went back to the apartment and got high laughing about what happened that morning. That night her Mom laid down the rules and we followed them to the T as far as she knew. We would sneak out late at night and go across to McDonalds and sit in the balls and get high. One Saturday we were coming from Taco Bell and there was this fine guy who looked to be moving in. I told Hope he is mine dog you have a boyfriend. He asked us later after we passed by for about the fifth time if we knew where to get some weed from and introduced himself as Kenny. I told him I could help him out. He became our weed buddy and instead of going to McDonalds to smoke his house became the party spot. He had a friend who would come by who seemed to be cool. Of course neither Hope nor I liked her. She could not drink and could not dance to save her life. Kenny loved reggae music.

As time went on I began babysitting his little boys on the weekend and at night because he worked late. He talked me into going back to school. I would catch the bus to and from school. I stopped selling weed and started going to church with Hope and her Mom. November rolled around and I had met this guy named James back in October on the bus. He went to Spring Woods High School and was kind of cute but annoying as hell. I really wanted Javier but he never made a move plus he still had a girlfriend that I never saw. We did a lot of talking but I never took him seriously and he never took me seriously as far as a real relationship went. He was a great listener and to me that is what mattered the most. James and I began dating. He came over for my 16th birthday.

James was 17 and was still a virgin. He loved to kiss and well I had not gotten any in a really long time due to Javier's schedule and girlfriend. I took his virginity while Hope played the DJ as I had done for her so many times when her and her boyfriend Tyrone would do it. I was upset that he did not even make it all the way through the song. I was so upset I sent him home. Hope just laughs and says I guess everyone cannot be Javier. I punched her in the arm and told her to shut up. He left just before Hope's Mom pulled up to take us to the mall. I quickly showered and we spent the rest of the day at the mall.

Back at home that night we talked about life and what we wanted to do. I just wanted to get high and have sex with my man all day I said. Hope said that sounded good and at this point that is all she wanted to do also. "What's up with Kenny have you hit yet?" "No girl not yet he does not make a move or anything. I think he is getting some from his little friend who comes over sometime," I say. "I see the way he watches you when we be dancing to the reggae music and bone thugs and harmony. He wants you," says Hope.

"Well after today he needs to come and get it because that was crap." The phone rings. We both look and start laughing. "Hello," says Hope. Snickering she passes me the phone. "It is for you." "Hello." "Hi Baby." I roll my eyes in my head. "Hey James what's up?" "I want to come and see you again." "Ok come on." "I can't right now it is 9 PM." "So do you have a curfew or something?" "Yes, I am not even supposed to be on the phone." His Dad then says, "That is right so get off before I come in there and whip your butt." I fall out laughing as James says bye and hangs up the phone. His Dad was really strict. He could not watch certain movies, hang out or even catch the bus to come and see me. After about a month of that I was tired of him letting his Daddy tell him what to do. I broke up with him just as we moved to some new apartments.

Hope and I became more and more like sisters every day. She had two older sisters who were cool but she and I were like glue. She knew my thoughts before I even got them out and I hers. As time went on I continued to baby-sit for Kenny. It was an easy legitimate way to keep money in my pocket. One night when he came home from work, he asked me could I stay for a little while. I had the music playing and the boys were already asleep so I said sure. I had cooked as I usually did so that he could have lunch and the boys could have dinner because he slept all day. He handed me a bottle of Boones Farm and said he would be out in a minute. He went in and took a shower. He came out and was smelling so good with water still glistening on his shoulders and chest. "You know I really appreciate you watching my boys for me," he said as he sat on the couch across from me.

Kenny had moved from California and was divorcing his wife because she was strung out on crack and would abuse the boys. She burnt one of them with an iron. Those boys were so sweet and timid. He told me how much he loved her and still wanted them to be a family but he knew he had to do what was right for his boys. "Ahh I do not mind watching them at all," I said as I poured me another glass of Boones Farm. "Do you want some?" I ask. "No," Kenny says. "I want something else. Come here." he says gesturing for me to come to him. I sat on the floor next to the couch, looking up at him. "You know you are really a beautiful young lady," he says caressing my face. "Thank you," I say putting my head down. "No I am serious," he says grabbing my hand gently pulling me next to him on the couch. "What are you going to do with yourself?" he asked looking directly into my eyes. "I don't know I guess go to college and become a lawyer or something and open my own dance studio on the side," I say turning my head away. "I think you will make a great lawyer and I already know you are one hell of a dancer," he says then leans forward to kiss me.

As he sits back I lean forward and kiss him back. He then gets up and changes the music. "Dance for me" he says. I had already hoped that this would happen so I wore my sexy red panties and red bra. As R. Kelly It Seems Like You're Ready plays in the background I began to dance. I did not even need him to touch me I was already hot from the music. He stood up and lay me on the couch and began to kiss my body. I moved sensually to the music and he then pulled down my panties. He took my legs and placed them over his shoulders and began to lick my private part as if I were an ice-cream cone. The feelings I began to feel were like nothing I had ever felt before. I began to shake and lose control. I tried to yell stop but I could only manage a deep groan. As I struggled to get my legs down I lost all control of my body. I could no longer hold it in I let out a loud wail of satisfaction and exploded. Sweat rolled from my head and finally after what seemed to be hours he let my legs down. He looked up at me and said don't move. I whispered softly I can't. My body was numb I had no control. He came back with a hot towel and began to clean me. As he raised my legs he kissed the back of my knee caps and I began to come all over again. He quickly went back down and tasted me more and more. After about a week of this I wanted to ride him. He would not allow me to. He said that it would not be right because his divorce was not final yet. So not once did he penetrate me but he quenched his thirst every chance he got.

As much as I enjoyed being tasted I had to restrain myself because the dick is what I really wanted. With him inside of me I had full control but with him tasting me I had no control and I really did not like that feeling. Somehow if I could not be in full control I was not fully satis-fied. It would not be until many years later that I realized this was a demonic spirit that desired this control not me. The end of the school year was rolling around and Hope's Mom had caught us smoking weed one too many times in the apartment, and decided we needed to do something constructive with our lives. Her Mom suggested Job Corps.

Job Corps was a program where teenagers were shipped off to a camp-like place to learn a trade.

My sister told me that Keisha was back down here from Louisiana and was trying to get in touch with me. Hope decided to go to Job Corps. We had a week left with one another before we would go our separate ways. Her Mom said I could go with her but I did not want to plus my Mom would have had to agree to it. I decided to go and stay with Keisha. Later that evening Hope and I went to see Kenny. When we got to the apartment there was a woman coming down the steps with little Kenny. "Hi Ms. Reyne," he says. "Hi baby boy," I say walking towards him. "This is my Mommy," he says hugging the woman's neck. I look her up and down in a nice way and say hello. Kenny comes around the corner and says, "Oh hi! I did not know you were coming today. This is Jessica my wife." "Your wife," gasped Hope. I elbowed Hope in the side. Reaching out my hand I quickly say, "It is nice to meet you." She shakes my hand and says, "Oh you must be the babysitter. I have heard so much about you. Jacob speaks so highly of you. You look quite young but he tells me you are 16." "Really," says Hope with an attitude. I give Hope a look to shut her up and say, "Yes you look young as well. Kenny tells me you are 23, one year older than him. So where are you guys headed," I asked trying to shift the subject. Kenny takes little Kenny and puts him in the car.

"We are going to take some family pictures," says Mrs. Kenny. "Oh how sweet," says Hope sarcastically. "Baby, you all go ahead and get in the car," says Kenny guiding her to the door and opening it. He led us around the corner and Hope begins going off, "You know you have some nerve." "Hope its ok. I knew about his wife," I say looking at him in the eyes and "I hoped she would get clean and come back so they could be a family." He walks over to me and pulls me to the side and says "Look she is clean now. She has been clean for about 8 months now. You know that I still love her and I told you that. That is why I never penetrated you."

I cut him off saying, "Kenny it is not a big deal. I know. I am not upset. I hope everything works out for you two and the boys." "Really," he says looking excited. "You are not upset?" "No I'm not. I am happy for you. I just hope that someone will love me enough one day to forgive me for all the dumb things I have done," I say putting my head down. "Ahh Reyne you are beautiful and trust me someone will, if they don't already do. Love is not easy it takes a lot out of you but never stop loving and always love like you have never been hurt before," he says kissing my hand. "Oh here I did not pay you for last week yet." "No keep it," I say pushing his hand back. "Girl you slipping now! You can forgive him and all but damn that get the money," says Hope taking the hundred dollars out of his hand. "Bye Kenny," I say walking off with Hope. "Be good," he says, "and get that law degree and open your studio."

Back at the apartment I began to cry while I was washing dishes as I remembered my Mom yelling and fussing at my sisters. I remembered how she complained about everything and only seemed to be happy when Mr. Roger was around. The more I remembered the more I cried. I thought of her slapping me when I asked her about my Daddy and how she beat me when I tried to leave the first time. "I want to die. I want to die," I began to say as I rocked back and forth. Hope came and grabbed me by my neck and began choking me. I began to lose my breath and I was not able to move hardly. "Do you really want to die huh? Do you? Answer me," she said while choking me. I began to hit her arm. She eased up and I grabbed my throat and begin gasping for air. When I caught my breath I asked her if she was crazy. "No are you crazy? You the one that said you want to die." "Yeah but I did not want you to kill me," I say rubbing my neck. "Well stop saying that crazy stuff," she says still standing over me. "It is just that every time I get close to someone they seem to leave me." Hope climbs up on the couch and pats the seat next to her. I get up off the floor and sit down next to her. She holds me in her arms and begins to sing His Eye is on the Sparrow to me while rubbing my head. I fell asleep right there in her arms crying. Ironically this was our last week together for quite some time but at least we got a chance to say goodbye to one another. Hope seemed very excited about going to Job Corps. I on the other hand was half happy half sad but thankful that I would see Joy soon.

That next week Hope left for Job Corps and I went to live with Keisha. Donnie was in jail serving time for drugs. He was scheduled to be out in July or August. Keisha, Joy and the kids and I danced and listened to music almost all weekend. During the week Joy had to go to summer school, so I mainly babysat while Keisha was at work. July rolled around and Donnie came home. Joy's sister Rita came with him to visit for a while. She stayed for about two weeks. We got into a big fight the first day I met her. This was the first and last time I got my ass whooped in a fight. Obviously she was Donnie's pet project before I came into the picture and she did not take too kindly to our relationship. By the end of her two week stay, Rita, Joy and I realized we all had something in common. In some kind of way Donnie had put his mark on all of us. Joy and I did not want to see Rita leave. She promised if she could that she would come back.

During that two week stay of hers she was not the only visitor we had. Lawrence popped up shortly after Donnie got home. Come to find out Donnie had been sleeping with Lawrence cousin's girlfriend and that is how they always knew when each other were in town. It took a while for me to warm back up to him especially after he told me he had had a little girl. Although I had been with someone else during that time he made it seem like he only wanted to be with me. We had an on again off again relationship. I really was not sure what to do; he was sweet but annoying at the same time.

School was getting ready to start again so we moved to a bigger apartment because Rita decided to come and live with us. She and I both got a job at Pizza Hut in July. Joy and I had worked together at a jewelry store but we had to cut the owner because he was a nasty pervert. I really enjoyed my new job. Joy would have the 40's on ice for me when I got off and we would get loaded and high then stay up all night listening to music and dancing. On the weekends when I did not have to work we would go to Fuddruckers and order our favorite meal, root beer soda and French fries with tons of cheese on them. Then we would walk down to the mall and shop like crazy.

Finally August came and school rolled around. Lawrence had been acting funny lately. That first weekend school started was the last time Lawrence and I slept together. After that I broke up with him. He continued to call for a while but I would not return his calls. When Donnie saw that I was not calling him back he tried to sleep with me again. I said hell no and walked out of the house. As I walked across the street, I heard someone call my name. I looked up and low and behold it was Anthony. "Hey girl. I have not seen you in a long time. Look at you growing up," he says looking me up and down smiling. I smile shyly and say, "Yeah I am a big girl now." He invited me to lunch, so we sat and talked over a good meal. He told me he understood my anger but I should not have stayed out of school so long. Anthony made me pinky promise to finish school and stay out of trouble. He also gave me his pager number and told me to keep in touch and if I ever needed anything to let him know.

That night at work I was prepping the items for the salad bar so that the person in the morning would not have to do it. In walks this yellow bone bow-legged guy. "Hi! I ordered some bread sticks," he says to the person at the register. I quickly walked to front and pretended to be checking for an order. Renee was busy closing out her drawer and Donnie was making pizzas. I told him it was not ready yet. "Would you like to wait for it," I asked? He smiled and said, "I tell you what. I work right next door. Why don't you bring them to me?" I smiled and said, "Ok I think I can manage that. We usually don't deliver that close but I can make an exception for you." "Good," he says walking towards the door. "I will see you in a few." I watch him walk out the door and I think to myself um I have to hit that. By this time Donnie and Renee are standing there giving me the shame shame shame finger. "What?" I say. "I am telling Lawrence," says Donnie. "Yep," says Renee co-signing. "Anyway," I say rolling my eyes," Lawrence and I are no longer together therefore I am free to do what I want and who I want. Thank you all very much." "Ok, do what you want. You would not say that if Lawrence was here," says Donnie. "Yes I would. Anywho…I will be back I am going to take these breadsticks over to our customer," I say boxing up the breadsticks. "Um huh whatever," says Renee rolling her eyes.

"Here are your breadsticks," I say. "Here is a movie I picked out for you and my number. Maybe we could watch it together." he says smiling. "Maybe," I say walking out the door. The next night he comes back and every night after that until I agreed to watch a move with him. We began hanging out and finally at the end of September I went to his house to watch that movie. Needless to say the movies watched us. He said wait and grabbed a condom. As we began to do it he realizes that the condom had broken He looked all over for the missing piece. We could not find it anywhere. I went to the bathroom and there it went. "Uh James I found it," I yell from the restroom. We threw it away and I took a shower and he took me home.

The next day he picks me up and we ride down to his college for him to get his books. As we pull up I notice all the trees and like a big kid I jump out and began climbing one. He yells at me and tells me to get down. I climb down and asked him what his problem is. He said, "Baby I am not trying to be rude but you have hair under your arm." "So don't everybody," I said. "Uh Yeah! But you are a girl. You are supposed to shave that," he says pointing at my under arms. "Shave what? You must be crazy." After he gets his books we go to the store and get some razors and shaving cream and I shave my under arms. I was sort of embarrassed but then again I was like oh well at least I know now. I also wondered why Keisha or my sisters never told me that. Later on while we are lying down watching TV, he starts asking all these questions. "Do you really like me?" "You cool," I say while watching the movie. "Do you want a relationship," he asked. "No," I say. "What do you want?" I ask still watching TV. "Well I um, I guess we could just kick it then," he says. I turn and say, "I can still hit right?" He looks at me with astonishment and says, "Wow, yeah why not," rolling his eyes. "Ok," I say turning back and watch TV. A few minutes pass and he says he needs to take me home because he has to pick up his Mom from work. When we pulled up I leaned over to kiss him and he gives me a dry peck. "Are you ok," I ask? "Oh yeah I am fine. We are just kicking it right?" he says with an attitude. "Yeah that is what you said right? You do not want a relationship right," I say. "Yeah sure. I have to go" he says. I get out of the car and head inside.

A few days later Lawrence starts calling again. "Reyne telephone," says Rita. "Hello," I say. "Hey Baby." "Who is this?" I ask frowning. "You forgot my voice already?" I say rolling my eyes and shaking my fist at Rita. "I miss you," he says. "Look I have to go. I have homework to do. Bye," I say hanging up the phone. At school the next day this guy named Daniel who had been trying to talk to me since the beginning of school gave me a letter.

That weekend at our usual spot at Fuddruckers I showed it to Joy. "Ahh that is sweet. Why don't you talk to him? I like him better than that James guy. James is a jerk. I do not like his attitude. Plus Javier is obviously busy with school and his girlfriend." "Speaking of Javier, I miss him but I do not think he misses me because he has not called me and you don't like James because I told you he said he was with not wanting a relationship." "So what at least Daniel is willing to commit," says Joy. After thinking about it for some time I told Daniel yes I would be his girlfriend. Two weeks later I began to get really sick. The doctor said I had strep throat really bad and stomach flu. I could not keep anything down. After the strep throat went away, I went back to school but still could not keep anything on my stomach.

Everything I smelled seem to make me throw up. Donnie's attitude towards me only got worse because I would not sleep with him and I threatened to tell Keisha. After about a week of throwing up I went back to the doctor. The doctor told me I was 6 weeks pregnant. I told him he must have mixed my chart with somebody else's. I took two more pregnancy tests and they drew more blood. I was pregnant. On the drive home Keisha ask me was I going to tell Lawrence. I humped my shoulders and began to throw up even more. Once at the house I told Joy and she comforted me. "So what are you going to do about Daniel," ask Joy. "I do not even know," I say shaking my head. "Are you going to tell Lawrence? Wait a minute didn't you and James do it once." she says franticly. "Yeah, but we used a condom and Donnie said if I use a condom I cannot get pregnant and Lawrence and I did not use one, so it is not his," I say. "Good I cannot stand him anyway," says Joy rolling her eyes.

That next week I told Daniel and he said he did not care that he still wanted to be my boyfriend. I told him I was not sure about that. I did not want to raise a child without at least trying to make it work with the father. He said he understood but would still be my friend and would be right there if it did not work out. After he left I walked down to the video store and told James. The first thing he said is well it is not mine I made sure we were careful. I just looked at him and said you're right it is not yours. It's my ex's and walked out. I do not know why his words upset me but it really ticked me off how quick he was to say the baby was not his. I did not believe it was his either but he could have been nicer about it. He called me a couple of times after that but I never returned his calls.

One day while Keisha and the kids were out shopping and Rita was at work, Donnie hemmed me up in the kitchen. "Now you carrying that nigga's baby" he said angrily while trying to force himself on me. "That is my stuff," he yelled. I wrestled away from him and ran out of the house. I called Anthony from a nearby payphone and asked him could I come over. He opened the door and immediately knew something was wrong. I told him I just had an argument with my cousin and I just needed to rest. He told me take his bed and get some sleep. I did not dare tell him I was pregnant.

The next morning he took me home and told me to take care of myself. I was really thankful for the fact that he did not ask any questions. When I walked in Lawrence was sitting on the couch. "I have been waiting for you," he said walking towards me. "Hello to you too," I say and walk past him. He grabs my hand and says, "Reyne I love you." Donnie comes out and says, "Man take that bullshit somewhere else." I roll my eyes and head to the patio so we can talk. "Were you going to call me?" ask Lawrence. "Yeah. I was I just did not know when," I say playing with my fingernail. "I love you and I want to be with only you. Please do not take this opportunity away from me. You know Kyla did not even let me see my child being born. Please I want to be with you and experience this with you," he pleads. "Please stop telling me you love me," I say and I began to cry. He grabs me and stands me up and says, "Why I can't tell you I love you? How about you tell me you love me you know you do," he says. I just lie on his shoulder and cry. I look up and see the blinds close.

As the months began to go by my sickness gets worse and I have to take off work. Daniel continues to bring me my homework. By this time I am about 5 months. One day while walking with Daniel to go and get Katy, Kerry, and Kyle, eight guys come out of nowhere and jump

Daniel. I try to jump in but Daniel yells no she is pregnant. As soon as he says it one of the guys begins stomping him in the jaw. I squirm loose and swing at one of the guys. An old Mexican man comes out and grabs me and begins yelling for the other boys to get off of Daniel. The boys run away and the ambulance pulls up shortly after. "Daniel are you ok?" I ask him holding his head in my lap. He was bleeding badly. The smell of it made me even more nauseous. I did not get to the school for another 30 minutes because I kept throwing up on the way. By the time I got there the principal had done called Donnie and he was pulling up as I walked up. "What happen to you?" he said seeing the blood on my shirt. "Daniel got jumped," I said out of breath collapsing on the floor. When I came to I was on the couch with my head in Lawrence's lap.

After Lawrence left that night I went to check on Daniel. Joy and I caught the bus to his house. He looked really bad but tried his best to crack a smile when he saw me. Come to find out it was some guy and his buddies who Daniel had got into it with at the mall a couple of weeks ago. He claimed he was going to take care of them. I told him to let it go and get better. His Mom thanked me for staying with him and calling her. She offered us a ride home but we insisted on catching the bus back.

On the bus Joy and I lay on each other's shoulders and talk. "Donnie sure has been acting funny lately," says Joy. "Yeah his attitude stinks. He gets on my nerves," I say trying not to throw up again. When we arrived back to the house Donnie told me to get my stuff and get out. He said he was tired of supporting me and that if I loved Lawrence so much I needed to be with him. I looked at Keisha and she just put her head down. I grabbed my stuff and walked out the door. Keisha took Joy home and made her vow not to say anything to me. I tried calling Lawrence but he was nowhere to be found. I called Anthony but he was not home. I stood there at the payphone with no more money to call anyone else. I asked the security guard could I use the phone and he said yes. I called my sister and she said I could come but she did not have a car to come and get me. The security guard said he would be off in twenty more minutes and he could take me. My sister gave him directions and we headed there as soon as he was off. I drifted off to sleep. As I slept I dreamed of being in that tunnel again, this time the light was clearer and I was almost to it when the security guard woke me up. "Do I make this turn right here?" I jump up "Yes right here, it is the 3rd house on the right. Thank you very much." As I get my things out of the trunk Lacey comes out and welcomes me with open arms.

That night I did not sleep much at all. As I put my stuff up I looked at the picture Joy and I had taken last month on my birthday at the mall. I began to cry and shake my head. I could not believe I was back in that house. I started going to church with my sister and I threw myself into my school work. I told her and Stacey I was pregnant. They were more excited than I was. The thought of having a child scared me because I was not sure if I would be able to give it what it needs. One thing I knew for sure was that I would not treat my kid like my mother treated us.

Lawrence would come and visit, but not often because Lacey refused to let him spend the night. In about my eighth month we broke up because he would not take me to my junior dance after he promised to take me. Joy would come and see me and sometimes I would go and see her. Hope had come home for Spring Break and we got a chance to catch up. She told me how cute I looked pregnant and that she could not even tell that I was. Seeing her felt good but she was somewhat distant. She was kind of stand-offish to Joy but we just thought she had a lot on her mind because she said life was really different for her in Job Corps.

After catching up on old times Hope left and went back to Dallas. My Momma came to visit close to the time for Elizabeth to be born. One night I was cleaning out the bathtub and I felt some water run down my leg. I called for my Mom and told her I think my water had broken. She gets me to the hospital and they take me up to labor and delivery. My Mom calls Lawrence to tell him that his child is about to be born. Because of my nausea the doctor gives me two shots of Phenergan and two shots of Demerol for pain. I was knocked out instantly. They woke me up to ask if I wanted an epidural. The nurses had to hold me up because the medicine had me so sleepy. "Do you want her to have the epidural?" the nurse asked my mother. "Yes" she said. They sat me up and stuck me in my back. I flinched a little and was out again.

"Wake up wake up it is time to push," they said. I said ok and opened my eyes. I saw Lawrence on one side of me and my Mom on the other. I let out a little push and went right back to sleep. I am not sure how long after that but the nurse woke me up said, "Here is your baby girl." I counted her fingers and her toes and handed her back to the nurse and went back to sleep. I did not wake up until the next after-noon. I had a hissy fit when I realized what had happened. "Oh my gosh," I started screaming, "Where is my baby?" I had been having nightmares that she died and I died. My Mom comes in with her in her arms at that moment. She hands her to me and we all move to another room. I ask the nurse why she had glasses on. The nurse informed me that she had yellow jaundice. I called Lawrence and he said that no one in his family ever had that and that he was coming up to see the baby tomorrow and that he loved me but needed to tell me something.

My Mom left and Joy came and stayed with me. "Look at my god-daughter," says Joy. "Yeah she has your feet. I should not have talked about you," I say holding Elizabeth's feet in my hands. We both laughed. There is a knock at the door. "Come in," I say still laughing at Joy. In walks Lawrence and some woman and a little girl. Lawrence says Kyla this is Reyne, Reyne this is Kyla. All the feeling went out of my body. Joy just looked speechless. I said hello and managed to stand up to hand Elizabeth to Lawrence. The news he had to tell me was that he and his daughter's mother had been back together but he did not want me to be stressed during the pregnancy so he did not tell me until after I had the baby. He and Kyla thought that would be best since I was so young. All I could do was shake my head because in all honesty I did not want to be with him either. I was just trying because I did not want Elizabeth to grow up without me at least giving her Dad a chance. We both look at Elizabeth as she lays there with her diaper on backwards under the light.

After they leave Joy climbs next to me in the bed and we just sit and talk about the love that we want. Five days after Elizabeth was born we went home. That same week I went right back to work. My Mom and sisters fussed at me because I went to work before my six weeks were up. I told them I have to do something. Lawrence is preoccupied and I am not going to sit around and depend on no man to provide what we need. Eventually they dropped it and realized that I was going to do what I wanted to no matter what anyone said.

My Mom went back to Louisiana mid-June. Stacey and Mitchell came to live with Lacey in August. School started back and I moved in with my Aunt Pat. My grandmother and two other aunts and an uncle lived in the same apartments. So I figured between all those people somebody could watch her while I went to school and worked. On days when no one was available to watch her I had to take her to school with me. It was somewhat annoying because all of the little girls who think they want a baby come running up wanting to touch her. Needless to say I kept her swaddled up well. All of my teachers were cool except for one. During that class my Life Skills teacher would watch her because it was her conference period and she rarely had parent meetings. I was almost done with school and things were starting to get hectic. I exempted most of my finals. If I could pass an advancement test I could graduate in December. My Mom came to visit in September and said she did not like the fact that I was leaving Elizabeth with this one and that one. I did not see anything wrong with it I was working two jobs and going to school trying my best to graduate early plus they were family.

My Mom suggested that she take Elizabeth with her to Louisiana and when I get out of school she would bring her back. I weighed the pros and the cons and figured it would be ok since she was so young plus I could work more. Joy and I said goodbye to my baby girl and I moved back in with Lacey. Stacey and Mitchell had moved out and were back at his Mom's house. In December I graduated and in January '97 I started at the Community College. Joy and I both had been working at Pizza Inn since September. The manager had to let us both go because he said we had too many off days on the same day and my school schedule began to conflict with my daytime hours. I began working at a video store close to the house during the week.

On the weekends I would go to Joy's house. I found out that Walter stayed right across the street one day when Stacey dropped me off. I got back in touch with him and come to find out Derrick was his roommate. I introduced Derrick to Joy. Javier and I, well let's just say we picked back up where we left off. We went to movies, and the book store. Javier and I loved the book store because we got to read about all the different positions and try them out. Everything was good away from home for a while. I had even got back in touch with Anthony. He and I hung out a lot and he would always stay on me about school. Lacey and I seemed to argue all the time. She put Mr. Roger out and always seemed to be angry about something. She and I did not talk much. I was having my own issues.

I had found myself pregnant again and had my first abortion. I tried to kill myself right after it. Joy stayed with me the whole time. She called Anthony and he took me to his church and laid me at the altar, crying and speaking gibberish that I could barely understand. I don't remember much else after that, just falling asleep as a gentle wind passed over my face. When I got back home I cried myself to sleep in Joy's arms and all I could think about was coming up with a Master Plan to get my own place and raise my daughter alone with no man to let me down. Joy's Aunt called the next day and she had to go home early. To make matters worse my Mom was coming in town to bring me Elizabeth the next day which was also Elizabeth's 1st birthday. Lacey and I could not seem to stop arguing and although I had the abortion I still felt emotional and lost when alone and not busy. As I lay in bed that night I only hoped that things would get better and that I could give Elizabeth everything she needed.

The next morning I woke up to my sister banging on the door telling me I had a phone call and to hurry up and get dressed because we had to get to the bus station to pick up Momma, Tanya, and Elizabeth. I opened the door and grabbed the phone without even speaking to her. "Hey are you ready to go and pick up Elizabeth," says Joy excitedly. "Yes I am ready," I say. "Your sister sounds really pissed," says Joy. "Yes, she has had an attitude for the past week now. I do not know how much more I can take," I reply. "Well, keep your head up and try and be nice you do live there," says Joy. "Hopefully not for long," I say putting my legs up on the wall hanging off the bed.

CHAPTER 6
From the Pole to the Cross

"Hm! something sure smells good," I say waking up stretching. "Well I see greedy has risen from the land of snoring," says Derrick. "Anyway," I say rolling my eyes, "you already know what I want," I say pointing at the Jack In the Box sign. "Give me your money," says Derrick reaching his hand out. "What, you got it Big-timer and besides, Javier will give it back to you," I say humping my shoulders. "Man," Derrick says going into his pocket. "Yawl two be breaking a nigga." "Ah, you'll be alright. Now hurry up and get to the house before my food gets cold," says Joy laughing.

"What's up everybody," Derrick says as we walk through the door. Pulling him aside I tell him I really do not feel like being around anyone right now and I ask if it is okay if we eat in his room. Not giving him a chance to answer, I say thanks and start going down the hall to his room. While ritualizing her sandwich as she always does Joy asks, "Are you okay?" "Yeah I'm cool. I am just trying to think of a legal way to make some cash fast." "Knock knock." "Come in," I say. "Hey Javier," says Joy. "Reyne I will be back in a minute," Joy says smiling. Joy leaves the room and Javier takes her place on the chair across from me. He looks at me with such sincerity but yet it is hard for me to see that he cares. "Are you okay?" he asked as he moved next to me. "Your eyes are shall I say me eyes are so puffy," he says and softly kisses the top part of my eye caressing me. "Why do you always kiss me eyes" I ask him? "I don't know" he says looking into my eyes quickly turning away playing with my fingers as I glare back into his. "You're just so damn cute," he says leaning in to kiss my eyes again. Derrick and Joy walk through the door in that exact moment. "Oops my bad sorry to interrupt such a romantic moment," says Derrick sarcastically. "Anyway," says Javier scooting from under me, "aint nobody being romantic." Joy and I make eye contact silently noting his behavior and mouthing you see.

I stretch and say, "Look it has been a long night and I am tired," giving Javier the eyes while watching him rise to the occasion. "Yeah I am quite tired myself" says Javier. "Whatever you two bunny rabbits" says Derrick. I hug Joy and tell her goodnight. She grabs my arm and asks me am I sure I am okay? "Yeah girl I am good. I just need some Prince in my life," I say looking Javier up and down and thinking that will make everything all better. She lets my arm go and tells me not to be too bad. "Oh don't worry I will," I say grabbing Javier by the hand and pulling him down the hall. For what seems to be an eternity after we enter the room we enjoy the comfort of one another's presence. He and I both explode in passion just in time to fall asleep to Purple Rain. In that moment of explosion all my troubles disappeared and I slept like a baby.

Sex became my escape and every chance Javier and I got we were intertwined in each other's arms leaving the cares of the world behind on the beat of every slow song ever made by Prince and every other great beat we could find. Sex was what kept me in control, I felt so full of power each and every time. It was the one thing in my life so I thought, that I could control. The next morning we awoke to a knock on the door. "Who is it," I sang. "Are you ready? I have to get home. My Aunt is going to kick my butt, says Joy. "Yeah I'm ready. I will meet you outside," I say putting on my clothes. I tell Javier goodbye and looking serious he says, "Bye Dot." "Hey, Reyne," he says standing up as I walk to the door. "I was wondering do you want to be my girlfriend. I mean seriously I want you to be my lady," he says half smiling. "Ha Ha, yeah right," I say laughing uncontrollably. "You don't even like to be affectionate in front of your boys." Shaking my head and waving my hand I say, "Nah I'll pass. When you get serious then ask me that again. Bye now."

Laughing all the way outside I spill the beans to Joy but strangely she does not join in on the laughter. "What? Why are you looking at me that way?" I ask her. "What?" I say humping my shoulders. "Did you laugh at him in his face?" she asks. "Uh yeah! Come on now I know you don't think he's serious," I say. "Well," shrugging her shoulders and looking at the ground as if she knew something I didn't, "what if he is? You know you him and Elizabeth could start a life together," she says looking me in the eye. "Whatever if you think he is so serious, what is up with you and Derrick," I ask pushing her. She just smiles. "Yeah cat got your tongue now huh?" I say grabbing her in the headlock. "Okay, okay," she says pushing me off of her. "All I am saying is that every time you get somebody nice you push them away." Very defensively I say, "No I don't. Give me examples," I say already knowing full well who she would say. Mocking her as she began talking, "Well let's see there was James. You took the poor boy's virginity then kicked him to the curb. Daniel, and not to mention the little boy that! What are you doing?" she yells as she turns and notices that I am mimicking her. "Are you mock-ing me," she says punching me in the arm as we run across the street.

Before entering the house we get our lie straight about why we did not make it back until this morning. Walking in first I say, "Hey Janet," and head straight for Joy's room. "Hi Aunt" says Joy. Janet yells, "Uh uh both of yawl come here and where is Elizabeth?" "Well Aunt Janet the reason we are late is because we missed the first bus," says Joy looking at me for help. "Yeah" I say jumping in, "and see Elizabeth is still with my Mom because I and my sister got into an argument." "Yeah," says Joy jumping back in. "And then she put her out and her Momma would not let her take Elizabeth so (together shaking our heads simultaneously) can she stay her for a few days," says Joy. "Two days and that is it. Then your uncle will be back and he is going to throw a fit if she is still here." "Okay that is fine. Thank you," I say. Once in Joy's room jamming to slow songs, primping in the mirror, I say, "It is time for me to get my hustle on. Give me the newspaper. Tomorrow I am going to start looking. Monday will start a new beginning."

"Hi, my name is Reyne. I am here for an eleven o'clock interview." I say to the receptionist in the front. "What position are you applying for?" she asked. "For a cocktail waitress" I say. "Hold up just one second. You can have a seat over there and someone will be with you shortly." Wow, this place is nice. I know there is a lot of money to be made here I think looking around. Yeah, but from the looks of these females, how far do you have to go to get I think to myself. "Hi, I'm Chris, one the managers here. Let's go into the office here. Do you have any waitressing experience?" "Why, as a matter of fact I do. I was a waitress at various restaurants around the Houston area. I did inventory and stocked the freezers as well. It is all here in my resume, I say handing it to him confidently. Anthony told me I should always have a fresh up to date resume when applying for a position. Chris makes a slight grin and says, "Pizza Hut, Pizza Inn excuse me honey but right now all the positions have been filled. Thank you for coming out. We'll hold on to this application." He gets up and walks me to the door.

"Okay thank you. Where is your ladies room?" I ask. "Right around the corner," he says not even looking at me as he goes back to his desk.

As I walked to the ladies room with tears in my eyes there are two mix breed girls waiting to be interviewed. Hmm, I wonder if he is going to tell them the same thing. I peek from around the corner as he takes them into that dim lighted cold office. But for some reason, it was not the air that felt cold to me. Once inside the ladies room I hop up on the counter and break out in tears. What am I going to do? I need a job and I only have one more day to stay at Janet's. Lord knows, I need this job. As I'm sitting there moping the two mix breeds come in giggling and laughing. Immediately, when they see me, one of them comes over and gives me a warm comforting hug. "What's wrong? Are you okay." she asked. "No, I am not. I really need a job, so I can get me a place to stay and my daughter back," I say wiping tears from my cheek. "He didn't hire you?" says the other sister. I shake my head no. "Why not? He hired us on the spot. He wants us to start right now. You know that is not right, he only did that because you are black," says one of the sisters. "Well we will just see about that. Come on," says the sister that gave me the hug. They dried up my tears and pulled me off the counter. Chris was not in the front, so we all sat down and waited for him.

"By the way, I am Kristin and this is my twin, Tristan," she says shaking my hand. "It is nice to meet both of you. I am Reyne." "As you can see we are mixed and we don't go for that racist crap. If he wants us then he has to hire you. We are only here for the summer anyway, after this we have to go back to Florida for school," says Tristan. "Are you in school? Yes, I go back in August." "Well good for you. Here he comes now." "Ladies are you all ready?...oh, what are you still doing here?" he says with a disgusting look on his face looking at me. They both squeeze my hands as my anger squeezes theirs turning them red.

"Look we do not think that it is fair that you did not hire her. She was here before us and basically if you want us then you have to hire her also. If you don't we will protest that this Gentleman's Club is a racist establishment, you discriminate against blacks. Because in case you didn't notice Mr. Manager we are black too!!" say the twins standing in his face. "Ladies, Ladies, Sweethearts, I am sorry. Okay how about all of you be back here tomorrow at 10 a.m. to start your paperwork and come in uniform, okay?" "Thank you we will see you tomorrow at 10 am," I say shaking his hand. We all walk out hugging one another and saying yes! "Thank you girls so much." I say hugging the both of them. As they drive off in their Mustang, with the license plate that reads TWINZ, I walked to the bus stop happy about the job and upset because of what I had to go through to get it.

The next day while at work things are going quite well. "Girl, how many tables have you had," asks twin wiping her brow. "Girl I can't even much tell you. I know I am hungry and those steaks sure look good." I say. "Where is your sister?" I ask. "Ain't no telling. She is probably hiding out in the bathroom. She can be lazy at times." "Well tell her don't be too lazy, I will take her tables." I say walking to the bar. "You are going to have to beat me to them first," says twin racing me to the bar. "You're on partner," I say catching up. "Hi, how are you doing today? Can I get you something to drink, a Heineken or maybe some Cognac? You look like a Cognac and steak type of guy," I say to the gentlemen at the table. "Oh really? Well I tell you what, how about you hop right up here next to me and have a steak with me," says the guy. "Sure but only if I can have dessert afterwards," I say. "You can have whatever you want pretty lady." he says smiling. "Well let me close out my other tables and make sure it is okay with my....oh here he is now," I say turning to Chris my manager.

"Well hello Mr. Bear," says Chris shaking his hand. "Hey Mike how are you?" he replies. "Well I see you're getting acquainted with our new pretty face," he says smiling at me. "Try beautiful face and as a matter of fact I am treating her to a steak dinner, dessert, and all the drinks she want," he says patting the seat next to him. "Well if that is the case let me take your tray lady. Order a nice bottle of wine," he whispers in my ear while taking my tray. Thinking to myself and rolling my eyes, what a fraud, they know they don't like me. "You all enjoy now, Bye-Bye," he says before walking off. "Um Chris be sure the young lady gets all of the tips now from her open tables!" says Mr. Bear. Chris just nods and smiles and says, "Yes sir, will do." I crack up laughing and Bear turns and says, "How about that bottle?" I look up at Bear and say, "I would really prefer a root beer and the money you would use on a bottle to go in my savings account." "Go ahead and get whatever you like. It is on me," he says slipping a hundred dollar bill in my pocket. "I'll take a root beer please, your biggest steak, a bake potato with extra, extra cheese and sour cream, no chives, ranch dressing on my salad and for dessert…" I say.

"Dessert? Are you going to eat all that?" Bear says looking amazed. "As hungry as I am I probably could eat two. For dessert, I'll take the ½ lb brownie with 3 scoops of vanilla ice cream," I say proudly finishing my order. "I'll have the same, disregard the dessert." he says rubbing his stomach. Waiting on the food he asks me what I am doing in a place like this. I tell him all about what I am going through. The food comes out and on the first bite I finally understand why men flock here so frequently during lunch. That was the best and actually first steak I had ever had. Bear's phone begins to ring and he turns to me and says, "Well, here is my card. When you are ready to move give me a call. I own a moving company." "Thank you so much Bear, I say looking at the card. "You go ahead and finish eating I have to go. Take the steak home for dinner," he says signing his credit card tab and telling the waitress to be sure I get the tip. "Alright, see you next week," I say waving bye bye.

Chris walks up shortly after that and says, "Here's your tray back and your tips from your table, your shift is over in about 20 minutes, so we'll see you tomorrow. Way to go with the bottle of wine, next time order Moet," he says handing me a bottle of something I cannot even pronounce. Turning my nose up as Chris walks away and I still think what a jerk. Back in the locker room twin says, "Girl you are going to have the dancers mad at you for taking their customers." "Hey he offered me a steak. I did not ask for it," I say smiling holding up the bottle of wine. "How did you do," ask the other twin." "I did very well; I was not expecting all this. I hope I can pull this in every day," I say counting all my tips.

One of the older waitresses said, "Don't count on it; we have a lot of slow days around here. The real money can be made at night." We all nod and say our goodbyes. While waiting for my ride I decided to call and tell Joy how well I did. "Girl, hurry up and get here, you have to come and get your stuff. I am moving. We are going back to Louisiana." says Joy crying. "What?" I say shocked at what my ears are hearing. "That's not all. I am pregnant, she says. "Oh no! Joy, how, why, who? No, you can't leave I need you, hell you need me, especially now," I say not able to think clearly. "I know but my Uncle is gambling all of the money away and my Aunt is sick so she can't work. I'm in school and well you know Monica is not helping. If you had your place I would come and stay with you," she says. Tears falling from my eyes I say, "Okay boo, I am on my way. We will get through this."

Walking out the door I bump into one of the dancers and spill my tip tray all over the floor. "Oh, I'm sorry here let me help you. Galee girl, you made more money than me today and I take off my clothes," she says kneeling down. "Yeah I guess today was okay," I say trying not to cry. "Are you okay, why are you crying," she asked rubbing my back. "My best friend is pregnant and her Aunt is making her move to Louisiana. I have to find a stable place to live and one stable person to baby sit my daughter while I work and go to school ASAP. These stupid managers here are racist and are giving me a hard time. Boo hoo, Boo hoo and, and…" I say no longer able to hold back my tears. "Ah come here," she says leading me to the sitting area. "Look my name is Tiny and I am moving into a 3 bedroom house next week. I have a nanny for my 2 kids. You can come live with me," she says. "Thank you but I really need something of my own," I say getting up. "Well that's even better. I already have a house, as soon as my divorce is final, I am going to move back in it. Right now my ex-husband and brothers family lives there, this way you pay half the rent and we split the bills and by the time I move you will be able to take over the house. We can go and talk to the real estate agent tomorrow, his name is Nick, one of my customers," she says standing. "Are you sure about this," I ask her. "I tell you what bring your things here with you when you come to work, we will put them in my car and go talk to Nick. If it does not sound or feel right to you, I'll take you wherever you want to go. Here is my cell and home number," she says handing me a card. "See you tomorrow. I got customers waiting," she says walking out the door. "Thank you," I say behind her. She turns and says, "Hey and don't worry. Everything will be ok."

"I'm sorry, how long have you been waiting," I ask Anthony getting into the car. "Not long actually. I just pulled up. What's wrong?" he asked seeing my tear stained face. "Joy just found out she is pregnant and is moving to Louisiana tomorrow and I have to find somewhere to stay. Tomorrow I need you to bring me here early please. One of the girls said I could stay with her. I'll explain tomorrow, but right now, just get me to Joy, ASAP without getting a speeding ticket," I say putting on my seatbelt. "What took you so long?" ask Joy hugging me tightly. Smiling and waving Bye-Bye to Anthony I turn back to her and start asking questions. "Did you call Derrick?" "No, I want you to do it, she says. "Nah ah, you do it. That is between both of you, I have nothing to do with that. Do you want to go over there?" I ask her. "No, call them and have them come over here. Tell them to meet us at Dairy Queen," she says still sniffing back tears.

"Where is Javier?" I ask Derrick hoping to see him before I have to move. "He couldn't make it he has football practice," says Derrick. "Tell him I'll call him once I get settled." I say. "I just wanted to say goodbye to both of you. I am leaving tomorrow. We will probably head out at 10 am," says Joy. I step aside and give the two of them time to talk. Finally, Joy meets me back at the house. "So, did you tell him," I asked. "Yeah I did," she says looking a little better now that it was out. "Are you going to have it?" I asked. "Yeah I am," she says rubbing her stomach. I sit next to her and give her $50. She asked me about my work day and where was I going to stay. I told her one of the dancers offered, and that she is getting a house and it may be mine after a few months.

The more we talked the more we cried. "I guess we can't get drunk one last time," says Joy. "Yeah too bad I sure could go for some Red Dog and Boones Farm right now," I say lying on the bed. "Shid me too," she says lying on my stomach. That night was a very gloomy night. As Joy lay on my stomach, I brushed her hair softly as we cried our-selves to sleep. Thinking to ourselves, here we are at a very important point in our lives. I finished high school, Joy with one more year and a baby on the way, so many problems at such a young age.

Morning arrived and it was time to say goodbye. "I love you and I will write to you every day and come see as much as I can," she says while hugging me. "I will call as soon as I get a home number. If you need me page me I have the calling card. I love you and I miss you already," I say waving at Anthony as he pulls up. Getting one last hug, she says "I know boo. We will be together again soon." "I will come and get you as soon as I can," I say releasing her. Once they drove off I got in the car and never cried again about it. Luckily Anthony, who had become sort of like a mentor to me, knew I did not want to talk, so he didn't ask many questions. I told him what Tiny said and he told me to give it a try and let him know how it goes.

Determined now more than ever, I not only wanted to get my daughter back, but to get Joy back as well. Tiny and I went and saw Nick, and being that I was underage I could not sign anything until my 18th birthday. We moved in the house and got settled. I worked long and hard for 2 months straight day and night. Some of the dancers began to complain that I was too friendly with the regulars because people were coming in just to see me. Eventually the day came when Chris decided to fire me because I was insubordinate by telling off one of the floor supervisors. He claimed that the customers came to see me for odd reasons against my job description of course. I was told that my job description was serve food and drinks not be a psychiatrist. I told all those racist pigs to kiss my ass and screw themselves. I felt as if I was alone all over again.

One day Tiny and I were having lunch and she began talking to me. "You know you could make a lot more money dancing. It is easier and less work." "Me dancing topless," looking down at my chest, "girl I am not sure about that. I do not have any boobs," I say poking my chest. "So what you can dance and you have a great body. You do not need boobs. White girls need those for a lack of," she said pointing to my butt. "Look I tell you what tomorrow we will go down to this spot I know and we will tell them you want to dance. I know the daytime supervisor and you can try it out. If you don't like it then you can just keep waitressing," she says. I hump my shoulders and say, I guess, we can try it."

I gathered all my belongings as well as my eight paying customers and went from waitressing to dancing in a better established club. At least, I thought it was better established, it turned out to be the biggest drug rink run by the head drug cartel, big shot lawyer, who only pur-

175

chased this club as a tax write off and a cover up. The next morning came around and I was a tad bit nervous as the manager showed us around the club. The dressing room was huge with the ugliest pink lockers I had ever seen. "Ok this is where you change and here is where you walk out on the stage. After you're done with your set you come down this same way. Be careful because the stage does get slippery. We try to tell the girls not to use oils because we do not want anyone to fall and break their necks, Campeche," asked the supervisor. "Campeche," Tiny says. "By the way my name is Jerome, yeah I know but I am white, right? Well my Dad is black and I am named after him," he says. "Okay," I say looking lost.

"Come on so you can meet the DJ, Vernon and pick your songs," he says leading us to the DJ booth. "Hi Vernon," says Tiny. "Why hello there Miss Lady. I have not seen you in a while. Who is your friend?" he asks. "This is Reyne," she says pointing at me. "What's your stage name?" he asks. I just stare looking lost. "What do you want your stage name to be," asked Tiny looking at me. I turn, uh, look around, uh, I look at the TV and Stacey Dash is on and I think, hmmm, she seemed to be every guy's fantasy that I ever liked so this is a fantasy place. I turn and smile and say," how about Stacey." "Stacey it is," said Vernon. "What songs do you want?" "Let me see, do you have UGK, Bone Thugs and Harmony." Vernon says placing his hand on my shoulders turning me around, "Take a look around sweetie. We do not have any of that in here."

Noticing my surroundings, I say, "Ok well let's bump it down a notch or two." "Uh, yeah," he says rolling his eyes irritably. "Ok how about Madonna Holiday and Luck Star," I say happily. "Ok that's good. You need one more," he says. "Why don't you pick," I say. "Ok I will surprise you," he says. "Do you want a drink?" asked Tiny. "Nah I am ok," I say looking around. "Well I am going to have one. I have been doing this for over two years now and I still get nervous when I go on stage," says Tiny downing her drink. Now coming to the stage, we have the lovely, the fresh, the new Stacey. My music begins to play and I run to the back and out on stage. Wow I think to myself, everything looks so different from up here. I began to move to the music and Tiny lets out a wild yell. I turn around and notice the mirror behind me.

As I began to sing the song, I forgot I was on stage and begin twirling around thinking back to dancing with Joy and Hope and my little sister. Oh I felt so free. Lucky Star came on and a guy walked to the stage and gave me two dollars. I continued to dance and then the final song came on. As the beat to R. Kelly, "You Remind Me of My Jeep," came on, I took off my top. As I took off my top I notice more people began to turn around. I took off my bottom wearing only a g-string and Vernon yells "Dang girl, you do remind me of my jeep." I leave off the stage with $58 by the end of the song. Tiny went right after me and made about $36. Back in the back she asked me how I liked it. "It was okay, I guess, easy money," I say putting the money up. "Yeah real easy. Now we have to go out here and sit with the men. One of them wants a dance from you," says Tiny. "But I don't know how," I say. "Yes you do. You will be fine just watch me," she says. I watched Tiny do her dance and I started mine to some rock n roll song that seemed to last forever.

I twirled around and put my butt in the guy's face and wiggled it a little. He gave me twenty dollars and said he would get another one later. By the end of the day I had $268. I decided it was cool, so I kept the job. About a week later, this middle-aged white man with hair like Einstein comes up to the stage and tells me he wants to see me when I get off stage. I go over once my set is complete and sit at his table. "You are really beautiful," he says. "Thank you. Do you want a dance?" I ask him. "Yes I do," he says. So I put my rat tail comb on the table along with my top and began to dance. As I turn around the man starts to move around. I turn back to face him and he has his shirt up pinching his nipples. The next thing I know with one hand still on his nipples, he pulls out his penis and rubs it and says, "Suck me baby, I'll give you an extra twenty." Without thinking I grabbed my comb and stabbed him right in the head of his penis and yelled, "Suck that," and stomped off to get the manager. "There is some pervert over there that pulled out his thing and asked me to suck it." The manager says laughing, "Which one, all of them who come in here are perverts." "Uh, hello this is not a laughing matter this guy is sick and he is pinching himself." Suddenly one of the floor workers come running from the front. "Call a medic, this dude is bleeding, he said some dancer stabbed him with a comb." The manager looks at me and I hump my shoulders and say, "What? What was I supposed to do? The guy's a freak." The manager shoves me to the side and says, "Oh no, we are going to have a lawsuit." I look at the floor worker and say, "Oh well, somebody should have taught him not to pull his stuff out in public."

Days later after all the action dies down, I then realize that a lot of the girls in there did those types of things. In the dressing room one day in August, I asked this Indian chick name Eva, why the white girls gave these men head. She said it was because that is how they made their money. As she made her statement, one of them came in and said, yeah Stacey we are all not blessed as you are. I just looked at her in silence. Something about her statement made me uncomfortable. Just as I was about to get up the manager comes in the back and says that the professor is not going to file charges due to the fact that he is a married man with three children and is a well-known teacher at a well-known college here in Houston. I just rolled my eyes and said, "Whatever! He got what he deserved." "Stacey you cannot go around stabbing people in the penis. It is just not cool," says the manager. "The men are only trying to live out their fantasies." "Oh well, they better learn some manners messing with me," I say. "You really think you are all that, says Cinnamon, one of the few black dancers at the club, who just so happen to be gay and very upset that I was not. I rolled my eyes at her and told her I did not think, I know. She then said, "I bet I could fix that attitude for her." I stand up and say, "Oh yeah" holding my comb! "Try it and I guarantee you'll be sipping your own piss through a straw with no tongue by the time I am done with you." She backs away and tells one of the other girls, "That bitch is crazy." Cindy and Erica, two other black girls tell me to lighten up and that I need to release some of my frustration. She was right. I had not been out just for fun in quite some time or had any sex. Now that Joy was gone I did not see Javier much and I had not found anyone else that I felt like being bothered with

That night we all went to the Pool Hall. This became like a regular routine. We would work during the day on Friday, play pool on Friday night, and work a double on Saturday. Dancing was great, but I wanted more, I was still not satisfied something was missing. In mid-August I saw that I was pretty stable and decided to go get my child. As I explained my living arrangements to my mother the arguments began. "Yeah right, you really think I am going to let you take her to be with a live in nanny. Where are you going to be?" she protested. "I will be at work and school. Look you said, if I get a stable place to stay, I could come and get her. I have that and a babysitter," I say pleading my case. "No, I don't think it is right. You need a place of your own and some form of daycare. I don't trust live-ins," she says shaking her head no. "Oh, Momma, this has nothing to do with you," I say throwing up my hands. "Where is my mail?" I ask walking out of her room. "On the top of the TV in the living room," she yells. I cannot believe her. What am I going to do, I think to myself as I look through the mail. Hmm! What is this? I'll be got damn. That is why she will not give me my daughter, she is receiving $158 for her. I cannot believe this. Along with that letter were my financial aid papers for school.

I left and went register for school. I was so angry. I had to focus on something positive so that I would not go off. I called Anthony and told him what was going on with my mother and why she kept making excuses not to give me Elizabeth back. I also told him I registered for school. He was quite distant to me after my suicide attempt after my abortion and told me we needed to talk. "Sounds important. What's wrong?" I ask. "I'm on my way," he says hanging up the phone. Waiting on him to arrive I could not help but remember how his behavior had been towards me over the last few months. He barely looked at me and gave me semi hugs. I had a bad feeling. Boy was I right. I was angry, but I had no choice, but to understand. After the suicide attempt from the abortion, and seeing me so vulnerable and always being there for me he said it would be best if he separated himself from me. To this day I still wonder if he blamed himself for the things I went through. He was the only positive male in my life at the time and I guess me pouring all my problems on him just became overwhelming.

That was it. I could not take any more heartache. Although we were not in a relationship I felt extremely close to him and thought he would always be there for me. The next 3 months, I threw myself into my work. I worked double shifts and went shopping occasionally. I was not saving any money for the simple fact that it seemed like every month my sister needed a hand out. After that last one I said no more. "Ladies and gentlemen, I bring to you Stacey, and boy she is making me hot," says Vernon introducing me. I step on stage and lazily put on a show to Toni Braxton's latest hit, "Makin Me Hot." A fat black guy walks up to the stage and tells me he will pay me $50 to dance to his song on stage. Sure, just give the DJ the CD. Of course being that it was rap they only played the instrumental. Boy when the beat dropped, I felt like I was at a house party back in the old apartment dancing with old friends. A tall Jamaican guy, whom I later learned is co-owner of the record label walks up and tips me $100 along with the $50 promised for dancing to the song.

Once my set was over, I went over and thanked them. "Girl, you got it going on and I am not just talking about your body. I mean the way you let your body flow to every bass drop in the song. That is talent, what are you doing here?" "Trying to make money, that's all." "We had asked your girls down there to do the song but they said no. Why don't you call them over here, we need some dancers and they can entertain my boys." I call Erica and Cindy with her jacked up attitude over to entertain the entourage. While they are getting paid $20 for a table dance, me, the artist, and the owners pull off to the side and talk business. "Okay before y'all make my heart jump out of my chest from excitement let me get this straight. You want me to choreograph your songs, be on the album cover, and do shows?" "Don't forget the T-shirts and coming with us on promotional sets." "Man are y'all serious?" "Yeah li'l mama, are you down? We don't fool with junkies and hoes." (Grabbing my arms to see if I shoot up or anything) "Nah none of that. I have talent, so I don't need to do any of that." (Pointing to a trashy white girl giving head in the corner, while the guy snorts coke off her back) "None of that." "Okay well here's the deal, you will be the lead dancer, we will pick you up tomorrow for the photo shoot. Are you girls interested in being dancers? Ask them." "Would you all like to be back up dancers for us?" "Yeah, sure." "Reyne or shall I say Stacey is going to be the choreographer, she will teach you all the routines for each song. The photo shoot is tomorrow." "Oooh, girl I have to get my hair done tonight then." "No, no only Reyne will do the photo shoot. You know one male artist, one main attraction dancer that is the vibe we need. We are not trying to be Luke." Cindy rolls her eyes and gives me a dirty look. "Okay, well we will see you tomorrow boo, here's our card and take care and keep letting the beat flow through you." No need to say that, I was hyped the rest of the day. I called Joy and told her everything. That night at the pool hall, I bought drinks for my peeps and kicked a little butt in pool. "Damn, she is fine, who, the little one on the end. I like the way she handle that stick." "Man, dog please my girl look better than all these bitche's in here. My girl is a model." Overhearing this conversation, I place butt on the corner pocket. The tall, bowlegged, chauvinistic pig, who made the remark is about to shoot his ball in. I do my butte shake and turn and say, "Hm, she must not be too much of a model, you scratched and spilled your drink," walking off. Giving my girl high five. Later at the bar they walk up and the short chubby one with the pretty hair tells Erica, he wants to marry her and raise beautiful babies in a fake Jamaican accent. Of course, she melts and instantly begins playing in his hair. I looked the tall one up and down and walked off.

The next morning waking feeling really excited I search for the phone to call and see if I have any messages. Right as I am checking the voicemail Erica calls and tells me the guys that we clowned last night want to take us out. I told her I would let her know and wrote the dude's number down. In all honesty the guy seemed like a jerk and I really was not sure I wanted to deal with that. After hanging up with Erica I finish checking my messages and began jumping up and down on my bed. Tiny walks in and says, "Who in the world is Mr. Drop-it-Low?" I fall out laughing and tell her the low down of how it happened. "Hey, do you want to dance with us?" "Girl no, I cannot move my butt the way you jiggle and pop yours. No thank you, I'll stick with stage modeling." "Suit yourself. If you want a lesson or two, let me know." The guys arrive to pick me up and I can barely contain myself. Sitting in the car my stomach begins to growl. "Are you hungry?" "Yeah I can go for a little grub." "Ok we will go eat after the shoot." Well, the shoot was more of a workout than I expected. Trying to hold in my big kool-aid smile it took about two hours for only 15 poses, because I kept smiling. It was a lot of fun though. "How much do you feel those two hours of work were worth?" All the dreams I've had since a little girl dancing to Janet and Michael Jackson videos… (Putting my hand down,

I see Darrin the CEO pulling out his wallet counting hundreds) "Oh, you meant cash." (Laughing) "I don't know, I mean I can't sign any contracts or anything because I cannot make a commitment to be with you all for years, you know. I have my daughter that I am trying to get back A.S.A.P. I tell you what, break me off whatever you think is proper and buy dessert to top off this Monte Cristo and we will be cool." "Okay, well here is $400. Promise me you can do this show coming up at home in Lufkin in November." "As long as it is not on my birthday and I don't have to fly I am game." "The show is at the end of the month right before Thanksgiving, so that means it is October now, you and your girls are going to have to get on the ball putting these routines together. We are performing four songs and doing an after party. You can make extra cash there." "Okay that sounds cool but what about clothes, food, hair, food, expenses, and did I mention food." "We will bring along a picnic basket just for you, shaking his head. For someone so small you really eat a lot."

For the next 3 weeks, I put up with double dates with Erica and her new-found friend and the male chauvinist, not to mention Cindy's nasty attitude, just to be sure the girls got the choreography correct. If I did not put in that kind of time Erica would have slept all day long. Boy, was I sore. "Okay ladies, I am going home tonight, we have 3 more days before we go to Lufkin. Let's relax and get ready for stardom. I hear this guy is really big out there, it's his hometown. Let me call a cab." Leonard says, "I will take you home if you want me to." "Oh, thank you, I don't live very far.", I say getting into the car.

"Your routine looks really nice. I think you are very talented and should not be stripping, but maybe dancing for real." "You think so?" "Yeah you're really good." (Yeah okay the male chauvinist hit a soft spot, so what, I'm not falling in love or anything) "What are you doing for Thanksgiving?" "I don't know, probably sitting around the house." "If you like, you can come to my house." "Oh, thank you. I will let you know, my birthday is the next day, so I am definitely going out." "Maybe I can take you out." "Maybe we'll see. Thanks for the ride. Bye-Bye." Hmm, thinking while I am lying in bed, that was nice. He likes my dream of dancing, he looks okay and he always listens to me and takes me wherever I need to go.

It is about time to settle down. "Let's just take it slow and see what happens," I say out loud while balling up the messages Tiny tacked to my door from 6 different guys. "Hey, we need to go to the mall out here, I need some boots and push-up bra, for the show." "Okay, but we cannot be in here all day, we have to do a sound check at 5:00 PM sharp. It is 2:00 now, we need to be out of here by 4:00." More like 4:45. Darrin bought us everything from bras to panties, to shoes, to CD's to cookies. Not to mention, he had just paid for our clothes to get out of the cleaners, plus our hair and nails. "I must be dreaming, please don't wake me," I yelled out loud once we were on our way to sound check.

It seems like as soon as we got there, we were leaving heading to the hotel to get situated. Knock, Knock, "Are you girls ready?" "Well y'all this is it. Let's show these Lufkinans what we got. Here we come, here we come." Running out of the hotel room all the way down the hall to the truck. Once at the truck with breakdown, the body shake, and hop in the truck, yelling come on to our managers as they stand in the hotel entrance laughing at us. "Ladies and gentlemen, homeboys and home girls, pimps and pimpettes, welcome our very own greens and cornbread fed Mr. Drop-it-Low." "Oh yeah it feels good to be back home. I got a special treat for y'all tonight. Oh, ladies…" (With the intro to the CD playing in the background, we each walk out one by one and do a butte shake and state our stage name. We took our positions begin to P-pop and the crowd went wild, first our tops down to our designer sports bras, then our bottoms down to our velvet butte shorts from Victoria Secret. Last but not least of course, we wore Lugz to dance comfortably. Dollars and flowers were being thrown all over the stage.

Cindy has a flash back and thinks she is at work and goes to the edge of the stage and pulls down her shorts to have money put in her g-string. I instantly get pissed off and slide over there and tell her to get her ass back to the routine, because the climax is coming. Poor Erica, she completely forgot the climax, so the hype man gave her some CDs to throw out with T-shirts while Cindy and I finish the set. (Back in the dressing room) "What is your problem, don't ever interrupt while I am making money." "First of all, I suggest you get out of my face, if you wanted to strip, then you should have stayed your stuck up ass at home." "Oh yeah, yeah what the fuck." "What do you want to do?" standing there in Cindy's face with my heart pounding and such embarrassment from her getting out of the routine for 3 damn dollar bills. Right then Erica walks in and gets in between us still holding T-shirts and CDs. "You guys better learn to get along while we work. I don't care what y'all do at home." "Oh shut up hype woman I have no words for you drunk ass either." Putting gear back on. Guy (body guard) comes in and sneaks us out the back to the truck. Guy is supposedly our Bodyguard, more like our Seeing Eye dog. He never takes his eyes off our butts. Drop-it-Low says, "You girls were hot." "Ooo wee, yeah y'all tore it up," says Guy's country behind. "Yeah it was alright, we could have been better as a team." "Yes I saw that," says Felipe, "we will handle that before next show."

Here it is one of my biggest dreams is happening right in front of me and I let my attitude toward that heathen get me down. I have to work on that. I could hear Anthony's voice all up in my head. "Where to now?" "It's time for the after party Baby. I have some big time people I want you all to meet, so be on good behavior. Oh and by the way Cindy if you want me to make you a few more dollars, you can strip there," says Darrin laughing. "Hah hah, ooo, says everyone in the truck." Ouch! Guy elbows me in my side as I cover my mouth and try to stop laughing.

Of course I get a dirty look from Cindy, but I could care less that comment made me feel ten times better. Upon arrival at the hotel that the after party was at, I instantly spotted a nice tall cutie. Erica followed my stare as I grabbed my bag out of the truck. "Go get him girl, you know it does not count when you're out of the state," says Erica. I look at her and say, "It is out of the country when it does not count and by the way, is that what you've been telling yourself for the past 3 years since you've been in Houston? You freaky slut." "That was a low blow, but I will let you make it, because I have a secret." "What is that?" "Damon is my boyfriend. That's right, my man, no more playing the field." "Okay, you and mister I want to marry you and have babies on the first time he sees you. Yeah right." "Okay you will see when we get home. Don't worry you and Leonard will be together soon also.

I've noticed he takes you to school and other places you need to go and I heard about him bringing you Thera Flu for your cold when you were sick." (Tickling my stomach) "So what?" (Pushing her hand and walking off) "He is just nice like that." Mumbling under my breath, "I ain't trying to settle down with him just yet, I have tall yellow bone with the pretty hair and green eyes on my mind right now." "What was that did I hear yet?" "No and stop listening so hard." "Hello there ladies, can I get you a drink?" "No, but you can get me a nice T-bone and baked potato." Darrin throws me a look. "Just playing, I'll take some water, strawberry daiquiri, and a Hurricane for hype woman." "Stop calling me that." In the back changing clothes, "Are you going to dance with us?" Cindy asks. "No, I am not stripping in here. It is only 5 females and about 30 men.

Hell no, 3 out of 5 is us. Y'all can strip, I'll walk around and talk business, maybe I can find you a singing deal, Cindy and Erica, well you just do what you do." "Well you do your magic we are stripping, I need some extra cash for my trip home to Pennsylvania." "Ladies, I would like to introduce you all to the head of In The Hood Productions, M.C.

Thick." "Hi! How are you?" After a brief intro, Cindy and Erica wander off as I'm held captive by Mr. Thick, the whole time, Mr. Cutie is sitting on the couch pretending not to be staring at me. I see you, boy, trust me, I see you. "So Stacey, can you teach me how to shake my butte like you shake yours?" "Well Thick, that's gonna cost you." "Okay, how much a hundred for the example and 150 to look at you do it right?"

By this time, everyone is laughing. Thick stands up and puts the money in my hand. "Okay turn on the music." I turn in yellow boy's direction and do the butte shake. Thick says okay my turn and takes off his shirt and stands on the table and begins to shake to do the butt. We all fall out laughing. I sneak off to the kitchen, I just could not bear to watch anymore of that 300 pound man shaking all his stuff. "Hey Stacey, I have someone I want you to meet." "Okay here I come," grabbing another water bottle. "This is our top DJ here at home, Lil Homey, oh and this is his cousin, R. L. Langley." "Soon to be Dr. RL. Nice to make you acquaintance."

Caught in a daze by those green eyes and the warmth of his big yellow hands, I wanted to say let's go somewhere so you can hold me and I can be caught up in the smell of you. But instead I retrieved my hand, reshaped my eyes and moved on to shake Lil Homey's hand. "Girl you got some talent. Are you coming out to the station next week for the interview, and then in another week to the record store for autograph signing? And not to mention the release party." Taking my hand from Lil Homey, RL pulls me to his side and pretends to write in his hands let's see. "After party tonight, radio show next week, autograph signing week after that Hmmm I think that leaves," looking at his Movado, "room for breakfast with me." Looking at Darrin, he gives me the go ahead and says have fun. "Be back at the hotel no later than 10 AM. We have a luncheon at 12 at Apple Bee's with the entire staff." Okay. I grab my bag and wave bye to Cindy and Erica. R.L. sees me wave and ask me why didn't I stay and dance?

I told I had made my money off of Thick embarrassing himself and besides I really didn't care much for stripping at private events. Niggas try to make you work too hard for pocket change. He opens the door to his pearl blue vet and tells me to get in. The car smells just as good as him. He wipes off the door handle upon closing it and gets in on the other side and wipes off the ignition. "What are you doing?" "Oh I'm sorry, force of habit, I am a neat freak." "Okay, I guess." "Where to, how about some food?" "Actually, Whataburger is fine. What I would really like is a nice hot soak in the tub and a massage." Grabbing the food he says, "Well that can be arranged."

We pull up to this castle and he parks in the curved driveway. Wiping off the door handles after letting me out, he says, "This is my parents' place, they're out of town on their 5th honeymoon. I stay here when I home from school." "This house is beautiful." "Yeah it is hah, me and my Dad sculpted most of the sculptures. Here I'll take your bag, you can eat right over there, while I get the Jacuzzi warm." Once my belly is full, I undress down to my panties and bra just in time for him to walk in the room in his midnight blue Ralph Lauren shorts and that 6-pack just yelling out come and feel these abs Baby. "You all done?" Looking over the well-figured package I have before me I look up and say, "Nah, I actually just think that I'm getting started. Hmmm! This feel good. Nice and warm. How about the massage?" As the night passed, we talked about everything from playing with jacks to designing toys for the future. He is really smart but there is something that does not click. "Wow time really flew by, you'd better get me back to the hotel before they send a mob after me." "Yeah that's true, the bathroom is over there." Once I brushed my teeth and changed, we headed off for the hotel. No sooner had I lain down in the bed here comes Guy beating on the door for us to get ready for the luncheon. "Yeah, yeah stop beating on the door," cries Erica from under the covers some-where.

"Let me guess, someone has a hangover." (Pulling the covers off of her) "And how was your night or shall I say morning hoochie." "Ah is the dikey wikey mad because no woman wants to be licked by the Big Bad Bitch." "Whatever!" "Okay you two don't start." Once the luncheon was over we headed back to Houston. "Did you girls enjoy your first show? We know you did Stacey." "Anyway, I am going to sleep." I woke up just as we pulled in my driveway. Darrin and I were the only two left in the truck. "Well, hello there sleepy head." "Man I must have been drugged, I didn't even hear everyone get out of the truck." "We will have a meeting on Saturday, about what happen at the show. Some changes are going to be made. You have a Happy Thanks-giving and a good B-day."

"Okay you too. Bye-bye." "Ow galee, Tiny watch it you almost knocked me over." "I am sorry, me and Marcus are going to Louisiana for Thanksgiving." "Marcus is from LA, I did not know that. What part?" "Hey girl, see you made it back. How was it?" "It was nice, I had a great time. What part of Louisiana are you from?" "Opelousas." "Ah come on your shitting me, I am too. I want to go, I have not seen my best friend in a minute." "Sure you can come but you have to hurry we are leaving now." "Okay." (Telephone rings) "Hello." "Hey." "Hey to you, who is this?" "It's me Javier." "Oh hi Boo." "I'm sorry I just got back in from Lufkin and now I'm going to Opelousas to see Joy." "You going see your girlfriend?" "Anyway, yes I am going to see my Joy. How have you been?" (Re-packing my clothes and throwing the dirty ones in the corner) "I just wanted to tell you Merry Thanksgiving and I hope you have a good B-day." "Thank you, that's sweet." "Oh boy don't start sounding gay, what I said was gay enough." "Everything is gay to you." "Except me and you." Beep, Beep. "Hey Baby I hate to cut you off, but I have to go my roommate is blowing for me." "I will call you when I get back and you can come see me." "Alright. Bye-bye."

Needless to say I slept the entire way there. "Hello, hi can I speak to Joy, please." (Calling from Marcus's car phone) "Hold on." "Hey Boo. What's up girl?" "Why don't you go outside?" "Go outside for what?" (Walking to the door) "It is a pretty day out here." "Yeah, well the weather out here….hey!" Running giving each other a hug! "You got me. Yeah you got me. Hi Tiny, nice to meet you Marcus." "Okay, bye, I'll see you all on Friday. Do you have the number?" "Yes, mother Tiny, I have it. Bye-bye T." "This is really a surprise." "Yeah I know I was not expecting to see you for a while but then when I got in from Mississippi, they were headed this way, so I caught a ride. Good coincidence hah.

Just so happened Marcus is from here also." "I knew he was not all white." "Nah, his parents Frenchmen." "You're getting big." "Getting, girl I feel like the turkey we are going to eat tomorrow. I am ready to pop." "Well who do we have here? Is that my little cousin coming to hug me?" I move aside and shake his hand, "Hi Donnie." "I can't get a hug." "Well, actually…" "Oh Lordi, Lordi, look who here y'all. I bet Joy go smile and be sociable now her buddy is here." "Who Reyne?" We hurry up and go in the house leaving Donnie standing there with his hands out. Phew, I and Joy both say. Saved by the loud mouth. That would be Joy's grandmother. After speaking and hugging everyone except Donnie, we go to Joy's Aunt's house, where she lives so we can have some privacy and I can get some rest. After telling her all about the show and RL, she asks, "Have you heard from Javier?" with a sneaky smile.

"As a matter of fact I did." I wonder how did he get my number. Hmmm! Those darn operators. "Hah, I got you the phone; is not in my name." "Okay," throwing her arms as if to surrender, "you got me. Derrick came see me last week and I gave him your number and address to give to Javier." "Okay, matchmaker, Javier is not ready for a real relationship." "Oh, and you are?" "Maybe?" "Yeah right." "I really do like being with Javier, but he is so young. I think I like older men." "I really don't like being here, but if feels good to be around family sometimes. Other times you know it is the same old drama." "I put my name on the waiting list for housing. I should get something in a few months."

"Do you still talk to that gynecologist?" "Girl, no I left him alone he was trying to get serious." "There you go running from commitment." "Girl please it is that he is 34. Imagine six years from now he will be forty." "True enough he has good pipe action but come on now. I have not reached my peak yet I need someone that can keep up." "You are crazy," says Joy. "I have been hanging out with that guy Leonard," I say looking away. "I thought you didn't like him," says Joy. "He is alright I guess," I say humping my shoulders, "I just had to get to know him a little more." "Hm, could this be a catch," ask Joy, "with that goofy smile on his face."

"No I aint trying to marry the boy. I am just chilling and besides when I need a ride somewhere he takes me and he don't ask for my butte." "Will he at least be your boyfriend?" ask Joy. "No Mrs. Twenty-Questions I am weighing my options right now." "Well okay but you do know that you cannot keep running forever," says Joy. "We all get hurt sometimes but we have to bounce back." I knew exactly what and who she was referring to and on that note I rolled over and went to sleep, trying not to think about that bastard father of my child. Those wounds were being healed slowly but surely.

Thanksgiving was nice. Seeing everyone was good too. It was not hard for everyone to tell how much Joy and I missed each other. We shared big hugs and crocodile tears as I got into the car to go home. "Call me when you make it home," she yells. Needless to say I slept all the way home. Before I even put my bags down good the phone began ringing. "Hi may I speak to Reyne," said the voice on the other end. "This is she," I say. "This is Leonard, are you just getting back?" "Yeah I went back home for Thanksgiving," I say. "How was it?" he asked. "It was nice. I got to see my Joy." "That is good," he says. "I wanted to tell you Happy Birthday. I got you something.

How about I bring it to you?" "Okay, but I have a meeting in about 45 minutes, do you think you could drop me off at Erica's house?" I ask. "Yeah I have to pick up Damon anyway." "Okay thanks," I say, "let me get ready." Stepping out of the shower I hear a knock on the door. "Tiny can you get that please?" No reply, shoot I think to myself she must have left already. "One second I'll be there right there." I run to the door in my robe and of course it is Leonard. "Come on in and have a seat I will be right out," running down the hall pushing my door closed.

Not realizing that it was not closed all the way I look up in my mirror while putting on my lotion and notice that he is looking at me. I quickly jump to the other side of the bed and laugh. I can hear him sighing because I moved. "Okay I'm ready," I say coming down the hall. He looks at me and says, "Here is your gift and I am sorry for looking at you." "Don't worry about it," I say opening my gift, "it is not like you've never seen a woman putting on lotion before. Ahh thank you I wanted this CD. Janet and I go way back. One day I am going to be in one of her videos, Alliyah too." "Reyne I have a feeling that if you set your eyes and your heart on something you will eventually get it no matter what it takes," says Leonard holding the door open for me. "Do you believe that for real?" I ask. "What?" he says nodding his head, "you would be surprised what people capable of doing when they put their minds to it." Hm I say thinking to myself he believes in me, point number two.

"Hey thanks for the ride," I say getting out of the car. When I walk inside there is a heated debate on stripping on stage and hype woman. Well cutting in, "Excuse me," I say stepping into the middle of the room. "I personally feel that when we met you guys you said you needed stage dancers, not strippers, stage dancers. If you are a part of this team and you want to strip then go and stay at Rome 21.

If you are a part and you just to be seen, then don't bother learning the routines. Stay in the background passing out t-shirts, posters, and CD's. All in favor say Aye," I say raising my hand. Everyone yells Aye except Cindy. "All oppose say nay." "I got yo nay you skinny bitch," says Cindy. "I do not like you and you will not come in my house." In the middle of her sentence I walk over to her (thinking to myself so what if she is bigger than me I am faster than her and as soon as she swings I am going to duck and uppercut her in that nasty coochie licking mouth of hers). "You nasty p-eating slut don't you ever," I say. Drop-it-Low jumps between us right before anyone can throw a punch. Darrin grabs me while Erica and Guy grab Cindy as she yells "Anytime bi---." "Oh yeah," I yell wiggling out of Darrin's arms and charge over to her. As I dive in I am lifted off the ground by my waist and drug out the door while yelling obscenities and kicking and waving my arms. Basically, looking like a fool once again. Drop-it-Low says "Okay that's it, Reyne get in the truck."

Turning to Garland he says, "Go in and tell them the meeting is over." Turning back to me he says, "You and I are going to recruit some new girls because this will not get it." "Okay can you have your watch dog put me down now please? Thank you," I say elbowing Darrin in the stomach. Those next few weeks were hectic. Between finals at school and two shows in Lufkin plus the autograph signing and teaching the new girls I was pooped, but it was all well worth it when I pulled up at Lafayette hospital and surprised my girl again a few hours after her baby was born on Christmas eve. She was so happy to see me and I was happy to see her and the baby. Looking at him I notice that he resembled my cousin Keith very much. But she said it was Derrick's not Keith's. I reminded her of that party at my Grandmother's when they snook off. She just smiled and said, "We used a condom. Anyway how long are you staying?" she says. "Unfortunately we are leaving tomorrow. I would love to stay but I have to go soon." "Well I am glad that you came." Giving her a hug I feel an overwhelming sadness thinking of my own baby girl, wishing she was with me. Before tears flow I let go and Joy grabs my hand and says, "You will get her back soon." "I know," I say. "I love you," and I head out the hospital. I run back in and give my charm bracelet. "I know you don't wear jewelry but I was not able to stop and get you a Christmas present." Holding it tightly in her hand, "I will treasure it," says Joy. "Bye now," I say walking out the door.

Once back home Darrin calls me to meet with them about the New Year's show and pleads with me to do the last show with Cindy and Erica. Of course I protested but he promised he would make it worth my while. Worth my while he did. He paid me $750 up front plus a new pair of boots. As we drove to Erica and Cindy's house I was very happy. The drive down was a quiet one. The show turned out to be a great success. Afterwards Darrin permitted me to spend the rest of my evening with RL and what an evening it was. Come to find out the uneasiness I felt came when I reached in his glove compartment for a napkin a picture of his ex-fell out. "Who is this?" I ask. "Oh that's Shelby." "She is really pretty," I say, "so what happen to her?" He looked puzzled. "What do you mean?" "Come on RL it is obvious that you love her, so you might as well spill the beans but after my shower first," I say pulling up to his house. Once out we climb up to the roof and lay out looking at the stars and the moon, cuddled in each other's arms and he tells me all about Shelby.

I tell him all about the kind of man I would like and how I hope that one day I would find him. One thing I told him though is that he must stop cleaning so much. Wiping off the roof after we go back inside is a bit extreme. The next morning he takes me back to the hotel. We share a long hug and say at the same time, "Go get your soul mate." Holding his hand, "Please if you love her don't let anything stop you unless she does not feel the same and in my heart I truly feel like she does. Goodbye RL." That was my last time seeing him and I was happy that we parted on such good terms and were able to help each other out.

The last I heard about him was that him and Shelby got married and were expecting their first child. I went home and decided to take my own advice. That night I made a vow January 1st that I was not sleeping with anyone else unless they were my boyfriend. I knew it was time to make a choice and of course my first pick was Javier. There were certain requirements that he would have to meet so as promised I called him up and he came right over. Not realizing that this was my problem, I always wanted what I wanted when I wanted.

This mentality led me to make the biggest mistake of my life yet it held one of the greatest blessings. "Hey come in," I say to Javier. "Nice house," he says. "Thanks, soon it will be all mine." "You still look the same," he says. "Well of course I do," I say flopping down on the couch next to him. After a little small talk and refreshments we pop in a movie but end up talking throughout the whole thing. I find out through our conversation that he is still hanging out with Derrick, drinking and partying. He still lived with his Mom and well nothing was sounding the way I wanted although I really liked him. After about three hours he says, "I'd better go, I have school in the morning and you don't live right around the corner," he says pulling me to a standing position. He kisses my eye and looks deeply into them. Feeling that tingly feeling in my back I reach up and kiss him fully on the lips. Feeling my legs begin to spread I stop myself and say "You'd better go." He kisses my eye again while standing at attention and says, "You know I meant what I said a year ago," walking towards the door. "I know," I say softly, "Just not right now.

I just don't believe that you're serious." He shakes his head and says, "Bye Dot." "Bye Javier," I say as he walks out the door. I sat on the floor by the door not realizing I just let the best lover and best friend next to Joy walk out because I was afraid of letting go. I wanted someone who did not party so much and who kept their priorities in order and could take care of me and me him. Besides he admitted that he would not tell his boys yet because he did not want to hear their mouths. I did not want to deal with that. Javier was only a year older than I and he could barely take care of himself at the time. Somewhere inside of me I longed for his attention and affection, though I eventually chalked that up to just being so close to him because of all the intimate moments we'd shared. However the case maybe I will always hold him dear and close to my heart. Even though he is the best lover more than that he is a great friend and always listens to me and encourages me. Probably what I needed the most, but I just could not understand his fear of being serious in front of his boys.

The next week I called Leonard and told him I wanted to go to the movies. We went to see Titanic and after he admitted to crying I tallied up all the positives about him and decided that maybe I would give him a chance. After the movie he drove me home and he mentioned how he was glad that there were no black people in the movie because they always end up dying first. "Yeah," I said, "I hate that also," walking into my house. "You can stay for a little while if you like." We talked for about an hour or so and then he leaned over and kissed me. The kiss was not bad and I thought maybe he is just nervous.

After that he said he needed to get home, so we said our goodnights and he left. I showered and went to bed still longing to be in Javier's arms trying to decide if Leonard was really what I wanted. About three days later and another conversation with Javier I made my decision after Leonard dropped me off at Erica's house so we could get to work. Once at work she and I walked across to the Beauty Supply store to get some stuff. "OO somebody got the hots for Leonard," says Erica. "Girl shut up," I say pushing her. Erica begins singing "First come love…"

I grabbed her and began tickling her. I really wish she would have never sung that because the next month went by like a rocket. When I got home I called Leonard over so we could talk. He says, "Wow you look like you had a long day." "Yeah I did," I say rubbing my legs. "Since things have slowed down with the record label I am trying to stack some extra cash." Scooting over to him I take his hand and place the bracelet in it. "What are you doing?" he asks. "Will you be my boyfriend?" He smiles really big and says "You beat me to it of course I will. I have wanted to be with you for quite some time now." "I don't expect you to wear the bracelet; I just thought it would be cool to give you something since you do so much for me." "I have the perfect place for it," he says and grabs my hand and leads me out to his car. He hangs it up on the rearview mirror.

The next two weeks we were inseparable. I called Joy and told her the news and of course her first question was so is he better than Javier? "Girl please," I yell, "hell no. Not even Prince the master himself is better than Javier. If I find a man that is better than Javier I am going to spend the rest of my life with him." We both fall out laughing. "Nah but for real I say he is ok. I need to teach him my rhythm but besides that we have really nice conversation and fun together.

He is a good listener and talker. He has a steady income and a good future. At least he is doing something with himself and not just partying all the time," trying to self-consciously justify my choosing him over Javier not even realizing it. "Well you have a point there," says Joy. "Have you heard from Javier?" "I heard he got back with his girlfriend." "Good," I say, "I want him to be happy." "And I am sure he wants the same for you," says Joy. "Besides the notes you have him hitting you could swear yawl are brother and sister as close as you two became." "Anyway," I say hearing Leonard pull up outside, "I have to go so I will talk to you later. We have to go pick up Elizabeth." "Ok kiss my god baby," says Joy, "and I love you." "Love you too bye now," I say hanging up the phone running outside. Once at my mother's I introduce her to Leonard and we head out with Elizabeth. That weekend with my baby girl and my new man was very fulfilling as well as the next four months. I felt like I had it all. Nothing could possibly take my joy away or so I thought.

A few weekends later we were coming back from the mall and I told Leonard that I think I am ready to stop dancing. "Yeah you need to," he says rudely, "and stop working with that fake ass record label also." "Excuse me," I say with attitude, "I am not stopping for you. I am doing it because I want to." "So what," he says cutting me off, "you are going to stop both." "Uh," I say to myself rolling my eyes I know this Negro didn't. I reach my hand out to turn the music up so that I do not have to engage in anymore conversation with him. He pushes my hand down yelling "Don't touch my fucking radio." "Oh hell nah you just hit me," I scream.

"Stop the car. Stop got damn it I am not playing with you," I say taking my seat belt off. "Reyne I did not hit you I just pushed your hand back." "I do not care what you did you put your hands on me in a non-affectionate way you black bastard. Let me out." "Fine then," he says stopping the car. "Get out and stop acting like a stupid bitch and give me my necklace. Yanking it off my neck I throw it in the car and start walking. While walking I am thinking to myself my own Daddy don't even raise his hand to me. This boy done lost his mind. Pulling up on the side of me he says, "Baby I am sorry I just get jealous sometime please get in the car." "No," I yell and speed up walking. I walk all the way to Linda's and on top of his Stepmom's car in the driveway and pout. He pulls up and I jump up walk in the house. I say I don't even want to see him. Linda asks me if I am ok. Leonard walks toward me and I began to yell and cry like a child. "No I am not ok he hit me and call me a bitch."

"You called me a bastard," yells Leonard, "and I did not hit you on purpose. I was just trying to stop you from turning up the radio." "No you were not," I yelled. "Son you keep your hands to yourself and Reyne all that yelling is not going to solve anything. Yawl go on and talk." "Do you want me to take you home are or you going to walk there too?" he asked sarcastically. "Don't tempt me," I say rolling my eyes getting into the car not realizing that for the next three years and another child later I would regret it. I should have not even stopped at Linda's. I should have kept going all the way home.

Woulda shoulda coulda woulda never saved anybody from trouble and I learned that the hard way. The next two months were a breeze. Leonard and I made up and there were no more outbursts from him. One evening while we were having dinner I mentioned since his sisters were home for spring break that he may want to spend some time with them. "So what is it Reyne you have to go out of town right?" "Yes as a matter of fact I do. I need to go to Austin with one the dancers. I need to make some extra loot because things are low with the record label right now." Looking frustrated he says, "When are you supposed to be back?" "Two days or so," I say. "Whatever I guess, if that is what you want to do.

I am going to miss you," he says pushing his plate away. "Ahh I will miss you too." "Maybe when we get back we can go paint." "Speaking of painting where is Damon?" I ask. "He is waiting for us at the game room so let's go," says Leonard. Damon and I had a good friendship. I admired the way he was always so honest with these females yet they all swore up and down that they would be the one to change him. Laughing about it Damon and I would just shake our head and say they were touched.

After the pool hall Leonard dropped me home and I began to pack for my Austin trip. After I had finally lay down and gotten comfy the phone rings. "Hello," I say. "Hi Baby were you asleep?" says Leonard. "Al-most what's up?" I ask. "I can't sleep," he says, "I have something on my mind." Growing impatient I say "What is it?" "Reyne I love you and I know we have only been together almost six months but I love you. When I first saw you I knew I was supposed to take care of you. My uncle is moving back to Huntsville and he asks me did I want to take over his lease. It is a 1 bedroom and well I was wondering if you would come and live with me." Waking up suddenly I say "Did you say you want me to move in with you?" "Yes I did," he says sternly. "So what is it going to be?" he asks. "Um let me think about it," I say, "why, do you love me?" Because he says, "Look at you, you are beautiful and you live so carefree as if nothing bothers you, you make me feel like a man. You make me feel good about myself. I think to myself I am so the bomb." "Let me sleep on it and we will talk tomorrow," not realizing that if a man does not feel like a man when you meet him than that is a serious red flag.

"Alright," he says, "let me know something soon." "Goodnight," I say hanging up the phone. Oh God I say holding my pillow tight this is really exciting. Okay I must get some rest I have to be up in three hours. I try and go to sleep but my mind was going a hundred miles an hour. At seven the doorbell rings and it is Nick our Landlord. "Good morning Nick," I say wiping the sleep out of my eyes. "I just came by to check the sewage line to see why the water bill is 600 dollars. Entering the backyard you can see where the line has been moved. No wonder the city's line is crossed with the house line," he says walking back in the house.

"I will call the city of Houston tomorrow so they can get this fixed." "Ok," I say walking him out. "Oh Nick by the way do you have some weed whackers, I want to cut down these bushes and plant a small garden right here." "Nice idea Reyne but this is still my house all you guys are doing is leasing it." "What are you talking about I am taking over the payments when Tiny moves to her old house and she is signing the house over to me." "I am sorry Reyne but you have been misinformed," says Nick. "You all are leasing not buying this house. It is not for sale." "What!" I say angrily, "do you have papers proving that?" I ask. "Sure they are right here." I read the papers and find out rent is actually only $700 a month and I have been giving her $500 thinking I am paying half.

"Thanks a lot Nick I will handle this by the way can you not mention anything to Tiny." "No problem you all take care and sorry for the misunderstanding." Going to my room slamming the door I say I cannot believe this cow. She has been stealing my money. I should have listened when my guardian told me not to agree to anything without getting in writing first. I pick up the phone and call her to let her know Nick came by to check out the water line. "I told him I was going to cut the bushes down you do not mind right since you will be moving in a few months and the house will be signed over to me right?" I ask aggressively. "Uh Uh I have to go," Tiny says nervously getting off the phone. That B I yell. I lie down and have my quiet time. God I am really angry with this girl. I want to beat the snot out of her. Ok calm down maybe she will tell me the truth and give me my money back then I can let her make it.

On another note God I really like Leonard and he wants me to live with him. I don't know if I will. I'll think about it. Turning on my music, I fall asleep not even realizing the time. Bbrrrg Brrrg. "Hello, Hello," I say knocking over the radio. "Girl I paged you four times. I had to call Damon to get your house number." "What time is it?" I say rubbing my eye. "It is seven," says Cindy, "time for us to go. Have you packed yet?" she asked. "Yeah I just gotta brush my teeth," I say looking around hearing a car horn. "Is that you?" I ask. "Yeah hurry up so we can get on the road." Hanging up the phone, "Hey I think your ride is outside," yells Tiny. "Hey to you," I say walking towards the door.

"By the way have you talk to Eduardo lately?" I ask. "About what?" says Tiny moving around busily. "What do you mean about what?" I say aggressively, "about him moving out of your house?" "Oh yeah," she says unpacking her dance bag, "he said about a month or two." "Well, I would like to start decorating and stuff," I say. "Ok well go ahead and start, I will be packing up soon moving the big stuff over to the house," she says humping her shoulders never making eye contact. Rolling my eyes I say "Ok Tiny we need to talk. I talk to Nick and I feel like you are lying." Before I could finish my sentence Cindy walks in saying, "Girl come on here we have a two hour ride ahead of us, and lots of money to make. We cannot be late." "Alright," I say grabbing my stuff. "Tiny we need to talk asap when I get back here." "Sure girl we will talk," she says rushing off into the bathroom.

Slamming the door closed to the car, Cindy asks "What is wrong with you and why do you have those angry lines in your forehead?" "No reason," I say rubbing my head, "just aggravated. Can I see your phone, I need to call Leonard." Cindy passes me her phone. "Hello hey I am on my way to Austin if you need me you can call me at this number because my pager does not work out there." "Okay Baby I love you be safe." "Uh okay bye," I say and hung up the phone looking puzzled. "What's up?" ask Cindy. "He said he love me," I say looking strangely. "So why didn't you say it back?" "I don't know that is not a word that I play around with lightly." "Girl please everybody says it," says Cindy shrugging her shoulders.

"Not me unless I mean it. Anyway," I say changing the subject, "have you heard from Damon?" "Yeah when I called him to get your number. He is a really sweet guy," she says smiling. "Who? Damon? Ha! Let me guess he told you he wants to marry you and have babies with pretty hair," I say with a dumb look on my face. "How did you know?"

she says surprisingly. "Wild guess," I say rolling my eyes in the back of my head. "Girl I am going to sleep," I say. About two and a half hours later Cindy nudges me and hands me the phone. "That is your man girl," she says. "Have yawl made it there yet?" he ask. "I think we are about twenty minutes away," I say. "Are you coming home tonight?" he ask.

"Depends on business, I told you I am trying to stack some loot. I may be moving," I say and then hit myself because I did not want to say anything yet. "What!" he says excitedly, "you are considering my offer?" "What?" I say, "look we are pulling up I have to go. I will call you later," I say hurriedly and hang up the phone before he can get another word out. Turning to Cindy I ask, "Are you sure they are going to let us work?" "Yeah girl. My cousin knows the owner and he already called and arranged everything," she says getting out of the car. As we go inside I immediately get an odd feeling but I soon get aggravated when I notice the girl behind the counter looking at us as if we are dirt. "Is Mr. Rogers in?" ask Cindy.

With a nasty smirk she picks up the phone and says there is two more here and we already have our quota for the night. Turning my head swiftly if looks could kill she would have dropped dead because I knew exactly what that comment meant. I tell Cindy, "Girl I aint feeling this place let's go," peeking inside the club. "Everything will be fine," she says, "Don't worry about it." "I aint worried," I say angrily, "I just don't like." Before I could finish my statement in walks Mr. Reynolds. "Hello Ladies," he says clearing his throat. (Looking at us as if we are dead carcass on the side off the road and he is the grandpa vulture #) "I deeply am sorry," he begins to say, "We have a full house tonight and are not taking any more."

His sentence was cut short by a tiny little waitress with a loud mouth. "Where have you been I have been looking all over for you? We are short on girrr...." Grabbing the tiny mal-nutrition waitress by the elbow pulling her away he says nodding his big bald head toward us,

"We will discuss this later." That was enough for me. I say you can keep this sarcastic bullsh--. "Shh!" Cindy says grabbing my arm and pulling me over by the door. "Girl calm down, you know how this business is." "No, actually I don't," I say snatching my arm away from her. "I don't really give a shit how it works." I walk over to the bald head vulture, "Look do you need girls or not. She just said that you were short." He says "I'm sorry ladies," motioning for Cindy to come over. Placing his nasty grimy hand on our shoulders he continues saying we just don't have. I quickly push his hand off my shoulder and began walking towards the door saying,

"Don't fucking bother you racist son of a bitch. Let's go Cindy, now." Cindy says, "Thank you sir and I am sorry for the outburst." Walking towards her I grab her by the arm and say "Girl bring you a— on here, and why in the hell are you saying sorry?" "Stacey you can't be that way," she says fixing herself once we get outside. "He might have let us work if you..." I stopped dead in my tracks and walked around to her side of the car giving her a look that shut her up dry. "Take me home now," I say calmly and sternly. "Well I am tired, maybe we could just get a room..." she says opening her car door ducking to get in, moving out of the line of fire.

"Fine I will drive myself," I say reaching for the keys. "You don't have a license," she says. "Look," I say getting in her face, "I am going home regardless if you take me or not." "Ok fine let's go," she says. It was a silent ride all the way back to Houston. Once we arrived she dropped me off at Leonard's Mom's house. "Thank you," she says when we pulled in the driveway. "This business can be hard and I did not have the courage to stand up to baldy." "No girl," I say "thank you, you help me realize that this business is not for me," I say getting out of the car. "You take care, bye." I never saw or heard from her again but I really pray that that moment changed her life. "Hey Leonard," I say walking into the garage, "Can you take me home?" Ray T comes out his Step

Dad and says "You look tired." "I am," I say walking to Leonard's car. Once in the car Leonard asks me what was wrong. "I am just aggravated," I say trying to regroup on all the activities of the day.

"Well what happened?" he ask, "Talk to me." "Well first of all I found out Tiny lied to me about buying the house. Come to find out we are only renting. I am going to talk to her and tell her I need my money back because we had an agreement and then on top of that the man at the place in Austin was a total dick. I cannot stand people that act like that. Racist son of a so and so, how dare him behave that way. That is so not fair, I say." "Well Baby life is not fair, and that girl is not going give you that money back, says Leonard." "Shooed she gone do something," I say as we pull up to the house.

"Um that figures she is not even here. I will just talk to her tomorrow. I have to go to school so I will just go in and get some rest," I say walking up to the door putting my key in. "What ah hell nah. I know good and well. I am going to beat the living shit out of her. What's wrong with this heffa go and get the locks changed. She done lost the li'l piece of mind she have." I get back in the car and ask Leonard to take me to her job please. "Hello, Hey Chris is Tiny there?" "Yes she just got on stage actually, are you coming up here?"

"Yeah but don't tell her." I get out of the car fuming mad. Leonard yells behind me, "Do not go in there acting crazy." "I got this. Hey," I ask around, "where is Tiny." "Oh she just left. I told her you were on your way here and she said she had to get home so I let her leave." "Uggh you idiot I told you not to tell her I was coming." "Sorry," says Chris. I go back to the car and tell Leonard let's go to Marcus house because that is obviously where she had to be going. "Hello Marcus is Tiny there?" I hear her shushing him in the background. "No she is not here," he says. "You know what the hell with the both of you," I say hanging up the phone. "Uggh just take me to get a room for the night please." "Look," says Leonard, "calm down ok." "Ahh damn."

"What is it?" he asks. "I need my books for school tomorrow." "Well just chill out," he says. "We will go by the house and check a window and the back door. Back at the house all the windows were locked as well as the back door. Leonard broke the small pane on the back door and got in that way. "There go inside and get your books and let's go," he says. With tears in my eyes I mumble to myself I cannot believe this. How could she do something like this to me? "Hey," says Leonard, "I will ask Linda if you can stay at her house tonight ok?" Leonard pulls over on the way to Linda's and ask me have I thought about what he ask me in reference to moving in with him if he takes over his uncle's lease.

"He already has furniture in there and besides I love you and I feel like I am supposed to protect you and take care of you." "Thank you," I say, "but I am not sure about that and I can take care of myself." I sat there and I thought about it I mean we are together and he is always there when I need him. When we pulled in Linda's driveway I told him yes I would move in with him. "How much is rent?" He said, "Don't worry about that I will pay all of that you can help with the phone bill." "Ok so when are we moving in?" I ask. "I go and pick up the key tomorrow," he says. Sitting in the living room exhausted and frustrated and confused, Linda hands me some blankets and tells me to get some rest. She is really a sweet lady whom I grew to adore. "I apologize for the last minute visitation."

She assures me that it is not a problem and goes off to bed herself. I grab Leonard's hand and say thank you. He sits in the chair next to the couch but before I could even start a conversation I was knocked out. The next morning I woke up to find Leonard asleep in the chair next to me. I thought Ahh that was so sweet he stayed in that uncomfortable chair all night. As I watched him sleep I wondered if he really loved me as much as he claims he does. In the middle of my staring his middle sister walks in and clears her throat loudly and says, "Good morning."

Leonard jumps up and hits his arm yelling ouch and good morning at the same time.

Looking at the time Leonard says, "Oh no you have to get to school." I say "Yeah I am already late so let's just go and get my stuff and get settled." Pulling up to the house I say, "Um I see she is not here." Leonard says "Well if she comes back just don't say anything to her ok? Get your stuff and let's go." We go in through the back door and I began packing my things. While Leonard carries my things to the truck I hear her pull up. She immediately jumps out of the car and begins to yell saying "I cannot believe this.

How did you get in my house?" Coming down the hallway I pass right by her and say nothing. I don't even look her way gritting my teeth the whole time. In walks Leonard and Marcus. "Hey Reyne," says Marcus, "you moving out?" Before I get a chance to answer Tiny yells "You black bitch, I cannot believe." Before she even finishes her sentence I dropped the box and am on her like white on rice. All you hear is her screaming for Marcus to help her. Marcus turned to Leonard and said, "Man is you going to stop her?" Leonard said "No and you better not touch her either." Tiny yelled, "Marcus help me." Leonard gave him a look and he just squealed "Fight back Baby." She managed to squirm away and run down the hall to her room. I did my best to kick the door down when Leonard said "Come on that is enough let's get out of here." We grabbed the last of my things and left. As we drove out of the neighborhood the cops were pulling into the neighborhood. Needless to say I never saw her or her cunt boyfriend Marcus again. I still wanted my money but getting to whip her ass was payback enough.

After getting settled living with Leonard I began contemplating on not dancing even more. On the phone with Joy I tell her that he is a cool guy and he works hard and makes sure all the bills are paid and that I am straight. "Okay beyond that Reyne, do you love him?" she asks. "He's cool," I say "and yeah I think I do." "You think," she says loudly, "girl take some time and figure out what you want to do. In the meantime breathe and enjoy someone finally taking care of you." "Alright girl I love you," I say. "Get some sleep and stop thinking so much," she says. Needless to say enjoy is what I did. Within a month or so I was pregnant. Sitting in the bathroom looking at the test, Leonard knocks on the door "Well what does it say?"

"I'm pre---." Before I could even get the words out of my mouth good he was on the phone calling his Mom, stepmom, sisters and best friend. Thinking to myself uh hello what about me but looking at how happy he was how could I steal his joy by telling him I wanted an abortion. I do not want another child he knows this. Grabbing me he says "Oh baby I love you and we are going to have a baby." I just smiled and said nothing. Within the next few months I got my daughter back from my mother, stopped dancing, and completed my third semester of school. The rest of the pregnancy went by quick. In my ninth month we moved in with his Mom until our apartment was ready due to the lease being up. On December third my labor was induced and just as fast as the labor went so did our move. We were in our new place in no time. Six months and two teeth later I stop breastfeeding and Leonard begins to discuss marriage again. I told him I would think about it and decided to start working. I prepared for my job interviews that night and said a small prayer. The next day I ran in the house and said guess what I have a job interview. Leonard says that is good without looking up at me. I ask him what is wrong with you. He says nothing and continues watching television. Well it starts on Monday I say going in to check on Larry and Elizabeth. That weekend I went to meet the babysit-ter and got her acquainted with the kids and was ready to go to work secure and comfortable that she would do a good job.

I stood in the bathroom getting ready Monday morning and I think to myself. Here I am with my daughter back, a six month old son and a man who wants to marry me. I never thought I would have a child let alone two. Suddenly I smile remembering a conversation Joy and I had a long time ago at one of our many luncheons at Fuddruckers. I remember saying, "Yeah girl I am going to have a girl and a boy and that is it." Joy said she wanted three or four kids and a husband. "A husband um I don't know, knowing me I will probably divorce the first one, live in marital bliss the second time around like those rich white women and not work only to learn that he has a whole other life, divorce him and marry the person I have known most of my life that was always my friend for love."

"Girl you crazy," Joy said to me. "It is going to take a life changing experience for you to settle down and get married." "Yeah girl you are absolutely right about that." Startled I look up and say "How long have you been standing there?" Leonard replies, "Oh just long enough to see you smiling." I began blushing and went back to doing my hair. "What were you thinking about anyway?" ask Leonard. "Oh," smiling again shyly "just Joy." He rolls his eyes slightly. "I just miss her so much and it has been a while since she visited, I really want to go and see her."

Irritated Leonard says "Um," walking out "hurry up and get ready so that we can go and drop the kids to Ms. Gloria." Now Leonard did not really care for Joy too much. She and I had a bond that no one could come between. I would sit up late at night and write her letters and sometime I would even cry because I missed her so much. This really frustrated Leonard, he just could not seem to understand the closeness that we shared. It was as if it made him jealous. Once in the car he started talking about us getting married again. "So tell me have you thought about us getting married?" Before I could answer Larry began to cry so I reached to the back and began tending to him totally ignoring Leonard's question.

"Hey let me drive," I say as we walk back to the car to go my interview. Now Damon Leonard's best friend had taken me to get my license a few Fridays prior to this, because Leonard had to go out of town for reserves. Leonard was not exactly comfortable with my driving but Damon on the other hand said I was champ behind the wheel. I took off slow and then quickly picked up gas and sped off to the interview. After about three hours of paperwork and testing came my interview.

The lady apologized for the test taking so long. She told me the secret to registering with a temp agency is to already say you have computer experience so that you do not have to test on everything. I was thinking to myself thanks for telling after the fact. She offered me a receptionist assignment that would last for like month it was only a temporary assignment but I took it. At home that night I told Leonard and how excited I was about work but he was more interested in the game. After that month the agency put me on two other assignments. It was honestly a blessing because the only experience I had to put on my resume what Anthony taught me how to do which was filing, distributing mail typing proposal letters, and answering the phone which is what I did as a young girl when I would go and meet my Mom after school at work at the college.

The next few months were cool and quite a learning experience. I began going to my mother in law's church Sunday August 16, 1999. The Pastor was preaching on Romans 8:28. He was talking about how God works everything out for the good of those who love the Lord who are called according to His purpose. As I sat in the balcony looking at my sisters and thinking about my life I began to feel heat. I looked up but there was no vent above me nor to the right or left of me. As the Pastor continued preaching it began as a curious thought. Then it escalated to warm feeling.

Then it moved to a fire that took flame from my chest to my feet and I had to move. I could no longer sit there. I was being called and I was a soldier in an army that already had the victory. The song began to ring in my head. My feet started to move by then and before my mind could catch up I was already half way to the front of the church marching, singing, "I'm a soldier, in the army of the Lord. I'm a soldier. In the army." Boy was I ready. I felt like I could take on the world at that moment. I gave my life to Christ and joined church. The rest of my life no longer seemed to matter at that moment. I received Christ as my Lord and Savior and knew I was saved just knew something was different. I did not feel alone anymore.

I did not feel like the weight of the world was on my shoulders. For the first time in my life I felt like I had a purpose. There was light at the end of the tunnel. I went in the new member room and took my picture. The lady asked me if I needed prayer. I told her no and she then gave me a pamphlet and told me to come to new member's orientation and welcomed me to the church. My sisters were really happy for me and thankful that I had received Christ. On the ride back to my apartment my sister Lacey says "Now you know you cannot be shacking. The Bible says you cannot fornicate."

I was like forni-who? She said "Yawl need to get married now or stop living together." "Oh," I said as I got out of the car and hugged them goodbye. As usual Leonard was not there when I got home. He would get up early on Saturday and Sunday and go play basketball. I called Joy and told her what happen at church. She asked me the same thing my sister did. "So when are yawl go get married?" "Girl I do not know if I want to get married." Why did I say that? She started her twenty questions. I put her on speaker phone as I laid the kids down for their nap and began cooking Sunday dinner. After about the fifteenth question I told her,

"Ok fine I will consider marrying the boy." By the time we got off the phone the food was cooked and Leonard was walking in the door. "Hey Baby," he yells towards the kitchen. "Hey the food is ready." "Ok let me shower first." After about twenty minutes he called me in the room. "I won all my games today." "Good for you," I say sitting on the bed. "How about we have a nice quiet movie evening?" he asks. "Cool we can do that but first I need to talk to you." Walking out of the room he says, "Can we talk over lunch I am starving." I fed the kids and fixed my plate and sat down next to him in front of the TV. "What is on your mind Baby?" "I joined church today," I said. "Really?" he asks. "Yes and I want you to start coming with me." "Now I am not sure about that you know I have my games on Sundays." "Well you all can play after church or we can go to night service." "Look I really do not feel like talking about this right now besides the game is on," he says turning away from me.

I got up and went in the room and pulled out my Bible that they had given me at church. I read over the passage in Romans and began thinking. Laying back with the Bible on my chest I thought about what my sisters and Joy had said earlier. They kind of had a point it was already two years since Leonard and I had been together and I did not seem to be going anywhere. The more time I spent reading and in church the worse I felt about staying with Leonard and we were not married. Being that our lease was up at the end of June I sat him down three weeks into the month and told him that I was going to move to my sisters. Now early on in the month we had had a disagreement that caused me to retreat from sleeping with him.

A female had begun paging him late at night and when I asked him about it he got a tad bit hostile and defensive. I politely took it upon myself to call the female and get the scoop with him on three-way one evening when I left to go hang out with a friend girl of mine. Once I got the both of them on the phone the girl stated that Leonard did not tell her he was in a relationship and that I needed to check him not her. Very well put, I excused her and told Leonard I would talk to him when I got home, if I came home. I went home at about 1 in the morning.

Lo and behold he was not even there. I stayed up until 3 AM waiting for him and I finally fell asleep after I drank an entire bottle of wine. At about 4:30 Leonard came in and woke me up. As soon as he woke me up I began throwing up. I rushed to the bathroom and caught the toilet just in time. After I was emptied out we both sat back and laughed because of how drunk I was. The next morning I vowed never to drink another bottle of wine again. He sat me down and told me that he did not know why he gave that girl his pager number. He said he just wanted to see if he still had game in front of his boys. I told him that if he likes living he may not want to test his game while I hold the title as his lady. I made him pinky promise me that he would never do something so stupid again and that he would get his pager number changed. "Oh yeah and by the way I am moving to my sisters." What he said. Yeah I told him in the midst of me getting drunk last night I decided that I did not want to live with him if we were not married.

He said okay and that we would get married soon but let him get a ring and everything first. I told him no rush I am just going to move in with her and we can still be together but no sex and no sleep overs. My sister would not have that. He kept questioning me and I told him I just did not want to live like that anymore. He then stated "It is because of church, huh?" "Yes according to the Bible it is not right." He stomped off mumbling under his breath. In all honesty I really did not know what was going on with me. All I knew was that something changed and I needed to make better choices. I only wanted to please the God who took the time to create me and love me and if not living in sin is what I had to do according to the church leaders then that is what I was willing to do. For so long I searched for this feeling and now that I had a taste of it nothing else satisfied me. This began a long painful journey that in spite of all the hurt and mistakes bought forth much needed fulfillment and peace.

CHAPTER 7
Out of Ignorance into Bondage

The following week his Mom came to visit and I rode back to her hometown with her after I moved my stuff to my sister's house. The kids had a nice time out in the middle of nowhere in some little small country town in Texas. That town was smaller than my hometown. She gave Leonard and me her car because she had purchased a new one. Leonard did not come to pick me up as discussed because he got called to his reserve unit, so I took that five hour drive back to Houston alone with the kids so I could drive the car back.

On the way back I really thought a lot about my life. I knew I wanted to finish college and get married one day but I was just not sure I wanted that day to be so soon. I did not quite understand why Leonard and I had to get married. As soon as I arrived at my sisters they told me that the Temp agency had been calling for me. I called them the next day and they told me about a job at the light company from 7 AM to 4 PM Monday to Friday. I called Ms.

Gloria and arranged for Elizabeth to be picked up by the bus driver in the morning and afternoon for school. Larry was only 7 months so she kept him all day until I got there from work. Leonard was excited about my new job but not happy about me driving all the way from the north side to the southwest side and then downtown for work every day. He switched cars with me and gave me his car because it had fewer miles than his mother's car. As time went on I got used to the drive and even met a friend named Faith who lived on the southwest side. Occasionally I would pick her up and bring her to work.

She worked as the admin assistant and I was the test administrator. Faith and I became really close over the next few months. She was pregnant and engaged to this guy named Nathan. She already had a daughter named Jasmine from a previous relationship. Being that I had a child from a previous person I felt close to her, so we bonded quite well. October rolled around and by this time my sister had begun to get on my nerves. She complained that I was taking advantage of her by leaving the kids with her on the weekends when Leonard and I would go out. It was not like I was not coming home every night.

My sisters believed that once you have kids your life is supposed to stop. Of course I begged to differ, plus most of the time they were asleep when I left or at least fed, bathed, and in the bed. At the time I really did not see it as a problem because she was right there at home not doing anything or going anywhere. So by November I decided to move back to the southwest side and get my own place. Leonard was happy about the move but I told him the same rules still applied no sex and no spending the night. During the move Leonard's pager went off. I went over to it and picked it up. When he walked in carrying the chair he said, "What are you doing?"

"Your pager is going off." He put down the chair and took his pager out of my hand and put it in his pocket. I told him I trust that that is not a female. He looked at me crazy and was like no it is not. I said ok and went on unpacking my things. That night he spent the night and the next day. I made him go home. The day after he called to come over and

I told him no he could not spend the night. After about a week of being told no and me sweating bullets from not getting any we broke down. He came over that Monday. I was not feeling well and he asked me to marry him.

After I caught my breath from throwing up I told him yes. We went down to the court house and got the marriage certificate. On the way back he asked me was there anything I needed to tell him before we got married. I sat there and thought for a minute and said no, not that I am aware of. I asked him about the girl who had paged him months ago and he assured me that he had never talked to her again since the night I called him with her on the phone.

The next day at work I went out for lunch. On my way back to the building I heard someone calling my name. I turn around to see James running towards me from across the street. "James, is that you?" I ask. "Hey Baby, you just up and disappeared on me. Where have you been?" "Around," I say walking ahead of him. "Where are you headed?" he asks. "I am going back to work." "In this building?" he says. "I come here to pick up my checks right now until they start my direct deposit next week. What company do you work for?" I ask. "Core staff," he says. "Really I work for them for the Light Company as a test adminis-trator."

"Would you work for them at American General?" says James. "Oh cool," but then I thought to myself not cool. As we enter the elevator he asks, "How is the baby?" "Well she is not a baby anymore she is four years old now," I say. "And how is her Dad are you all still together?" "Actually no we broke up not long after she was born. I have a picture," I say getting off the elevator. "Hey James," says Faith. "Hey, Faith." I stop in my tracks and say, "You all know each other?" "Uh yeah," they both say at the same time.

"James lives in my apartments." "Well I do not live there but a friend of mine does and I am over there a lot." I look at Faith and mouth, "A girl?" She nods her head yes and hands him his check. "How do yawl know each other?" asks Faith. "Well we use to be friends back in the day," I say handing him the picture of Elizabeth. His face turns beet red and he asks, "Now how are you and her Dad getting along?" I say, "Why?" looking at the picture and looking at him. Faith sits up and says, "Oh my gosh," looking at the picture, "that is your child," and then covers her mouth and sits back in her seat. I look shockingly at him and the picture and say, "Oh well I guess we will find out for sure tomorrow.

Lawrence filed child support on himself and had to take a paternity test." James just stood there in shock. Finally he gave me the picture and said, "I am willing to pay child support and be in my daughter's life once those results come back." I said, "Well we will see tomorrow give me your number and I will call you. As he wrote down his number Faith just stared big eyed and shook her head. "Reyne," says James. "Yes James." "Don't just use my number for the results, we have a lot of catching up to do," he says smiling and rubbing my hand. "Uh James I have to tell you something," I say nervously.

"Oh I know before I was not ready for a relationship but now we have a child and all I want to do is be a part of yawl's life." "James I am getting married on Thursday." His smile quickly turns to a frown and he backed away and was like oh oh okay well just call me when the results come in and he walks out. Faith says, "Wow Reyne, I hope he is not suicidal. You could have told him better than that." I looked at her like what humping my shoulders. "He will be ok," and went back into my office. On the way home that day I kept asking ok God what was that all about?

I picked up the kids and called Leonard and told him I had something to tell him. "Remember how you asked me if there was something that I needed to tell you. Well here goes." I ran the story to him about Lawrence and James. Now being that we had already been together two and half years of course he had met Lawrence, but knew nothing about

James. His reaction was calm but curious. He could not understand how I did not know if you used a condom and it broke you could possibly get pregnant. I told him my cousin taught me that you only get pregnant if you do not use one. Plus I was young and ignorant and did not know any better.

The next day the results were delivered to me via FedEx and as soon as I opened them the phone rang. Before I could even get a word out Lawrence cursed me out and hung up the phone in my face. I placed the phone back in the cradle and Faith walks in and says, "James's?" I shake my head yes and sit down in my seat. I left work speechless not knowing what to do or say. Four years had gone by and I thought Elizabeth was Lawrence's child because we had never used condoms, and here it is the time I do use one and bam I got pregnant. At home I told Leonard and he sat right there as I called James and told him the news. James was happy but sad because I was getting married.

The next day my stomach was upset again but I still went on with the plans. As we arrived at the courthouse I tried to feel good about my decision but I was suffering in a pool of guilt and grief. I felt convicted about living with Leonard all the more now than when I first received Christ. I knew or so I thought that in order to get in right standards with God I had to marry Leonard. I never voiced how I felt to him. I really did not like talking to him about God it was as if he did not understand. I really did not have anyone else to talk to about it either. All I had was the Word and it was slapping me all over the place.

The church leaders always talked about shacking and having children out of wedlock. It was a lot to bear and I felt like I had messed up so much with God already that I had to fix it. Not realizing that that was one of the first misconceptions of being saved we, us, me, humans trying to fix our past mistakes. Duh, this was the sole purpose of Jesus dying for us for past and future mistakes. This is why he turns things around for our good but I had yet to learn and understand this as well as one heck of a journey getting free from trying to fix my choices. After the judge married us I felt like I had just gotten a bad tattoo or something.

Leonard was happy but it was not an 'Oh I love you' happy it was more of an 'I won the prize' happy. That weekend he moved all his stuff in and we began life as a married couple. The New Year came and went. February rolled around and on Valentine's Day I came home from work to find a teddy bear with a ring around its neck and a note. The ring was beautiful. It was a princess cut one and half carats.

I slipped it on my finger and he came running from the back laughing and smiling. Things were cool for a while, then at the end of March Damon came back. All hell began to break loose. Leonard started staying out late at night. Faith had her baby and had gotten married to Nathan and was now ready to hang out again. She and I began going out. I would ask Leonard to go with me but he claimed he did not like clubs. I told him it would really bring me joy for my husband to go out and dance with me. He always told me no.

Towards the end of April I was released from my position as test administrator due to all the positions being filled for the particular test I was administering. That month of April was spent in hot heated arguments with Leonard. It seemed like every day we were fussing about something. One day he was tripping because I went to go and check the mailbox in some shorts. Coming from the street I really did not take too kindly someone yelling at me about stupid stuff, so I ignored him. He then pushed me and I had to catch myself because before I knew it my hand was next to his balls ready to rip them off. I told him if he likes living he better not ever put his hands on me again.

He walked out of the room and went out the door. After a few hours I called him several times and he never called me back. When he did come home he yelled and cursed at me and called me stupid bitch and a hoe. I politely grabbed my white stuffed animal tiger and went to sleep in the living room. These kinds of things happen for about two months. By this time I had a new job at this company called Check Care Systems. Damon had left and went back to working offshore. It seemed like as long as he was gone things were cool, but as soon as he got back Leonard would begin to show his tail. It did not matter where we were.

Even in front of his step mom he would cut up. One evening I received a phone call from my sister. She told me that Freddy's mother had passed. Now I had never ever told Leonard about Freddy so I knew I had an argument on my hands. The only guys I told him about were Javier, Walter, Derrick, and Anthony because these guys meant a lot to me and I defined them as true friends and I told him from the gate that if they needed me I would be there for them. His first response was so, what does that have to do with you; yawl can't be that close if I have not heard his name mentioned in the past four years that we've been together. I rolled my eyes and told him he could act stupid if he wanted to but I was going to Freddy's Mom's funeral.

He shoved me in my temple and told me to get out of his face. I pushed his hand back and told him to keep his fucking hands off of me. He then pushes me down and begins cursing me. I jumped up and cursed back and he shoved me in my face and walked out. I went to the funeral and Freddy and I had a slight chance to catch up. I talked to Faith and told her about the hitting. She said it was my choice what I wanted to do but I needed to do something. I wanted to kill him but did not want to spend the rest of my life in prison because of it. As time went on I began to resent him more and more. It was a battle and truly a struggle for me not to kill him. This time in January '01 when Damon came back we all began going to the gun range together. I became an excellent marksman in less than a week by visualizing Leonard as the target.

My job was cool I had received my second promotion and had moved up to office manager in spite of all the stress at home. James really did not spend much time with Elizabeth and seemed to have an attitude each time I spoke with him. I was already going through hell with Leonard I was not about to listen to him whine. One evening my side was hurting really bad. I went to the doctor and the doctor said they would run some test. I went back home to find Leonard in the closet hiding something. I asked him, "What are you doing?"

"None of your damn business," he says walking out of the room. We were not on the best of terms due to another lie he had told me about his whereabouts. He grabs his keys and says, "I will be back." I asked him where he was going because we needed to talk. "I do not feel like talking right now," he said. As he drives off I go to the closet and search for whatever it was he was hiding. Just when I was about ready to give up I notice that his jacket was not in the same place that it usually is.

I reached in the pocket and lo and behold there was a medicine bottle with the label torn off. I open it and pour one of the pills in my hand. I take it to the bathroom where the light is better and read the name. "Momma," says Elizabeth. Got dog it I drop the pill startled by her voice. "Yes bay what you want." "I am hungry." "Ok go sit in the living room I will fix you all something to eat in a minute," I say bending down to pick up the pill. As I kneel down I notice the wrapping in the toilet. I get a hanger and pull it out. Once I got it out I laid it on the counter and blow dried it with the blow dryer. After it dried completely I put it in my purse and fixed the kids some dinner.

The pain in my side begins to come back so after they ate I went to bed. The next day I called the pharmacist and told them I got the wrong medication. I gave them Leonard's name and his social and they told me no that was the right medication for an STD. I called my doctor immediately and he said that he did not find any negative results and that I did not have anything. Luckily due to all the arguing I had stopped sleeping with Leonard for like a month before this happened. I told my doctor about Leonard's STD and he said I was clean and did not have anything and that it could just be stress.

I told Faith and she said that it was nothing but God that kept me covered. I thanked God and went and got a second job to start saving to leave Leonard. That next week Leonard's pager went off at 3 in the morning. I grabbed it and recognized the number as ole girl number from 4 years ago. I called her the next day and she told me that Leonard had come to see her one night and his head was bleeding and she cleaned him up and told him to go home to his wife. She also said that Leonard told her I was crazy and that I hit him in the head. In essence I knew exactly what incident she was referring to because it left me with a black eye that I had to cover with makeup and lie and tell my boss that I had pinkeye for about a week.

His head had gotten cut open when I ducked and he hit the corner of the picture on the wall. I confronted him about the STD and he lied and said that the medicine was for a bladder infection. I also asked him about the girl and he said he has not talked to her since that day. "Leonard I am going to ask you one more time and I really pray that you tell me the truth. Did you or did you not go to the girl's house that night you gave me a black eye and tried to tear the head off my white tiger." He looks at me right in my eyes and says, "No.

I picked up the phone and called her and put her on speaker, he sat there with his mouth open in disbelief and then began to explain. I hung up with her and he said that he did go see her but they never did anything. I asked him how long had he been in contact with her. He said him and Damon ran into her one night at the pool hall. My final question, "Did you sleep with her before we got married?" He said no but she had told me different. Later he admitted that they did kiss before him and I got married. For me that was it I was done I just simply stood up and said ok well we are married now and if you say you did not sleep with her than I guess I cannot divorce you.

Because I cannot prove that you cheated. We went to talk to his Mom and she said that according to the Bible God hated divorce and I could not leave him if I was not sure that he cheated. After another fight I finally decided to roll out. Our lease was getting ready to end and we were planning on moving to a house. I packed up all the kids' stuff and took enough clothes out for about two weeks. Then I packed all my stuff and did the same. Leonard asks me why I didn't pack his stuff. I told him, "Oh honey I was not sure what all you wanted to keep out for the next two weeks so after you separate your stuff then I will pack it."

The next day after another argument he got up and went to play ball. I called my babysitter and asked her to come and help me move. I signed my new lease, and moved out. Just as he was pulling in the gate we were pulling out with the last load. He jumped out of the car saying, "Baby I have a gift for you." The neighbors that were outside barbecuing laughed at him because they knew I had moved out but he did not until he went upstairs and saw all our stuff gone.

Once settled in my new place I called my sister to check on the kids. "Are you okay?" asked Lacey. "Yes girl I am fine just getting situated. I will be there to pick them up tomorrow after church." I called Leonard to talk to him about seeing his son and to my surprise he was out with Damon. Hello I say loudly, I see you did not waste any time getting to the club. "What are you talking about?" says Leonard, "I love you." "Nigga get off the phone, here come some dimes," says Damon and then the phone hangs up. "Oh hell nah," I say picking up the phone calling Faith. That night we went out on the town, I wore my Fuck him dress and we celebrated being free.

Faith had left Nathan and I left Leonard. A few months ago she had mentioned the problems they were having and that she wanted to leave. I could not understand why Faith did not want to come and live with Leonard and me at first but after seeing how going to the shelter turned out to be a blessing I understood. The shelter gave her an apartment with the rent paid for six months. The liberation that you feel after getting out of such a bad relationship is exactly what we both needed.

Once we arrived at the club I headed straight for the dance floor. Wearing my red spandex hook around the neck dress I walked right in front of the guy who I had been ignoring for the past four months that Faith and I had been coming here. As his eyes bulged he began to speak. I gently covered his lips with my finger and told him to shush just dance don't talk. Just as he stepped under the rail the DJ noticed and put the light on us. I wrapped my leg around his just as the beat dropped for Flex by Mad Cobra.

As the reggae music continued to play I forgot all my troubles and danced with him until the lights came on. Once the music stopped and the lights were on I quickly thanked him and for the dance and headed on my way. For the next two months or so every Friday night we would go to Club Phoenix and dance our troubles away. One night after the club at Chachos we heard some guys talking. One of the guys told his friend not to even think of approaching me because the only person I dance with is Desmond.

I thought to myself so that is his name. Although Desmond and I had never held a conversation I still felt somewhat guilty for dancing with him. In May I received a promotion at work that put me in a position to save a little money. Leonard was calling more and more reminding me of my words that I would never keep the kids away from him. So finally we decided to meet at his mother's house. Everything went well and we even arranged a schedule for him to spend time with his son. James was keeping Elizabeth every weekend, so in a lot of ways it worked out great for me. The kids were spending time with their dads, I would go out on Fridays, practice on Saturdays and church on Sundays. One Sunday Pastor preached on family and how the family should stick together.

Now James was by no means a fool. So after church I told him as I picked up Elizabeth that Leonard and I had to take a break for a minute but would be back together. I could no longer take him questioning me about the situation and trying to get with me. As I drove off I began to cry because I wanted to tell him the truth but I knew he would kill him dead. As I looked at my face in the mirror and rubbed the back of my head where my hair was growing back, I thought to myself is it that I still wanted my family complete or the fact that I wanted to kill him myself? Elizabeth says, "Momma, are you ok?" "Yes Baby," I say, "Why do you ask?" caressing her cheek. "Well at first you were crying and then your eyes turned black."

Gasping slightly and turning away, "No baby girl I am fine. Let's go get your brother and go home," I say changing the subject. Pulling up to Leonard's apartment I take a deep breath and we get out of the car. As soon as the door opens Larry runs and gives me a huge hug. Leonard asked me to sit down and talk but I quickly declined not wanting to hear his begging me to come back today. "I will call you when I get home and get settled," I say walking out of the door. Once at home I fed the kids the food James had cooked for us and we all laid down for a nap.

When I awoke I noticed I had nine missed calls on my phone and you guessed it all of them were from Leonard. I called him back and he began to fuss. After he finished I just said ok and he began his spiel about how much he loves me and misses us all being together. I informed him that his actions did not show that. He then promised that he would do anything to fix it, church, and counseling, whatever it took to prove to me that he loved us. He calls and sets a counseling session with Rev. Jackson. I did not like the fact that our first session has to be one on one but I went along with it. After about our third session together I realized that I was dealing with an egotistical chauvinist who felt like occasionally flirting outside the marriage was okay.

I quickly nipped that in the bud. Although we stopped going to counseling we kept our weekly dates. At the end of June, the arguments started back. Some girl named Latasha had been blowing Leonard's phone up. I politely grabbed my kids and prepared to leave; Leonard pushed me and told me I was not leaving. I of course yelled and pushed him back and hurriedly put the kids in the car. As I closed my door all I saw was a foot. The window broke and I put the car in drive. Just as I put my foot on the gas, Leonard jumped through the window pushing glass in my arm trying to grab the wheel.

As the kids were screaming I began to drive the car straight into the gate. I can honestly say it had to be an angel that flung that gate open because I had no intentions of stopping. Seeing that I was not stopping, Leonard retreated just before he was hit by the pole and fell to the ground. I wanted so bad to put the car in reverse, but when I looked back to do so, I only saw the terrified eyes of my children, red and full of tears. I put the car back in drive and drove to my apartment. I did not even realize that one side of my body was full of blood until I opened the car door. I hushed the kids and checked them to be sure they were okay and had not been cut by the glass.

Once inside, I locked all the locks and slid down to the floor, trying not to cry. Elizabeth ran upstairs and got some tissue and some peroxide. As I watched the tissue trail from the bathroom to where I was sitting, I squeezed back the tears remembering all too well how my little sister had run down the hall with the tissue after my mother had beat me with the shot gun. Once I cleaned up my arm, I laid the kids down for bed. Larry had already fallen asleep on my legs. "Good night baby girl, I love you," kissing her forehead. "I love you too Momma."

As I showered, I cried. God help me please. Standing in the mirror I looked at my phone, as it was ringing. I picked it up and turned it off. Placing it on the charger, I picked up my bible and turned in the back to marriage. As I picked glass out of my arm, I read 1 Corinthians 7, where it says that if the unbelieving spouse is willing to stay with the believing spouse then the marriage must remain. The next morning, I check my messages and all thirteen of them were from Leonard apologizing and begging for forgiveness. I called Linda and talked to her about getting a divorce.

She told me that God hated divorce and that I could not divorce him just because we argue and fight. Week after week as we continued our dates, I battled with wanting out. By the beginning of August I decided to give it my all. I prayed daily and threw myself into my work. At the end of August, Leonard and I moved into a house. I was excited about the move, because the kids had a yard to play in. Things were going well. Leonard and I were communicating better and I was actually considering going back to school in the spring. Of course, once things were better, he stopped coming to church, and started playing ball on Sundays again.

Things were even cool when Damon came to visit. In September Joy came down for her birthday. We had a blast up until when Leonard decided to complain about our music. "Turn that bull shit down." "Excuse me," I said. "Turn it down," he said. "Whatever," I said, turning back to Joy. Leonard walks up behind me and pushes me in my head. I get up and the cussing begins. Joy pulls me back and gives me a look and then looks at her bag. I shake my head, no and look back at Leonard. I turn the music off and tell Joy let's go. "What are you going to do about him hitting on you?

How long has this been going on," ask Joy. "It has been off and on for a few years now." "Years (while we are riding in the car) and he is still breathing," said Joy. "I know, I know." "Do you love him," she asks. "Honestly, no I don't. I have been dealing with that reality for a while now." "Well what are you waiting on," she asks. "Peace, I am waiting for peace to leave and not be condemned." That night when we got back to the house, I found my stuffed animal tiger in the middle of the hallway. It looked like it had been stepped on several times. Joy picked it up and gave it to me. As I lay on her back that night, staring up at the ceiling, I prayed, "God, I know that you hate divorce, and you also hate lies.

I feel like I am living a lie. I do not love him. Please speak to me. I don't want to do anything that is unpleasing to you." I got up and got my Bible and turned to Corinthians. Again, the scripture stood out that says, if the unbelieving spouse is willing to stay with the believing spouse then they have to stay, but if the unbelieving spouse wants to leave, then they are free to do so and the believing spouse is not held responsible. I closed the Bible and thought about that word believing. By the time I fell asleep, it was time to get up.

Leonard had already left for work and I had to drive Joy to the bus station. Embracing, "Reyne," says Joy. "Hmm?" "I love you," lifting up my head, "and you and the kids can always come to Louisiana with me. I know there is no mall, but at least you will be closer to your Dad and me." I smile and tell her, "I know, but I have to do it right. I have to make sure and I need Him to release me." Frustrated she says, "Okay girl, but please Reyne, don't make me kill him. I am shocked to know that he is still breathing this far." "Bye girl," I say shooing her to the bus. On the way home, I laughed and cried remembering all the hell Joy and I had been through.

I thought about the night my sister put me out and us sitting in front of a closed grocery store, waiting for Derrick to pick us up, the time she got pregnant with Andre and had to move back to Louisiana. Pulling back up to the house I sat there and concluded that Joy would be in my life forever and I would do all that I could to be there for her no matter what just like she is there for me. The following week was very strange. The world seemed extra sensitive. On TV they were showing excerpts from the 9/11 crisis that happened.

The more I watched, the more I thought to myself, "Do I really want to die unhappy, without experiencing true unconditional love and then go to hell?" Just the thought of such darkness saddened me all the more as I took a real good look around my surroundings. Later that evening Leonard came home with the kids and a gift for me. "Hey Baby," he says. "Hello Leonard, how was your day?" I ask while hugging my babies.

"Good," he says while walking towards the room. "Hey do not come in the room until I call you ok," says Leonard. "Okay," I say and continue playing with the kids. "Did you all have fun at Grandma Linda's house?" I ask Leonard and Elizabeth. "Yes, Momma we did. We played and watched TV. Grandpa Ray barbequed and..." "Reyne, Reyne," yelled Leonard. "What," I say. "Come here," says Leonard. "Alright hold on," I say irritated with him already.

I sat the kids down on the couch and went into the bedroom. "What's up?" I said to him, while he was sitting on the bed with this goofy look on his face. "What?" I say irritated. He just smiles and stares at me. "Leonard, come on now what do you want I was talking to the kids. What?" He says nothing still smiling. "Okay whatever," I say while turning to walk away. As I turn to walk out the room in the corner of my eye I see it. I rub my hand across it and say "Oh my you got me my own vanity table. Thank you so so much." He comes up to me and gives me a hug and says lifting up my head, "Now you can practice your make up without having to cover-up any scars," and he kissed my eye that he had blackened two years prior.

Weird thing him kissing my eye felt so wrong, something inside of me shivered and I pulled away. I felt completely violated even more so than when he would hit or curse at me, but for the life of me at that moment I could not figure out why but it continued to baffle me. He attempts to kiss my lips but as his lips got closer to mine I tensed up even more and closed my eyes. I saw a vision of me being in a tunnel and at one end there was a light and the other end was a tall dark figure that had a tight grip on me.

I pulled back just before his lips met mine and looked him in the eyes and I heard Hope's voice in my mind saying do not go with the tall dark man. He is not safe. He will hurt you. At that moment I realized those seven years ago when Hope and I were sitting on the stairs getting high she had warned me about this very situation that I now find myself married to. Trying not to show it in my face I backed away and told him I was going to check on the kids.

I went to the kid's bathroom and cleaned my face as hard as I could with soap. I scrubbed my eye so hard it hurt. Hope's birthday was coming up soon and so like I did every year I called her Mom's house and left a message telling her I miss her and Happy Birthday. The next few days' things were smooth or so they seemed to be. I talked to Leonard about church and he said he knew God but just did not want to be in church all day. Whenever I would say let's pray or read the Bible there was always some kind of conflict, so I just decided to leave it alone. By October we really had no relationship.

We were like two strangers under the same roof. I was light, he was dark. At about five one morning after Leonard had gone to work I got up to see what this irritating beeping noise was. I looked around and could not figure out where it was coming from. It sounded like it was by the door but when I walked over there the noise sounded further away. I stood in the middle of the bedroom closed my eyes and realized the noise was coming from the computer.

I click the mouse and lo and behold it read Steve 101 you've got mail. I say out loud who in the hell Steve is. I click open the message and it reads, "It has been really fun talking to you this past two months. I am looking forward to meeting you this weekend. Be sure to call me so I can give you directions," signed Lisa. Okay I am thinking maybe she sent this to the wrong person. Surely Leonard is not cheating also. So I go to the inbox and his profile sheet is flashing. I click on it and it says three new messages. All of them are from this Lisa person. I went to the deleted items but it was nothing there.

Then I checked the history and recycle bin and what you know a whole relationship had formed between the two of them. Nowhere did the messages mention him being married or in a relationship. It did state that he has a three year old son. He failed to mention anything about Elizabeth or myself. On his profile he has his name as Steve, single, and one son. I was more than livid. I wrote down the girl's number and waited until after the weekend to make my move. The next day after obtaining this new information I went out and got a second job to start saving my money to leave him for good this time. This was the icing on the cake I was completely done.

Friday night Leonard did not come home until almost five AM, neither did he answer any of my calls. I played it cool and did not bother mentioning his inconsiderateness. I reminded him that Saturday was my day to grocery shop so I needed some money. As he reached for his wallet his face suddenly changed and he jumped up and began searching all around, first his pockets, then under the bed, then the car. "Never mind," I said. "I will just stop on my way home from work." I kissed the kids goodbye and left him standing there looking dumbfounded.

Once at work I called Lisa and pretended to be an old friend from high school. I told her I would be in town and I wanted to see her. I got the idea from a story she put on her page about her most memorable moment in school. She said 8:00 would be good for her and gave me the directions. Of course I arrived extra early so I could case the place and right at 8 I called her to have her come outside. As she walked up to the car and I got out she instantly says "You're not Carol." I said "No I am not Carol. I am Reyne." "Reyne who are you and why did you say you were Carol and how do you know anything about me," she asks looking nervous.

I tell her look that is not important. What is important is the status of the man you have been talking to over the computer the last few months. "You mean Steve," she said. "Yes and his name is not Steve his name is Leonard," I said as I pulled out our family picture and showed it to her. "Oh my," she said, "you are his wife?" I raised my hand and declared that I was not there to hurt her only to get facts. "Have the two of you been intimate?" "No," she says quickly pulling herself together. "We just met in person one weekend." I asked her "So do you want to, did you all talk about it?" and then I stopped and caught myself. I backed away and told her "Never mind he will be free in a couple of months," and got back in my car.

I drove to the nearest store and stopped. I looked at myself in the mirror and said out loud, "What are you doing? You cannot divorce him unless he actually commits adultery." I throw up my hands and say God is this not enough. So what if he has not been intimate with her yet. The talking is bad enough. Please please God give me a way out of this. I pick up my Bible and turn to Corinthians again. The same scripture that states the believer is not held accountable if the unbeliever wants to leave keeps coming up. I closed my Bible and drove home seriously contemplating the pros and cons of divorce. As soon as I got settled here comes Leonard charging me up about calling the Lisa girl. "Excuse me," I said standing up. "How do you ask me about calling another female that you should not have been talking to in the first place? You have lost the little piece of mind you have left." He then pushes me in my head and begins calling me all kinds of names.

I grabbed the kids and I left. I went to talk to his stepmother Linda and she said that if I could not prove that he committed adultery, I would have to stay married to him. His biological Mom stated that I should just stay and finish school and then leave. I thought to myself both of yawl is crazy. They both were married to men that they did not really want to be with anymore. I went home and Leonard and I had a nice to the point talk. I told him, "Look this is what it is. I am willing to try one last time to work this out. I understand that you have not committed adultery, so according to what I have been told I have to stay. This is how it is going to be.

The holidays are coming up and the kids deserve to be in their home to celebrate a good Christmas. That gives you the rest of this month and all of November and until Christmas to get your act together, counseling, church, etc., whatever needs to be done. Handle it or I am out and I am never coming back ever." After that talk he played it cool for a little bit but needless to say no counseling or going to church took place. Damon came back in town and things just got worse.

One day he promised that we would have family time together after he came back from getting his license because of course he still had not found his wallet. He did not show up until 11 o'clock that night. I remained calm up until about six weeks later around the middle of November when the new license still had not arrived in the mail. When I asked him about it he jumped on the defense and began cursing and yelling. I was standing in the kitchen washing dishes as he continued to act a nut. I open my Bible and began reading the Word of God out loud.

He pushed it down and spat on me, continually yelling that he did not care about the Bible, about God, etc. I picked up the knife and as I got closer to him I looked into his eyes and saw pure evil. I dropped the knife and ran out of the house and drove straight to the church. "Please somebody pray with me." Sister Jackson, Rev Jackson's ex-wife prayed with me and told me God would forgive me for anything that I did. I went back to the house and through the rest of the month we slept in separate rooms. Larry's birthday came and went.

His party was nice and it was as if Leonard and I were the happiest couple ever although we barely said two words to one another the entire night. Finally Christmas came and after getting cursed out, hit and carried in the house by my neck and several nights of the kids and I sleeping in the car at the park it finally happened. Christmas day Leonard and I got into it about him buying a Christmas gift that he claims was for Linda when he is the one that stated we were not buying anyone anything for Christmas outside of the children.

After the argument the kids and I left and went to Linda's. I really needed someone to talk to badly but she said she did not want to be involved and it would not be a good idea for us to stay there. Being that it was Christmas I did not want to impose on any of my friends so we ended up just going back to the house. I would not dare tell my family what was going on because they would flip and I knew this was something I had to do alone because I had left once before and came back. So this time I needed to be sure that I did my best before I left.

The kids went to their room to play. Leonard was watching football and I was on the phone with Joy passing down the hall when I felt the remote hit me in the back. Leonard yells "Don't be talking about me you stupid bitch." "Girl this muthafucker done lost his mind. Let me call you back," I say hanging up the phone. I threw the remote control back at him and he comes charging down the hall and smudges my head into the kids bedroom door that I am so thankful was closed. I could hear them crying through the door. I kicked him as hard as I could and ran to the den to find my keys. He jumped me from behind and caused us both to go toppling over the Christmas tree.

Now I could hear the kids screaming as they watched what was happening. I yelled for Elizabeth to take her brother back in the room and close the door. Leonard then put his hands around my neck and began choking me and cursing me out. I kicked and pulled at his eyes as best as I could until finally he let go. As I grasped for air I picked up a box and hit him with it. I got up, grabbed my keys and ran out the front door. I got to the nearest payphone and called the cops. Just as the 911 operator came back on the line from placing me on hold I saw him speed by in the truck.

I screamed I know he did not leave my kids in the house by themselves. I told the operator, "Send the police he left my children," hung up and sped back to the house. I walked back in and Larry and Elizabeth were lying on the floor holding each other crying. The house looked as if a tornado had run through it. I grabbed them both in my arms and soothed them until the cops arrived.

The cops took pictures of my face and neck and the house. They told me I would have to come down to the station and file a report on Monday. After about three hours or so the kids finally settled down and fell asleep. As I tucked them in their beds I knew I had to get them out of here quick. I had saved two and half months' worth of checks in a separate account that Leonard did not know about and was skimming daily off of our main account to get us a place. Leonard came back and was still angry and began asking for the phone.

"I am about to call Joy," I said dialing her number. He snatched the phone out of my hand saying, "Give it to me you stupid bitch." I said "Do not call me that or snatch anything out of my hand again." He then threw the phone at me and I grabbed the iron. Just as I was about to hit him over the head with it he took it out of my hands and threw it at me. I heard a voice clear as day saying, "Leave now." I ducked and the iron hit the wall but the cord hit my eye. "Ahh hell no," I said, "I am gone."

I grabbed the phone to call the cops on my way out the room to grab the kids. He came and pulled the phone from my hands just as the operator was talking and punched me. I yelled, "Send the police," and crawled to the door. He threw the phone across the street and kicked me in my ribcage with his size 13 foot. I could not move for a good minute. The kids were awake by this time and Leonard had done jump back in his truck and was gone. I could barely move by the time the cops arrived. They put out a warrant for his arrest and I gathered enough items for a week and moved to Faith's. I still needed some more money before I could get my own place. After getting the kids settled one evening I went back to the house to get a few things. But on my way there I stopped by the police station and they said an officer would be there shortly. I walked in and the first thing out of his mouth is, "Where is my son?" I ignored him and grabbed what I needed and just as he was about to start arguing I walked out. I could hear the sirens coming as I backed out of the driveway.

I parked at the curb and walked back to the house just in time to see him being carried out to the police car in handcuffs. We made eye contact and he mouthed as they put him in the car "I am going to get you bitch." I gave no reaction, thanked the officer and began packing all the kids and my stuff. Although we could have stayed with Faith it was just too much for me, my children, her children, my drama, her drama. Uggh I just needed to get in a quiet place and think. Although Faith warned me not to, I went back to the house anyway.

Sitting there looking at all our stuff packed up I decided to call the landlord and show him the police reports and explain the situation in detail. This time I do not know if it was the bruises in my face or my out of place rib that made them change their mind but they finally let me out of the lease. Back in October when I had gone to them they gave me a pat on the back and told me to stay and work it out because all young couples start off having problems.

Sad to say it took them seeing the torn up house and all my bruises for them to finally understand that I was serious. They just kept apologizing. For the next few days I was tormented by Linda and Rev Jackson's voice telling me I could not get a divorce.

Again I turned to God and began to cry out. "Dear God I am sorry. I need you I am desperate Lord. I am anxious to leave but I need to be sure you will not be disgraced if I do so. I do not want to shame you. Please forgive me for being a failure at this. I am so sorry God." I cried and grabbed my Bible. I turned to Philippians 4:6-8 that says, Be anxious for nothing but in all things through prayer and supplication with thanksgiving, make your request known to God and He will give you the peace that surpasses all understanding and will guard your heart and mind in Christ Jesus. After reading that, I began to pour out my heart out to God even more.

As I poured out my heart I had a flashback to the day Leonard knocked my Bible to the ground and spit at me and cursed me and said he did not care about God. I also began to remember how funny he would act when it came down to going to church. Surely he could not be saved. Upon that revelation an overwhelming sense of peace came over me. "Oh God I thank you. I thank You Lord God for releasing me from this. Thank You Lord Thank You Lord," I shouted, "and please provide the finances so I can move."

The next day at work we received our W-2's early and I filed my taxes that day. The very next day I got my money and was approved for my apartment that Thursday and began the moving process. To my surprise my best friend Joy came down from Louisiana to help me move. By the time I dropped the kids off to my sisters Friday and picked her up from the bus station I only had the mattress, the 27 inch TV, and three boxes left to take to my new place. I dropped her off at the new place and went back to the old house to get the last of the stuff. On the way I was thinking how in the world am I going to get this mattress and this TV in this little bitty car.

In the midst of Leonard's stupidity he would threatened me about taking his car so I went out and got my own. It was a little red Passat. As I walked in I saw the torn up Christmas tree and began to remember all the drama. I was even more determined to hurry and get out of there as those memories began to flash in my mind. I found some rope and folded the mattress in half and tied it up and drug it down the hallway out the front door. Once out the door I unfolded it put it on top of the car and tied it down with the rope knotted on the inside. "Whoo," I say, "thank You Lord," wiping the sweat from my forehead. Now the TV.

I do not know where the strength came from but the Word does say when we are weak He is strong. I got the 27 inch TV in the car and placed some blankets around it, loaded the last three boxes and headed to my new home never to look back again. Riding down the street in my little red Passat I felt so thankful and liberated and was eagerly looking forward to my future without Leonard in my new place with myself and my children.

"This is definitely something I am going to have to get used to," I say to Joy while kicking up my feet on the couch. "What," she says, "being single?" "Yes Girl," I say. "Ahh Girl you will be alright. It is not like you are going to be single very long. You always have a list of options to call up if you feel like being bothered. And besides there is always Javier the master of lovemaking himself," she says tickling me on my side. "Yeah that is true," I say remembering his smile, "and the way he would always kiss me on my eye." I shudder at the thought because now I know why I felt so uncomfortable when Leonard kissed my eye. "Right now I have to focus and handle my business for my babies and me." "Well remember," says Joy, "yawl can always come home with me. We could get a house and raise our kids together."

"Thank you and I love you but no," I say shaking my head. We both laugh and then suddenly Joy stops laughing and grabs my hand. "Are you sure you are ok?" she asks sincerely. "Yes, Boo I am fine," I say with tears in my eyes placing my hand on hers. "I am just happy to be out of that relationship. I really wanted to kill him. But now I am just glad to be free and in my own home where my children can be happy and grow up without all the drama." Sitting up Joy grabs a handful of chips and says "Hm I am surprised you didn't. Why didn't you call someone, your family, Derrick, Javier, Walter, Anthony, anybody, somebody?" Shaking my head, "I couldn't. I had to be sure I did everything I could possibly do before I called it quits. I did not want

God to be angry with me or get anyone else involved and then end up going back or staying.

You know, I never wanted a failed marriage, so why get someone else involved and then end up going back. That just doesn't make any sense to me." Nodding her head, "Yes I understand that." "Besides you know Derrick'nem would have killed that boy and he is not worth me losing one of my partners over." "Yeah you right," she says shaking her head grabbing more chips. "Maybe if you would have called Javier's bluff some years ago you would have not went through this." I give her a look and say, "Girl now you know he was not ready for real." We both began to laugh and reminisce about all the fun times we had with Javier and Derrick.

Argument after argument is how my days seem to go. Shortly after Joy went back home Leonard got out of jail and was furious because I had taken everything. Oh he called day in and day out claiming that he wanted his family, when in actuality he did not even know what he wanted, each conversation ended in a screaming cursing match with the kids looking at me as if I was crazy. For a month and a half I cried out in anger almost every night. I had so much rage inside and was so furious with him as well as myself for putting up with it for so long, I did not know what to do.

Nothing seemed to soothe me except my Friday night ritual of going out. After a while even that got old. I would spend time with Javier here and there but even that became a dead end when I realized he was not ready for both the kids and me on a full time basis. His way of saying goodbye was to write me a poem about how much he feared the way I made him feel. I threw that in the bullshit a pile along with every other excuse I had been given in the past.

One day about February 2 or so Leonard called me and asked if we could do counseling because he wanted to at least try to make things right between us for his son. I told him fine but there was no way of us getting back together. In my prayer time that evening I acknowledged the fact that I was wrong for sleeping with Javier and my divorce was not final. Although Leonard and I were not together anymore it was still wrong because Javier and I were not married and Leonard and I were not divorced on paper yet. "Help me to deal with this anger; I have so much animosity towards Leonard," is what I cried out when we went to counseling. The Pastor decided that we needed to at least be friends for the kid's sake. He suggested that we go out together occasionally with and without the kids to develop trust and respect for one another again.

Of course I did not like this idea but was willing to give it a try if it meant getting rid of the rage. So on Valentine's Day of 2002 I let him take me to dinner. Big, big, huge mistake. I actually had fooled myself into thinking that Leonard and I could actually be in the same room for longer than five minutes without arguing. Back in the truck he began his usual ignorant behavior and I simply waited until we got to the red light, opened the door and stepped out. With each step I took I felt the anger leaving me. It was as if weights were being lifted.

I began to remember the scriptures that I had searched for in the Bible to help me deal with Leonard's stupidity and my own shortcomings. Each time he got closer to me in the truck I would cross the street. Finally he pulled up just close enough to throw my Valentines gift at me and call me a dumb bitch and sped off. I politely kept walking but suddenly stopped. I went back and picked up the gift and said out loud this would make a good birthday gift for someone. By the time I made it to Linda's to pick up the kids he was already there.

I walked in, said goodbye to Linda and hopped in my car that I had parked in the driveway when I met up with the nut for the stupid date. As we got in the car he came out yelling and cursing. I simply backed out and drove away. "Did Momma's babies have a good time?" "Yes Ma'am," they both replied with fear in their eyes as I backed out. That night I lay on my bed remembering the scared look on their little faces. I promised that I would never again allow him to hurt me or let them hear us arguing and fighting. Needless to say by March I broke that promise.

I was doing my usual at work on my break. As I pulled out to go and make the deposit a young boy in his early twenties swerved around a truck and hit my car sending me flying on top of the median. I was not injured, but my car was torn up pretty badly. My only concern was can I still drive it. Lord knows I did not have the money to purchase a new car. My supervisor came running across the street to see if I was hurt. I told him I had a little pain in my shoulder and neck area. As the ambulance arrived the young man who hit me gave me all his information and told me I better call it in quick because his 'Dad was going to kill him so he may not be around to testify.

As I argued that I could still drive the car with the tow truck driver I began to feel lightheaded near fainting. The EMT specialist took my vitals and said I should go to the hospital. My supervisor said he would handle the car. I begged him please do not let them take my car to a storage I do not have money for that please. God gave me favor because the tow truck driver took my car right to my apartments and parked it in the back. Once I was done at the hospital they diagnosed me with an anxiety attack and told me to get some rest. I was offered medication for future headaches but I refused because I despise taking medicine. I called my job to let them know I was okay.

It was Thursday so he told me to take Friday off and be in on Monday. I had no one to call for a ride so I took a cab home. In the cab I watched the meter and thought about how years ago we would dodge paying. I just laid my head back and realized I did not have the energy to do so if I tried. Once we pulled up I paid him the $15.71 and walked slowly to my apartment. When I walked in I sat on the floor and called the guy's insurance company. The man on the phone told me since I received the citation that they were not held responsible because I was in the wrong.

Needless to say I was furious. I began crying and screaming not knowing what to do. Shortly after my outburst my phone rang. Wiping tears and sniffling "Hello," I said. "Ms. Williams?" "Yes this is me." "Mr. Wilson with State Farm Insurance, you were in an accident today with my client. We are willing to pay for the damage to your car up to a certain amount but first we will need to have our guy come out and take an estimate." I agreed thankfully and hung up the phone. I called Linda to see if she could pick up the kids for me. She told me to call Leonard and have him pick me up. I begged her and she said no we needed to be able to work together in times such as these.

I called him and after a twenty-minute argument on him meeting me at the store and not at my new apartment he finally said ok. I walked about two blocks to the Randall's just so that he would not know where I lived because I still did not trust him at all. We arrived at Ms. Gloria's. I told her what happened and told her I would pick them up from school the next day. On the way back Leonard starts acting stupid and saying vulgar things about my driving as well as myself. I yelled for him to shut up and he cursed at me and threatened to put me out. His younger sister just sat in the front seat laughing as I commanded the kids to cover their ears so that they would not have to listen to such stupidity. With that said he pulls over and gets out of the truck. Comes to the back door and begins pulling me out cursing me out. I fight as much as I could but still weak from the medication I lost the battle badly and ended flat on my butt on the side of the road. I yelled as he drove off, "Give me my kids." I could hear them screaming in the back as he drove away, I chased the truck but he slammed the brakes and u-turned. I began to walk not exactly knowing where I was going.

Suddenly from behind I hear a car. As I turn Leonard yells "You stupid bitch I hope you die," and throws a cup of sprite all over me speeding off quickly. That was it. I was so angry I could not even cry. I made up in my mind that he would never get that close to my kids and me again. I realized I was right by the church so headed in that direction. Once I arrived I was compelled to go into the sanctuary. Pastor was teaching on tithes. One of the ladies handed me a packet that said New Members Orientation.

I thought to myself I have been a member at this church for 5 years and have not even thought about orientation. As he spoke he said that no matter what we should pay our tithes on everything we get. I raised my hands and asked, "What if your light bill is due and you only have enough money for that, do you still pay your tithes?" He said yes indeed my child the word says right there in Malachi that if you do this God will rebuke the devourer. That word was like fire to my heart. After class was over, one of the ladies that Linda had introduced me to a while ago asked me if I was ok. I told her no and that I needed a ride to get my children and back home. She called Linda and Linda informed me that the kids were there and that she was aware of what happened and that she deeply apologized. At that moment

I could care less about her apology because if she would have just helped out in the first place none of this would have happen but then again I would have not heard the teaching. Ms. Katrina drove me to get the kids and then home. On the way I told her about Leonard and she assured me that God would restore all that had been given up and lost and that I would be ok. She also encouraged me to come out to Woman Christian Fellowship every night at 6:30. I thanked her. My neighbor was pulling up as I opened my door. She asked me if that was my car in the back. I told her yes and she offered to take the kids to school and me to work. I thanked her and went inside. I hugged my babies and bathed them and went to sleep.

I was exhausted. The next morning my neighbor took me to take the kids to school and dropped me at the rental car place. I had paid off my credit card and was literally debt free other than my normal monthly bills. I had to keep the rental for two weeks until the adjuster came out and looked at my car. During those two weeks I emailed the youth and young adult Pastor about my anger towards Leonard. He then emailed me back and told me to write down everything that bothered me and find scriptures to put with it and read those and study Jesus' character in different situations. If nothing else I learned that Jesus was a healer and I spoke those scriptures over my children every time they got a cough and immediately it would be gone.

The scriptures even helped me to not argue with Leonard. Now I just put down the phone and said ok when I figured he was finished. The more I read the Word and learned who Jesus is the more I changed. After the adjuster came he summed up the damage to be about $2500. My car was picked up by the mechanic of their choice and I was given a loaner car until mine was to be completed. In about a week and a half I received a call from the mechanic and he said my car was totaled and was not worth fixing. I called the insurance company and they paid the car off. I asked could they come and pick up the loaner car from the car dealership because I was going to get me a new car. They said yes so I called Anthony and he gave me $300 to put down on a new car.

Once at the dealership I walked around to see what I could find. It felt so different actually doing this on my own. The last time Leonard was breathing down my back throwing in his own opinions, never really letting me say what I truly wanted. I was determined to get a truck. I wanted a Ford Escape because that is what I felt I had finally done escaped the drama of Leonard. The price was not too bad but from the looks of things there was no way I would be able to get my payments under $400 without putting more money down. The sales person that was helping me insisted that I put at least $1000 down. I called my brother and agave him the details. He told me not to do it and to get something new not used and only put $300 down and stand your ground at least until my note was under $350.

I did exactly that and ended up gaining the attention of the manager of the dealership, Mr. Bud Reed himself. "Hello there," he slithered like a reptile, "how can I help you?" "I would like to leave here today driving a new 2003 vehicle with a note under $350." "Ok no problem, I can make that happen. Let's go and take a look at the used cars," he says turning towards the door. He looked back and said, "Aren't you coming?" I looked up at him and said, "Did you not hear what I said, I do not want a used car I want a new car. New meaning never been driven, never been rode in, new fresh off the truck." He stepped back, cleared his throat, and said, "Yes mama; I will show you whatever you want. Let's go look at the new cars." Once outside in the new car section he took me over to the Ford Focus, and asked how about this and began describing the details of the car.

I looked at the car and said no. Next he took me to the 4 door Escorts; I said no, then he took me the Taurus I said no. "Well madam what is it that you want?" he asked. "I want a Ford Escape," but thinking to myself remembering what my brother had told me about my driving being too bad, because they may flip over, "I think I will stick with something small, like that over there." Over and way down towards the end of the lot were the Ford ZX2. "This is it, this is what I want." The price was good and I liked it. "Does it come in blue?" I asked him. "No I am sorry we do not have any blue ones," he said. "Ok that is fine I'll take the light gray one." Walking back he began to ask questions about my job and my life.

He mentioned the fact that I seemed like a young lady who knew exactly what I wanted and got it no matter the cause. I told him I just have a way with people that seems to always get me my way. "Well you surely do because here I am the owner of this dealership and out here in this heat walking it trying to help you find a car." "Good, I said, "so that means you are doing my paper work as well right?" I said walking into the building heading towards his office. As the process got started I called Anthony and told him that I could put $300 down and my notes would be less than $350, I assumed because the ZX2 was cheaper than the Escape. Anthony said cool and I went from there. Bud came back into his office and said, "You really do not make enough money to get this car.

The bank will not finance you unless you can put more money down." I leaned forward and said, "Question, are you the owner?" He said yes. "Ok and you can override and overrule decisions right?" "Yes, but there is procedure and protocol." Waving my hand to silence him, "I am not concern about protocol nor procedure, there is some kind of way that you can get me financed for this car with $300 down and my notes under $350. He backed up slowly with a twisted smile and said, "I will do my best little lady to make you happy." About an hour had gone by and my stomach began to growl.

Bud looked up from his desk and said, "Are you hungry?" I chuckled a little grabbing my stomach and said yes. He said "There is a McDonalds up the street, you can still catch breakfast it's only 10:08." "Well I have to wait because I already had the people from the mechanic shop come and pick up the car." He pulls out this black little square box and says "Here take mine." I picked up the box and said as I fumbled with the box, "Where is the key?" He took it out of my hand and pushed a little button and out popped a silver key. I took the key and said "Which car is yours?" He looked at me strange and said "That one," pointing out the window, "the Black 545 Mercedes Benz." "Oh ok, do you want anything?" I asked.

Reaching in his pocket he hands me a fifty dollar bill and says "No just get whatever you want, and you have to move the seat up from the side." I open the door to the car and sit down. The car was huge enough for me to sleep in. I tried my best to find the button to push the seat up but after several minutes or so Bud came out and reached over me and touch some button and the seat began to move up. With his face being so close to mine I could not help but see into his eyes. I raised my arm as to move him and said thank you, shaking off what I thought I had seen. As I close the door he says, "Be careful now it's a big one," smiling that sleazy smile. I shook off the chills that ran up my spine and continued on to McDonalds. I arrived just in time for the breakfast. Heading back I looked around the car and it looked as if he lived out of it. There was a gym bag and towels and shoes all in the back. I thought about my old self and wondered should I rob him and then quickly dismissed the thought because surely I am not that person anymore.

Back at the dealership I pulled in and he told me that I would be getting financing through Ford Motor Credit. I called Anthony from another room and he said cool. Back in Bud's office once I finished my breakfast he asked me was I married. I told him no, and that I was getting a divorce. Then he went into how some men do not know they have a good thing until it's gone. I said "Oh well how much are my notes going to be?" He pulled the paper work and said approximately $420 a month. By the time I finished my note had gone down to $326.40. I drove off with one year of free oil changes, a five-year warranty on the car and a lifetime warranty on the parts, brakes, battery, etc. Oh yeah and a coupon to come back next week for a fill up and a detail. Also one of my latches was loose so they would fix that next week. Mr. Bud asked could he call me I told him no. Once on the freeway I smiled from the inside out happy that I had my own car again.

I went to Linda's to pick up the kids that next day and lo and behold guess who was there. No sooner had I walked in the house it started. "Why did you send them over here without a toothbrush, and why is all his clothes wrinkled?" I politely walked by and gave Linda a hug and told her thank you. "Come on kids lets go," I said heading towards the door. Once outside Leonard comes behind me yelling and cursing saying "Bitch I know you hear me talking to you." As I open the door I told him to leave us the hell alone. Needless to say that started an uproar. As soon as I closed my door he kicked it and I began to get out but the kids screaming and crying "Let's go home" made me rethink that. I told him he would pay dearly for that. Shortly after that incident his truck was repossessed. As soon as I got in the house the phone began ringing off the hook. Once I got the kids calmed down I answered it. Yep you know it was Leonard with all kinds of threats and obscenities.

I began to yell, curse, and scream back at him, and of course the kids began crying again. I slammed down the phone and unplugged it from the wall right when it began ringing again. I got the kids calm again and asked them how their weekend was as we curled up on the couch together. With Larry just turning four and Elizabeth coming close to seven I knew I had to do the right thing by my children. "Momma is that our car?" "Yes it is baby girl; we have a brand new vehicle." "Momma why did my Daddy kick your car?" asks Larry. "Momma do I still have to call him Daddy, I don't like him. He is mean," says Elizabeth. "Whoo, one question at a time. Elizabeth what is a Daddy?" "A Daddy is someone who loves you and spends time with you and takes care of you making sure you have everything you need." "Do you feel like Leonard does that?" "No Ma'am," she says. "Ok well it is up to you if you want to call him Daddy." "No I don't want to." "Ok well you do not have to. Larry I do not know why your Dad kicked the car. He is angry and bitter." "Momma are you supposed to cuss?" ask Larry, "Because you said some bad words while you was on the phone." "No Baby we are not supposed to curse and Momma has to work on that." "Have you prayed about it?" asked Elizabeth. "No but I need to and I will."

That next week I went back to the dealership to let them fix my handle and detail my car. Mr. Reed asked what happened and I told him. He suggested that we go for a ride and grab some lunch because it would be at least an hour before the car would be ready. We climbed into his Range Rover and headed to Jack-In-The Box. I knew I could have gotten a steak dinner but I was hooked on those Ultimate double cheeseburgers with lettuce and tomatoes. On the way back he asked again could he call me. I told him yes. In about the third week of April he called and asked could he come by to talk. I had just finished an argument with Leonard so I could use the conversation. He bought pizza and the kids ate while we talked. 8:00 rolled around and I put the kids to bed.

I tried to escort him out before I did that but he kept talking, because I had them on a specific schedule I had to put them to bed. Back in the living room he asked me was I looking to get into a relationship. I told him no and I was not interested in anybody. He then said "Not even me? I have a big house and lots of money. Not to mention I know you liked driving my big Benz," he said lustfully. I stood up and said "YUCK, first of all I was hungry and you let me use your car because the loaner was already in use. Secondly I do not care if you had five big houses and fifty dealerships." He stood up and said "You mean I got you all those good deals and warranties and you not go give me none?" "What you black son of a so and so if you do not get out of my house I will skin your balls and make you eat them for dinner.

Get the hell out of here now you dirty bastard. I do not want you I thought you were being kind, get out." He walked to the door opened it and never looked back. In about three weeks about the second week in May I went to work anticipating my third year annual review. I just knew I was going to get a raise. Finally at about 2:00 my boss John Smith called me in his office. Once I walked in and sat down I did not have the same happy feeling I had had all day. Simian my supervisor was inside and their faces did not look like I would be getting a raise. Jeff began by telling me how much of a good worker I was and Simian nodded and agreed. Then it hit. "Due to your personal life seeming to affect your work environment we are going to have to let you go.

Your ex-husband cannot keep calling here plus we are downsizing anyway because in one month the office will be closing and everything will be handled from corporate. We are sorry. Here is your last check." I took the check and looked at Simian and walked out. On the drive home I began to cry. I noticed it was time for the kids to get out of school so I went by Ms. Gloria to let her know that I would be picking them up and they would no longer be coming. She told me that was fine and if I needed her to keep them while I go on interviews she would. I called my Mom and told her and she told me to call the dealership and asked them what could be done being that I had just purchased my car. Of course Bud laughed in my face and told me nothing and hung up the phone in my face.

I later found out that I could defer a payment by calling the finance company. So my payment for May was deferred. I picked up the kids and when we got home they seemed severely hungry. I was down to two packs of meat and my check was only enough to cover my tithes and the bills. Not to mention on top of all of that I had to give a testimony at church about my recent deliverance out of a bad relationship, to the youth.

Once I arrived at church I went to the restroom and looked in the mirror. "God who am I to stand before these individuals and give my testimony? I am nothing; I have made so many mistakes and am no-where near perfect. I have been bluntly disobedient," and "Oh Hi," I say startled to find a young lady standing there looking at me with such questionable eyes. She said "Don't be nervous you will do fine. I am sure whatever you have to say will help us and they'll love you. Don't be afraid. Bye now." Wow I thought to myself and straightened up. I walked out and signaled that I was ready. Kevin called me up and introduced me and from that moment on my life changed because I took a position to speak the truth and uncover my sins that I was once so ashamed of.

Right after that the Choir Director Ms. Joyce asks me to join the young adult choir workshop. I told her I was 23 years old. She said that was ok and told me that I encouraged her by standing up speaking about such a true reality for so many women. I thought to myself, all I did was told how I left an abusive man whom I should not have married in the first place and how through reading the Bible I was healed from all the penned up anger. One of the songs we learned in the workshop is titled God Can. The Director and his wife taught us the song and I sang that song so much that even my kids learned it. They liked it so much we put it on the voicemail at home singing it. One night at rehearsal a guy named Tyler asks me to join his singing group called Purpose.

I informed him that I was really not a singer but I could dance. He told me to sing something, so I did. He then said "We can work with you. You are an alto." He introduced some of the people in the group to me and one of the girls just so happened to be the young lady from the bathroom the night I gave my testimony. "Hi I am Samantha," she says smiling. "I am Reyne." They began discussing practice times and dues and things like that. I quickly made them aware that I had just lost my job and was not too sure about paying any dues. That following Sunday one of the matrons of the youth choir called me to her after church.

As I approached she told me that she had something for me. So, cautiously I walked over to her car with her. She popped open her trunk and what do you know it was full of groceries. I fell to the ground thanking God because just the night before I was crying out to Him because I was down to nothing. Elizabeth had spilled the last of the milk and I broke. The kids politely left the kitchen and began playing. The Spirit of the Lord spoke to me and said "Get up, look at your children. They do not worry about anything. Why then should you?" And now today here it is God has blessed me with food. I later in life came to realize that the blessing had already come the moment God spoke and gave me peace.

The food was just a physical manifestation. I could go on and on about those three months from May to the end of July about how God blessed me with everything I needed physically and mentally but that stuff is a given that will come when you begin walking in faith and repentance. Not one bill went unpaid. There were places that helped pay lights and rent. Although the process was nerve wracking if you want your bills paid you will do it. After the workshop I began assisting with the youth ministry. In my doing so I realized that there were a lot of things that I did not know about the Bible or God.

One night about mid-July I came out of Bible Study overly excited. "What are you so happy about?" asked Tina, one of the girls from the group. "I just found out that once you receive Christ in your heart you cannot go to hell. Isn't that amazing? The entire...wait a minute," I say, "you don't look excited. Where is William?" William was Samantha's brother. He played the keyboard for the church as well as for the group. I turned and walked off excitedly with the kids tagging behind me. "William, William!" I yell, across the parking lot. "Yes, Reyne, are you ok?" William asked reaching out his hand to steady my fall. "Am I ok? I am more than ok. I am overjoyed." "Great, I am happy for you." "Did you know that we cannot go to hell because Jesus lives in our heart?" "Why yes, Reyne, I did and that is exciting," says William. "I knew you would understand," giving him a hug. As I walked back to my car I did not realize the stares and murmurs that were directed my way from individuals in the group.

The next night at rehearsal, a young lady named Beautiful, who had watched the kids for me a few times, mentioned that she wanted to move. I told her she was more than welcome to come and live with me but remember I am not working yet, it is truly the grace of God that has and is sustaining us this far. That night she drew up a contract and a set of rules. We discussed them over dinner and she called her Mom in the Bahamas for me to speak with her. That following Saturday she was all moved in and settled. I had rehearsal that morning so she offered to keep the kids for me. In rehearsal the whispering and eye rolling began again.

As time went on I grew more and more irritated. How is it that we could be standing there singing about Jesus and how much we love Him when we really did not love one another nor like each other for that matter? "I cannot take this anymore," I yelled and walked over to Tina the ringleader of it all. "Why is it that you don't like me? What did I do to you?" I ask with tears in my eyes. "What, I just don't like you?" she says with an attitude and shocking look on her face. "I don't understand that. How can we sing praises to God and yet when I walk in here you all treat me like dirt. Is this what love is all about? Is this the way we are to display Jesus? Look," I said walking down the steps turning to face everyone. "This is it; the point is God is sovereign. Yes I sinned. Yes I lied sometimes. Yes I was selfish and may still be a little. But all in all God is God. There has been purpose in the midst of the pain, even after I thought I completely surrendered. There is still lessons to be learned; lessons, to be taught and lessons to be lived out, one story today and another story tomorrow." "Regardless if you do it now or do it later you're going to do it. This is not a game, its real life. Jesus died for you and me because we were sinners. No I don't have a big fancy house nor a luxurious car but what I do have is freedom.

Freedom from sin, freedom from Egypt, freedom from lack of understanding, and more than anything freedom from self, the captivity of Babylon. You see having faith, believing God for the impossible is not about name it and claim it, it's not about sowing a financial seed, it's not about being seen, it is about Jesus. No not just the man coming down and giving His life, not just the name that we yell when things are not going right, but Jesus the Savior, the Redeemer, the very Lamb of God, God Himself who hung bled died yet rose for you and for I. You see struggling and hardships are not so much about the pain but about the knowledge you learn from it. Being ridiculed and ridiculing is not so much about the hurt, but suffering and being humbled is about Him, the One who hung, bled, died, for you and for I.

This life is neither about us nor our troubles, situations, circumstances, but it's about our Redeemer being revealed in this world. Not just the One that hung but the One that as He hung He bared all of our sins that they may no longer be hung over our heads. Not just the One that bled but the One that as He bled you, me, we became cleansed, cleansed from that which was hung. Not just the one who died to self, conquering death that we too may die daily to overcome, conquer, and destroy that which brings death making us as He to take part in the rising of the newness of a victorious life no longer bound by sin. The focus of what Jesus did is not that He came here as a sinless individual but that His obedience fulfilled all of our disobedience.

So to sum it all up, yes we've all made some bad choices but through the burial, the bleeding the dying and the rising we too like Jesus come to a place of obedience. The only sin that inhabits the world is disobedience. The only Savior from that is Obedience, Jesus, Yeshua. So basically please stop talking about me as if you all have never done anything wrong and if we are going to sing about Jesus than sing with meaning and understanding, not what is popular and sounds good. Dang," I say walking out the door shaking my head. Not realizing that I had just spoken and prophesied not only of my past but my future as well, I sat in my car and began to cry. As I drove home, I just could not seem to understand why I always seemed like the outcast. Everywhere I went and everything I did people did not like me for it.

Once I reached home Beautiful saw my expression and sat me down and told me to pour it all out. I told her what happened and had been happening through sobs. She held me and prayed my strength. Beautiful had become a dear friend over time. She always encouraged me and tried to warn me that everyone was not who they appeared to be. It was hard for me to see this because I really wanted to believe that everyone could play in the sandbox together but I was about to learn that surely everyone cannot be in your front row. Once I was settled she let me go and I thanked her and went in my room to shower and go to bed. Looking in the mirror the thing I found the strangest though was I could not get angry at these people for their two faced ways.

Usually I would not deal with females like that or anybody for that matter but something inside of me was changing. I was nice to people that were intentionally ugly towards me. Weird I know but that is one of the many things that happen when you allow God in your heart. At one service a prophet came and spoke. She told me that God would restore all that I had given up for Him. She told me that I would have a marriage and we would walk in ministry together over youth. She also told me that I could not walk in the fullness of what God had for me until I married. I would have another house. Deep down I guess that is truly what I wanted, what I did not have as a kid and a home with two parents in it raising the children and a yard for the children to play in.

I opened myself up to this prophecy only to hear it three other times from people all in the offering line. Javier and I had gotten back in touch with one another and would spend ample time together but it did not take me long to realize he was still not ready. Don't get me wrong I enjoyed his company but church was not really a part of our daily conversation or should I say nightly. Jacob and I would talk every now and then but I had absolutely no interest in him whatsoever. He still proclaimed that I was the only woman for him. I constantly reminded him we were 10 and he stole a kiss. Finally in July a company called me for an interview.

Shortly after that call three other companies called. I went to each interview and was offered a position from each. I chose the one that not only paid the most money but was closest to my apartment. I was so happy to be working again. The Company needed a receptionist. Samantha had mentioned she was looking for work so I told her about the position. She was quite skeptical at first so I told her look you can ride with me. I also informed her that she could ride in the back for all I cared; I was just trying to help her out. After my outburst at rehearsal everyone was somewhat distant. She took the job and we became very good friends. We would pray every day together but her behavior would change at practice and around Tina. I did not care though; I still treated her nicely which was sort of a challenge for me and amazing that it came so easily to me.

One evening after an event we went to go eat at Denny's. Sitting at the table Samantha and I were talking when I looked up and was captivated by what I saw. He was tall, with smooth milky chocolate skin and a smile that would make even a dyke quiver. Samantha immediately said, "Nope he is mine." I asked her was that her man she said no. I asked again out of respect, "Do you plan on having him as your man?" She said, "No." "Call me crazy but a no to both of those questions means that this brother is free and unattached, right?" I asked her. She said, "Yes," and I just smiled and said "Hm." Not to mention she was dating someone. I asked her one last time if she liked this guy and she said no she was just playing. So I made my move. Growing up in the 90's we had rules about dating someone we knew a friend or semi-associate was interested in without permission.

Sadly I did not know that this younger generation had no such rules. We made eye contact and it was over from there. About a month or so later we found each other's company to be quite comforting. He was a nice young 19 and I was four months away from 23. Not that much of an age difference. Something about this young man Dominic intrigued me and something about me intrigued him. Because I was always at the church in practice or bible study the kids became quite familiar with the members of the choir and the group. It was a blessing having people to help me out with them.

One night Dominic and I decided to go out. We had a blast. It was his first time in a club and well since I was not having sex, since Javier decided to run off claiming he was fearful dancing was my way of releasing all of my penned up energy. When we got back to the house I showered due to all the sweat from dancing and he cooked me an omelet. Not only did he feed it to me but he massaged my feet as well and my back and neck. I was amazed at the skill level this boy maintains, not knowing that he had studied all his moves from romantic movies and love songs. Dominic and I became not only lovers but each other's comfort zone. The comfort I used to get from Javier whom I missed dearly I begin receiving from Dominic. Although Javier was the best homey lover friend I ever had up until I met Dominic who has the most unique way of making love to my mind with the conversation that in all honesty had nothing to do with lovemaking.

Dominic is a charmer but is very intelligent as well. Javier was a good listener and lover but Dominic challenged me to think and re-search. He pleased more than just my body. He ignited passion in me that I did not know was there. Although I sensed the same fear in him that Javier wrote about in the poem he gave me I just told myself I would enjoy the time I had and move forward from there. This way when and if he left I was mentally prepared and not shocked or con-fused. The thing that drew us together the most was the challenging conversations we dabbled in which I have to admit were very intriguing and a huge turn on.

When he tore his ACL I prayed with him. When Tina's mess got overwhelming or Leonard's insults overbearing he prayed with me. It quickly became about the peace that surrounded us when we were together rather than the sex. When he whined and got down on himself I reminded him of who he was and told him stop acting like a wimp. Upon him getting better he moved back to Louisiana. I was happy for him and wished him the best. My life went on and about September that is when the counterfeits started. First there was Henry, a guy I met on my sister's Dad's side of the family reunion in Louisiana. We exchanged numbers and shortly after that he asks me to marry him. It had to be about two weeks after we met.

The prophet said that it would be a quick engagement and that it would not take long so I thought maybe this is it. Not to mention he was involved in helping the youth at his church as well. The only dilemma was I was not moving to Boston, he would have to come here. While he worked on a transfer from his job he came here to visit. We had a blast. He fit right in with the church people and the kids seemed to like him but I was still not sure. In November he asks me to come to Boston. This was my first plane ride so of course I was a little nervous. I asked Samantha to come with me and she did. She actually hooked up with one of his friends and we made it a double date. I felt bad for her though because the dude was not handsome at all. She handled it like a trooper though and made it work. While visiting some things did not sit well with me about the relationship between him and his child's mother. They seemed to still be together.

Samantha and I headed back to Houston. I called him to let him know I made it home and that is when he told me the truth. I was disgusted but chopped it up and kept on moving. At church another prophecy came for me not to give up on marriage. One day I was taking a nap when I saw a figure walk across a stairwell in my sleep. I began clutching at my chest and grasping for air while I was sleeping. Beautiful must have heard me because she came into the room and began to shake me awake. She grabbed my hand and loosened my grip on my necklace. She asked me if I was ok and I told her that I had a dream.

The next day I got a phone call from Ray saying that Damon, Leonard's best friend had died last night around the same time I was taking my nap. Come to find out he went upstairs to lie down and his lungs collapsed. They found him with his necklace in his hand ripped off his neck. This shook me but I knew what it meant. It meant that the dreams were back. I called Leonard at work and spoke to him briefly. He was very sad and to make matters worse the day before he had just signed the divorce papers, I went to Damon's funeral against my own rules about not going to funerals to be a support system to Leonard and Erica. Samantha came with me as my strength. After the wake everyone gathered at Ricardo's house. Samantha and I went.

It was funny seeing the people that Leonard would hang out with all night when we were married. They knew of me but no one had ever seen me other than Damon. Damon and I were pretty cool. He was happy for me when I told him I left Leonard because he did not agree with him hitting on me. The next day standing at the funeral looking at the body next to Leonard it was almost as if I could feel Damon smiling down at me saying I am proud of you. I smiled warmly inside and headed to Ricardo's for dinner afterwards. At dinner there was a guy there named Lewis. I noticed him the night before but I never said anything to him.

This time it was not that easy to get by. He pulled me over by the stairs and began talking to me. He told me he heard Damon mention me before but never knew I was so beautiful. We exchanged numbers and for about two weeks I ignored his calls. In Bible study one night some-one said if a man tries to talk to you invite him to church. Beautiful had been trying to get me to come out on Monday nights to hear this man speak and I would always say no. This time I decided to say yes and I invited Lewis to come with me. There were only two seats left in the front. So we had to walk to the front and sit there. The man speaking called Lewis up and began to tell him things about his life. Lewis began to shed a few tears and then he asked him who I was Lewis said my wife but she does not know it yet.

The man said you are right you are just waiting on God to tell her that. You all met at a funeral and when you saw her you knew she was the one. In my head I'm thinking yeah right, I am not trying to marry this man. I am trying to get my house and take care of my babies. Well it was almost as if the man heard what I was saying and said you worried about a house. This man is go put you in a million dollar home in a million dollar neighborhood. When yawl get married yawl go get 20 million. Then he said he will put you through school and you all will be ministering together.

Upon saying that, he asked for his bull horn and poured oil in it and then anointed Lewis to preach God's Word. He told him he did not have to wait to go to school to start preaching but that he could do it as soon as he finished the assignment God had given him which was to read the entire Bible. On that note I bought into it. Hook line and sinker. In about two months my lease was up and I could not renew it because I was making too much money to live on that property because it was low income housing. Lewis had just sold his house and suggested we just get a place together. Beautiful had already moved in with her boyfriend and his Mom. They had gotten married and were saving for their own place. So I went and found a place and did all the paperwork. I was a little shaky because for one, I could not really afford the place by myself, and for two, I vowed to never live with another man unless we were already married. Lewis assured me that no matter what happened he would help me with the rent and that we would be married soon anyway so it would not hurt.

We moved in together and for a while things were good. Almost a year into it he began to ask me to do things that I was not comfortable with. He said that he wanted to have a threesome before he started preaching to get it out of his system. He began suggesting friends that I could ask to join us and told me that he knew I would be woman enough to handle it because I was very secure in myself. For a moment I thought about it and my girl and I joked around about it but we both said no after careful consideration. The more I tried to plan it the more something did not sit right. So I went to God about it. Immediately a big NO came, I told him that I would not engage in such activity and I was offended for him even asking me to do so. Needless to say his behavior changed and he started to treat my children differently from his own.

On that note I began to devise a plan to leave him but there was only one small factor. The apartment was in my name and I needed his half of the rent. For Thanksgiving we went to his Mom's house and he acted a plum fool, so much so that I spit in his face because he had the audacity to tell me that he would have his threesome with someone else and come back to me when he was done so we could go on with our lives. I spat directly between his eyes and dared him to come near me or my children again. I really tried to be patient and wait for December's rent money but I could not take any more. He packed his things and got to stepping. I was devastated. I was madder at myself than anything for even allowing him to talk to me about such a thing and to exclude my children from certain activities because he claims they were too young.

Yeah true enough his kids were older but still you are supposed to teach your younger sibling's basketball and football no matter if they understand the game or not. Sitting in that apartment feeling like a fool, no furniture only my kid's beds and dressers because I had given all my stuff away, I had no idea how the rent was going to get paid. They had fired both Samantha and me back in October when we got a new CEO who did not want prayer in the office. I had used most of my savings and was out of luck. I could not ask my family because I was lending them money. I bit my tongue, called him and asked him for the rent money reminding him of his promise. He just hung up the phone.

The next day I got a call from his cousin. A few weeks prior to our break up they tried to tell me that he was not a good match for me and I should consider ending the relationship. I informed them that I was contemplating that and thanked them. They came to visit and gave the kids two bags full of brand new toys and a check for the amount I needed for December's rent. Larry and Elizabeth were so thankful for their Christmas gifts. All I could do was thank God for providing for my children and me again after I had messed up once again. As we sat in the empty living room eating dinner I told them that Lewis and I were not together anymore. They both said, "Good," and began to tell me the horrible way he treated them when I was not at home. He would make them go to their room and stay in there while he and his friends played dominos.

They told me that they did not like him and were glad he was gone. After putting them to bed I cried like a baby because I could not believe I had been in a relationship with this man for nine months and did not see that my kids could not stand him. I felt like a horrible mother. I was so involved with work and church that I did not even see that they were unhappy. I was glad this relationship was over but not glad that I was still in that apartment. I tried to make a payment plan with the management but they were not trying to hear it. The apartments had recently gone under new management because the old management was not abiding by the rules. Come to find out the lady who leased me the apartment did not even verify my income she just gave me the apartment.

The requirements were you had to make three times the rent, and I only made two. Management was not willing to cut me slack so I turned in my notice and moved out without paying the finals month's rent. I moved in with my friend Keisha and her two boys. She had just recently gone through a break up and could use the help. I got a job at a collection agency which for me was short lived because I could not stand calling people harassing them for money. I went to a temp agency and they sent me on an interview for a church that needed a receptionist. I got the job and was very happy. Faith came back in town in January and her, Keisha and I went out and celebrated her birthday. The three of us turning 25 was no joke. That was like a landmark for us all. I got my belly button pierced and began getting my nails done and my eyebrows arched on a regular basis. Funny because I was always such a tomboy I never thought I would enjoy those things but I did. I even started wearing dresses and heels with my jeans to the club.

One day in February the phone rang. I had transferred my phone to Keisha's house since she did not have a house phone. "Hello," I said. "Hello to you, Ms. Williams." My heart started to beat hearing his voice. "Hello Mr. Perry," I replied. It was Dominic. We talked long enough for him to tell me he would be in town in two weeks. Those two weeks could not go by fast enough. I took the kids to my sisters for the weekend and was looking forward to another omelet and massage. Well no omelet, and no massage, he called me and told me he would have to reschedule due to some family situations. I was so disappointed. I really thought I would not be alone for Valentine's Day. My girls said well you might as well join the party. We had shrimp, chocolates, champagne, chocolate covered strawberries and a 'fuck every man whoever hurt us or lied to us' hat. As I observed the scene after the girls were passed out drunk, I stared out the patio window and prayed. "God I do not want to be alone, send my Boaz to me." I cried gently and went to sleep dreaming of how wonderful things would be when he finally did come.

CHAPTER 8
Counterfeits: Confused but not Condemned

You see I still had not got it yet. Although through all this time God was showing me how much he loved me and desired to be close to me I was still searching for love in a human being. Time went on and yep you guessed it too many cats in one house. With Faith moving in and her habits and me being a neat freak we all started clashing, I went to my friend Charity, the lady I had met in the apartments Lewis and I used to live in to look for a place on her computer. Charity is older than I and began to drop some grown woman wisdom on me. I really appreciated her for this and began helping her with her expos and art shows. The kids and I stayed in a hotel for two weeks after a big falling out with Keisha.

By March I had moved into my own apartment close to Samantha and a few other people from the group. This worked out perfectly because I went to school at night and was in need of a sitter. Samantha or Tina would watch the kids for me. One night I got a call from Charity asking me to help her make some baskets. "Yeah I can," I told her.

"Tina is with me so can she come too?" Tina says, "Charity?" "Yeah, long story," I say, "I will explain later." "Ok that's cool, the more hands the better." Charity was always on me about people not being who they pretend to be. Much like Beautiful she too was protective of me but of course I did not listen. Always wanted to see the good in people.

Once at Charity's we started putting baskets together. Charity and Tina began to converse and the kids were watching TV. My phone begins to vibrate. Before I even pick it up my heart begins to beat fast because I know who it is. "Excuse me, ladies this is an important call. Hello," I say. "Hello there, Ms. Williams or shall I say Good Samaritan?" "What are you talking about?" I ask. "I was told that you have taken in a stray." "Oh," I say, "that I did but I am sure any good Christian would have done the same." "Your heart is too big, baby girl." After about 20 minutes of talking to him Charity yells do not cum on my sheets, I just washed them. I told her I wouldn't, I was saving that for his arrival. I made it very clear what I needed and expected from him for the week that he would be visiting.

I told him I was being very selfish and wanted him all to myself, so to see and spend time with his family while I was at work because I wanted his full attention. He quickly said "Yes Ma'am" and told me his bus would be there at 11:20 Thursday night. The night we talked was Tuesday so I waited anxiously for Thursday. I arrived at the bus station at 11 PM. 11:45 came and no Dominic. 12:15 still no Dominic. I went home furious that he was not there and had not called. I called him the next day and they said he was at work. I left a message but did not hear from him at all. That Friday I took the kids to my sisters and watched movies. By Saturday I was very upset. I told Tina the hell with him lets go somewhere. Her cousin in Baytown had called and asked if we wanted to go to Kappa. I really did not want to go to Kappa but I did not want to sit in the house either so we went. Needless to say it was a very degrading experience. It was half naked women wandering around being groped by men and not even getting paid for it. I stuck out like a sore thumb because every guy that tried to touch me got his fingers pulled out of place, slapped, or kicked.

You see I was not used to this type of behavior. I could have made a fortune off of those stupid girls letting these boys touch them for free. But that was the old Reyne and I was trying to be better. After her cousins saw my reactions they decided that we should leave before we all ended fighting because some guys were just real ignorant. They suggested a party back in Baytown that one of their guy friends was having so we headed that way. Once we pulled up I realized that we were in Little Jamaica. I could not have been happier. I danced for about two hours straight felt like, and ate some really, really, really good food. There was this really tall cute guy that I could not take my eyes off of. I thought about what happened the last time Dominic stood me up and could not let that happen again.

Eventually before the night was over we ended up talking. He was from the Dominican Republic and I had to concentrate really hard to understand what he was saying. Later we all went back to Taylor's house and hung out. Taylor had to be at work by midnight and Tina, well, she was occupied so I was left alone with Antonio. I told him I was going to take a shower because I was drenched from dancing. I sat in the bathroom contemplating if I really should shower, knowing full well that once I was clean and if he was thirsty and tried to taste me I would not stop him. Besides I needed a release and my girl was only to be penetrated by one man and he was definitely not it. So quenching his thirst would not hurt anything. I went against my better judgment and showered anyway. I figured even if he was not thirsty I could at least be held. Surely that was harmless. Right when I got out the shower my phone began to ring.

I said hello harshly because I did not recognize the number plus it was three in the wee hours of the morning and no one ever calls my phone that late. "Hi, Baby Girl." "Don't baby girl me. What happen to you? Do you know I went to that damn bus station?" "Baby Baby," pleads Dominic. "What," I say. In a very calm and soothing voice he says, it's cold, I am tired, and I have been on a bus full of people for the past seven hours. Please Please come and get me and then you can fuss all you want." I thought about it and peeked out at Antonio and told him ok but it would be a little while because we were all the way in Baytown. I rushed and put on my clothes, grabbed Tina, and told Antonio a friend of mine had just come into town but I would call him soon and rushed out the door. Tina said, "Why are you all wet?" as she drove to the bus station. Feeling the breeze of the cool air against my wet skin I laugh and said, "Oh I had just gotten out of the shower when D called so I just threw my clothes on, got you, and out the door we went. Tina laughed and said, "Um I am going to need you to dry off, he can wait a few extra minutes or two." I knew he could, but could I? I thought to myself as I grabbed my shirt and dabbed off.

Dominic was only supposed to stay a week but ended up staying two weeks. His plans were to finish school in May then go meet his best friend Denzel in California to hopefully be drafted into the NBA to support his Mom and Dad back home. One day before he left after church we were discussing our futures. I told him about the dance studio, the mission trips, working with the youth and maybe dabbling in the FBI or becoming a private investigator. His plan was the same as always, get drafted in the NBA and if it was God's will come back to marry me.

We joked about being married quite often. I told him more than anything I valued our friendship but if the good Lord decided I could go further I would not complain. During those two weeks I re-evaluated a lot of my ways. He had such a smooth way of helping me to realize that the world did not revolve around me. No man other than Javier has ever been bold enough to tell me that or should I say succeeded in telling me that. I decided to show him the house that I was led to some time ago. The inside was open so we took a tour. There was a huge fish tank dividing the foyer from the living room. The house had to be over 6000 square feet. As we left the house I told him, "Ok now, you go get drafted and come back and buy me my home regardless if we get married or not. I believe I deserve that much all the nights I held you and listen to your sob stories," I say poking him in the side .We both laughed and enjoyed our last evening together.

I took him to the bus station and we said our goodbyes. We both kind of held on to the 'if it was God's will' thing and went on with our lives. At least he did. Not even aware but for the next two months I did not date or even talk to anyone else. Somewhere in my heart I wanted him to be the one. Although Javier would come to mind time after time I scratched him because when he had the chance he coward up and went elsewhere so without even noticing I found myself waiting for Dominic. As time went on things became ugly between Tina and me. Being that I had only heard from Dominic three times in two months I threw myself into work to stay focused.

One Sunday Antonio came to visit me but ended up being stranded. Being that I had to go to work I let Tina keep the car to take him home. 6:00pm rolls around and no Tina nor have my children been picked up yet. By this time I am pissed. 7:45 rolls around and she finally pulls up with my children in the car big eyed and my car wrecked. She did not pick up the kids until late and did not take Antonio home until after that. She knew I had a strict rule about the kids being around men they did not know so as we drove to the apartment and she began to explain. At this point I really was not listening and was really trying to calm down.

By the time we got home Larry and Elizabeth were exhausted. After their baths I kissed them good night and put them to bed. As I walked in their bathroom to put up their lotion I noticed my underwear on the floor in a part of Tina's shorts. It looked as if she just stepped right out of them and left them on the floor. I dropped the lotion and ran out. Reyne where are you going she asks? I grabbed my keys and my jacket. I will be back I mumbled. I drove to Samantha and William's house. Samantha was not at home but William notice my distress and took me right in. As I laid out what happened, he comforted me with prayer which was a great solution to the problem. Samantha came home and joined in the prayer. They also told me that this is not the first time she has behaved this way. As I drove back to my apartment I knew what I had to do. The next day I called her Mom and asked her to come and pick her up. I left work early to prepare.

I called Gabrielle and Samantha over as witnesses just like I told her Mom I would so there would be no mess. While packing her things I found out that not only did she wreck my car, steal and wear my under-wear more than once but she also stole money from me and wasted my children's food. When she arrived at the apartment to find her things neatly packed in the middle of the living room and her Mom as well as Samantha and Gabrielle sitting there she immediately jumped on the defense. I was not the only one to find my items mixed in with her stuff but so did Samantha and Gabrielle. I told her I loved her but taking food out of my children's mouths and wearing my underwear was the last straw. I could not take it anymore. She told me whatever started grabbing her stuff and said I could have come to her instead of making a scene and left.

Once she was gone there seem to be a tremendous peace in the apartment, even the aroma changed. By the end of May things were back on track. One Tuesday evening after work I invited Sue and Gabrielle over to watch a movie and eat. Sue had used my car that day to go to an interview and on the way home I told her I really missed Dominic and hoped that he would get drafted soon because I was ready to move in my house. A few weekends prior to that day I had taken Gabrielle and

Sue to see the house I showed him. While we were all walking up the three flights of stairs I asked if they could help me put my bed together. One of my church members had given me a bed and a TV for the kid's room. I jokingly said while unlocking the door, "I wish Dominic was here to help me put it together." Sue said, "Hm be careful what you say he might just pop up." I smiled as I opened the door and heard the phone ringing.

Immediately there was a jump in my stomach and I knew it was him. "Hello," I said. "What would you give to see me right now?" "I don't know it all depends on what you have in your hands when I see you," I say motioning to the girls to let them know Dominic was on the phone. "Well I guess we will just have to see in about three minutes," he says. I ran to my balcony and began to scream, "Where are you? I know you are close I can smell you." He simply laughed and hung up the phone. I told Sue, "Girl he is here." She fell to the floor and starts saying, "Bless you, Jesus." Gabrielle and I look at each other then back at her and shake our heads. As the kids ate I hurriedly got cleaned up for his arrival. Not even five minutes later I hear his voice in the house. I was so excited to see him. The kids were too. We all had written him a letter that he joked about with them as I came out of the room. Gabrielle and Sue decided they would leave and take the movie with them while D and I talked. He was only in town for the night and was leaving the next morning.

To my surprise and pleasure we did not have sex that night. Was very happy not to break my abstinence. Once we put the kids to bed we talked about him heading to California and how badly this had to happen for him to take care of his family. We fell asleep in each other's arms as usual but without the lovemaking feeling but just a comfort that only friendship can bring. On my way to work I dropped him off at the metro transit center to catch the bus to the bus station. All day at work I had an eager anticipation that I would see him again really soon. Just as I suspected that night while on my way to my little sisters award ceremony he called. I exited the freeway and luckily I was right by Downtown and scooped him up. He said he had been there all day not able to get his ticket because his last check had not been direct deposited and he was trying to get the money from his Dad or Uncle but neither one of them had it.

After Tanya's ceremony I stopped at the ATM and got out $160 for his ticket. He promised he would pay me back. I told him with a reassuring smile that I knew he would. I dropped the kids off at school and came back to a nice cooked breakfast. After we finished eating Dominic touched my hand and said, "Reyne, as much as I would love to marry you and be all that you deserve, my prayer is for you to be happy." I smile and shake my head. "No really, Baby Girl, listen, I pray that God blesses you with exactly who you need and what you desire. I am not sure if I could be all that you deserve but He knows." I smiled and said, "Amen." "And I really hope it is you." At the time I knew this was guy talk for you know we are not going to be together right but we will always be cool.

Although I knew that the words meant that, I still cherished and felt the geniuses in him wanting me to be happy regardless of whom I was with. That was the most important part. As I pulled up to the station I knew this was goodbye. "I love you, Baby Girl, and thank you so much. I promise I will get this back to you." "I love you as well D and just keep your word. And if it's God will get drafted and…" we both said at the same time, "Come back and buy me my house," laughing. I drove off and headed to work with an assurance that married or not D would always be a friend just like Javier although I was quite disappointed with him for leaving. The kids started summer camp that Thursday and I was really thankful to have them with me all day at work.

It was very convenient and I was blessed not to have to pay anything. I poured myself into my studies at school and at home. By mid-

June, Larry had taken a liking to a guy that worked at the camp named Sean. He was a funny looking little guy, yet kind of sexy in his own way. One evening Larry was scheduled for a haircut with Sean and I had to go to class. Sean told me to go ahead and he told me that he would take him home. Elizabeth and I went to my class and Larry hung out with Sean. When he brought him home, after the kids went to bed, we sat and talked for a while. I told him about my divorce and no child support and some of the others that came along while sitting on the couch cuddling my white tiger. He picked it up and told me you have to get rid of this. You can't hold on to the past and expect something new.

That came as a shocker to me. I really had not thought about that nor was I ready to get rid of my tiger. It was a comfort to me, but I knew he was right. The abuse that I endured showed in the tiger's broken neck and worn out body. It was as if all the abuse I received had not had any effect on me but had showed up on my tiger. It took a lot of courage but the next morning, I called my best friend, Joy, and told her what I had to do. She gave me encouragement as I journeyed to the dumpster and said my final goodbyes. It was not easy letting go of something that I did not realize I was holding on to. The next few weeks, Sean and I became really good acquaintances. I had sincerely prayed for a good male influence in Larry's life and he was definitely it. Not only did he help with Larry and cut his hair, he also got me new tires, oil changes, and lunch almost every day for the rest of the summer.

One thing I did notice in the times that we were alone together, he never tried anything and I was thankful for that. In July, I heard from Dominic. He informed me that things were going well. He had gotten a job and he would mail me my money on his second check. Of course, I was excited to hear from him and still anxiously, secretly, hoping for the day that he would come back and marry me and buy my house if that was God's Will. Sean was a sweetheart, but made no initial advances. I was okay with it because it allowed me to be me, the vulnerable me around him. On a beautiful weekend in July, Kate's mom got married. A lady whom I had never seen before came up to me after the ceremony and looked me straight in my eyes and said, "You know you are next right, but the counterfeit always comes first." I nodded my head ok and kind of shook off what she said. Dominic had four more years of school and I was definitely not interested in anyone else other than Javier but I figured and just accepted that he and I would just be friends the rest of our lives.

I caught the bouquet at the wedding and by August, I was preparing for another wedding, my friend, Samantha. I was so happy and excited for her and Lord knows we have been waiting on this day. Although summer camp was over, Sean would still stop by my office and say hi sometimes and cut Larry's hair. I was very thankful for his friendship but could not honestly bring myself to develop feelings for him. I believe this is the reason that he never made any attempts with me. We soon found out later that we were just not each other's type but not before that counterfeit that I had been warned about showed up. His name was Erwin Paul and I

met him through Kerri, a mutual friend of Samantha and mine. We met at the end of August and by the Tuesday after Labor Day, he proposed. Like a fool I accepted because we had clicked so easily and it happened so fast, just like the prophecy said it would. One thing though, he was in the Marines and lived in Oklahoma. I knew that I was not moving to Oklahoma. He was there for all my fun moments and even attended Samantha's wedding with me on October 16th. I was glowing just as much as she was with my $1800 dollar princess cut diamond with baguettes on the sides. The engagement was cool and when individuals found out I was getting married they offered to pay for everything, even the place. There was one small problem though, his parents lived in New York and did not approve of their son with no kids marrying a divorced woman with two kids that was three years older than he.

This caused major issues. The tension led to frustration and I eventually needed a release and the night after Samantha's wedding I got it. Towards the end of October, I met with Sean for lunch. I had not really talked with him much due to the wedding and my engagement to Erwin. When I told him I was getting married and showed him the ring, he became very quiet for what seemed like an eternity. He then exhaled and said, "I am happy for you as long as you are sure." To be honest I was not sure. I still cared for Dominic deeply but had accepted the fact that maybe it was not God's will for him and me to be together. For some strange reason I felt guilty about being engaged to Erwin and I felt like I did a horrible thing by telling Sean. Although the prophet told me that my marriage would happen quickly, something just did not feel right about this. I sat out on the balcony that night after I came back from bringing the kids to my sisters and thought back to the last time I had sat in this very same spot.

It was the night Samantha was perming my hair for her wedding and Tina walked in geeked about my engagement. She asked me out loud and in front of everyone, "So Reyne what are you going to do when Dominic comes home?" My body froze for about a minute and in that moment I knew I had a decision to make. Shaking my head, too overwhelmed to think about him, I switched my thoughts to the day back in June when Samantha came to pick me up. It was early one morning in June. I was still exhausted from the excitement of Byron Cage's testimony about his house and his future wife. Samantha and I went to the house I had found and prayed and anointed the entire house with oil. We even put our feet in the water and laughed and prayed about the day Dominic would get drafted and come back and buy me my house.

We prayed over every crook and corner of that house, before we went home. That was another issue. I really believed this house is mine but I could not see how Erwin fit into the picture. I looked up at the sun while out there on the patio and said, "Ahh great memory." My phone began to ring and it was Kerri saying she was pulling up. I grabbed my weekend bag and was out the door for Oklahoma. The entire time we were there I felt very uncomfortable in a sort of weird way. Not to mention we were on a gated military base and anybody that knows me knows I do not like restrictions. Kerri was excited about her and her husband's new home and I was kind of happy to see Erwin. I did not like being on base at all, being that period seemed to make my skin crawl.

Erwin was distant and each time his parents called he grew more and more quiet. This I did not like at all. I need communication. I began to do my homework which was a rewrite of the Book of Lamentations in the Bible based on my new life. It seemed like the more I read the more I knew that Erwin and I were not meant to be together. Upon completion of my assignment I realized how defiant I had been towards God. Here I was in another engagement with everything paid for still having pre-marital sex and sending up a stinky worship to God. I cried the whole entire night begging Erwin to repent of his sins with me as I repented but he would not. The next morning Kerri and I left. I cried the whole way home. She thought it was because of Erwin's parents not accepting me but that was far from the reason. I cried because in doing that assignment I realized my unfaithfulness to my one true love, God.

That evening October 31, 2004 Erwin called me and told me he could not marry me and the engagement was off. I was ok with that part yet I yearned in my spirit for him to come to a place of repentance. Naturally I prayed and cried. I stayed in my prayer closet for hours asking God why my heart was open to Erwin. Once I received my answer I called his mother and informed her that her son needed Jesus in a major way. Yes we sinned but I pleaded with her to talk to him about repenting immediately before it was too late. It seemed as though

I was not getting through to anybody. It was almost as if no one recognized how serious this really was. I continued to pray. About three hours after the conversation with his Mom he called me cursing me out saying send him his ring back.

I politely said no and hung up the phone. This went on for some hours until I called him back to get some answers and was only welcomed by rude remarks from him. I went to work the next day and I told Sean what happened. He hugged me and said, "Don't worry, your mate will come." I wanted to believe him but at this point I did not even feel worthy of a mate. Throughout that month I constantly asked God why. Then I finally asked what his motive was. At about the second week in December on a month long vacation in the Bahamas I received my answer. I was at one of Allen's friend's houses when 'mummy' called to tell me to call home immediately. I hurriedly called home thinking something was wrong with one of my children but when I called Gabrielle whom had been living with me since the second week in November informed me that Kerri wanted me to call her ASAP.

I said ok got an update on the kids and called Kerri. "Reyne I have some bad news and I do not know how you are going to take it, says Kerri. Erwin is getting married tomorrow to his ex. He was only trying to marry you because you had kids and if he married someone with kids rather than without kids he receives more money when he leaves for Iraq." Not knowing what to say or how to take her calling me while in another country with this bullshit I just took a deep breath and said, "Kerri that really could have waited until I got home. Goodbye." "Reyne wait are you going to give him his ring back now?" "Uh no this is my ring. It was given to me and besides it's payback from the money I spent on his, because I cannot get my money back." "Reyne that is not fair he spent $1500 and you only spent $200. I don't believe that is right and I do not want to be your friend anymore," and she hung up the phone.

I laughed to keep from screaming as I dialed Gabrielle back to tell her about the stupidity of the phone call from Kerri. She agreed and instructed me to enjoy the rest of my vacation and stay out of trouble. The next day as I walked on the beach I became more and more aggravated with the entire situation. I just did not understand why this marriage thing seemed so hard. The prophet said all that I lost would be restored. He said that the marriage would happen quickly. All that he said seemed to be happening but nothing lasted. I did not understand. God's word is true and holds strong and never returns void so I could not understand why none of my many engagements seem to make it.

Not to mention anytime I talk to the leaders at the church I was working at, they told me I lived in 'la la land' because of my faith. I enjoyed the rest of my vacation in the Bahamas. It was great spending this time with Beautiful. She always knew just how to comfort me and pray over me to restore my strength. Truly she is a pillar God sent to me just as I was to her. Beautiful had moved back home shortly after I broke up with the wanna be preacher man. The Bahamas was beautiful and although I was excited about going back and starting Theology school I was distraught about leaving. At the airport I cried like a baby because I was torn between staying and going home. Something had happened to me down there in the Bahamas and it was quite unusual. Usually women go to another country and get laid by some sexy island man who can barely speak English but I had the total opposite experience. Sex was no longer a necessity for me.

Sitting out there on the beach being so close to nature and beauty all I wanted was to be clean, to be whole, to be new, and to be a virgin again. I knew from this point on I had to make some new choices. No longer could I live the way I was living. It seemed as if my life and my ways were forever changing since that beautiful day back in August some years ago. As I nestled in my seat on the plane I laid my head back and whispered a tiny yet firm and meaningful "Yes Lord."

CHAPTER 9
Total Submission

Once I reached home it was back to work as usual. My babies were happy I was home and once I arrived I was also. Charity called me to volunteer with her at the Stella Awards no sooner had I walked through the door. Although I was tired I went anyway. I had a blast meeting the gospel singers and laughing at how crazy they are. The first night went well and on the way home I told Charity about the Bahamas and what happened and that with God's help I would abstain from sex, and just being held until he saw fit to bless me with my husband. She laughed at first but realized I was serious when I did not laugh back. She supported me and told me that I could use her extra vibrator if I could not take it anymore. She always kept a brand new one just in case she burnt one of them out. I said yuck, nasty, you know I do not like toys. We both laughed. The next night was the dinner and pre-show.

I must say we looked pretty damn good in our evening gowns escorting all the singers and speakers to their seats. It was a really fun experience but by the end of the night I was ready to go. While Charity took her last few pictures and closed her last bit of networking I received a tap on the shoulder. I turned around to face one of the twins from a mime ministry that used to come to my old church. Come to find out he was stranded and needed a ride back to his hotel because his brother had left early. Charity and I gave him a ride and he asks me to walk him up because he wanted to give me something. I walked with him only for him to tell me that he believes I am his Ruth and that he remembers me from the church and cannot seem to get me out of his head.

He told me he was considering moving to Houston to be over the youth ministry at my old church and he knew he was ordained to be youth minister. My heart skipped a beat but I was cautious and watchful. We exchanged numbers and spent half the evening together the next day before he left to go back home. We talked off and on for approximately a week or two. When I asked him to fast with me to seek God's direction for us he quickly backed down and said he was not sure about that and would let me know. I found that strange especially since he claimed God told him I was his Ruth but I said ok and did not push the issue. I began to pray and ask God to reveal his heart to me. Upon praying that prayer I remembered that while we spent the day together he was very touchy feely and kept trying to kiss me.

Then it hit me he was not trying to get married he was trying to get some ass and obviously had discerned that I was seeking a husband so used that as a decoy to try and get my goods. I was devastated and immediately began to pray more and more and more for God to remove off of me whatever it was that attracted these counterfeits to me. I asked him to give me an eye to discern the motives of individuals before they even got close to me and the wisdom to deal with them. This He did. For the next two years I remained sex free, fondled free, and orgasm free. This was not an easy process for me to undergo. Sometimes that sexual urge would come over me so badly I would have to lock myself in my room and scream in my pillow until it went away. As I studied the Word of God more, the more I realized how filthy it was. A huge part of this change in lifestyle had to do with Gabrielle. Gabrielle was a virgin and loves God very very much.

While she prayed against masturbation within herself because of the thoughts she would have, I prayed for God to sustain me so I would not go and get any. I remember one afternoon in March after Gabrielle had moved out I was in my prayer closet and I was crying out to God to purify me and cleanse me with hyssop. I began to scream and try to tear off my flesh in repentance. The Spirit of the Lord was showing me how funky my worship was unto Him because I kept giving in to sex. Suddenly everything went black. I am not sure where I went or how long I was out, all I know is that when I came to I felt like a new person entirely. I went to the mirror and I even looked new. My skin was glowing and I felt like I could run a marathon. Something had happened and that something was God Himself had delivered me.

I began to praise Him. I ran in the living room and put some praise music on, grabbed the kids and began exalting the Lord. I was free and redeemed. Cleansed and purified with hyssop. A new creature. That sex demon was gone. I kept feeding my Spirit man with the Word of God, telling myself that I was to present my body as a living sacrifice holy and acceptable to the Lord. I would remind myself that I am the temple of the Holy Spirit each time I looked in the mirror. Whenever I would get a twinge the good Lord would satisfy me and I would be ok.

One day at the end of March I was in the nail shop. I was telling my nail lady Ginger about my deliverance and that I was ready to get a house for my children and me. One of the other customers overheard my conversation and gave me a card and told me to give the realtor a call. I took the card, thanked the lady, and said my goodbyes to Ginger. Once at home I pulled the number out of my pocket and said, "Lord, I do not have any money for a realtor. She is going to want a down payment, closing cost, and other fees and well you know that I don't have that." I shook my head and sat the card on the bookshelf. After a movie with the kids I tried to go to bed. I wanted to get to work early to look for houses on the computer, but I could not get to sleep at all. I kept having this strong urge to pack.

I got up and started packing at about four AM in the morning, only to wake up at seven rushing to get the kids to school on time. Each day that week I looked at the card but just shook my head thinking about the money required. My lease was up that month and I knew it was time to move. By that Saturday I gave in and called the realtor. Her name was Renesha Johnson. I informed her that my lease was up at the end of the month and I was looking for a home. I also let her know that I was a woman of faith and was told to call her by a stranger in the nail shop. She replied Praise God; I am a woman of faith also. She asked if it was possible for us to meet about an hour or two to discuss details about purchasing a house. Now I know that many people feel that some things in life are just coincidence. I am not one of those people if you have not realized that by now.

I believe everything that happens has reasoning behind it and some sort of purpose. Nothing just happens. Although we don't know or always understand the reasoning as well as the purpose, indeed there is a purpose and a reason for us not knowing the purpose in the particular moment of the reason. Follow me. I met with the realtor and actually continued meeting with her for several months after that. She became like a mentor in a weird way.

When I went to visit her that day come to find out she had been to the exact house that I felt the Spirit led me to and she knew the owner through mutual friends. The owner tuned out to be a professional basketball player. After several weeks of praying and fasting and working out, Renesha tripped on me one day while walking the track. She told me that I was young and stupid for believing that God would bless me with a million dollar home and I did not even have millions of dollars in the bank. She basically told me my faith was a joke and she really did not want any part of it. Now the odd part about this is that this is the same woman that told me her own faith story about a particular man that she thought was her husband and how time has passed but they have never gotten together yet everything keeps leading them back to one another some kind of way.

She was also the one that suggested we fast and pray until the owner of the home got back in town so we could go and meet him and tell him all about what I feel the Spirit told me about the house. I was saddened, not necessarily because she went off on me but because she let go of what she believed was for her. I walked off the track and went to her car. She drove back to the place where her niece and the kids were. I grabbed my children and I left. To make matters worse at the end of my lease I had moved in with a co-worker of mine from the church we worked at. Each time I tried to get in a quiet place to hear and study she wanted to go out or go eat with some guys that she had just met. It was becoming quite nerve wracking. Not only that, at work it seemed as though I was the laughing stock of the nation because people I had prayed for in the office received all that we together went before God for yet I looked like a fool to them for standing in faith believing I would receive this home.

I had told them about the realtor and given away all of my furniture except my children's beds in faith that I would be moving in the home soon. I had to do something different. My mind was in an uproar and I was in desperate need of a break. Expo time was coming up and I knew Charity would need help presenting her pieces so I called her. She could tell I was down and offered for the kids and me to come and stay with her. She said could use the help with the rent and some company since her teenage daughter was now living with her Dad on a trial run. I quickly accepted the offer which came right on time because Mesha had family coming in town that weekend and well we had to move out anyway. Before leaving Mesha and I had sort of a little pow wow. At work I had shut down due to the laughs and ridicules I was receiving because of my faith.

Not to mention I was shunned by the Pastor's wife because she told my supervisor that I could not wear jeans on Thursdays but everyone else could. Claiming the reason to be because I was at the front desk, yet the other secretary could. I knew it was for another reason but I chose to let her have it and just did not wear them. Mesha told me that I should stop telling people my business because everyone is not out to help me. She also said I was acting a little stuck up because I did not want to hang out as much anymore. It was not that I was trying to be funny it was just I no longer had a desire to sit in some guys face to get a free meal when I could pay for my own. I did not feel like being bothered with men and felt like my time was too precious to be sitting there knowing full well I was not interested and would not be getting any or giving up any for that matter.

Mesha just shook her head and said whatever. I talked to Pastor Joe about what was going on and he told me to just be patient, and wait on the Lord. I just could not understand how everyone I had prayed for received their stuff but I chose to rejoice with them in spite of because it let me know that God is real and some things just take time so I moved in with Charity and continued to wait. Finally in a space where there was peace and quiet I began to seek the Lord for myself more and more. This was at the end of July. The kids had enjoyed a full summer of camp and their cousins and were looking forward to school. So funny I believe I have the only kids in the world who actually enjoyed going to school. I think the most part about that was they were excited to tell their friends about all the cool things they got to do over the summer.

Living with Charity was truly what I needed at that particular time. Charity bestowed upon me a lot of Wisdom from an older woman's point of view and I taught her a lot from a spiritual standpoint. We both loved God and we helped balance each other out. Where she worked too much I did not work enough, so we definitely kept one another on our toes. She is a huge reason that this book is complete today. Around September a really bad hurricane hit New Orleans and killed tons of people and the whole city had to be evacuated to other places. Houston being so close a lot of people were brought here. This was a horrible and sad time yet the church I worked at did not seem to care. This disturbed me to the utmost and I lost all respect for certain individuals. I began volunteering and attending another church that actually opened their doors as a shelter to the hurricane survivors. It was a tragic situation and I was thankful to be in a place where leadership cared and were willing to pull clothes out of their own closet to place on the backs of these people who had lost everything materially. We washed hair, permed hair, cut hair and polished nails. Those people were back on their feet in no time yet a lot of their hearts were still tremendously heavy.

In October when Houston was under warning for the same type of disaster a lot of people left town while others were stuck on the freeway out of gas. Again my place of employment did nothing to encourage the people, not even the employers. I was truly devastated and realized the heart of man. I prayed for mercy to be upon all of us especially our church leaders. By the 3rd week of November Pastor Joe called me into his office and let me go. I had never been so happy to be fired from a job in all my life. I went home and celebrated. I had money to hold me over for at least a year, but I took another temporary assignment anyway. I had joined Charity's church but was not liked there very much. The Pastor and her husband seemed to had taken a kindness to the kids and me and, well, other members were not too fond of that.

I was called a wannabe and a jezebel because I came in helping with the entire hurricane stuff and organizing and putting together ideas whereas members that had been there for years did not do nearly as much. I ignored their sarcasms and got my praise on anyway sitting right in the front like I belonged there. I began to realize that the presence of God in me is strong and some people do not know how to perceive that. This revelation caused me to repent because I really thought it was me the reason I got almost everything I wanted and seemed to almost own every place my feet entered. It seemed as though all the Pastor's messages were about staying encouraged and keeping your head up in spite of people talking about you. Hold on to what God has promised and walk in victory.

More prophecies about things being restored and the husband came to me. One Thursday I was in a meeting for the youth there at the church when I received a phone call. Lo and behold it was Dominic. He was in town and needed a ride. I left the meeting and went to pick him up. On my way there I prayed and said ok Lord I have been doing so well on this journey of no sex, dating, etc. by your grace. Please, please you know this is not a strong area for me so please cover me. I want to remain pure and holy before you. I am yours Lord God and I do not want to hurt you Lord nor myself. Tears began to flow from my eyes and I could feel a presence around me that comforted me and guided me throughout the next few years.

You see Dominic in his own way was going through a lot that I did not know about. He asked me about marriage that night and of course I was totally excited but very cautious for some apparent reason. It had been a year and a half since we last spoke and now he was coming back talking about marriage. I knew something was up but because this was my deepest desire I went with it. After the holidays he went back to California. He asks me to come visit him for the weekend but being me I decided to come early to scope out the scenery. One thing you have to remember Dominic and I had become good friends so I was not crazy.

I knew he had been tapping something during his stay in California and I wanted to see for myself what this unsettling feeling was that I had. Needless to say things were just as I suspected but wished not to be true. He was on the verge of eviction. I prayed with him and really got on him about his spiritual walk but it was as if he was lost. Something had a grip on him and I knew in that moment that this trip was not about us being together but about standing in the gap for my friend that was trapped in a whirlwind of darkness. Things got too strong for him because he told me he was going to work that morning and did not return. He was running, something he did quite often when not wanting to surrender to God. I was thankful that Father had equipped me with unspeakable strength to understand that he needed a friend, a spiritual confidant at that that time, not a mate. So, that I was. I fasted for the entire the next day and left California the following morning. I told his roommates to be sure not to eat his pistachio almond ice cream and be sure to tell him I purchased it for him and that I was not mad.

They could not seem to understand the point of telling him about the ice cream. But I knew he would and indeed he did. He told me later that he knew it meant that I was his friend and not upset about the marriage thing. D and I always had a way of speaking and ending things without others having a clue what we were talking about. Although I understood my purpose with D I needed healing. I could not understand why this marriage thing just seemed to not be happening for me. Every time I turned around it was another counterfeit, even after I stopped dating. I hid from men. I only went to the store early in the AM and barely went anywhere on the weekends. I met a young African girl at Wal-Mart that introduced me to a church where a guest minister was speaking from Nigeria.

This man seemed to speak right into my heart. I had stopped going to the church I volunteered at due to the Pastor's husband's advances towards me and the mess that surrounded the individuals there. My heart ached for a place that would be purely about worship and serving not how it could make me feel or what I could get. Pastor Chigbo was a

God-send. He ministered directly to my heart issues and caused me through the raw uncompromised word of God to see errors that caused me to make ridiculous decisions based upon prophecies that were not completely accurate and man's view. After the service he asked to meet with me the next day. I went to meet him and explained to him all that I had experienced. He cut me off not needing to know the details and went to the core of the problem.

I had been operating out of the lust of my own flesh and based upon serving man not God. I was like wow I never even realized that. It is amazing how we get in some of these churches and get so caught up in serving the leaders we miss what Father is saying. He even helped me with the Dominic situation. That night Hope came to see me and we watched the Juanita Bynum no more sheets. Watching that DVD with the person who would be in the closet playing my DJ when I was doing my thang and I hers was like a huge slap in the face to the enemy because we were being restored. Everything we gave away and took we prayed would be restored and for redemption. I was happy to be back in touch with her and glad we both were on the same page. Charity had moved to Boston for a while to take care of her mom who had recently become really ill.

So I sort of had the apartment to myself. The next day while sitting in class I began to cough really badly. I got up and went to restroom. My chest began to heave and my heart carried on really fast for about 30 to 35 seconds. Then I felt my breath leave me and when I opened my eyes I was ok. Just as fast as it started it ended. I was not sure what that was all about so I washed my face and returned to class. After school I had to return something at the mall. While inside I got a phone call telling me my Dad had just passed away around 11:30 from a mild heart attack. I was in total shock. Here it was February of 2006 and my Daddy who was 84 years old was gone.

I had just spoken to him the night before and he told me he was ready to go home. I sat the kids down and spoke to them about his passing but had no idea it would happen that quick. I informed my brother that I would come down that weekend to help him with whatever he needed help with. I really did not know my siblings on my Daddy's side and had only met two of them once when I was like five or six. When I picked the kids up from school I told them what happened and Larry insisted on being baptized that day. I called Pastor Chigbo and he told me to come to the house where he was staying during the duration of his visit and he baptized Larry right then and there in the bath tub. I still don't understand why after hearing about my Daddy's death Larry insisted on being baptized but I did not have to understand it. It was something that had to happen. Pastor Chigbo and I kept in touch and he became like a father to me. The impartation that took place over the next few nights from sitting under his teaching led by the Holy Spirit was something I had never experienced in a church setting before. My heart had been opened and I could no longer be satisfied by prosperity and emotional messages. I was hungry for truth.

As I cleaned out every physical thing that had anything to do with him my spirit man became clean. I would stay up hours at a time reading and studying the Word of God. It was as if I had stowed away from the world and retreated to a mountain top. I had no contact with the outside world, other than bringing the kids to school and picking them up, and occasionally Wal-Mart. I went vigorously before God in pursuit of relationship with Him, to understand His will and desire for my life, to honor His statutes and commands. Theology School did not come close to satisfying my aching in my soul for the Word. It was those moments alone with Him in His loving arms, learning of Him that help me to understand the pain and disappointments I had been through. I confessed, repented, prayed, interceded, cried, moaned, lay silently, praised Him just Him and only Him for three months.

The peace that came from that time of truly seeking Him and being willing to be changed, broken, split apart, pressed, brought me into a place that nothing created could remove me from. I had come into the knowledge and reverence of His love for me, as His daughter, servant, vessel, creation. Though I was not complete yet and understood that I would not be until Jesus returns I had received from God an assurance of salvation and peace that cannot be shaken. The scripture had become evident and real, alive and active in me. I was truly a new creature. I released every prophecy, every word that man had ever spoken over me as well as my own agenda. I still understood His purposes for my life. He had just matured me to a point to remove my hands and lift them in reverence and praise instead of trying to make something happen.

At the end of April I received a call from Hope. I had not spoken to her since she accompanied me to Louisiana to help with the arrangements for my Dad's going home service which I did not attend because I did not want to remember him lying there in a casket because I knew he disliked funerals just as much as I did ever since I saw him cry at one when I was little. We met up and hung out for a while at Red Cat jazz Café. It was funny to us how grown we have become over the years yet we still look like teenagers. At the Red Cat we met a gentleman who does plays. I read the script for him and he told us to come out for auditions the following Saturday.

Well as usual Hope and I had a minor falling out over her not getting her way but leave it up to her and she would say it was me not getting my way but we eventually worked it out. I ended up going to the audition by myself. Roderick the writer of the play through conversation found out that I praise dance and gave me the part as the Angel that would minister to the teenager in the play and the understudy for two of the main characters. I was excited and nervous at the same time but through the power of the Almighty I excelled in each role I was given. I also met a young man that as I was going out to minister came and prayed for me. He too was a worshipper and understood the shakiness that comes right before going out to minister in dance. At the end of the night we talked and exchanged numbers. I was not feeling too well so he followed me halfway home to make sure I arrived safely.

We ended up staying on the phone the next night after the play until 630 in the morning. I kind of liked him somewhat but was not budging nor making any moves. I heard that Javier was back in town through Derrick when Hope and I went to see him when we came back from Louisiana but when I tried calling I got no answer, so I was pissed because I wanted to tell him about my Dad. I just left it alone and figured that was a dead end anyway but I had been praying hard and knew in my gut that something was coming. I studied the Isaac and Rebekkah passage of scripture for those three months and asked God for a sign myself much like the servant did to know who Isaacs's wife would be. Well one Sunday while sitting at Denny's with Jonathan the young man from the play and the kids I received my answer.

I was presented with a white tiger stuffed animal on that very day. The sign I asked for was a white tiger because my other one I threw away as a symbol of letting go my past abuse and hurt. This time this one was a symbol of assurity. It was security alright. Assurity that I did not need a sign to believe, but it unfortunately took me four years and another divorce and losing some loved ones to realize that. Jonathan proposed the following week and I gladly said yes believing that this was truly it because I had received this sign. During that first year of marriage no one could tell me anything. We ministered to so many people and did so many workshops. I just knew that this was where I was supposed to be. Although the sex was few and far between I figured I could handle that as long as we were accomplishing Father's work. I never thought to question why he would sometimes tell me no or seem so stand offish once we did have sex. I mean hello we were married you

would think I would have gotten it every day.
WRONG!!!

I guess the biggest thing for me was dealing with the fact that in our first year of marriage, I was patient, supportive, encouraging, giving and self-sacrificing. He asked me not to work, so I did not work. True enough I enjoyed that part until we started lacking yet he still asked me to remain an at home wife. So out of trying to be submissive I did. I spoke of integrity matters and gave my body wholly and freely, only to find out that Jonathan was cheating. I went into my wedding renewal believing that I was truly loved and cherished by my husband of one year but in actuality I was the butt end of an ongoing joke that I did not find out about until 10 months later after a 3rd child was born which I was not expecting nor desiring.

My honeymoon only holds one good memory and that is sitting out on the balcony of my suite alone looking over the golf course and Abba's beautiful creation knowing and trusting in that moment that You, Abba Father, were and always will be with me and that my completeness is found in Your love for me and my love for You alone. I acknowledged the fact that my wholeness is in you, not in any man. I was submitting to sharing our time with Jonathan but still stealing away to be alone with You Lord God while he stole away to send pictures of himself to others. Another couple Samantha, the young girl from church I used to sing with and her husband who I nourished and considered a friend, knew of this ongoing transgression but bothered not to tell me, but instead pretended that I had married the right man that would love me and protect my children and me.

Yet three months in Samantha, herself, indulges in the transgression. To make matters worse, while sick and throwing up everywhere, Jonathan is getting sexual favors from others and living a whole other life on the computer and at work. To add to my physical uncomfortableness, I began to have dreams about him being unfaithful and doing all that he was doing. Of course, naturally I rebuked it and assumed it was someone else. Never have my dreams been about the actual person so I began to intercede as I always have because I know my dreams don't lie. But not in my wildest dreams would I have guessed those dreams were about my husband for real. So here I am just living, thinking that I have a man that loves me and a real friend that cares about my well-being when the whole entire time I was being played.

My baby shower comes around and Samantha is really distant and rushed. She behaves as if the shower was just something to scratch off her to do list. I ask her about it and she just claims she has a lot to do when in actuality the fling between her and what I thought was my husband was at a high. They both professed they loved me to my face that day and to the face of my family and friends yet they knew the secret they held between the two of them. So, there I was pregnant with my 3rd child, 3rd baby daddy, and 2nd husband, happy as ever that I finally got it right, or so I thought. Dreams began to become visions and the closer I got to having the baby, the more they came, so I rebuked, and rebuked and rebuked some more.

Finally, the moment arrived to give birth to our precious new addition of the family. And of course, I wanted what I thought at the time had become one of my best friends there since Joy nor Beautiful could make it. So there I am in one of the most vulnerable phases in a woman's life, to my right a friend or shall I say foe. To my left, my husband or shall I say stranger. The both of them scratching my back yet behind my back holding secret conversations and meetings. Still so innocent and unknowing after delivery and recovery sitting there with the baby book, Samantha begins to fill it out for me. I am there, kind of out of it, yet trying to work through all the different feelings I feel. Once the little one came out I began to feel like myself again yet I did not feel alone. There was an assurance but a darkness also.

About a month or so later I get the gist of all those visions, dreams and emotions. Kim, a young lady I met through Samantha sends an email needing the number of a lady we went to church with. I call her to answer her email to my husband and I also take the opportunity to make amends because I sensed friction from her the last time I saw her. In that conversation, she tells me that I am a wonderful person and she is so sorry to have hurt me. Me, clueless immediately kick into ministry mode. She then goes on to say how after we met her at Samantha's son, James's birthday party, she and my husband began an email and picture sending relationship. She blamed her actions on being jealous of the fact that I was having a baby and she could not have any. I prayed for her, forgave her and ask God to bless her womb.

On top of all of that she then told me that Samantha knew about all of this before Jonathan and I renewed our vows and that she just stood there and watched and said nothing about it and she ventured to Miami with me and still did not say anything. Lo and behold evening came and Samantha came to do my perm. I played it cool although she knew that I knew she finally confessed. I told her I would let her make it since she was just getting into a deeper friendship status with me but had it been Joy or Beautiful I would not be having this conversation. On that note she sat me down and said Reyne there's something else.

Spilled beans everywhere she gave me the email account and the password and there my eyes, heart, mind and soul were penetrated with the filth that flowed between the two of them. I was weirdly disgusted, but ok. Disgusted by what my eyes had seen. Kim asked me if I would be willing to pray for her and could she come over for me to do so. Now I do not know if this was supposed to be a mocking or if she was really sincere. No matter her and Samantha's motives for wanting prayer I was sincere and Father knows their hearts far better than I do. I was not always innocent so who was I to turn them down when they asked.

This really freaked me out after the fact because surely the Holy Spirit had taken over my body because Lord knows I am not that nice.

We all sat at the table in hopes that everyone would repent including Jonathan and not just the girls but he refused to admit all he had done. So I took Kim and Samantha in the room and asked the Father to have mercy on their souls and bring every person involved to repentance and deliverance. I prayed for Kim's womb and that Father would bless her as He saw fit with a child. I called Ms. Brenda to pray my strength and sanity. I had a newborn to nurse and two other children to tend to and could not allow such foolishness and betrayal to wipe me out. Where the strength came from only God knows that.

To this day I still believe I had to be walking in some heavy glory for the woman and so called friend that were messing with my husband to come to me and ask for prayer on the very night they decide to come clean. What made them so sure that I would not murder them? For when we are weak He is strong and strong He was and is. The next day Ms. Brenda came and did somewhat of a deliverance process. He supposedly confessed everything. I forgave him based on his repentance. Time went on and Samantha left me a Dear John letter on my apartment door saying she could no longer be my friend.

Now I was devastated. I had forgiven her, spent an entire day with her and then she leaves me at a time like this saying she was never my friend. This hurt, I believe, more than what Jonathan did. All of the dreams and visions were true and no matter how much I rebuked them the reality was evident. This almost caused me to question my spirituality and my gifts but it gave me understanding and I realized that I am saved because I truly forgave them and moved on and I even stayed with Jonathan. Not sure why but at that time I knew that I could not leave him yet. This was all really strange for me because this was totally against my nature but I stayed. He told me they reduced his pay at the

University so he wanted to quit and get something else. He lied, only to quit and pursue network marketing.

He got a good job through the help of one the ladies at the church. We moved to his parents' house, supposedly for 3 weeks and put everything in storage. Well, it's been over a year and the stuff was still there. His mother suggested that he come to her job and I told him not to leave. He left and we lost the car. Not to mention I listened to him and traded my paid off car in. Thank You Lord that my name was not on that Altima. I had lost my sex appeal slowly and no matter how I tried I still felt dirty and used. I would push these feelings aside and continue to be a wife. March rolled around again and we house sat for an associate of mine. During this time, I completely supported Jonathan's dream. We barely had money or food. Yet I did not get a job.

I respected his wishes not to work and I suffered with him. We walked a lot and through it all God yet provided. I really felt like if we pushed really hard we would come out of this rut. Well come out we did because my friend Gabrielle leased the condo and told us we had to go. I was really hoping she would have given us another week but the answer was no. Her discernment worked slightly better than mine. We moved in with Harry and Ann and their five boys. I then found out that I was pregnant right when Jonathan was finally contemplating me going back to work. I was horrified and felt really bad because our living situation was not good, but I kept smiling and being supportive. Sickness came and went yet I was not prepared for what happened next.

Jonathan got a job at Little Caesars. While we were in their home I walked in heavy deliverance starting with the head, then the oldest son and then to the middle son. I had no idea what I had done. One night I got word that my friend Derrick was dying. I had not seen or spoken to Derrick since Hope and I went to visit him after my Dad died. That night at the age of 33 he died from cancer. I knew Javier would be devastated because Derrick was like a brother to him. I was determined to be there to support Joy and see Javier.

Although I hated funerals I knew I had to go plus I needed closure if I was going to stay with Jonathan. That mishap with him and those women really got me to thinking about who I should be spending the rest of my life with if anybody. Walter picked me up to get my Mom's car so I could go to the funeral, to support my best friend, Joy and catch a glimpse of Javier even if it was just for a moment. After the funeral Joy and I went to eat. It was wonderful catching up with her and I was looking forward to her coming to Javier's house with me but her aunt was ready to head back to Louisiana so I dropped her off and headed over to Javier's to chill. I had already informed Jonathan how much these guys meant to me so he was not tripping about me going to his house.

In all honesty Jonathan really did not trip about anything but I guess under the circumstances I understand why now. Once I arrived at Javier's home I tell him I need closure. He seemed oddly surprised at my words but said ok if that is what I needed. After catching up I decided I had better go home. Being that I accepted reality that he and I would just be friends I hugged him and he kissed my eye as always. I went to my sister's house to bring my Mom back her car. My sister's sat me down and had a talk with me about Jonathan's and my living situation. They knew how much I hated the north side but insisted we come and live with them. So that very day we moved to my sister's house. That next week at my 16 week checkup, the doctor told me that the baby did not have a heartbeat. I walked around another 5 days or so with a dead baby inside of me. The day of my delivery of this dead child, Jonathan asked me how I was doing.

I told him I kind of had my hopes up to be able to have this last child without the violations of the first one we had. He just smiled and put his head down. The delivery was hard and painful, worse than delivering a live child. Shekinah came out while I used the bathroom. I caught her frail, undeveloped body in a bowl. It was out, my final hope of her having breath was gone. I let go of her and the bowl full of blood and death. The synopsis was that a knot had gotten in the umbilical cord and she suffocated, losing all oxygen. I too felt as though I was suffocating. The dreams of Jonathan came back and I asked him about his behavior and he said no so I rebuked them. Shortly after that we got put out with no apparent warning by my sister, I had a revelation.

Sitting on that hotel room floor in the hallway looking at my children, it finally hit me, enough is enough? I told Jonathan that something different must be done. We had two options, a shelter or back to his parents. We felt the best choice for the kids would be his parents. We went back to their house, used their car and Larry went back to his old school and Elizabeth started a new school. She was ok, but upset because she had to leave her cousin, Ben. This was October. By December I found out I was pregnant again. He went to an interview for work in November and often went back and forth because he did not want to work a full time job. Finally in November he began working at Red Robin and American Eagle.

At first, it seemed to be getting better and better, but I did not feel right when he would touch me. We barely had sex anyway and the fact that I seem to get pregnant the two times we did do it in the past year did not help. I really felt eerie around him and I knew something was off. When I went to my doctor's appointment they did an ultrasound and could not find the baby. I had lost another one. Dr. Jenkins said this time no baby developed just the sac. I was devastated and kind of relieved at the same time. I told Jonathan and he seem very nonchalant yet relieved. I thought that being pregnant explained why I felt eerie around him but I was sadly mistaken. Going into the hospital for D&C surgery flooded me with memories and an assurance that I was not having any more kids. I had to be put to sleep. So for a while I was shaky and out of it.

I was not too out of it to realize that Jonathan was back to his old ways. I came downstairs the day after my surgery only to catch him on the computer again, looking up the same people. He had allowed that spirit to come back. I was livid not because I was his wife but just for the simple fact that he belongs to God and he had supposedly been done with that lifestyle. I was crushed physically and spiritually had prayed and fasted so hard and so much and he turned right back to his own vomit. It was hard to deal with. It was not as easy to forgive and let it go but instead I tried to deal with the emotions. I had been meeting with my Pastor for several weeks prior to this incident.

Meeting with her really helped me to realize a lot of ways that I behaved was not appropriate, because I let everything be on his shoulders. But I only did that because at the beginning of our marriage she told me I was too aggressive and should let him lead. She helped me to realize that everything is not black and white; some would prefer to stay in the dark gray areas. So I had to deal with the emotion and learn how to put myself in others shoes and see things from their eyes before I act. Although the session helped I still left somewhat confused and on the defense because now I was being told that I am the woman the one who holds everything together and I should have put my foot down earlier.

I began working a week after my surgery and Andrew started daycare in the afternoons. That was big for me because he had never really been away from me. Tax time came around and his dad sat down and did a financial plan that Jonathan agreed to. Well he did not stick to it and we argued constantly about him taking money out to buy coffee for this network marketing company from what we needed to get established. Well, February rolls around and by that time I had separated the bank accounts and we split everything in half. The simple fact that we had to do this made me lose all the more respect for him. With the little respect I had left, it quickly flew away when he took money from the taxes that was for the car and got into another business.

I told him it was me or the business. He stayed and still is in the business. I informed him that the company was fraudulent yet he chose to stay in it. Finally, after many tears, mind struggles and long conversations with Dominic, we decided to call it quits. Much like Javier, Dominic had a wonderful listening ear, and well since Javier and I really had not spoken much since the funeral Dominic was the next best shoulder. This decision, to us, is the best decision we ever made. Though our leaders did not agree, we were at peace with it. Jonathan and I realized that we should not have been married but God's grace covered our every wrong decision.

We hate that the kids were involved but he has committed to taking care of and supporting them. I am at peace with this decision and I prayed that eventually our leaders at the time would accept this and see that we are finally good and the kids are great as well. You see during the past four years Jonathan and I were used mightily in ministry. We danced, taught the youth, did plays and various workshops. My life was everything I thought I had ever wanted it to be. In spite of all the mishaps in the marriage we both enjoyed and learned so much from the church we were attending. Although Jonathan and I have gone our separate ways the seeds that were planted and lives that were touched were pure and genuine.

No one is perfect and everybody makes a bad choice here and there yet God still used our mess and made it a blessing and encouragement to others. Dominic had been a great confidant to me during my decision making time of what to do in deciding if I should divorce or stay. This would be my second divorce and again I did not want this on my head but in my heart I knew I had to do what was best for my children and me. Dominic helped me to see clearly from an unbiased point of view. He told me not to dwell on the wrong or the right but what was necessary to better my children and myself. In many ways during that time we helped each other. Although I had obtained all this great spiritual insight and revelation I was still empty. I felt as if I had no purpose anymore.

CHAPTER 10
The End or Shall I say the Beginning

Would I like to say the struggle ended there? Of course I would. Would I like to say the pain ended there, of course I would. But can I say that? The honest answer would have to be no but what I can say is that my eyes were open. I moved out and attempted to deal with my hurt and pain in the only way I knew how by pouring myself into others. I was confused in some ways and severely hurt in others. Not having the support I thought I should have had from the church did not help either. This caused not only my church life to change but my prayer life as well. As I poured myself into helping others reach their goals, my own goals began to slip from under me. My moments alone became few and far between because alone I was surrounded by un-dealt with mindsets and pain. I just wanted it to be like every other time. I move on you know. Get my own place, a decent job, make sure my kids are good and move forward. You know that thing we like to call survival. Surviving, this time would not be enough. You see something happened to me the last four years of my life. Although I was in a faulty marriage my yearning and desire for God was not faulty. During that four years I was pushed, challenged, and dropped into areas of ministry that I myself would have never imagined or even wanted to be in. I experienced God in areas of forgiveness and fragrance that I never dreamed possible. I remember when I first got involved in church I would hear people say that being chosen or anointed is costly. True I can agree that it is but the underlying factor is Jesus paid for it so that we would not have to. You see I was led to believe that I could not walk in the fullness of who I am without the covering of a husband. This faulty mindset led me to seek after a husband so that I could serve God fully. First lie of the enemy.

The Bible says God is our covering. He is Our Head. It is Jesus who sits at the right hand of the Father interceding on my behalf not a husband. The next lie was that of seeking a sign. A sign is exactly that, a sign of a lack of faith. The Bible says a perverse generation seeks after a sign. We believe what we believe about God not because of a sign but merely because of faith, a choice to believe that He is I Am that I Am, The Creator of the heavens and the earth, The One who tells the ocean when to stop and the river which way to go and how far to flow. He is The One who strategically placed each and every star in the sky and knows the number of hairs on each and every one of our heads. You see That One, The One, The only One, He would not allow me to drown in a pit of self-sufficiency.

He said, "No My Daughter, my beloved, my child, my Servant, I Your Maker, Your Master, Your Creator, Your Father, and Your Savior said: 'You will live and not die. You will walk and not grow weary. You will run and not faint. You my child will breathe. For it is I that has blown life into you. Breathe my child, take a deep breath and breathe. I did not call you to a mediocre lifestyle of survival. I called you to have life and have it more abundantly through Christ who has redeemed you and made you righteous by the pouring out of His blood in obedience to Me."

At first I did not understand why I could not be content and settled in my new apartment. Everything I needed physically, I had, but yet there was no peace, no fullness of joy. Don't get me wrong. Father was with me but there was more to be obtained. You see I tried to hide behind helping others, and having my own place but soon Father allowed that to be taken. Though the words never came out of my mouth, my Spirit cried out for more. I was not satisfied with my own place and a decent job, or helping others. I was empty and the more I tried to fill myself with what the world would consider success, the emptier I became until finally Father said, "Enough." I took Andrew to live with Jonathan and Larry moved in with His Dad. I continued to throw myself into helping others not realizing I was only being used or should I say not caring. Elizabeth and I tried to hang in there but before long I had to leave the apartment due to the job not paying me the agreed amount in the interview. Elizabeth ended up at a different school that caused even more heartache and trouble.

Everything I once had was now gone. I continued to throw myself into my sisters, Mom and Jacob. That was my first mistake. In all honesty most of my saved life had been based solely upon me trying to be obedient so that it caused me to forget I was saved, because alone I cannot be obedient. It took this last pitfall for me to truly understand what it means to be saved by grace and come out of self-righteousness and religion. Jacob was like the last guy on my list. As a matter fact he was the guy that never even made it to the list; the one that if the world ends and he is all that is left and you just can't take it any more than you would say ok and even then you might still say no. He had been in and out of my life since we were ten. If you recall he is the one I beat up for stealing a kiss. While trying to cope with the reoccurring nightmares that had begun to haunt me I some kind of way fell into a relationship with Jacob.

This was totally the wrong thing to do but at the time at first I thought it could possibly work if everything he said was true. And wrong. This was almost a reenactment of Bobby Brown and Whitney Houston without the drugs. He for me became a place where I could live in the world and have an 'I don't give a fuck' attitude. Being with Jacob took me back to the old Reyne where I was alone and felt like it was me against the world. I have to be honest and admit I felt comfortable in this place for a little while. I was angry, embarrassed, hurt, ashamed and sad to say I did not recognize any of it at first. Before Jacob and I started this forsaken relationship I went to see Javier a few times. A part of me wanted to remain in his comforting presence because in that place I was the total me, but after a few dinners he told me he was getting married.

I was shocked at first but than the old Reyne did not really care. I was happy for him all together but still shaky about it. Something about it just did not sit well so I quickly dropped it and told him to be sure that she pleased him in every way because he was worth it. One morning I saw him at Kroger's buying breakfast food and I asked was he cooking her breakfast. He said yes and for the first time in my life I felt a twinge of jealousy. I quickly shook it off and smiled and moved on literally. I figured we had had our time and no matter what or who came into either one of our lives he would always be my friend. From the look in his eyes every time I saw him there-after I knew he felt the same way or so I thought. After allowing Larry and Andrew to go and live with their dads, I let Elizabeth stay with my sister so that she and Ben my nephew could go to the same high school like they have always wanted to.

After losing my apartment and almost everything in it because the complex would not let me out of my lease due to the job change not paying me what I was making from my old job I moved out to El Campo with some Pastors I met through a good friend. I had visited their church several times and enjoyed it quite a bit. I had lost everything. I felt so empty and being with Jacob drained everything I had left yet it was almost as if I was addicted to him. You see every title I carried was wiped away in the blink on an eye. Everything I thought I had accomplished was like a vapor in the wind.

Upon Jonathan and me going our separate ways we both got sat down from the dance ministry and from working with the youth. This devastated me more than I even knew causing me to find my comfort in Jacob more and more. It was not so much as him as a person because he turned out to be a total jerk that needs salvation badly but for me it was the fantasy that surrounded our past. The guy who has always loved me, never asked me for sex, always told me how beautiful I am, did anything I told him to do, even married and divorced someone with my almost same name and skin color and height.

The boy was consistent for over twenty something years with telling me how beautiful I am and I was the only one for him. So that is what I buried all my hurt, pain, anger, and disappointment in. So I was wrong because I used him although at first I thought all those things he said were genuine and true but after I found out the kind of person he really was I still did not have the strength to walk away. I knew this guy was no good for me. This is why I had told him no for the past twenty something years, yet I took the risk anyway. I moved back to Houston in November of 2010 when I could not find work in El Campo.

I stayed with my Mom for a short period but most of my time was spent in bed with Jacob. No one knew of my relationship with Jacob except my sisters and his family. In all honesty I was quite embarrassed by it. Not as much as with him but with myself for being with him, someone who had no goals, no job, no money, no morals, and no standards. He only had two good things going for him and that was good pipe and good cooking. Which were both two things that I really did not need in my life. After some time the Spirit of the Lord in me began to rise up as I continued to seek the Lord for direction. I knew I wanted stability and to marry again one day but I also knew Jacob was not it and I had to get away from him but I just could not let it go yet. I was still harboring hurt and disappointment that I did not realize had taken over my senses and caused me to want to stay in this fantasy world I had created in my mind about Jacob. I in all honesty knew better but just did not care and was not being true to the essence of who I am. Although I helped Jacob finish school and get his CDL and a job I still felt empty and unfulfilled.

I applied back to my old job and was told I could start back to work in January. I was very excited about that and took up residency back on the West side of town where I belong. My goal was to break up with Jacob and when I came back to Houston in November start working and pursue my dreams. Unfortunately after one last romp in the hay I found out I was pregnant. I immediately called and scheduled an abortion and then contacted my three female best friends to get the money to pay for it. I told him I was pregnant and his eyes lit up. You see Jacob was the type of man who prided himself on making babies and thinking you would stay with him because yawl have a child together. Backwards right! His facial expression quickly changed when he saw that I was not smiling with him. He has been claiming that Elizabeth should have been his child and here he thought he finally had the opportunity to fulfill what he has always wanted.

Looking at him through open eyes now I see that he was a user, manipulator, and a compulsive liar and in my head I was like there is absolutely no way I will carry the title of this fool's baby mama. I just have to add a side note here on how we as humans do things. Now I know full well that I did not like nor respect this person as a man yet I continued to give him one of my most precious possessions because at the time I had lost all respect for myself. I was in a very dark place and the sad part is no one knew and if they did they dare not tell me because

I was always Mrs. In Control. Not to mention I purposely stayed away from Dominic during this time.

Although we have no ties to one another I felt somewhat bad for giving my goods to Jacob rather than him. Plus I knew he would tear me a new asshole if he found out how low I had allowed myself to stoop. Jacob and I tried to make things work at first. He changed his behavior somewhat but it was not long before his true colors came shining through and I quickly informed him that I would never ever carry the title of his baby mother. Neither one of us really wanted any more children nor were we in a position to handle another child. My own children were not even with me at the time. I was so angry with myself and ashamed.

So on top of the undealt with hurt, disappointment, confusion, rejection, and pain was shame, guilt and embarrassment. For my spiritual folks the enemy was making his bed in my heart yawl and it was hard getting free from that because I allowed and put myself there. Jacob and I began discussing other options and he said the choice was left up to me. I knew in my heart and mind I did not and would not be with Jacob so surely I was not about to have his baby but I could not bring myself to killing it or leaving him. He appealed to my flesh, my pain, my disappointment, my shame, all the emotions that I had not dealt with properly. You see Jacob had issues too. He was beat as a child, rejected, cast aside, made to feel inadequate, prostituted out because of his looks, taught that good dick is all you need and the world will fall at your feet. We were a terrible mix of darkness and light.

My light was dimming and each time I reached up for help he pulled me back into his darkness. Around December I talked to Beautiful in the Bahamas and she informed me of a lady and her husband who had been trying for over eight years to have a child and they could not. The lady called and for several months we prayed and talked together in preparation for me to come there and give them the baby. I was to arrive there in April and her and husband would take care of all my expenses up until I come back to the states. I was relieved and so was Jacob, yet deep down he really wanted me to keep the baby. Turns out the pregnancy was the best one I ever had. I was not sick and barely showed for a long time.

I started work as scheduled in January and anxiously awaited my departure for the Bahamas. In February Elizabeth and I went to Kerrie's wedding and lo and behold Samantha and Tina were there. Samantha had just lost a baby two weeks prior to the wedding. It was weird seeing her because she still seemed very nervous around me. Tina on the other hand was happy to see me and was pregnant also but I dared not tell any of them about my recent mishap. During the wedding I received a much needed revelation. When the facilitator of the wedding asked if anyone knows why these two should not be joined together, she went into a detailed explanation of how if anyone knew something and did not speak up they were held accountable and the marriage would be considered unlawful and void in the eyes of God.

At that moment something in me broke. I was both relieved and angry at the same time. Angry because Samantha was sitting right across from me at the same table and did not even bother to glance my way and say sorry. She stood as the maid of honor in my wedding knowing full well of Jonathan's infidelity. I just shook my head and Elizabeth my wonderful daughter squeezed my hand and mouthed its ok Mommie. I was happy overall though because leaders of my old church could no longer try to hold me accountable because according to what was just explained Jonathan's and my marriage was unlawful from the gate and could have been annulled, had Samantha big head self-spoken up. But Father knows best and the purpose and outcome of each and every situation. After the wedding I gave Tina a ride home. By March Jacob finally got a decent job but it was putting a strain on me helping him get back and forth to work every day.

One day on the way back from picking him up from work this lady stopped in the middle of the road going through a green light and Jacob rear ended her and totaled my car. Thankfully no one was hurt. My sister came and picked us up. He stayed behind with the car to wait for the tow truck. I let him keep my phone because his was dead. This sorry excuse for a man never even apologized but only complained that this accident would go on his cdl. On top of all that he used my phone to text some broad and told her he wrecked his car. To add insult to injury because of course by this time I was no longer sleeping with him he had birthday sex with one of his baby mothers that he so say cannot stand and don't want anything to do with all so that she could bring him back and forth to work. I will not sit here and lie and say that I did not sense that he was using me but because I had not dealt with myself I let it happen by lying to myself saying maybe he really does love me. Well those three situations were the defining slaps in the face that I needed to snap me back to reality and what I know I am worth. I had forgotten who I was and almost forgot whose I am.

That was the life-line that I had been praying for to leave. Finally I had the strength to leave this Negro alone. Pissed at myself because it took me having to lose my car and have a car note now to realize that his ghetto trifling behind was only tearing me down. Let me not judge, yes Jacob has some issues and then some more but much like myself at that time I was wrapped in my own flesh and that is where he is. The only difference is I chose to come out because I know what the love of the Lord feels like and looks like and I knew being with him was not it but it took tragedy for me to finally stand up and move around. I tried to encourage him to pray and surrender to God but I had to finally walk completely away.

For a while he called with the same old stuff but by then it was too late that lost hurt woman that I once was that allowed so much foolishness was gone. I began to repent and seek God like never before. I had fallen so far yet my Father never left my side. How awesome and loving is the God we serve. April came quickly and I had to see Dominic before I left for the Bahamas. The only people who knew of my condition were my two older twin sisters, their Pastor, my roommate, prayer sister, and a co-worker. I dare not tell Dominic for fear that he would be upset with me. I had been calling and calling for about two months.

Finally I prayed and sure enough he was at my doorstep. It was as if no time had passed at all. We talked for hours and I told him I would be going to the Bahamas next week. He was happy that I would be getting a much needed break and refreshing. I could not bring myself to tell him about the pregnancy. I wanted to tell him all that I was going through but I could not. I did tell him about all that I found out about Samantha. Come to find out the reason she did all she did with Jonathan was supposedly some kind of payback for him and I hooking up back in 2002. He shook his head and said, "Baby Girl it is not even worth discussing. Some things are just meant to be left alone. It is crazy how church people are the ones with the most issues." I told him "Yeah you're right." Sitting there talking and laughing reminded me of why I have treasured the friendship we have for so long.

As I went throughout the next week Karen called and stated that she could not send the money because her mom-in-law had to have surgery. I was somewhat disappointed but said ok. We moved the date to May 7th. May 7th came and went and I did not hear from her nor did Jacob keep his word about helping me with my car insurance. I was pissed not only at Karen and Jacob but at myself more than anything. I felt so stupid for trusting Jacob to keep his word when all the evidence was there that he wouldn't. May 13th rolls around and I finally call her after not being able to wait any longer to hear from her. All of my arrangements were made. My daughter was settled with my sister. Larry was scheduled to go to my sisters when he came home for the summer and Andrew would be going to her house as well on my weekends.

My roommate was going to keep my car and pay the car note and insurance on it until I got back, leaving me with only two bills, my storage and cell phone. Jacob was supposed to be paying the storage but of course that never happened. I reiterated all of this to Karen and to my surprise she could not seem to grasp why I was so upset. Her reasoning for not calling me was as she put it she did not want to give me another excuse for not sending the money. Supposedly some lady that she did some work for did not pay her. I informed her that none of that is an excuse if indeed it is the truth. I told her communication is vital because my livelihood is basically in her hands. Once I hand over my keys and leave my job I have no other provision for income. She apologized and claims that she understood and she would get back to me with a final date. She called me the next day and said the 17th would be the day. I had intentions on turning in my now one week notice as soon as I came back in my from my route but my supervisor and I always seemed to just miss each other.

My dear friend and co-worker had grown tired of Karen's excuses and told me I may want to consider other options. I had given Karen my word and could not bear the thought of going back on it or giving in to Jacob's begging and pleading for us to be a family. To make matters worse Karen had another excuse. This time the Pastor at the local church had not paid her. I was so glad I had not turned in my notice. I would have been jobless. I tried to look on the bright side at least I would finish out the school year and have a good foot in for next year in spite of all the lay-offs they were considering. I immediately called Dominic and the next day he came right over, only to find me more emotional than ever. My sister called me the night before and told me her husband said I needed to come and get Elizabeth. I was devastated. Supposedly she had reached her strikes three strikes.

I knew nothing about three strikes and could not help but wonder, what she could have possibly done that was so bad. Just as I thought it was nothing crucial just regular teenage attitude stuff rolling eyes, not wanting to clean little stuff that one good back-hand could easily cure. I asked could she at least finish the school year and my sister said of course, but come get her on the last day. I just said okay because by this time I had no strength left to argue. Still not informing Dominic of exactly what I was facing as always he was gentle, loving and supportive just as I was to him. He helped me out financially and was a good listener when I just needed to breathe. During those next two weeks I prayed and cried, prayed and cried, prayed and waited. I had no idea what. I was going to do. I had only made arrangements to stay with my roommate until the end of May.

It was bad enough that I could no longer afford to pay her what we had agreed on in rent, now I had to get Elizabeth. We would be home-less, carless, and jobless. I called Karen and informed her of what was going on and she said it would be no problem with Elizabeth coming there. Of course I would have to find the money for her ticket and passport, plus she would have to start school late. The biggest battle I was facing was the fact that I would have to tell her I was pregnant. I felt like a failure as well as hypocrite. Seeking the will of the Father I battled with still trying to figure things out. There were days when I would live reading books on God's deliverance and strength.

As I continued to seek him my strength began to increase. I still did not know what the outcome would be but I had an overwhelming sense of peace and strong reassurance that everything would be alright. Slowly I began to get the picture. Somewhere along the line I became self-sufficient, dependent upon my efforts and dealings. Father quickly showed me that this behavior is unbecoming and unacceptable. Though He allowed me to walk in it for a certain amount of time I became so drained and empty. You could see it in my eyes that I had nothing left yet I was still going, running on nothing but fumes. Finally I surren-dered. As I stated at the beginning of this book life can be odd to some and normal to others. Looking back over things I would not have expected to be used by God, nor even chosen by God but I am. Believe me I am not bragging, in no way shape form or fashion but I am boasting.

Boasting in the fact that Jesus is real and He does love us. He has blessed us with His Holy Spirit. Taken away our old man, the one that used to curse at everything and everybody. The one that was seductive and manipulative, conniving and deceitful. The ignorant one that just wanted to love and be loved, Me! He gave me His Spirit and called me by name. Delivered me from the works of the flesh and caused me to walk by the Spirit. Have I arrived? By no means have I done any such thing. This walk is a lifestyle and this flesh must die daily. God is not mocked and we do reap what we sow so be aware of your motives, for God judges the heart of man. So say what you want, criticize where you like but know that before My Creator my heart is pure. My only prayer is that at the end of my days He Himself will call me faithful for He surely has been faithful to me.

I quickly changed my focus after receiving this confirmation of peace and truth to my attention to my daughter. I informed my room-mate of what was going on and told her by the following Tuesday. The last week at work Serenity my co-worker and dear friend hung out a lot. She gave me lots of encouragement and kept me fed with some great homemade Jamaican food. Lying on the couch at home my thoughts are on my children. I pull out my Bible and turn to John 14:12-17 which I came to the conclusion after looking at the definition of the words and reading the commentary that when Jesus says whatever we ask in His name, He will do to glorify the Father; it means whatever we ask in Christ's name that shall be for my good and right for the occasion proper and fitting to my position life he (Christ Jesus) shall give it to me that the Father may be glorified.

This revelation of this scripture took me into praise like no other. I understood why some things I had prayed for were not happening. Don't get me wrong my needs were and are being met but I realized that the answers to my prayers were coming according to the revelation and meaning of that scripture. I began to think back on all I have prayed and fasted and stood on it and the only thing I could do was thank Father God Abba for his timing, wisdom and provision. You see He did not give me those things that I sought after, one: because of my mindset, and two, those surrounding people that meant me no good had to be removed. Although the removal of those individuals hurt it had to be done and now that I look back I can understand why, and am truly grateful.

I now know how to love my enemies. I now understand what compassion and mercy is because I've had to show it to others, not through my own power but by His Spirit for without it I am nothing. The next morning coming from work I continued my prayer for stability and permanency for my children and myself. That night I barely slept. If only I could be blessed with my own house is what I thought. Karen could just come here and get the baby and life would be good. I continued reading the Word of God and praying the John 14 scripture which is also the same passage of I read out loud seven years ago when Samantha and I went to the house and prayed over it and in it. I thought of Elizabeth and how it is an awesome thing that she is coming home now. Our relationships are not your usual mother daughter type. You see we are total opposites and clash a lot but one thing is true, she is definitely a trooper and survivor. She had just turned 15 at the beginning of the week and is at a stage in life where she really needs her mother. I began to pray for Father to bless me with balance and understanding to be her friend as well as her mother.

I love all three of my children and was looking forward to all of us being under our own roof finally with our own rooms without any man around to ruin or bring in drama. One thing I can truly say in spite of the two failed marriages and three disappointing engagements my children have been blessed tremendously and have never gone without. Although we moved a lot and they had to change schools a lot they have never been homeless or hungry or without clothing. God has and still is keeping His promise to accomplish all that concerns me and supply all my needs according to His riches in glory in Christ Jesus.

Though I do not like the fact that my last marriage was all a big fake, Andrew and the ministry that came forth during that time is real. Andrew though if I would have known of Jonathan's indiscretions probably would not be here. Is here and I am honored and blessed to be called his, Larry's and Elizabeth's mother. I finally drifted off to sleep only to wake up five hours later to the sound of birds chirping and my roommate leaving for work. I got up showered, dressed and headed to look at a home. The same house from before was on the market again and although I had long ago let go of the false prophecies, I just wanted to see. Arriving at the sales office I sit with an agent and her first question is do you have a realtor. I tell her no and she pulls out a card calls the realtor and hands me the card. The realtor is unavailable so she leaves a message and says I hope she calls back soon cause we've all been dying to see the inside of the house.

I smile and say me too remembering the elegance and framework of the home. While waiting she gives me as much information as she could think of to make my transition a smooth one. She even printed the forms to petition the price to be lowered for the taxes as well as a print out to file the home as a homestead property. After about two hours of paperwork, demographics and a list of my eight neighbors she called the realtor again and left my number on her voicemail. I left with all my papers feeling very confident. One thing she asked me before walking out was if I planned on having a mortgage. I told her no. She smiled and said great that is what I thought, you have all the documents you need then. With a thumbs up and a handshake she saw me off. Driving down I-10 I quickly remember that there is only $300 in my bank account which was going to be used to pay my cell phone bill and car note.

Immediately I prayed Lord I need money to purchase this home and to maintain it. Please provide in Jesus name amen. I got to my sister's house and was gone in record time. Stacey's attitude was not the best and I was still grasping the fact that that she knew Mitchell wanted Elizabeth gone before I was scheduled to leave to go to the Bahamas on the 17th but yet she did not call me until the 19th. What if I would have been gone? On the way back to the apartment the realtor called me and told me that we would have to schedule a time with the listing agent in order to view the home. She also told me I would need to fax her proof of funds to purchase the home. In full confidence I said, "Ok, will do." My mind went to praying and I decided I better play the lotto. After purchasing my ticket Ms. Diana the realtor called me and told me the listing agent said noon would be good. I said perfect and Elizabeth and I went to the apartment.

With one situation down I rested and prepared for another. After our nap and recuperating from the heat we went to dinner and a dance show at Miller Outdoor Theatre to celebrate her turning 15. Before leaving I told her I was pregnant and that is why I was going to the Bahamas to give the baby to Karen. I told her that I was sort of a surrogate. She said she kind of figured but was not absolutely sure because I did not appear sick like I usually am. Her next question was how it happened. I told her that part was what we would discuss at a later time. She said ok and we enjoyed the rest of our night. The next day I checked our numbers and to my surprise we had not won. I said, "Oh well, Lord you must have another way to bring this to pass." I called Mrs. Diana and told her that the funds had not reached yet. She said that was ok, meet her at twelve. We arrived at the sales office at noon.

She informed us that we could ride with her to the property and offered me Starbucks coffee. I told her I did not drink coffee and gave it to Elizabeth. I thought that was a really nice gesture to buy your client coffee though. Elizabeth enjoyed it very much. Inside her truck she was listening to Paul Wilbur which happens to be one of my favorite worship artists. We began discussing Davidic worship and our Hebraic Roots and ended up going the wrong way to the house. I told her the house was on the other side of the community and we both cracked up laughing. Pulling up to the house we got out and met Ms. Dionne, the listing agent. As they gave us the tour of the home I asked if the items inside would be staying. Dionne told me whatever I wanted to keep put it in the contract because everything was negotiable. Upon completion of the tour she asks me how I knew the owner of the house. Now I want to pause here and say it takes a really special person to tell this story to complete strangers knowing that you only have $300 in the bank and here you are standing in a million dollar home with only faith the size of a mustard seed and a Word.

Well call me special because I stood there and told my story in detail to two total strangers. Ms. Dionne teared up and the heat in my chest began to increase. I knew it was time to pray and obviously so did Mrs. Diana. We all grabbed hands and each person prayed. After completion of that prayer the realtor ask for oil and anointed Ms. Dionne's feet and hands and prayed a special prayer for her. She thanked us and told us that we do not know the depths of how that prayer and my story of faith in spite of the betrayal and disappointment she had experienced blessed her. We all hugged and said our goodbyes. Before getting in my car I thanked Ms. Diana again and Elizabeth and I headed back to the apartment with tears in my own eyes.

Tears because of how wonderful God is. We were not even supposed to see the house without proof of funds, yet He made it possible plus allowed us to be a blessing to one of His children. I told Father although I do want a home really badly as well as need it, if that praying for Ms. Dionne was the only reason this whole thing came back up, I was thankful and honored to be used by Him to encourage His own. After that I completely let it go. I threw away the lottery ticket and said if Father wants me to have this house or any house he will provide when he sees fit. Days came and went. Cassandra my roommate told me Elizabeth and I could stay but I would have to pay her $250 by the 15th. I did not have $250 and would not have it being that I did not make provision for income for the summer since I was supposed to be gone. I called Karen and let her know what was going on. I asked her to send the $250 and by the end of June I should have the money for Elizabeth's ticket and passport.

To my surprise she texted me back a rude and disappointing no that she would not pay my rent and that it was not right for me to ask her to do so. I was livid at this point. That was the last straw for me. I was completely done with her. All this time had gone by and I did not go through with the scheduled abortion because: one, I could not bring myself to do it, and two, I had given her my word. Her sister, my close friend Beautiful, called me and told me I was out of line and needed to humble myself. I was even more shocked. My thoughts were, well yes, true enough this is my fault because I got myself into this predicament but I am only still in Houston, jobless and damn near homeless because Karen never sent the money neither of the three times she was supposed to send it. Now here it is my first time asking for help and what I need and this is the response I get.

My heart was crushed. After getting off the phone I began to talk to Father. Karen called and asked if we could talk. She told me basically she has the money to send for me now but because of my attitude she was not sure if she wanted me to come. She also stated that she was afraid I would change my mind and keep the baby so that is why she would not send the rent money. At that point I lost it. Nothing pisses me off more than praying in faith with somebody for months at a time and going through all that I went through for them to allow fear to creep in. I could not believe my ears. I was no longer quiet and nice. I told her she had until Monday to decide if she was sending the rent, ticket, and passport money or the deal was off because I could not have the well-being of my child nor myself in the hands of a wishy-washy individual, and hung up the phone. I informed my roommate and she told me to just keep her posted.

She was scheduled to have friends coming from out of town for the summer. Elizabeth and I were already sleeping on the floor and I just could not bear people in the little one bedroom apartment. Elizabeth and I spent the rest of the weekend between Gabrielle and Serenity's house watching movies and enjoying laughs in spite of our current predicament. By Monday I had worked it out to where Elizabeth and I would use buddy passes to get to Ft. Lauderdale and catch the cruise ship over to the Bahamas from there. I texted Karen only for her to tell me that she had still not talked to her husband yet. I reminded her of the date and told her Wednesday is the 15th and either I have to pay rent or move out, so I needed to know something by the end of the day.

Two hours later she texted me and tells me he said ok but they would send the money on the 30th. I sat there as if I could see and hear for the first time. I politely finished my lunch and went on to enjoy the rest of my lunch date with a new perspective on what I had to do. The next day I went to my Dr.'s appointment and I received some bad news. He told me Wisdom's stomach was growing 3 weeks behind the normal size it should be for how far along I was. He said it was sometimes normal but they would run more tests and do ultrasounds every week just to be sure. I asked him if he knew anyone that could not have children and he told me to speak with the secretary and she could help me. She referred me to an adoption agency.

As soon as I got in my car I called and headed that way. Elizabeth sat out in the front while I went in the back and broke down in the meeting room no longer able to be strong. I was at my wits end. For the first time in my life in spite of all I been through and made it through I finally admitted, I need help and I could no longer do this on my own. God I trust you but I am alone, tired all out of request and strength. My only cry is help. The ladies embraced me and said that is exactly what we are here to do. I was under the impression that I was just going there to find parents for Wisdom, but lo and behold it turned out to be a blessing beyond measure and anything I could have imagined. They informed me that not only will I be able to pick a family but they would take care of all my expenses except my car note and insurance.

I was so relieved. You see when God blesses there is no sorrow. I began looking for an apartment as soon as I left there. I could not find anything ready on such short notice. So the agency placed us at the StayBridge Suites for two whole weeks. We absolutely loved it. There was breakfast every morning and dinner three nights a week plus an Indian soap opera that Elizabeth and I became quickly addicted to. Our first night there I cried and thanked God for His provision. Before I moved in with Cassandra I had looked into staying there but could not afford it after the car accident because my savings went towards a down payment for a car, since I could not find a decent cash car or someone willing to let me make payments. During our stay I continued to search for an apartment only to find that I still could not get approved for one because I did not make three times the rent.

This was becoming very nerve wracking and on top of all that I received a call from Diana saying someone put a bid on the house. I told her ok and what God has for me is for me in His timing and that I would call her as soon as I got the funds. Also during that two week time frame Karen texted me and threatened me, then criticized my relationship with God then added insult to injury by offering me $5000 if I reconsidered. I had texted her our first night there and told her I decided to do something different and would continue to pray for God to bless her womb as He sees fit. I was really hurt and dealt with a mental battle about changing my mind but what else could I do. As always I have prayed and done all I can.

The following week Elizabeth and I after desperately looking for an apartment were placed at another hotel. I asked Father for stability and cleanliness because I could no longer take all this back and forth. It was beginning to take its toll both physically and mentally. The agency found me a place all bills paid with cable, phone, internet and maid service once a week. Serenity's sons helped me get all my stuff out of storage and moved into my place. I got Jacob to sign the paper relinquishing his parental rights and although he still claims to regret signing and letting me go I did not care. I picked parents and looked forward to the day they arrived here in Houston and I placed Wisdom in their arms. I know I will have a wide variety of emotions once I deliver and a lot of choices to make. As of now I was settled with a roof over my head and food in the fridge for the next three months. Dominic and I defined our friendship and that is just what it is: a friendship. He had become a crutch to me and me to him. But finally after careful consideration I had to let him go by the grace of God.

We concluded that when the right person came along in both of our lives we would no longer feel the magnetic pull or need the emotional tie that we seemed to maintain between the two of us. After an endearing hug we said our goodbyes. This experience has taught me so much about life and myself. I can truly say that now I have a sense of redemption. The giving away of this child and transition of revealing my true feelings about what I really want have been very liberating as well as starting to embrace my emotions and not push them to the back burner. I have not seen my sisters or my Mom since June but I am taking the time I need for myself.

All of my life I felt the need to go out of my way to take care of others, help others, support others, and to be there for others. All of this was done because I was not dealing with who I was, and what I needed. I was trying to fill a void to be needed, wanted, and appreciated when in actuality I was not appreciating myself. To desire to serve is one thing but to need to serve is a warning sign that one is neglecting oneself. And surely that is what I was doing because I had not realized that I am worthy and that I did not need anyone to tell me I was because Father had already done so. I just had to accept it. Please do not get me wrong this characteristic of serving others will continue but this time with God's wisdom that I have attained from all that he has carried me through, knowing that it is a gift to have a heart to serve and not a need for recognition. Huge difference. You see I realize through each and every word written in this book that I am not an island. Though I have tried to be, I realize that I need to be taken care of, supported, and helped. And for the first time in my entire life I am open to admit and receive the help. God has been, and is here with me and always will be. He orchestrated each and every event. It is by His majestic and sovereign rule that I am who I am today.

Once I thought my life was worthless and had no meaning. Finally I surrendered. Looking back over things, I would not have expected to be used by God, nor even chosen by God but I am. Believe me I am not bragging, in no way, shape, form or fashion but I am boasting. Boasting in the fact that Jesus is real and He does love us. He has blessed us with His Holy Spirit. Taken away our old man, the one that use to curse at everything and everybody. The one that was seductive and manipulative, conniving and deceitful. The ignorant one that just wanted to love and be loved, Me! He gave me His Spirit and called me by name. Delivered me from the works of the flesh and caused me to walk by the Spirit. Have I arrived? By no means have I done any such thing.

This walk is a lifestyle and this flesh must die daily. God is not mocked and we do reap what we sow so be aware of your motives, for God judges the heart of man. So say what you want, criticize where you like but know that before My Creator my heart is pure. My only prayer is that at the end of my days He Himself will call me faithful for He surely has been faithful to me.

Today I know that I have all the worth and meaning that my Father intended for me to have the day He created me. True enough I still don't have all the answers or the full outcome of what will happen next but what I do have is a blessed assurance that yes just like every other created being I was Destined to Fail but Ordained to Glory and can now finally breathe.

Epilogue

Unlike myself when I was born, I made sure that everything for Wisdom to enter into this world was in place. One part I could not change was the rush of it all but Father knows best. You never know how precious your children are until you come across someone who does not or cannot have any and get to share in the joy of them receiving their deepest desire and prayer, a beautiful child.

Brrg, brrg (phone rings) "Hello." "Hello." "Um Ms. Williams, hi. This is Sonya here at Memorial. Were you sleeping? Wakey Wakey! We've been expecting you. You were supposed to be here at 5:30 for induction." "Today?" I say shocked, rising up on the bed in a panic looking at the clock. "Oh no I have to call Rachel." "Ms. Williams, how long will it take you to get here?" "Um, I am not far away," I say and began to scramble. "Let me call the Mom and I will call you right back." "Ok hurry. You need to be here in the next thirty minutes. Call me back now quickly," says the nurse. Calling Rachel while glancing at the clock, not able to remember what time her flight leaves, all I can recall is her saying six something and here it is already 6:19. Shoot her voicemail shaking and throwing things in my bag, "Rachel this is Reyne. The hospital just called I am scheduled to come in today. Oh please, check your messages before you get on the plane. Please Rachel I need you. Call me back," I say hanging up the phone. "Larry and Elizabeth, wake up babies, time to go to the hospital." Brrg Brrg "Come on pick up the phone please." "Hello," a sleepy voice rolls out on the other end of the phone. "Hey T can you please come and get me, the hospital just called and said I am scheduled to come in this morning for delivery." "Right now, or can I shower first?" she asks. "No right now I have to be there in the next 30 minutes." "Ok I am going to put on some clothes and be on my way." "Ok thank you." The next few minutes went by so quick that I did not realize I was contracting until I sat down in Serenity's truck headed to the hospital. I quickly called and told them I was fifteen minutes away.

Lying in the hospital bed with intimate gentle worship music humming softly to Grace Williams throughout the delivery room I finally breathe. Everything is in order. Larry's Dad is scheduled to pick him up from Serenity's. Jonathan is scheduled to drop off Andrew and Elizabeth is equipped to stay at Serenity's until I get out of the hospital. Everything was moving too fast until I spoke with Rodney, Wisdom's adoptive father. He asked to pray for me and upon him praying a flood of shalom washed over me. With Serenity by my side and about twelve good contractions and an epidural later plus four big pushes Wisdom departed my womb and arrived smoothly into a relaxed atmosphere of worship and still yet productive calmness. Finally the easy and long awaited part was over and the hard yet interesting part would begin.

Looking down at Wisdom as she pulls on my breast I have a range of different emotions washing over me. Although she came out of my womb and I carried her for nine months that initial feeling of this is my Baby was not here. All I could think was I wish Rachel was here. I was happy and sad. Happy that Wisdom was finally out but sad that Rachel missed her coming out. I had been informed that their flight was delayed an hour and would not be arriving to the hospital until like 10:30 or 11pm. Here it was 2 in the afternoon and I needed her there badly and quickly in order to complete, carry out and finish what had to be done. After a short recovery period and Serenity taking pictures, Wisdom was moved to my room.

Once settled in I left to tend to her family and I was left alone with Wisdom. Such a joy and a treat to be blessed with such a beautiful purpose I thought to myself as I watched her sleep still feeling like a mother yet knowing I would soon be placing her in the arms of another. One who had been crying out and praying to our Creator to bless her and her husband with a child that they could raise and call their own. Who knew that nice breezy day in November of 2010 while having break up sex such beauty was being conceived in the midst of pure ignorance? By the time I got that knock on the room door my emotions were in an uproar. No sooner had Rachel gotten through the door I was in her arms bawling like a little girl who needed her Mommy really badly. As she stood there comforting me, painfully holding back her own tears I just held on and cried. At that moment I did not care any more about being strong. I was as vulnerable as a kitty cat in the middle of a pack of German Shepherds.

Yet as hard as it was she stood there strong holding me tightly and took it all in. I wanted to stop, I really did. I could feel strength leaving me but I could not. The impartation and transfer that took place in that moment was immaculate. Here it was in this little bitty white woman from Maryland all that I am and will ever be Pure, Unadulterated, Beauty and Strength. Ahh, I exhaled and the embrace was released. Hugging and finally meeting Rodney for the first time, the man with the calming voice was the cherry on top. His cool calm demeanor held the tension of balance in the atmosphere as Rachel held Wisdom, her cry, the answer to her prayers in her arms for the first time. The next two days went by like a blur. My sisters came to visit and I finally got a chance to explain to them everything that happened since the day I picked up Elizabeth from her house. Rodney and Rachel decided I should have one more night alone with Wisdom and I did not object but quietly thanked God for hearing my heart's desire.

The next and final day as we began the paperwork and while Rodney interacted with Andrew and Elizabeth , Rachel anxiously peeps around PJ from the agency as she reads one of the papers to me that I have to sign. I ask PJ if in that moment people really change their mind and say no at this point of the process. She said yes and sadly she is the one that has to break the news, to the overly filled with joy awaiting parents. How cruel I thought. Upon hearing her response Rachel's and my eyes met and we smiled reassuring each other that yes this is real and no neither one of us is changing our mind. After a rude presence of disagreement from one of the nurses I became emotionally overwhelmed and could not see straight or even hear properly. I asked Rachel to sit next to me and she swiftly moved to my side sharpening as the iron she is. With that out of the way we went to the final document. As Ms. PJ read I asked her to re-read the part with Wisdom's name on it proudly proclaiming in the atmosphere her life starting off promptly and correctly with her identity fully intact.

As PJ got to the part about all that I was relinquishing light tears flowed from the corners of the signers eyes. Realizing I was not giving those things up but had strategically placed everything in order for Wisdom's future. Not to mention hearing Andrew's voice in the background as he nestled under Mr. Rodney playing the game counteracted any thought of robbing the world of such joy, because had I found out about what Jonathan was doing sooner Andrew surely would not have been but glory be to God He knows what is best for us and is in total control. Upon signing the last of the documents Rachel and I changed Wisdom into her going home outfit. Rachel passes her to Serenity then Serenity passes her to Elizabeth, then I pass her to Andrew and we say our blessings and goodbyes. I place Wisdom in the arms of her new parents in honor of Father Abba God! They thank me and hug me. As we embrace I know that this is not the end or the final departure yet the arrival.

The arrival of a long awaited and anticipated blessing for Rodney and Rachel and the arrival of newness and clarity into the unknown for me personally yet fully confident and assured that old things have departed and behold all things are becoming new. At home after a nice and delicious meal cooked by my darling firstborn daughter Elizabeth. It was nice reflecting with my dear friend Serenity before she goes home, Andrew gives me some comforting words and kisses and Larry calls me just to say hi and I love you right out of the blue. In spite of the past years events, mistakes and decisions I can truly say that I am blessed beyond measure and would be a fool not to recognize and acknowledge it. I may not know what my tomorrow holds but I know who holds my tomorrow for I am my Beloved's and my Beloved is mine. Thank You Yeshua, Lord God Adonai Nissi. You are blessed.

The next day upon awakening I realize just how fragile my body without Wisdom in it is. Though fragile it somehow seems strong. Looking at myself briefly while brushing my teeth I feel newness and freshness pumping through my veins yet the outer shell could use a tad bit of work. Although my stomach was right back flat like nothing was ever there I could use a workout. Back to bed I go, too early to be awake and I needed more rest anyway. My life feels so different to me now. I am more aware of things and my emotions than I ever have been before. My tolerance level for foolishness is zero. I know what I want and refuse to settle. Now that I have begun to embrace my emotions and Wisdom is born, each day I awake there is a sense of incompleteness and an urgency to deal with situations that keep rehashing themselves in my mind. For the next week or so I went through the wringer. I was an emotional wreck until I finally got on my knees in repentance for trying to be so self-sufficient throughout these last ten years.

The more I confessed the more emotions rose up in me. I felt as if I was in a tug of war. Now I know how people feel that have addictions. I even stop taking my pain medication because I found myself just taking it so I would not have to think and anyone that knows me knows that I do not like medication of any kind. During that time every emotion that I had not dealt with since I was 13 years old came rushing back to me like a tsunami but glory be to God He did not let any of it overtake me. Elizabeth was so understanding during this time and would sometimes just simply sit with me in silence. She is such a pillar of strength. As I began to relive past hurts and disappointments closure began to come. I began receiving and making phone calls accepting apologies and making some of my own, all the way back to the abortion. I spoke with the guy and he expressed that he has felt horrible all these years and why he called me last year when his wife of four years was having their baby just to say he was sorry but at the time he could not get it out.

He cried and poured out his heart and I let him know that he was truly forgiven. At the close of that conversation a door in my soul was closed and sealed never to be reopened again. With each phone call and or visit doors were closed, hurts were erased and pain was washed completely away. I even got a visit from Freddy. Yeah Freddy, Mr. Disappearing Acts himself. To my surprise I had not realized it was God's ordained season for the New Year according to the Jewish calendar. All that is celebrated and observed during that time took place in my life. I even spoke with Samantha and we both were able to truly release without anyone else's opinion about the situation which is now buried and long gone. Her friend Kim who started the whole situation with Jonathan was even blessed with twins.

I will never forget praying for her womb to be blessed the day she told me she was having an affair with my now ex-husband. My healing had become complete. I was back visiting my Mom and sisters on a regular basis and even made it to Tanya's birthday party which I would have missed had I been in the Bahamas. Jacob was no longer an issue and I finally understood that assignment and that door too is closed permanently. He tried to come back and propose and offer his car and for us to get a house together, but the moment I told him I was not having sex with him nor living with him he quickly retracted his proposal. You see men will only do what you allow them to do. And if you played the fool once it does not mean you have to play it again.

I learned a vital lesson and was presented with a choice. I could have settled for a lie but instead I chose the truth. You see the same weekend that Jacob came and proposed I had lunch with Javier. Out of all the men in my life Javier has been the most genuine and respected man out of each and every one of them with no hidden motives next to Dominic. I have never had a bad bone in my body towards him. Except for the time he gave me that poem and moved to Oklahoma approximately 10 years ago. But today is a new day and although I had my list of priorities that I intended to follow to the utmost until I reached my goal, my Father in heaven obviously had something else in store for me. All that I have gone through, all that I have lost, all that I have felt pain from is being restored. In my heart I knew I wanted to get married again but I wanted stability for myself and my children first. After leaving the apartment that the agency had gotten for me in October, Elizabeth and I ended up living with a co-worker who I had just met on my second day of work. You see I could not go back to my old job in Katy because I lost my car. Through much prayer and thanksgiving Father has given me peace and closure about everything in my life.

You see the weekend Jacob proposed Javier put it all on the table and let me know that he was no longer afraid and ready to commit to me. He left the ball in my court to choose. He expressed his desire for marriage to me. After careful conversation and consideration I agreed and the planning began. Although I had my new list of priorities that did not include a relationship nor marriage, my deepest desire beyond the house and stability at the root was still someone to share it with. He created me to be a helpmeet. And no matter how much I tried to run away from it, one thing that I have learned is that you cannot run away from your ordained purpose in glory. So yep you guessed it, shortly after Elizabeth and I moved with my co-worker, Javier and I got married and moved into our apartment.

Here it is almost two years later after Javier and I are married and I am as happy as ever, not because I am married and have a husband because I dumped that foolishness a long time ago but because I am happy with me and at peace with myself and my decisions. I am thankful that Javier is a part of my life but in all honesty with or without him I would be just fine because these past years of looking for love has taught me that God is love and no matter how much you show a person you love them or they show you how much they love you it will never mean anything if we do not first recognize genuine unconditional love within itself; God.

I must admit this has been the most challenging marriage I have ever had due to the fact that Javier is no way near the way he used to be and I am more aware of me and what I really want and learning what it really means to be a help-meet. Help-meet does not necessarily mean wife. As women we carry a gift to help men and they help us to be the best we can be as individuals. I had to learn to stop confusing the two. Life has changed the both of us and sometimes people are put in our life to help us reach a certain point. It is not always about marriage or being boyfriend and girlfriend but sometimes it takes that to be inside of the circle to accomplish the purpose at hand. You see we both still had undealt -with issues and although the marriage appeared great after one has been through so much you learn to settle and take what you only think you can get if you just choose to give up. By now you should know giving up is not an option for me, marriage or no marriage.

My center is God but there was still something causing me to continue the repetitive cycle of confusing help with mate. One day I received a message from Katy to call her dad Donnie my cousin. This was strange because I have not talked to or seen Donnie in years and the last time I did see him I really did not talk to him much. I called him only to find out that he was trying to get in touch with me to apologize. He gave me free reign to ask anything I wanted and described how his life went downhill after he put me out due to jealousy of not being able to have me for himself. I know it is sick and sad but people build emotional bonds mentally and physically which are called soul ties spiritually that cause some to do and say much distorted things.

As I listened to his side of things he mentioned that he knew he was the cause of all of my hurt, pain, and shame because he was the root the very beginning of it all. He only realized this by meeting other women who had been molested and taken advantage of by someone they trusted. He told me my wish was his command. I told him my only request was that he would pray to my heavenly Father to restore unto me the purity and innocence that he stole from me. He told me he has prayed that prayer every day and that he prays that I can now love freely and respect men genuinely without always wondering what if or looking over my shoulder, without any fallacies because of the wrong he had committed unto me. I thanked him and at that moment I changed. The final hurt had been healed. I then realized that we as people confuse someone being there for us as being in love with that individual and turn things into something that it should never be. Having a listening ear and a kind heart does not mean that person should be your partner or spouse. This is why it is crucial to be whole and complete before one settles into a marriage or an intimate relationship. Defining these things can save a lot of people a lot of money and time.

Two years in and I realized if I did not get some counseling I would literally explode. Although everything had come full circle except the prophecy about the house I still found myself legitimizing and making excuses for why it was necessary for me to prove my forgiveness to people. My marriage was becoming seriously affected because of me taking everything so personally. Although Javier had some faults of his own we both benefited from counseling. For so many years I had listened to others allowing them to lean on my shoulder when I myself did not lean back. After two months of arguing and pending divorce papers Javier and I got the help we needed. He refused to walk away. He made it his business to walk by my side and carry me throughout this process until I got better.

Although that should have been comforting I must admit it was quite scary at first because now that meant I would have to open up and up until this point I had gotten along with just opening up a little bit with not only to him but to Dominic as well. Both of these men are vital influences in my life but I had never really given either one of them my all. My exterior began to break apart even more as I read a book called Women Who Love Too Much. The book discussed patterns from our childhood where we as women either always tried to keep peace and accepted everything that happened or took care of a parent with an addiction. This behavior carries over into our adult life causing us to find partners that we can control or that need us. Being trained by my perverted sick cousin to never show weakness unless you are using it to get what you want but to learn everyone else's and use it to your advantage had caused me to have a two-folded view on life.

Being a Christian and sadly under religious rule did not help that mentality but thankfully being a believer in Christ and understanding the truth of His word bought forth healing and right thinking and repentance as well as open confession. During counseling when I began to confess it is not okay and named the things that were not ok that had been done to me I felt such a weight lifted that transformed me into a new person. I spoke with Dominic several times during this time and as always he supported me with encouraging truth and much accountability. My Pastors at the church I found who also are friends turned out to be one of the best things that could have happened to Javier and me.

Ironically my Pastors are the young lady I ministered to in the play and her husband. In my individual sessions I realized that I spent so much time trying to show my forgiveness that I never dealt with the pain of the betrayals I experienced. As I released every hurt and deleted the individuals I need to delete from my life I became liberated. There are no hard feelings towards anyone only the truth and I am thankful for that. Javier and I worked out our differences and began going to church together and spending more time together. As our communication opened more we gained mutual understanding and respect for each other's differences. After renouncing all foolishness and negativity spoken over our lives the heavens opened up.

Javier and I bumped heads several times during this opening up process. And although I would say we may not be compatible for marriage I stuck it out. I wanted to run so many times and even tried but each time he refused to let me go. He has reminded me of my dreams and challenged me to pursue them by giving me the space and time to do so. He has allotted me the comfort ability that sadly many of us as women do not take; the time to heal. Because of this friendship, this anchor I continue to move forward with great stride and accountability. While continually pursuing my goals a miracle that I had been praying for happen. I was put in a position to afford any and everything I could ever imagine. I immediately paid off my little bit of debt, purchased my home and am about to start my dance school.

Today, sitting here with my feet up under my gazebo I know beyond a shadow of a doubt that God is love, Jesus is the manifestation of that love, and the Holy Spirit is the proof. I am blessed, healed, delivered, highly favored, finally ok with being alone and indeed set free. Although it took a painful and interesting journey to get here, I am here still standing stronger than ever. Am I saying there will never be heartache again, or mistakes, or even bad choices? No not at all. But what I am saying is that my mind is in a good place and Jesus will be with you and me the whole step of the way if we will only be honest with Him, trust, lean, and depend on Him. He will see you through as well as those attached to us. I am no longer bound by the religious rules of man and church but free to live a life totally submitted to Father and still have my occasional margarita and night on the town with no setbacks or convictions. Elizabeth, Larry and Andrew are growing and can see that I am happy and learning life for themselves now. Life is about freedom and the only way to embrace that freedom is to not be a victim of circumstances and desperate choices.

Face it shit happens but the beautiful part about shit is that it makes for a great fertilizer and well Father never said we would not get dirty but He did promise to clean us if we allow Him. The most beautiful flowers bloom from fertilizer. Will I ever find love? The answer is yes. For I have found that and more in every display of forgiveness and act of kindness that has passed though the tablet of my heart. Love is not about being married or having a mate it is about God and forgiveness and helping others out of genuineness not ulterior motive or comfort ability. In this lifetime I can truly say no matter what happens I have been blessed to find love in various places not by looking but by simply giving and receiving.

Thank You Lord God for this is truly the end or shall I say the beginning of righting of every wrong!

THE END

SHALOM

About the Author

MarSha Andrus is a first time author. She currently is the owner and founder of Carrier of The Flame incorporated a non-profit Fine Arts School. Serving in the local school district and her church MarSha takes out time to volunteer, teach, write and mentor in her local community.